Guess and Pray

KIM SWIZZ

Cover Art by Ink and Laurel

Developmental editing by Annie Meagle at Spare Words Novel Editing

Copy editing and proofreading by Hannah at April Editorial

❀ Formatted with Vellum

Books by Kim Swizz

<u>Wilcox Grove Stories</u>:

Barefoot Lake

In the Stars Rewritten

Guess and Pray

For you.
Thank you for visiting Wilcox Grove.

Playlist

Homesick – Noah Kahan
Little Bit Better – Caleb Hearn, ROSIE
Safety Net – Bea and her Business
Manchild – Sabrina Carpenter
Iris – Boyce Avenue
Talking Body – Tove Lo
I Think He Knows – Taylor Swift
Why – Sabrina Carpenter
Wasn't Expecting That – Jamie Lawson
Little Bit of Love – Tom Grennan
If You Love Her – Forest Blakk
The Best Day – Taylor Swift
Electric Love – BØRNS
Love the Hell Out of You – Lewis Capaldi

Author's Note

Guess and Pray is intended for adult readers aged eighteen or older and contains explicit language and intimate scenes.

Some readers prefer to dive into a story without any hints about where it may go, while others prefer a heads-up regarding certain topics. There is no right or wrong way to read a book, so readers can find full content warnings and a spice guide at the back of the book after Acknowledgements.

/ *Eli*

PROLOGUE

LAST AUGUST

"Thanks for your help, man." Jake squeezes my shoulder as we watch the police car with Troy Basel in the back seat pull away from the curb outside Literary Lake.

While I don't think either of us saw tonight going this way, it's pretty fucking fantastic that it did.

The sound of Scott's laughter draws my attention, and I find the birthday boy with his head thrown back, cackling at something one of his guests said. I can't help but smile. Troy's been a dick since the day he was born, especially to Scott, and having his reign of terror come to an end at Scott's surprise party is some glorious retribution. The fact that Troy could face jail time for attempted arson is icing on the birthday cake.

"I've always got yours and Scotty's backs," I assure Jake, but he already knows that. While Jake and I are close in size and build—both well over six feet tall—Scott is Jake's *actual* brother. The three of us have been family for our whole lives, though, inseparable regardless of whether we share DNA.

Jake nods. He's a man of few words. Then, I see his expression change in a way that can only mean he's spotted his girl, Alice.

"Go," I say, jerking my head toward her once I pick her brown ponytail out of the crowd. "I'm gonna see if anybody's interested in getting to know a small-town hero better."

Jake scoffs with a smile, rubbing a hand over his short beard and shaking his head at my douchey comment before heading for Alice.

Literary Lake, our little bookstore, and Barefoot Bake, the café attached to it, are filled with most of the residents of Wilcox Grove, all here to celebrate Scott. Seeing faces I've grown up with my whole life at every turn, I know this isn't the night for picking somebody up. I just didn't want Jake to think he had to babysit me. I'm well-acquainted with going with the flow.

I wander for a bit, shoot the shit with Grateful Bob, say about a thousand hellos, and watch Alice's best friend, Piper, proclaim her love for Scott in front of everybody. All-in-all, it's turning out to be a damn good party.

After congratulating Piper and Scotty on finally realizing they're perfect for each other, I head toward the brick archway that separates the bookstore and café, my sights set on a birthday cupcake or two. Maybe I can help Hannah or Leslie—the couple that owns this fine establishment—with something. My dad always taught me *when in doubt, find a way to be useful.*

As I step into the café, somebody stands from the table tucked against the wall, and a shimmer of hair crosses my line of sight just before a body collides with mine—hard.

"Oof!" a quiet voice huffs out as warm skin lands on my forearm. My hands cup elbows as I help right my assailant.

"I'm so sorry!" she apologizes with a hand to her chest at the same time I ask, "Are you alright?"

That golden blonde hair shifts back over her shoulders as she looks up at me with one green eye and one hazel one, both startled. Her cheeks are pink, and her red-painted lips are parted. I'm a big guy, so our crash was definitely harder on her than on me, but I inexplicably feel like I'm the one who can't breathe.

She's stunning, and my stomach flips uncomfortably as I stare at her.

"I'm ok. That was completely my fault. I'm usually so much more attentive. Are *you* ok?" the stranger rambles a bit, seemingly frazzled by the contact. She takes a step back and pulls her hand from my arm to run it through her hair. I watch the strands slide through her fingers and wonder if they're as soft as they look.

The place where she touched me tingles, and my gaze falls to it, like I'm expecting to find the ghost of her fingers resting there. I realize I'm still holding her other elbow and release her, my hands hovering uselessly like they didn't want to let go.

She crouches a little and looks up to get my attention since I still haven't answered, and an expression I can't quite place settles on her face.

"Oh, it's you," she says, a hint of a smile on her lips.

It's *me*? I smile at the realization she recognizes me. That feels like wonderful news. But I'm *sure* I don't know her.

"I'm Eli," I say, finding a use for one of my hands again as I extend it toward this woman. I step closer, certainly closer than is socially acceptable, but I *want* to be near her. She's unfamiliar, beautiful. Magnetic.

A coy smirk tips her lips further up as her eyes trail down to my hand. Politely, she takes it, grasping firmly. My skin tingles again at the contact, and I decide I like her playful expression. I need to know what she's thinking.

"You don't remember me, do you?" she asks, still smiling. She's collected herself now and seems more comfortable having found something familiar in me.

I look her over, my eyes lingering on the way her denim

shorts hug her jaw-dropping curves. But then I notice the high neckline of her sleeveless top and the sure expression on her face. This is not a woman to be trifled with. I think she's someone who likes to be in control.

I have the immediate desire to rattle that.

"If we'd met, I'd remember you," I say, relaxing and trying to appear suave.

"Apparently not." She laughs, and joy suits her. She seems to know she has the upper hand here and is enjoying that fact.

I rack my brain to try to find some hint of recognition, but I've got nothing. How could I *possibly* have forgotten this woman?

"Hey Eli, could I borrow you?" Leslie calls over her shoulder to me from behind the counter where she's unsuccessfully trying to maneuver a tray of cookies. She blows a chunk of hair that slipped from her go-to ponytail out of her face in frustration.

She had a pretty serious mountain biking accident a few months ago and is still on crutches, so this is likely to end badly. She's got one of the crutches hooked into the side of her overall shorts, and I feel confident that's not the right way to use them.

Inwardly, I groan. Leslie's timing couldn't be worse.

I ignore the fact that the whole point of me coming into the café was to see if I could be helpful. Well, that, and to stuff my face with tiny cakes.

But now…

"Yeah, I—" I start to answer Leslie but cut myself off, looking back at the woman before me. I don't want to step away from her. I want to play this guessing game, feeling more curious about someone than I have in a long time. But I'm physically incapable of denying a friend when she's asked for help.

"Go," the woman says, tilting her head and patting my hand still holding hers before letting go. Just like when I released her a moment ago, I don't like it. "She looks like she needs you."

"I'll just be a minute. Stay right here," I instruct, flashing her one of my most effective smiles. I've been told I'm very charming. "I want to keep talking to you."

She chuckles, and I hope it's a good thing.

I hurry to help Leslie set out the cookies. I'm not gone for more than two minutes, but when I get back to the little table, the woman is gone. I look around the café, able to see over most heads from my height. She could be in the bookstore, but though I can't explain how, I just know she's not.

A white paper cup sits on the tabletop, a name written neatly on its side.

Maybe she's outside. Maybe somebody here knows her. Maybe Leslie remembers something about her from when she ordered the coffee.

My eyes scan the street through the front window before I realize what I'm doing and stop.

Get a hold of yourself, Eli, I chastise myself. I'm not the *romantically-chase-after-the-girl* kind of guy. I have my rules for a reason.

I shake my head to clear out the momentary insanity and pick up the cupcake I came in here for. Then, I disappear into the crowd, eventually meeting a lovely young lady named Lindsey, who's visiting her friend in Wilcox Grove. She saw the commotion before and is very impressed with how I restrained Troy until the police arrived. She's sweet, unencumbered, and interested, and after we hang out for a while, offers an eager *yes* to my invitation to get out of here.

Later that night, when I'm finally alone after Lindsey's headed home, I spot a faint smudge of red lipstick on the shoulder of my shirt, and I know it's not Lindsey's.

As I look at the mark, I wonder again where I could have met the woman who left it there, but rather than do battle with the stain, I toss the shirt aside and fall on my bed, determined to put the mysterious stranger out of my mind.

But the name on that white paper cup is vibrant behind my closed eyelids.

Iris.

CHAPTER 1

Iris

"**S**ammy! We've got to go!" I call up the stairs, earning a panicked shriek in response.

Olivia and I share a curious glance across our little kitchen table as I zip up my daughter's lunchbox.

"What could cause that kind of panic for a four-year-old?" she asks, adjusting her messy bun of red hair, succeeding in only making it messier.

"It could be anything." I shrug, loading the sack into a rainbow unicorn backpack. "But don't let her hear you call her four. She's '*almost five.*'"

"Mooooooooooom!" Sammy's voice carries over her thundering steps on the staircase. How such a tiny person can sound like a herd of stampeding animals is beyond me. She flies around the corner and into the kitchen. "I can't find my sparkle pens," she cries, exasperated.

Ah, that explains the catastrophe. Today is the first day of preschool after winter break, and Sammy has been talking about showing her friends those pens since she opened them on Christmas morning.

"I already packed them for you," I assure her. I pull their

pouch from the backpack in my hands and see relief wash over Sammy's whole body.

"Thank you, Mama!" she squeals, rushing forward to hug me around my thigh.

"You're very welcome, lil' one." My phone buzzes on the counter. I quickly read the text from my sister, Lemon (yes, my parents named my sister Lemon. Thankfully, the unusual name from some rich ancestor fits her perfectly), before conveying her message. "Auntie Lemon says good luck on your first day back. Now, get your shoes on. We need to get out of here, or you're going to be late."

Sammy's expression is one of horror yet again. Like her mother, my kid *loves* school and likely considers few things a worse sin than being late for class. In a flash, she's shoving her tights-clad feet into purple boots and is yanking her coat off its hook.

"Oh my god." Olivia laughs. "I see more of you in her every day."

I smile but secretly hope I didn't pass *all* my neuroticism on to my kid. I'm an anxious person. I always have been. I overthink, I catastrophize, I disassociate. Years of therapy made me very familiar with these words. We're old pals by this point, but I don't want Sam to be like that. I want her to know joy, peace, and love.

"Mom, let's goooo!" Sammy yells, pulling me from my worrying. She's hanging dramatically on our locked door, thankfully still unable to reach the deadbolt. Otherwise, I'm certain she'd leave me behind without remorse.

"Alright, I'm coming." I deposit my coffee cup in the sink and head for the door. "We'll see you later, Liv." I turn to Sammy. "Say bye to Olivia."

"Bye, Livvy!" her little voice calls before she looks up at me, her eyes pleading for us to go. "Oh! And thank you, Auntie Lem," she adds, like Lemon can hear her. I'll text my sister back later.

I slip on my heels, throw my coat over my arm, and lead the way, Olivia's farewell carrying us out the door.

Drop-off is a flurry of reunions, storytelling, and hugs. I watch my social butterfly flit around excitedly and tell myself I've at least done *something* right with her. Sammy is still chatting away with her best friend, Georgie, beside Miss Evvie when I wave to them from the deafening silence in my car and pull away.

Transitions from school to breaks and back are always a little jarring. I've got a really cool kid who I'm obsessed with, and I love spending time with her, but that doesn't mean my days don't objectively get easier when she has school. It also doesn't mean I don't have crippling guilt for even thinking that. I love being her mother and always say I'm a mom first, second, and third, but it's been weeks since I've had quiet like this.

I stew in my feelings for the short drive over to Sutton and Associates, my uncle's law firm. My plans for law school got derailed when those two blue lines showed up on the stick, but I still get to be in the industry as a paralegal and legal secretary at his firm. The law has rules, structure. I *like* rules and structure. They help me feel like things are a little less out of control. I'll take what I can get.

I see Uncle Harry's round face through the front window as soon as I park and feel a wave of calm wash over me. He and my dad are allegedly brothers, but you'd never know by looking at them. Where my dad is tall and stern, Harry is short—like me—and happy. It could be because he's got a full head of hair, and my dad is bald… but I think it's because Harry seeks out happiness, and my dad is allergic to it.

Harry and I have always been close. My dad and me? Not so much. Or at all.

As kids, Lemon and I spent every summer with Harry and his husband, Kenny, in Wilcox Grove while our parents were gallivanting around the globe. I learned a lot about what family is supposed to feel like in their house. Wilcox Grove is also where I met Olivia. We were thick as thieves every summer.

As I look at Harry, I'm hit once again with the realization that this town really is my home now. At the end of each of those summers, I'd wish I didn't have to leave, and now I don't. It's been eight months, and sometimes it still surprises me that this is my life. I am grateful for what I have, even if some aspects are not exactly what I'd always planned for. This is what I get to have.

After I graduated college, I wanted to get the hell *out* of the life waiting for me with my parents. But a pregnancy rocked my world my senior year, and my last semester started with the arrival of a tiny baby, so I ended up moving back in with my parents at their Newport mansion. For such a huge house, it was stifling, and I felt like a trapped kid all over again.

There are a lot of responsibilities that come with being a Sutton. A lot of events, a lot of fake smiles, and a lot of fucking lace. If I never see another tulle skirt, it'll be too soon.

Growing up, everything has always been *big*. I lived in a big house with a full staff. I went to a big school in a big city. A hundred eyes have always been on me, waiting for me to mess up, ready to report to my mom, poised to critique.

Let's not beat around the bush. It fucked with my head. A lot.

I wouldn't do that to Sammy.

So, when Olivia called and asked me to move into the three-bedroom house her parents were giving her in the town I've loved my whole life, I packed our things as fast as I could. Sammy and I were on the road in less than a week.

Now my life is small and quiet and so unbelievably beautiful.

A light snow is falling when I climb out of my car, so I hurry across the small parking lot. Wearing my heels instead of just bringing them with me was a mistake, but I thankfully make it to the wraparound front porch without landing on my ass. Maybe those awful ballet classes *were* useful.

The building is stunning, an old Victorian-style home Harry and Kenny completely remodeled so it could serve as the law office. It's a warm, welcoming building, which I always thought was a nice touch since people rarely come to see a lawyer when things are going well. There's no reason for the place they feel most vulnerable to be scary and impersonal.

Harry started this firm when I was a little girl. After law school, he did a handful of years at a big firm in New York before deciding to start his own business in little Wilcox Grove, a place his family had visited once. Maybe he wanted a smaller life too.

Somehow, he convinced his law school classmate, Isabella, to take a leap and become his partner a few years after that. For a while, it was just the two of them. Then, a couple years back, as Harry and Isabella neared the start of their fifties, they added an associate. And last year, they recruited another and added me to support the lawyers. It's a well-oiled little group here.

Uncle Harry comes to meet me by the door as soon as I open it, taking my coat before handing me a steaming cup of tea.

"It's not going to stick," he says with a longing sigh, looking out the glass panel beside the door at the snow.

Harry has always adored the snow, something he passed along to me. Where others see terrible roads and the annoyance of shoveling, Harry and I see a sparkling winter wonderland, where everything gets quiet and peaceful, and magic has a place to enter our world. Sadly, we haven't had a good snow yet this year. It was *not* a white Christmas. It was almost sixty degrees, and Uncle H and I were devastated.

"It's still early in the season. The snow will come," I assure him with an encouraging squeeze of his arm.

He stares out the window for another moment, as if in longing, before snapping into business mode.

"What do we have going on today?" I ask as we walk into the front room.

When this building was a home, it would have been a parlor, but they knocked down a wall so it connects to the kitchen and serves as a reception area. Directly across from the doorway to the hall is my desk. To the left is a collection of couches and chairs in front of a bay window that looks out front, and the kitchen is toward the rear of the room. It's not often clients need to wait to be seen by one of the lawyers, so I like to consider the space my office.

I am greeter of clients and keeper of the coffee. It's a true position of power.

"Well, somebody gave a New Year's kiss to somebody they weren't supposed to, so Mrs. Carter is coming in to talk divorce," Harry says with a glint in his eye. He's always loved small-town gossip.

"Didn't they just get married in December?" I ask, aghast.

I never said I didn't love small-town gossip.

"That they did, Iris. That. They. Did."

It's going to be an interesting day.

CHAPTER 2

Iris

Half an hour after I settled in, Mrs. Carter arrived for her meeting with Harry. Five minutes later, Mr. Carter came flying in, begging for her forgiveness. After all, his indiscretion was just a one... oh, *two*-time thing.

Mrs. Carter didn't know about the second time.

Things did not go well for Mr. Carter after that. Mrs. Carter called him a good-for-nothing sack of suds and swore to take him for everything he had. She also told him his receding hairline *was* noticeable.

It was the commentary on his hair that finally brought him to tears.

Listening to them go at it had me thinking maybe being a single parent is alright after all.

It wasn't just the morning that was dramatic though. Maybe everybody is energized after taking a few days off for the holidays, but it feels like the phone hasn't stopped ringing all day.

I know it might sound a bit masochistic, but I like the busy days. They fly by, and I enjoy feeling useful. I have a good memory and a careful system—a place for everything, and everything in its place. Today, I *thrive*. Today, I don't need to be a lawyer. This is enough for me to give Sam what she deserves.

I keep trying to get just *one more thing* done and end up having to hurry out the door for school pickup. Still, I shove my notebook and laptop in my purse before taking off. I might be able to wrap a couple more things up after Sammy's bedtime.

On Mondays, Wednesdays, and Fridays, Sammy stays for the afternoon daycare at school, but it ends at 4:30. On those days, my early evenings belong to my daughter, and I pick up work after she's gone to bed if I need to. On the other days, she comes back to the office with me for the afternoon, where Harry has a room set up just for his favorite great-niece to spend her time. She has a whole chest of craft supplies, shelves of books and puzzles, a little table, and a squashy play carpet. With her child-sized couch, it's a sweet setup.

As I hurry to my car, I'm splashing through a muddy, slush-filled lot, likely causing irreparable damage to my poor shoes. Uncle H was right about the weather today; the snow didn't stick at all, so the world is a cold, wet mess outside in spite of the continuing flurries. Anybody who thinks this is better than a real, solid snow needs to get their head examined.

The drive to the preschool isn't long, so I pull up exactly on time. Then, Sam is filling my arms, and I'm listening to a detailed retelling of her first day back.

"We all used my pens when we traced letters, and Miss Evvie gave me this." She thrusts a piece of paper into my hands. It's a certificate for sharing.

"Samantha, this is wonderful!" I beam. I love that I've got a kind kid.

I buckle her into her car seat, and we're on our way just as she starts telling me what everybody had for lunch and who she sat with.

"Mama?" Sam says suddenly, cutting off her story.

"Yes, lil' one?" I answer, peeking in the rearview mirror to see her looking out the window with her brow furrowed. We just passed the turn that would send us back to the house.

"Where are we going?" Nothing gets past her. She's observant, aware, meticulous, just like her mama.

"It's a surprise for your first day back to school," I say, continuing along Main Street until I find a spot, park, and cut the engine.

Sammy squints her eyes as she scrutinizes the street out her window before realization dawns on her, and she whips her head around to look out the opposite side of the SUV and across the street.

"The bookstore!" she squeals, spotting her favorite place in town.

"You can pick *one* new book to buy," I say once I get to her door and release her seat's harness. She's bouncing with excited energy.

"To *buy*?" she repeats, her little mouth falling open when I nod.

With how quickly Sam consumes books, we're frequent flyers at the lending room upstairs in the bookstore—Wilcox Grove doesn't have its own public library, so the town came together to make a substitute—but buying books for keeps is reserved for special occasions.

Once we're across the street and inside the bookstore, I remind Sam that we don't run inside, but that girl does the fastest speed walk her short legs can manage to the children's section, peeking over her shoulder to make sure I'm within eyesight before settling in. Sam can be fiercely independent, but she's still my little girl.

"Iris!" a familiar voice calls to me from behind the register, and I quickly spot Piper Price, the newest part-owner of Literary Lake.

Piper has to be one of the prettiest people I've ever met in my life. She's tall and poised in a way I know my mom wishes I was, and her beautiful brown skin always seems to be glowing. Today, her bouncing curls are down, framing her smiling face and pouring over her shoulders.

Hannah and Leslie, friends of mine and the couple that opened Literary Lake and Barefoot Bake, asked Piper to be their business partner after she completely upgraded and transformed the bookstore while Leslie was healing from two broken legs last summer. She's all patched up now, thankfully.

Piper's a Wilcox Grove transplant, like I am. She came up here around the same time I did, looking for some Wilcox Grove magic. Selfishly, I'm thankful she found it and decided to stay because I got a friend out of the whole situation.

I scurry over to Piper, relieved that Sammy is completely engrossed in the stack of picture books she's collected. The girl is a regular bookworm, which is why I'm so excited about my plan.

"Hey," I say, giving Piper a quick hug across the counter. I then lower my voice so Sammy can't hear. "How's my good friend, ol' pal, generous, sweet, kind buddy, Piper doing today?"

"I'm doing fine…" Piper answers slowly, looking at me with narrowed eyes. "What did you do?"

"Nothing yet, but I'm about to ask you for a huge favor, and I'm really hoping you say yes." I give her my biggest smile for good measure.

"Alright, lay it on me." She still looks wary.

"How would you feel about hosting an adorable five-year-old's birthday party at the bookstore? It would probably be about ten kids from her class, some parents, and a handful of other adults from my friends and family. I'd like to surprise Sammy with it." I hold my breath while I wait for her response.

"Are you serious? Holy shit, immediately yes." Piper's eyes glitter with excitement. "When's her birthday?"

"February nineteenth, so would the Saturday after work?"

Piper turns toward the store's computer and clicks through a few things. "Calendar's wide open. This is going to be so much fun!"

I pull out the notepad where I'd listed ideas for games and food, plus a tentative attendee list to show Piper. I am nothing if not prepared. As we start planning, part of me wants to tell Sammy about the bookstore party because I know she'll be thrilled, but thinking about the look on her face when we show up here as a surprise keeps me from spilling the beans. It's going to be *perfect*.

Speaking of looks on people's faces, the one now on Piper's tells me that her boyfriend, Scott Preston, just walked in behind me. I turn, following her line of sight and, sure enough, find Scott looking at Piper just as dopily as she's looking at him.

Scott is a respectably-sized person, but beside him is a wall of a man, smiling brightly at something Scott must have said. My stomach swoops at the sight of him, like it always has. If you want to know about the kind of chaos I *don't* know how to handle, it's Eli Chambers.

As Eli looks forward, focusing on me and Piper, a few strands of his wavy blond hair flop onto his forehead, sparkling from the wet snow still falling outside.

Since August, he's grown in a full mustache and beard. The neatly trimmed facial hair suits him. I didn't know I liked mustaches until right now… but it seems like his face was made for one. Unlike when we first met years ago, the round boyishness is gone. He's been all man for some time.

When we first met, Eli was everything I wasn't—confident, charming, outgoing, carefree. I've always been reserved, careful, calculated… boring. It's ok. I don't think of it as an insult. It's just who I am. And because Eli was so different, he absolutely *fascinated* me.

Apparently, he still does. Not enough to speak to him when I've seen him around town, always flying here or there—usually I avoid him, except for our literal run-in on Scott's birthday—but enough for me to listen a little more carefully when I overhear somebody talking about one of his escapades, and enough to have a full body reaction to him walking toward me.

But I'm just a mom, and he's… Eli. Still confident, charming, outgoing, carefree, and a little wild with his *personal* life. We simply do not fit.

As the men get to us, Scott steps around the counter and reaches up to kiss Piper on her temple before shaking the snow out of his mini mullet of curls, making Piper shriek with glee.

Even though I'm still watching Piper, when Eli leans against the counter, he's close enough for me to smell snow and earth and leather on him. For an office guy, it's surprisingly rugged, and unfortunately for me, intoxicating. I focus all my energy on remaining—or at least appearing—unaffected.

"Hello, princess," Scott whispers, and I feel like I'm intruding at the sound of the intimacy in his voice. Piper gives him a shy smile.

I look away and find Eli staring intently at me. I feel a little stunned.

"What brings you here, Eli?" Piper asks, and I jolt at the sound, somehow having forgotten she was standing right there in the point two seconds since I looked away from her.

"I was just giving Scott a ride over so he can head home with you," he answers her but keeps looking at me.

"Oh!" Piper jumps into introduction mode. "I'm so sorry. Do you know Iris? She's the one who saved my ass with the Mia event last year. Iris, Eli."

The way Eli's smile slides onto his face is practically pornographic.

Is it hot in here?

"We actually met last year at your birthday party, Scott." He glances at his friend for a moment but looks right back at me. "And apparently before that too."

CHAPTER 3

Eli

I ris.

It's been almost five months since I last saw her, but she immediately has my interest once again. I've thought of her a few times since August, curious about our alleged first meeting and wondering what she's been up to but determined not to fixate on her. Standing before her again, I now *desperately* want to know more. And I want to know how she knows me.

She is not a forgettable woman.

I thought it would be fun to allude to that mysterious meeting, but Iris seems none too pleased that I've revealed our prior rendezvous… rendezvouses?

With her narrowed eyes scrutinizing me now, I do think there's something familiar about her expression. But I can't tell if that's just me trying to force myself to recognize her. Maybe I just like looking at her, whether she's annoyed with me or not.

Our staring contest is interrupted when a miniature person comes barreling into Iris's leg, a book clutched in her hands.

"Mama!" the little girl's voice says just before she catches sight of me and clamps her mouth shut. Ever so slowly, she slides sideways until she's behind Iris, peeking up at me with enormous eyes—one green and one hazel, just like *Mama.*

Apparently, Iris is a mama.

The little girl's hair is pulled into a ponytail, and my eyes catch on the curls. They're blonde. I'm blond, but that doesn't mean she got that from me. Iris is also blonde. All kinds of recessive genes could have given this little girl her hair color.

My stomach plummets to the depths of hell. Please, whatever higher power exists, don't let this kid be how Iris and I know each other. It's not possible.

Having forgotten a night with *Iris*? Not. A. Chance.

My gaze jumps up to Iris's face, and I can only imagine what I look like. I feel clammy and nauseous, and whatever horror-stricken expression I'm wearing pulls a sudden huff of laughter from Iris.

I don't find this funny at all.

She must notice, because she puts me out of my misery, shaking her head. I almost fall over with how quickly my blood starts circulating again.

The kid isn't mine.

I quickly check Iris's hand to make sure I didn't hit on a woman wearing a ring and find it bare. Sure, it's winter, but there also isn't even a hint of a tan line, so I think it's safe to assume it was bare in August too. Curiosity rears its dangerous head once more, but I remind myself to mind my damn business.

My boundaries, and creating distance, are key to my survival.

"Do you want to say hi?" Iris asks her daughter, but the girl's eyes just expand to resemble saucers.

"Hi there," I offer. I'm the adult. Now that I know she's not my accidentally abandoned daughter, I remind myself to be a polite human being. "I'm Eli."

"Hi," the girl says softly, still staying mostly behind her mom but looking up at me inquisitively now.

I look at Iris to make sure it's cool with her that I keep trying, and she shrugs, the motion saying *it's up to her.*

"Could I see your book?" I ask.

My approach is always to talk to children the same way I'd talk to adults because they're people too, just smaller. Despite my reaction to thinking I had a surprise kid, I actually really like them. Kids say what they think, and I find that kind of honesty really refreshing. It also feels like they always seem to see things adults overlook in their important, busy lives.

When the girl narrows her eyes at me, she looks like Iris's perfect clone. It feels like she's assessing whether I'm acceptable, and I guess I pass because she stretches her hand up to me, holding a picture book about a capybara.

"I *love* capybaras," I say truthfully, flipping through it and dropping down into a squat. "I think this is a great choice."

Her eyes light up at that. I return the book to her, and it's like the floodgates have opened.

"Did you know capybaras are kind of like really big rats? But I think they're cuter. They eat plants. And they're everybody's friend." The girl rattles off her list of facts energetically, finally emerging from behind Iris.

"I didn't know that. Very cool." I *did* know, but I like how excited she is to tell me and am not about to crush her spirit.

"I'll be your friend," she decides suddenly, and I'm honored to be chosen. "I'm Samantha."

"It's very nice to meet you, Samantha."

I look back to Iris and see her smiling proudly at her daughter. She lightly brushes back the loose hairs on Samantha's forehead and sighs. The tender moment hits me in the chest. The kind of devotion on Iris's face is something special.

Also, not my business.

Iris watches me as I stand back up and mouths *thank you.*

But she's got nothing to thank me for.

"We should get going so we can have some dinner," Iris says, lifting Samantha. "Give Piper your book so we can buy it," she instructs, shattering whatever moment was starting to form there.

It seems like Iris has boundaries and rules too. And I'm feeling like I'm on the outs.

Once they wrap up, Iris gives Piper a meaningful look. "If you need anything about *things*, text me."

"Will do," Piper promises.

With a wave from both Iris and Samantha, they leave, Iris's eyes passing right over me as if I'm any Tom, Dick, or Harry.

De-nied. Again. And this time before I could even give it the ol' college try.

At least Samantha thinks I'm alright.

"What was that all about," I ask Piper once they're gone.

"Literary Lake is going to host its first kid's birthday party, a surprise for Sammy," Piper says as she collects her things. Then she pins me with a pointed look. "More importantly, what was whatever that was between *you* and Iris? Did I sense something brewing? And what do you mean you met before Scott's birthday? When?"

Scott and Piper had been quiet for the last several minutes—it was exceptionally out of character, especially for Piper—but I'd be dumb to think they weren't watching every moment. Everybody in this town is nosy, and even though Piper is a new arrival, she's taken to hoarding town gossip like a native. I just know Alice—and by extension Jake—will be getting a play-by-play later.

"I don't know." I shrug, looking at the door Iris disappeared through like it holds the answers to all my questions. "That's just the problem. When I talked to Iris in August, she said we'd met before, but I swear I don't know her."

"You didn't hook up with her?" Scott offers.

"Not a chance. I'd never forget a woman I was with. It's not my style, and especially not a woman like her." This is a point of pride for me. I fuck around, but I am *not* a fuckboy. I respect the shit out of women and quick, faceless fucks aren't my style.

"Maybe you just walked past her at the grocery store or something, then," Piper says with a noncommittal wave of her hand.

Clearly neither of them is as intrigued by this mystery meeting as I am. To me, it feels like a puzzle, a game. And I want to win. I want to figure Iris out.

"She acted like I *should* have remembered her," I say. It's possible it was just a passing meeting, but I really don't think so.

"She only moved here last May, like me, so there really haven't been that many opportunities for you to have meaningfully met her and then forgotten," Piper notes.

"There's no way I met and forgot her between May and August. There's got to be something I'm missing," I insist.

"Why are you so hung up on this?" Scott asks. "*Is* something brewing? Is somebody catching feelings?"

"Definitely not." As great as Iris seems to be, I don't do feelings. It's one of those unbreakable rules for me. Feelings lead to attachments that are too fucking risky. Being that connected to another person when anything could go wrong? No. I can't. "I just want to know."

"I'm sure it'll come to you," Scott says, clapping me on the arm as we all head out.

CHAPTER 4

Eli

Once in a blue moon, I feel a rare, sudden connection with one of the women I'm with. Each time, I wonder for half a second whether I should try something more, but then I remind myself how much pressure comes with love, knock sense back into myself, and will myself to move on. Usually, that's the end of that, but sometimes we become acquaintances or even friends, comfortable existing in the same sphere without issue. To date, it's worked without fail.

I can't stop thinking about Iris's eyes. Sure, the colors are unique, but it's more than that. When she looks at someone, those eyes seem to see deep into them, unraveling their secrets. It's intense, memorable.

So why the fuck can't I remember her?

Every few days, she pops into my thoughts without warning or reason. I feel like I've been infected, and it's kind of making me an irritable asshole.

I'm a happy guy. I'm a nice guy. I'm a fun guy. I am *not* the irritable asshole guy. That's Jake (lovingly).

I find myself flipping through the pictures in my phone, my texts, socials, alumni groups from college… *anything* that can give me a clue. I can't think of anywhere I've gone or anybody I've met in the last year who could have put me in Iris's path. For the first time maybe in my life, I wish I had some kind of organization system for my stuff instead of the jumbled mess everything exists in. Half of my contacts don't even have full names. They exist on pure vibes.

I end another one of these thought spirals with an immature huff. I push back my chair and abandon my desk at the nursery.

Jake watches me snatch a piece of paper from the printer like it insulted my honor before marching into the greenhouse, but he doesn't say anything. He's an "I'm here if you need me, but I won't pry unless I'm worried" kind of friend. At moments like these, when I'm being entirely unreasonable, I appreciate the shit out of that about him.

I pick up a clipboard and pen from behind the register before descending into the greenhouse, starting at the very back and counting plants, marking them off my inventory list as I go. Checking inventory isn't glamorous work, but it has me on my feet, and I can't sit at that desk for another minute.

It could be in my head, but I think breathing in the earthy, damp smell of the enclosure helps relax me. After a couple hours of monotony, I feel better, less hyper fixated on Iris. This is good.

I head back to my desk to get my coat and drop off the clipboard, feeling lighter. Tonight is the night I shake this.

"Hey," Jake says as I pass him. "Wanna come to the Corner Post? Piper wanted wings, so Scott and the girls are already there."

See? My day is turning around. Wings with friends is exactly the kind of thing relaxed, not-obsessed-with-a-woman Eli says yes to.

"Oh, yeah. Count me in." It's a good way to end the week.

I follow Jake on the short drive to the bar and park beside him in the gravel lot.

The bar is noisy with raucous chatter that hits us like a wall as soon as we pull open the front door. We say hey to the owner and bartender, Penny, before Scott waves us over to a half-booth. He's in one of the chairs, and across from him are three women who all look up when Scott spots us.

There's Alice, Piper... and Iris.

God *damnit!*

I will not let this derail my progress. I am calm, cool, collected. I try to imagine the earthy smell from the greenhouse.

"So, we meet again," Iris says with a smirk as Jake and I walk up. It's hard to tell in the muted light of the bar, but I think she's flushed. I glance away before I'm caught staring, pretending to look for a server.

With Scott already sitting across from Piper, and Jake immediately claiming the seat across from Alice, the only empty spot is in the middle across from Iris. She shifts when I sit down, pulling her feet away sharply when I bump one with my shoe.

Happy. Nice. Friendly. *Don't be a dick.*

"Haven't we been here before?" I try, aiming for playful while still hoping to get a clue about our past.

"Nope, not here," she says with a smirk, immediately catching on to my attempt.

I groan and decide to change the subject to avoid torturing myself.

"Where's Samantha tonight?" I ask.

"She's got a playdate with a friend," Iris says, and I find myself looking again at *that* finger and wondering about her story. Maybe she's a single parent.

Nope. *Still* none of my business.

Our server pops up, and I welcome the distraction. I've been here enough times that I basically have the menu memorized and so does Jake, so we're happy to go with the plan to get a bunch of different things for the table to share.

I'm trying to discretely observe Iris to jog my memory when Piper catches me.

"So, does this mean you haven't figured it out yet?" she asks loudly, causing silence to fall over the rest of the table.

"No," I grumble, before realization hits. "Wait, do *you* know?"

"Oh yeah, I texted Iris as soon as we left the bookstore Monday, and she told me." Piper appears rather pleased with herself. Iris is ripping her napkin into tiny pieces and making a pile of the scraps beside the saltshaker.

"And then they both told me today. Party planning turned into yapping, and Iris is one of us now," Alice adds. Iris looks up, seeming pleased about being recruited into the girl gang.

"*I* think you should have remembered her," Alice adds. "Maybe it just wasn't as important to you," she adds.

I don't think Alice meant anything mean by the comment, but the look on Iris's face—a mix of embarrassment and hurt—has me feeling like a real asshole. Iris quickly covers up her reaction, smiling at Alice instead.

Piper nods, agreeing, and the three women take synchronized sips from their drinks. Then six eyes stare me down. This is the problem with friend groups. They get too comfortable, and then they adopt new friends who also get comfortable, and suddenly it's pick on Eli night.

"Come on. Help a guy out," I plead.

"No way!" Alice laughs in my face. That's not fair. She's supposed to be too nice to laugh in my face. "You're Mr. Memory, so you need to figure this out. Besides, it's funny to watch you squirm. Usually, you're unshakeable."

Can I say *uncle*? I feel sufficiently shaken.

"Why don't you make him ask questions for clues?" Jake suggests to Iris, either already knowing or having figured out what's happening. While being with Alice has made him less stoic, I expect he still wants to move things along rather than watch our conversation go in circles.

Scott is immediately on board with turning this into a game at my expense.

"Shouldn't you two be on my side?" I grumble to the men who are allegedly my *brothers*. Fucking traitors.

"No, I like this idea," Iris says, and her confidence builds. She thinks for a moment and crosses her arms. "You can ask me five questions, but they have to be yes-or-no questions only."

Iris looks at me, and it feels like a challenge, like she's saying *You should know me. You should understand.*

Alice and Piper are practically giddy with amusement.

Beers for me and Jake arrive. After I take a drink, everybody is still looking expectantly at me.

"You all suck," I say, but I start thinking of a question anyway. Got it.

"Did we meet at some point between when you moved to Wilcox Grove last May and Scott's birthday party in August?"

"No," Iris says and offers no further detail. I guess she's really only going to give me a yes or a no.

Maybe I shouldn't have wasted a question on that. I *knew* there was no way I'd forget her so quickly.

"So, we met somewhere other than Wilcox Grove?" I blurt before I realize that's my second question.

"No," Iris says again, and my eyebrows shoot up.

She was here before she moved to town? I don't say this question out loud, though. I only have three left, and I want to make them count. I go quiet as I try to think of something good.

An enormous plate of wings arrives, and I take a flat one, pulling the bones apart while I think. I can feel everybody's eyes on me, but I don't let it shake me. They can wait.

"You have to ask all your questions tonight," Alice pipes up, clearly impatient. "I want to be around to hear them."

"You can't make up new rules," I protest.

"No, but I can, and I agree with Alice. Use 'em or lose 'em, bucko." Iris holds my gaze. She's *daring* me to solve her puzzle.

I stare flatly back, but she just doubles down on that look. I take what is meant to be a menacing bite of my wing but fail spectacularly. First, because it's biting a wing—hardly menacing. And second, because it's shockingly spicy, and I fall into a coughing fit.

"Smooth," Scott mutters not at all quietly.

"Shut up," I rasp once I can breathe again.

"Did he hit on you?" Scott asks Iris, ignoring my peril.

"No," Iris answers after a pause, like she's not entirely sure of that answer. She must be mistaken.

"Why?" I blurt. She's fucking beautiful, and I can't think of why I wouldn't try to shoot my shot like I did last August.

"That's not a yes-or-no question. You have to play by the rules," Iris admonishes, even going so far as to wag her finger at me.

I raise my eyebrows at her.

"Ok, teacher," I say automatically.

She quickly pulls her finger back and sits on her hand. If she wasn't flushed before, she *certainly* is now.

"If it's not a yes-or-no question. It shouldn't count toward the five," I insist.

"Fine, that doesn't count since I didn't answer, but Scott's question does count. You've got two left."

I glare at Scott. He doesn't give a shit and opens his mouth, potentially to use up another of my questions, but I wrap my arm around his head and slap my hand over the lower half of his face, crushing him against my shoulder effectively in a headlock.

Penny comes by with sliders, cheese fries, and grilled veggie kebabs—so we can pretend this is a balanced meal—and eyes me and Scott.

"Y'all good over here?" she asks.

"All good, ma'am!" I answer while Scott waves for help. "Ignore him," I add.

Penny looks between me and Scott again before shaking her head and muttering "not my circus" as she walks away.

"I'll let go because I want to eat, but nobody gets to use my last two questions," I say. Scott gives a thumbs-up, and I release him.

Piper and Iris thankfully start talking about Samantha's upcoming birthday party while we work our way through half of the Corner Post's menu, so I have a second to *think*.

Iris lights up the second she starts talking about how thrilled Samantha will be once she finds out she gets to celebrate her birthday at the bookstore. I may not have known Iris long (or maybe I have), but I think it's safe to say that little girl is her whole world.

"You'll all help set up, right?" Piper directs her question to the whole table.

Scott immediately agrees. He'd flay himself if it would help Piper.

"I'm sorry, but I can't," Alice says. "I've got tutoring on Saturday mornings."

"I'm at the nursery Saturdays," Jake grunts. Then, he looks up with a foxlike grin. "But Eli doesn't need to be there."

"Perfect! Eli and I will be setup crew," Scott chirps.

"Does Eli get to decide where Eli needs to be and what crews Eli will be on?" I ask uselessly.

"No," Scott and Jake answer simultaneously.

"I'd like to go back to being an only child again. You're both fired from being my brothers."

Then I catch Piper's eye, and she's looking at me with wide eyes and an enormous pout.

"You know I'll help." I cave instantly.

Piper's expression flips to one of glee. I knew she was manipulating me, but it didn't matter. I don't want my friends to be sad, even if it's fake sad.

"You're too good to us, Eli," Piper says.

"I am." But I like to be needed.

"I appreciate all of your help," Iris says, and I don't feel so annoyed about being volun-told after all. "If you want to put it in your calendar, it's on February twenty-first," she adds.

Scott pulls out his phone right away to get it down, and when Iris looks at me, I'm reminded of a teacher yet again.

"Oh, Eli doesn't use his calendar," Scott explains, and I pull out my phone to show Iris the completely blank app.

"How?" The shock on her face confirms my suspicion. Iris is a bit of a control freak. That woman is wound *tight*.

I shrug. "I remember things."

"Except meeting Iris, apparently," Scott unhelpfully adds. He quickly scoots his chair away from me when I glare at him.

I turn my focus to my food before I get roped into doing anything else. I need to think of my last two questions anyway.

I eavesdrop on the chatter around me and get more information about Iris, though it doesn't help me place her. I learn Iris works for her uncle and is originally from Newport. She went to college in Boston and had Samantha during her senior year.

I also went to college in Boston, but if Samantha is about to turn five, and Iris had her during her senior year, we wouldn't have overlapped. Plus, Iris already said we didn't meet outside of Wilcox Grove.

"Alright, enough about me before I give up even more free information," Iris says as she leans back in her chair. "It's time for your last two questions, mister."

"Did we meet through a mutual friend?" I ask.

Iris looks thoughtful for a few moments, like the answer isn't straightforward. Eventually she says, "Yes."

I can only ask yes or no questions, so I unfortunately can't ask who we both know, though I expect that would give me all I need. I've only got one question left, and I'm no closer to figuring this out.

Iris's phone alert tone sounds.

"Sorry," she says, pulling it out and checking it. "I just leave the sound on for Sam. It's time for me to go get her."

She motions for Piper to let her out, and Iris hops to her feet and passes some cash to Piper before pulling on her coat.

"Wait," I say, pushing my chair back since it looks like Iris is about to bolt. "What about my last question?"

"Sam comes first," Iris says with a smile, and of course she does, but it's just one more question. Iris *really* sticks to her schedule. "You can ask it *right* now."

I don't know what to ask. I actually don't have a single thought in my brain.

"Uh..." I say stupidly.

"Tick-tock, tick-tock," she taunts. "Last chance..."

I can't think of anything to ask.

She makes a sound like a game buzzer. "Sorry. I've got to go."

She turns to leave, and I jump to my feet, telling the table I'll be right back.

Iris moves quickly and is already at the door, so I hurry after her.

"Wait, Iris!" I call once I'm outside. Even in the dimly lit lot, I can see her golden hair glowing like a beacon. She pauses for a moment, and I catch up.

"Did you like me when we met? Like, was I nice?" I blurt when I reach her, feeling dumb as soon as I do. What good is that to know?

Her eyes dart to mine.

"Yes, I did, and you were," she says quietly. She breathes in, and I get the distinct feeling she wants to say more. Instead, she pulls her gaze from mine and looks over her shoulder, presumably toward her car.

"Thank everyone for inviting me," she says when she turns back to me.

"I will." I look into those all-knowing eyes. "I really didn't hit on you?"

"I guess not," she says quietly, and it again feels like there's more to this story.

With a wave, she's gone, and I'm more curious than ever.

Iris, who are you?

CHAPTER 5

Meet at the bookstore at 9 for the bus.

Can't wait!!

I stare at our group chat with a mix of anticipation and dread. On the one hand, I'm thrilled to celebrate Alice's birthday tonight, but on the other, going out really isn't my thing. Plus, it means being away from Sam, which makes me feel guilty as hell. She's already only got one parent, and I don't want her to feel abandoned or like spending time with her isn't my first choice.

But after spending my first eight months back in Wilcox Grove mostly with my uncles, my daughter, and Olivia, I don't want to decline an invitation from my new friends. I might not get another one, and it feels nice to be included. I just wish it wasn't an invite to go out to some club. Even before I became a mother, I was a stay home and watch a movie kind of girl.

Tonight's plans are *far* from that. Surprising as it may be,

Wilcox Grove's night scene is… lacking. We have one bar. It's a good bar, but it's not really a dancing bar. Alice picked some place in a nearby town that has a DJ, and Piper booked a bus so nobody has to drive. I don't know exactly where this place is or how long we're staying or who all will be there.

To say I'm stressed about the whole thing would be an understatement.

While I contemplate what to say to the girls, a ping from my laptop alerts me to a new email, and I reflexively groan before reminding myself that *I love my job*. Harry's forwarded some more random, disorganized notes about client accounts. I've been helping pull things together so our tax guy can file the firm's return and figuring out both Harry's and Isabella's *systems* has been… challenging.

My printer whirs to life, spitting out the newest additions for my pile of random scraps—notes, receipts, and bills—when another series of texts come through.

ALICE

Here's to turning 30!

PIPER

Alice. You're turning 31…

ALICE

But turning 30 sounds more fun. Thirty, flirty, thriving and all that jazz.

The message is followed by a super close-up picture of Alice's face, eyes squeezed closed and mouth open in glee. She looks *so* damn happy. I smile to myself and make the split-second decision to commit for the birthday girl. I can do this. Besides, I can hardly call myself a girls' girl if I bail on her *birthday*. If all else fails, I can hide by our table and guard everybody's drinks.

ME

I'll be there!

Piper adds a heart to my message while Alice replies with a string of the excited screaming emoji that looks remarkably like the picture she sent a minute ago. I find myself smiling wider, even as I flip open the tax binder.

As I peel away the temporary tattoo paper and reveal my silver glitter freckles, Sammy gasps, and I really do feel pretty.

"What do you think, lil' one?" I ask, turning my head back and forth so the freckles shimmer.

The entire contents of my closet are piled on my bed—a problem *later me* is going to curse out *current me* for. After much searching, followed by ransacking Olivia's closet too, I finally settle on a black denim vest, skinny jeans, and black cowboy boots. I feel stupid dressing like this when it's still January, but I'm planning ahead for a crowded, hot club.

"You look like a princess," Sam exclaims from where she sits cross-legged among the mayhem that is my bed. She must be focusing more on the sparkles than the cowboy boots.

The vest is a little cropped, and every one of my curves is on full display. I'm about as far out of my comfort zone as I'm willing to venture tonight, but I tell myself that's not always a bad thing. It's good to celebrate this body and the amazing things it's done for me, especially when my daughter is looking at me. I read a *lot* of parenting books when I found out I was pregnant, and I like to hope those authors would be proud of me in this moment.

"Thank you," I say as I plant a kiss on top of Sam's head. "I think I'm ready."

And it's a good thing, because just then I hear a knock coming from downstairs.

"Go get your backpack," I instruct Sammy, but she's already taking off to collect her sleepover bag.

I head downstairs and open the front door for Kenny. Beyond him, I can see Harry sitting in their idling car.

"Well don't you look nice!" Kenny says as he instructs me to turn around. "It's good to see you do remember you're still in your twenties," he teases.

"I'm ancient on the inside," I joke back, though some days it doesn't feel very joking. My life is what it is, and I'm not sure much will change when I am old. That's ok. It's not a bad life.

"Uncle Kenny!" Sammy cries as she thunders down the stairs and crashes into him at full speed. "What are we going to do tonight?"

"I don't know. Do you want to watch a movie?" Kenny suggests.

"It is already way past your bedtime, missy," I remind them both.

"Mooooom," she whines.

"Yeah, moooooom," Kenny joins in, and I roll my eyes.

"Just be good for your uncles," I relent. One late night won't kill her. Besides, she'll probably pass out ten minutes into whatever they put on.

The two of them still cheer like they won a major victory and proceed to brainstorm movie options while we put on our coats, on the walk to the car, and for the whole drive to the bookstore where I'm getting dropped off.

Piper opens my door and hollers a "good night!" as she pulls me out of the car and into a hug. I can see Scott, Jake, Leslie, and Hannah standing next to a small bus with blacked-out windows. I wave at them over Piper's shoulder.

"You made it," she squeals in my ear, crushing me against her. "Just so you know, Alice pre-gamed with Leslie and Hannah."

The warning comes just in time because next thing I know, Alice has popped up out of nowhere and thrown her arms around the both of us, nearly taking us all to the ground. Even with the heels on my boots, I'm still significantly shorter than both of them, so I'm thankful Piper helped keep us from toppling over.

"You look *hot*, Iris," she bends to say in my ear. I think she intended to whisper, but failed spectacularly, basically shouting at me instead.

"So do you, birthday girl," I say on a laugh before turning my head back to Piper. "I need to be on her level."

"Me too," she agrees. "Once Eli gets here, we can go."

As if summoned, Eli's Jeep pulls up, and he parks at the curb. Since Alice still has both me and Piper in a bear hug, we turn as a discombobulated unit toward him as he unfolds all six-foot-what-ever of himself from the driver's seat.

"It's time to go!" Alice squeals before disentangling herself from me and Piper and running off on surprisingly steady heels toward the bus.

"I'm going to make sure the driver is all set since I doubt Alice is up to the task," Piper says before following after the birthday girl, leaving me as Eli's welcoming party of one.

Usually bright and cheerful, he's all dark and broody tonight, and I can't look away. He's like a walking shadow in a black button-up and dark jeans, every inch of fabric looking like it was made for him. I force my eyes away when he unbuttons one cuff at his wrist and begins folding back the sleeve before shutting the driver's side door.

For the love of all that is holy...

"Iris," Eli greets me with a polite tip of his head. While he's subtle about it, I watch his eyes trail down my body, and it feels like he leaves a trail of fire in his wake. He whistles low, and even though he doesn't say a single word about my appearance, his approval hits me somewhere deep in a way that Alice's blatant compliment from moments ago did not.

"Hello," I reply, sounding steadier than I feel.

When he offers his arm to escort me to the bus, I'm pleasantly surprised and accept it, goosebumps erupting all the way up my arms when I do. I tell myself it's because it's cold out.

I need to get a grip.

Once we're at the bus, Eli shifts his hold to my hand and helps me up the stairs.

"Thank you," I say politely, releasing his hand and stepping up into the bus. I'm glad it's dark so he can't see how I've turned scarlet.

I breathe slowly to regain control of myself as I climb the remaining steps onto the bus. I'm a responsible adult. I should act like it.

Suddenly, I'm bathed in swirling, colored lights.

This isn't just a bus. It's a *party bus*. The rest of the group is already loaded up. I feel Eli step up behind me, a heat at my back, but I don't turn, instead taking in the scene before me. Alice is unsurprisingly already dancing with Hannah, and Piper is popping a bottle of champagne.

"Surprise!" she exclaims as bubbles drip over her fingers. "I thought it'd be more fun to travel this way."

Sticky glasses are passed around, and Piper calls for a toast to Alice. We're all tipping our heads back as the bus pulls away from the curb. I stumble to the side at the abrupt movement, but a strong hand wraps around my upper arm to steady me. I look up… and up… and up—damn, Eli is *tall*—and find warm eyes looking down on me.

"Thanks," I breathe out after far too long a pause.

Eli doesn't comment on the delay, though. He just smiles and slowly releases me, making sure I'm steady before letting go completely.

This is dangerous territory, and it feels nice. When Eli turns and leans over to say something to Scott, I can't help it, I tilt my head and admire the view of him in those jeans. Shameless, sure, but *damn* it's worth it.

When Eli straightens back up, I come to my senses and scurry away to claim a seat between Leslie and Piper, wedging myself into it. The rest of the ride is a blast, and part of me wishes we could just spend the night driving around, but we soon pull up outside a club with music loud enough to hear from inside the bus. I feel a bit of my buzz fade when I spot the length of the line, but Scott steps out first and after talking to the bouncer for about a minute, waves us over.

A quick ID check later, and we're being ushered inside. Is Scott a secret celebrity?

I guess none of the bus drinks count because Piper hollers "I said first round on me!" and waves us all over to the bar. We squeeze between clumps of people in the quickly-filling space, and somehow Piper spots the other couple we're meeting here—a woman named Ila and her husband.

I'm squished next to Piper, so I can hear when she orders a round of tequila shots. I catch her and Scott sharing a secret look, intrigued by the sly smile that quirks up the corners of her lips. There's a story here for sure.

"Hey!" Piper protests when Scott hands his card to the bartender. "I said I had first round."

"Soon enough, my money will be your money, and this won't matter." Scott sighs, clearly reiterating something he's said before.

"Is this you proposing, Mr. Preston?" Piper asks, leaning into him and batting her eyelashes.

"When I propose, it won't be in a sticky bar where I can't hear myself think. This place is for questionable decisions, not proposing," Scott answers.

Piper narrows her eyes at him but laughs when he snakes an arm around her waist and pulls her off balance, yanking her against him and kissing her deeply. I look away, wishing there was a way to give them any more privacy.

Scott quickly signs the receipt the bartender brings back, and Piper starts handing out the shots, offering limes too. I notice she doesn't take one herself, but I certainly do. We shift around until Alice is in the center of our crowded clump.

"To Alice!" we cry, and it's bottoms up.

I'm biting my lime and trying not to let tears fall from my eyes when I feel my phone buzz. I pull it out of my pocket and see a text from Olivia. She's finally done with work.

"Oh! Tell her to come meet us! She can ride back with us, and someone can come with her to get her car tomorrow," Alice insists. I'm impressed she can read the screen upside down. Drunk Alice is impressively functional.

I pass along Alice's invite, and after a little bullying, Olivia says she's on her way. More drinks are ordered, and with a cool glass in my hand, I'm somehow shuffled with our group onto the dance floor.

I quickly learn it doesn't matter whether you can dance or not when the floor is this crowded because you can barely do much more than jump up and down. It's loud, and I'm being jostled among sweaty bodies, and my fingers are damp from my drink sloshing over the rim of my glass. It must be the magic of bus champagne mixed with tequila because I don't mind one bit. It's messy and disorganized, and I think I might be having *fun*.

Time loses all meaning, but eventually I catch sight of Eli parting the crowd and coming right toward me. I look around, but I've somehow separated from our group. It's just me and Eli.

"Iris," he greets me, and his voice sounds deeper than it did earlier tonight. It scratches my brain and makes me smile.

"Hello," I say, mirroring our earlier greeting.

My head feels a little fuzzy, and I'm much less inclined to be responsible. His eyes catch mine, playful and smiling, and I feel that rush again. I want to be bold, so I hold my ground as he inches forward, invading my space. My hand lands on his exposed forearm and slides up toward his elbow.

My phone is buzzing in my pocket again, and I know I should check it, but I'm having a difficult time pulling my eyes away from Eli's. The vibration stops for a second before picking back up.

I must make a face because Eli asks, "What is it?"

For reasons unknown, I find this very funny and giggle.

"My phone keeps buzzing," I say.

"Should you answer it?" Eli asks, looking like he's enjoying the ridiculousness of having this boring conversation in the middle of a dance club.

"Probably," I admit with a huff.

"Let me," he offers, reaching his arm I'm not holding hostage around me easily and into my back pocket. He's just so *big*.

I like when the screen of my phone illuminates his face. It's such a nice face to look at, especially when he's smiling like he is now—with a big grin, like he's just discovered something wonderful.

I don't pull back when Eli bends low, so his lips are right by my ear. My heart is hammering. He's strong and kind. He makes me feel… well, he makes me *feel*. Maybe I could let this happen, just once. Maybe my worries about a just-for-fun guy like Eli— worries that I can't seem to think of right now—are wrong. It wouldn't be such a big deal, and it would feel *so* good. I feel myself lean further into him, until his lips brush my skin.

"I remember meeting you now, Iris," he says loud enough for me to hear him over the thumping beat.

I turn more and catch his eye as he straightens up, that wicked smile on his lips. My head is swirling.

He what?

Then, he flips my phone around. There are a couple of texts from Olivia, letting me know she parked and asking where I am. But behind it is a picture of three faces squished together: mine, Sam's, and Olivia's. Eli's thumb is tapping by Olivia's cheek, trying to draw my attention to her, but my eyes are on Sam.

What was I *thinking*?

CHAPTER 6

SEVEN AND A HALF YEARS AGO, SUMMER

I poke around the big bucket of ice, but all I can find is light beer, and I really hate light beer. I should have let Liv get our drinks. These are her friends, in her town, by her lake, and she knows where the good stuff is hidden.

I look up, trying to find her so I can summon her to my rescue, but she's surrounded by a group of people, all enthralled with whatever she's saying. Olivia has always been like that. People are drawn to her. I don't fault her for it—it's how we became friends too—and she always makes sure I've got a spot right by her side whenever we're together, but I can barely hold a conversation with a single person, let alone keep the attention of a whole gaggle.

Maybe I shouldn't have come at all. This really isn't my scene, and that's ok. I like who I am. I'm smart, responsible, reliable, the person you come to for notes when you miss class. When I stick to things meant for girls like me, I get along just fine. It's when I venture out into unknown territory like this that I get tripped up.

I groan and try to find the least offensive beer in the tub.

"Hey," a voice softly calls, trying to discreetly get my attention.

I look up and see a giant of a man standing beside the picnic table a couple yards away and waving me over. Stupidly, I look around before pointing at myself.

Me?

He nods and gestures more urgently. I nervously pull the strings on my hoodie, tightening the opening around my face. I probably look like a psycho with the hood up in the middle of summer, but it's too late to change that now. I scamper to the stranger, lumbering clumsily as the sand slips between my toes. I don't know how hot people run so majestically on sand. I can barely walk.

"I don't think I know you. Are you new in town?" he asks once I'm close enough, smiling brightly at me.

Being so near to him now, his face kind of stuns me. He has deep blue eyes and a wide smile, one that makes you want to trust him with your secrets. He seems easy to like, and there's no denying this whole dashing blond, boy-next-door-if-the-boy-next-door-was-built-like-a-house thing he's got going on works well for him.

I really wish I didn't look like a turtle hiding in my enormous sweatshirt right now.

I try to speak, but words aren't working out well for me, so I just shake my head.

"Who'd you come with?" he asks, and I point toward the growing clump of people around Olivia.

His smile grows the way most peoples' do when they look at Olivia. Her light is infectious. But then he looks back to me and hunches over, lifting the corner of a red and white checkered tablecloth, revealing a cooler hiding underneath.

"Don't tell," he says, holding a finger to his lips and silently shushing me.

*I crouch down by his side to peer under the table and instinc-
tively pull back my hood to see better. When I glance at the guy,
he looks surprised for a moment, his eyes bouncing all over my
face before his sweet smile reappears.*

*He reaches forward and hooks a finger around my ponytail
before coaxing it out of the neck of my sweatshirt and letting it
fall over my shoulder. I feel like a frozen baby deer for the whole
interaction.*

*"There you are," he whispers as he slides his fingers to the
end of my ponytail, and I can feel his breath on my face. It smells
a little like beer, and maybe I don't hate beer after all.*

*"Hey, Eli!" somebody calls from across the park where the
cornhole tournament is set up, and both the giant and I jump.
"You're up, man!"*

*"Shit," the man apparently known as Eli hisses, his brow
furrowing. Does he not want to go? He groans and rolls his eyes
like he's engaging in an internal battle.*

*"Sorry," he says, standing up straight. "Coming!" he calls
back to his friend before looking back at me and tapping the
cooler under the table. "Remember. It's our secret. I'll find you
later?"*

*When I nod, his eyes crease with the intensity of his smile, and
I'm dazzled. He gives me a two-finger wave before turning and
running across the sand. Of course, he's one of those people who
can make it look effortless.*

"Bye," I whisper to the empty air.

*I pull vodka from the cooler and make a couple mixed drinks
before tucking it back into its hiding space and heading to Olivia.
She immediately spots me and parts the crowd to pull me through.
I feel so much better with her arm looped through mine.*

*"Oh, nice!" Olivia says when I hand her one of the plastic
cups, clearly pleased I didn't bring her nasty, beer-flavored water.*

"Ooh! You got to the good cooler! That officially makes you

one of us," Olivia's friend, Leslie, says from Liv's other side. She's always been kind and welcoming to me.

I smile back, but it doesn't feel genuine, no matter how much I wish it did.

Chatter picks up around us, and I can't think of a single thing to say. Olivia glances toward me and must see something in my expression.

"Do you want to go watch the cornhole game?" she asks suddenly.

Of course, I want to say yes. Even from here, I can see Eli's blond hair. Either his team is winning or he's just the happiest guy ever. Another guy jumps at Eli, and Eli hoists him up in a giant bear hug. I can feel myself staring, but I don't want to look away.

But then, from the corner of my eye, I catch Leslie looking longingly over to the bonfire where I know a woman is toasting marshmallows, a newcomer to town who Leslie's been trying to get the courage to speak to all night. I think she might need some help, and I'm the kind of girl who helps.

There's another burst of cheering from the game area. The quiet bonfire is better for somebody like me anyway.

"Maybe in a bit," I answer Olivia. "I need Leslie to show me the bonfire first."

Leslie's eyes go wide when she looks at me, ready to protest, but I just spin her toward the flickering light and give her a loving push. Olivia looks over at the fire and quickly catches on to my plan.

"Ooh, gotcha. Have fun you two," she says with a giggle. "Find me after."

Ignoring her attempts to resist, I force Leslie forward, walking over to the empty log beside the new girl and shoving Leslie into the seat beside her, plopping myself down on Leslie's other side.

"Hi, I'm Iris, and this is Leslie," I brazenly introduce us while

Leslie stares at a spot in the sand between her feet. When it's for somebody else, I've got no problem finding my voice.

"I'm Hannah," the woman says, extracting her skewer from the fire. She easily sandwiches the marshmallow between some chocolate and two graham crackers. "Can I interest either of you in a s'more?"

"Oh, they're Leslie's favorite," I say, basically forcing the poor girl into the chat.

"Then I made this just for you," Hannah says sweetly as she holds the s'more out to Leslie.

Leslie finally looks at Hannah, and I swear I can feel them fall for one another. They don't notice when I stand up, intending to go find Olivia.

But Olivia doesn't see me. She's being led to a truck by a tall, blond man.

My phone buzzes in my back pocket.

LIV

> I'm headed out, but please text me when you get home. Breakfast tomorrow morning?

I watch Olivia slip her phone into her bag and toss her hair over her shoulder. Eli's eyes are glued to her.

Olivia finds me on the dance floor and shoves past Eli to give me a hug. I sink into her, wanting to cling to her forever as a tether back to control.

"Where's Alice?" she yells, lifting onto her toes to try to spot the birthday girl.

Don't go, I want to say, but Eli, a head above both me and my roommate, directs her through the crowd.

Once Olivia has slipped away, Eli stands before me again, arms crossed, playful expression on his face.

"You're Olivia's friend. And you have been her friend since we used to have those stupid parties at the park on the lake," Eli recounts.

Stiffly, I nod in confirmation. Just like on that day, I want to leave. I don't belong here. I should be home with Sam.

"Aw, come on Iris. Don't be mad at me. It's been like seven years, and if I remember correctly, you didn't even speak to me. You can't hold this against me forever."

"I never held it against you," I say, hoping he can hear me.

His brow furrows.

"Are you alright?" he asks.

Somebody pushes through behind me, and I lurch forward. Eli's hands quickly wrap around my biceps to steady me. I jump back like I've been burned.

"Iris, are you ok?" he says again.

"I have to go," I say to Eli before turning and disappearing into the crowd without giving him a chance to respond.

CHAPTER 7

Eli

I hate winter.

That's not fair. I don't hate winter. I hate feeling like garbage on Monday because I dared to go out on Friday. Thirty-one isn't old, and I don't often *feel* old, but my hangover on Saturday, and my day spent vegging out on my couch on Sunday, overthinking how Iris ran away from me *again* make me feel old.

Clearly, she isn't interested, and I need to accept that and move on. I'd be no good for her anyway. I can't offer the stability that a woman like her deserves, not when I've never once wanted a second date or any of the responsibility that comes with a relationship.

So maybe I'm just in a shit mood, and I don't actually hate winter.

I do, however, hate tax season.

As an accountant who was not forced into the profession, I understand the irony of my feelings. It's almost as ironic as somebody who lives in northern New Hampshire saying they hate winter. Which I don't, to clarify.

It's just so cold and dark and shoveling snow is the fucking worst. Plus, since we live in the middle of nowhere, our electrical grid isn't the strongest, and we lose power at the slightest hint of a snowstorm, which makes things even colder and darker and more miserable. *And* tax season falls right in the middle of this cold, dark, miserable excuse of an existence. It ends up being so much time *alone*, which is really not my favorite.

Ok. Maybe I do hate winter. I'm just saying. That groundhog had better not see its shadow today…

At least I'm not Jake, I think as he comes clambering into the office at Wilcox Nursery after a stint braving the elements in our fields. Jake pulls off his beanie and a wet clump of slush slaps on the floor with an unappealing squelch.

Jake seems surprisingly unbothered by his general state of dampness or the seventeen layers he has to wear to avoid catching hypothermia out there. In fact, he's positively chipper. It's a pretty bizarre turn of events since usually I'm the optimistic one, and historically, he's been as cheerful as a rabid honey badger.

I've never actually encountered a rabid honey badger, but I feel confident in the analogy.

Jake catches me looking at him with what I expect is a perplexed expression on my face.

"The new drainage system we put in this summer is working in spite of the temperature." He shrugs like that explains his honestly alarming smile.

"Ah, yes. Nothing like functional drainage to put a man in a good mood," I say with a chuckle.

I know as well as he does that his whole personality did a one-eighty after he finally got together with Alice the year before last. After they got engaged last Christmas, he's basically had rainbows coming out his ass.

"Hey, snow mold is no laughing matter," Jake says.

Jake, Scott, and I jointly own Wilcox Nursery, but Jake is our resident farmer, a responsibility he takes very seriously. He loves being out in those fields, helping everything we offer to grow and flourish.

I also love our fields, just when it's at least fifty degrees warmer.

When the weather is like this, I appreciate being the back-of-house guy here. Most of my quality time is spent at my desk, organizing our files or on the phone with vendors. During tax season, I also help a lot of the businesses around Wilcox Grove with their filings. Most of our town's economy is made up of small, family-owned establishments whose "recordkeeping" consists of a box of crumpled receipts, so I step in to help them avoid unintentional tax fraud.

It all started a few years ago when I overheard Hannah and Leslie arguing about how to complete their return while I was picking up a cup of coffee, and my little side hustle has grown steadily since. I don't like saying *no* when somebody asks for help, so I don't.

Scott is our third and silent partner here. He's legally an owner because Jake's portion of the cash to buy this place came from life insurance money Jake and Scott received jointly after they lost their parents. Initially, Scott's portion of the profits from the nursery were set aside for him, but he's chosen to reinvest it in the business or make donations around town for several years now. I have a theory he's secretly rich or something, but I haven't worked up the nerve to actually ask him about it yet. Besides, that would be nuts.

As Jake disappears into the greenhouse attached to the office, I look back over the list of businesses I'll be helping this season. I have a couple I still need to confirm scope of work with, but it's going to be a busy stretch of time here for me pretty soon.

Jake can't have been in the greenhouse more than fifteen minutes, but when he reappears, his sleeves have been shoved up, and he's got dirt up to his elbows. I think he'd live in a dirt hut in the woods if Alice would let him.

"Hey man, I hate to ask, but is there any way you'd be able to pick up Waffles from the house? Alice is trying to leave for class, and the weather is supposed to get bad later, so she's worried about leaving him there alone," Jake asks as he approaches my desk.

Waffles is the golden retriever that Alice adopted for Jake's birthday last May. He's the sweetest dog but does get a little nervous when the wind picks up. The lakeside houses in this town are old and can get noisy when wind whips against them. Last time he was home alone in a storm, he burrowed straight through Jake and Alice's bedroom door, poor thing.

"Of course I can," I say, already standing and putting on my coat. I pull out my phone to check the forecast. "Is Alice going to be ok getting to the college?"

Her job as an English professor isn't too far from Wilcox Grove, but the backroads are dark and winding.

"She should be alright getting there and back. We're mostly worried about the wind knocking out power and heat," Jake explains. Jake points a soil-covered finger toward his desk. "My keys are in my coat in case she has to take off before you get there. I really appreciate it, man."

I look down at the list of businesses on my own desk. "Happy to do it. Is it alright if I take Waffles to a few places around town before I come back?"

"Whatever you need." Jake shrugs, already heading back to his dirt.

I unplug the space heater that had been blowing on my chair, pull on my hat and gloves, and step outside to brave the elements.

I must have just missed Alice because the house is empty except for Waffles when I get there. He greets me the second I open the front door, jumping up and placing his paws against my hip. I'm probably supposed to scold him for hopping up without permission, but that's his parents' job. I'm the uncle who gets to spoil him.

He's gotten so big compared to the little fuzzball he was last May, but he doesn't seem to have noticed. As far as Waffles is concerned, he's still a little baby puppy who needs and deserves constant love and attention. Looking into his enormous eyes, I can't disagree.

"Do you want to go for a ride?" I ask as I pull his collar and leash off a hook behind the door. The way his tail starts flying back and forth tells me he was born ready. I clip his collar on and slip back outside. While I lock up, Waffles looks as unbothered by the cold as Jake did. Like father, like son, I guess.

After a quick bathroom stop for Waffles, I lead him to the back of my Wrangler, where I've already folded down the seats. He easily jumps into the Jeep and flops down on the blanket I arranged for him. When I get in and crank the heat, he repositions himself so the center vents blow right on his face.

Like I said. He's just a baby.

In no time at all, we're cruising down Main Street, and Waffles has his head on swivel mode to take everything in. We swing by the pizzeria before heading to Barefoot Bake.

"Waffles!" Hannah cheers from behind the counter when we walk in.

"I see where I stand in the order of importance," I joke. "It's fine."

I'm ignored. Maybe my joke wasn't a joke after all.

A second later Leslie appears from the back of the café.

"Did I hear you say Waffles?" she asks, quickly spotting my

furry companion and hurrying over to kneel beside him. I remain invisible. If my ego was smaller, this would hurt.

"Do you mind if I give him a c-o-o-k-i-e?" Hannah asks, careful not to say one of Waffles's favorite words around him, solidifying the fact that I exist solely to serve Waffles.

"He was very well-behaved when we saw Mark at the pizzeria, so he's earned it," I say, though we all know he would have gotten the cookie either way.

"What brings you by, Eli? Can I get you anything?" Hannah asks after passing the cookie off to Leslie, who has Waffles going through a series of commands before he gets his treat.

"I just wanted to confirm you needed help with your taxes this year and see if there's anything I should know about before we start," I say. "But, since I'm here, I'd love a hot chocolate, please."

"Ah, I see. You brought the dog to make taxes not boring," Hannah says on a laugh as she makes her way back behind the counter and starts washing her hands.

"That wasn't my intention, but his presence certainly doesn't hurt," I admit before holding up my hands in surrender. "This isn't my fault though. I didn't write the Code."

The smell of molten chocolate quickly fills the space. Hannah wouldn't be caught dead using the powdered stuff. She melts real chocolate for her hot cocoa, making it rich, delicious, and the equivalent of crack.

"Well, since you understand it, and I don't want to figure it out, yes, please help us again," Hannah confirms as she hands me the warm paper cup. "You already know we made Piper a partial owner at the start of Q4 last year, and that's the only major difference from the year before. Is that ok?"

I take a careful sip of the steaming drink. It's heavenly. "You could tell me you restructured everything the day before year end, and as long as you keep supplying me with these, I'd be fine with it," I say, a little dazed from the decadent drink. "I'll write up the statement of work and email it to you in a few days."

When I glance down, I see Waffles looking up at me hopefully.

"Sorry buddy," I say, lifting my cup even further out of his reach. "This one isn't for you. Go bother the ladies, and maybe they'll give you another cookie."

His ears perk right up at that, and his head whips to Leslie again. He's a clever one.

After Waffles has conned both the café and the bookstore out of treats and pets, we're on our way again. I have one more stop before we head back to the nursery.

Waffles and I head up the creaking steps to the front patio of the beautiful, old, dark maroon building before heading inside. After I wipe my boots on the mat inside and watch Waffles try to adorably and jerkily mimic my motion with his paws, I hang my coat on a peg, and we head down the narrow hallway. We turn into the reception area, and I spot a familiar head of golden blonde hair behind the desk.

"Well, look who it is," I say.

Iris's bright eyes look up and lock with mine, shock on her pretty face.

CHAPTER 8

A deep, smooth voice cuts through my focus, and I blink a few times when I see Eli standing before me... with Alice's dog?

Spending the weekend hyper fixated on how mortifying it was that I completely unraveled Friday night was apparently not punishment enough from the universe. It felt the need to send the witness of my tragic crash out to see me... looking like *that*. My gaze trails down from his windswept hair to his broad chest and dark jeans hugging *thick* thighs.

I *cannot* lose control of myself again. While I was wrong for thinking I didn't deserve to be out with my friends having fun for Alice's birthday, I wasn't wrong to realize I can't have an Eli sex fling.

Ever since Olivia hooked up with Eli, I've known he doesn't do relationships. He won't become somebody's person. Gossip around town has confirmed his outlook has not changed. I think that's great for him, but as a mother and a woman with a plan to hopefully be settled and supported, sexcapades aren't really in the cards. I need to be serious about my future and my daughter's.

While I didn't think I'd see Eli so soon, I prepared myself

yesterday for the possibility, so we could put this whole thing to rest and avoid any misunderstandings.

I mentally recite: *I am a mother. People rely on me. I have goals. I have a five-year plan. What Eli offers doesn't fit with the life I want.*

"Hello," I greet him curtly. It's cold, but Eli's presence here can't throw me off balance again. I can't have him showing up at my work to continue this little game we've been toying with. I can't play at all anymore.

Eli steps forward until he's just on the other side of my desk. He places one large hand on the hard wood and leans forward ever so slightly until he fills my field of vision.

"It's nice to see you," he starts and flashes me one of those brain-altering smiles. "I—"

Nope nope nope nope.

"Look. This can't happen," I blurt and keep barreling forward while his mouth hangs slightly open, mid-word. "I don't know how you found out this is where I work, but I can't have you here. It was nice to see you again, and our little game of you guessing where we met was fun, but I'm not being fair to you. This can't happen between us. You're nice and obviously attractive and I'm flattered, but I have Samantha, and I can't get involved with what you offer women. No judgment—I respect it and respect you, but I need to be practical about my circumstances and what it does and doesn't allow me to do. I can't do *that*, and I hope you understand."

I'm familiar with the saying "it's so quiet you could hear a pin drop," but I've never actually experienced it until now. After what feels like an eon, Eli slowly closes his mouth and rubs a hand against his chin and jaw. It's impossible for me to feel more uncomfortable than I do right now, waiting in this heavy silence for his response.

"Iris," he starts slowly, and I pray he isn't going to plead his case. I don't *want* to reject him, and I don't know how much my resolve can handle. "I'm here to talk with Harry or Bella about preparing the firm's tax return. I didn't know you worked here until Waffles and I came into this room."

I was wrong. Apparently, it *is* possible for me to feel more uncomfortable than I did a minute ago.

"I'm not here to pick you up. I *did* try at Scott's birthday last year, and I don't regret that, but the flirting—the game—was intended to be friendly because I had kind of thought we were becoming *friends* since this is a small town and my friends are your friends. And I like that."

The way he emphasizes the word *friends* makes me wish the expensive carpet beneath my feet would open up so I could disappear right into the floor. Of course he wouldn't think of me like *that* again, not after he met Samantha earlier this month. I've been so focused on reminding myself he isn't what I need that I didn't even think about how *I'm* not what *he* wants.

I feel like such an *idiot*.

I'm trying to think of something, *anything*, to say to help remove my foot from my mouth when Harry appears behind Eli.

"Eli!" It's almost comical how far Harry has to crank his neck up to greet Eli. "It's good to see you."

Eli turns and the men shake hands while the dog starts furiously sniffing Uncle Harry's shoes.

"Are you here to talk taxes?" Harry guesses.

"You know I always come by with the most titillating conversation topics," Eli jokes.

"Why don't you come to my office," Harry suggests, holding out an arm to lead the way.

Before he goes, Eli looks back at me, not a hint of reaction to my mortifying speech on his face, but just imagining the pity he feels for me makes me want to die.

"Do you mind if I leave Waffles with you?" he asks.

I stare dumbly back at him. It's possible I'll never speak in front of Eli again, for fear of saying something stupider than what I just said.

"Go say hi to Iris," Eli says, unclipping the golden retriever's leash before he and Harry walk away, still unbothered. I hear Eli asking about Kenny before Harry's door snicks shut.

Waffles trots over to me and gently lays his large head on my thigh. We've met a few times now when I've hung out with Piper and Alice, and I think he can tell I need comforting after that fiasco. My hand finds his soft fur and begins stroking.

"Thanks, buddy," I whisper, and Waffles sighs in response, leaning his whole body against the outside of my leg. I keep one hand on Waffles's head but get back to reading the case on my computer screen.

Half an hour later, I hear Uncle Harry's door open, and Eli's rich voice is once again filling the space. I consider fleeing to the bathroom and hiding out until Eli leaves, but there's no way to do so without passing right by the men.

I can't make out what they're talking about, but they're getting closer with every passing second, and both Eli and Harry are laughing a moment later. I thought taxes were supposed to be daunting, not amusing. I put on my best mask of professionalism just before the two men re-enter my "office."

"Well, lucky for you, my niece, Iris, has started working here. She'll be helping create the binder and will be available to help you with anything you need," Harry says as he comes up to my desk. Of course he'd make me point person on this.

I see Eli's eyes flash to the nameplate on my desk and watch him read Iris *Sutton*.

"Ah," he says with realization, looking between me and Harry before settling on me. "Of course. You said you worked with your uncle. It's all coming together, now."

"You two know each other already?" Harry gestures between

me and Eli. "Even better. I have a feeling this is going to be our easiest year yet."

"Here's to hoping," Eli agrees, shaking Harry's hand. A ringing phone sounds from down the hallway.

"Oh, that'll be for me. I'll leave you two to sort out next steps, then." Harry hurries back to his office.

Even Waffles's presence fails to provide any sort of buffer, so things feel awkward as soon as it's just us left in the room. Eli puts his hands in the front pockets of his jeans and rocks back on his heels.

"So..." he starts but seemingly hasn't planned anything further.

"I'd appreciate it if we could both forget about my little outburst before," I request calmly, trying to portray a neutrality that is entirely contrary to the churning I'm feeling in my stomach. "I think I had a momentary loss of sanity."

"Hey now, it wasn't that bad," Eli tries, but there's no denying exactly how horrible it was.

"I never should have assumed..." I start but can't bring myself to say *you thought of me that way*. It's way too after-school special. I start over. "I'm sorry for accusing you of all of that."

Eli's brow pulls together, and he looks displeased. He has every right to. I was way off base.

"Iris, it's not that I—"

"Please. Let's forget it. You said friends, right?" I'm not sure friendship can survive my little speech, but I'm grasping at straws. Anything to move on from this part of the conversation.

"Yeah, friends. And maybe partners in tax return?" Eli takes a seat in one of the chairs on the other side of my desk.

"Ok." I desperately clutch to his offer of talking about work and dive in. "Harry got me started on the tax binder early, and I'm mostly duplicating the type of documents that were in the one from last year, but if you could walk me through what you need, that might help make sure I don't miss anything."

"For sure," Eli says, leaning forward to rest his forearms on his knees.

He begins listing off what he needs, slipping between rattling off tax code sections and explaining what they mean so I can follow along. His voice is deep and soothing, and I slowly feel the stiffness seep from my spine as he goes on.

While I'm furiously taking notes on what he says, he recites everything from memory. He's out of my league in so many ways, and another wave of embarrassment washes over me when I remember I thought he was interested in *me*.

It takes me a second to realize Eli has finished speaking, but I recover well enough. I quickly scan my notes to make sure I don't have any questions and then take the binder I'd started out of the bottom drawer of my desk.

"I can pull some more things together, but I can give you what I have already, if you want." I slide the binder over to him.

"That would be great," Eli says with a smile, taking the thick book and flipping it open. "I'll take all the time I can get. Things can get a little hectic closer to filing deadlines. Since the firm is a partnership, that'll be mid-March."

I stay quiet while his eyes run down the summary page I included up front. After checking a few other pages, he looks back up at me.

"I was just sucking up to your uncle before when I agreed that this year would be the easiest yet, but with you doing work like this"—he taps the binder—"I think it just might be. I've never gotten something this organized from a client before."

I know part of the praise might just be Eli being nice after my floundering, but the recognition feels satisfying, nonetheless. I take a lot of pride in my work, and my color-coding is pristine.

"Thank you for saying that. As you're going through things, if you need anything done differently, just let me know. I have my card in the front pocket, and it has my cell on it. Otherwise, I'll try to wrap up the last few matters as soon as I can and get them over to you. Maybe we can set up a schedule for me to get additional documents to you?"

"Whenever they're ready works for me," Eli says, absent-mindedly waving a hand. "I'm flexible."

I'm not, but I don't want to say that and sound like a stick in the mud. I couldn't imagine just winging it. I think I'd probably break out in hives.

"Ok then," I say, already mentally creating a schedule for myself anyway.

Eli nods and lifts the book as he stands, snapping his fingers twice. Waffles reluctantly gets up, but I swear he's dragging his feet as he goes to Eli's side. After reattaching Waffles's leash, Eli pauses.

"How are you at reading Bella's handwriting?" he asks.

"Excellent. Why?"

"I might need your help with deciphering it."

"I'm happy to lend a hand. You're welcome to text me."

Eli is about to turn into the hallway when he stops and looks back at me. He opens his mouth but shuts it again.

"Thanks again. See you around," he finally says.

I think we both know he's not going to text me. There's no way this friendship thing happens after my outburst.

CHAPTER 9

Eli

"That took a while," Jake says from his desk when we finally get back to the nursery. "Is everything ok?"

"As good as tax season can be. Meetings just took longer than expected," I say, unhooking Waffles's leash.

He briefly stops by Jake's chair to receive a welcome scratch behind his ears before going to lie directly in front of my space heater, which Jake must have turned back on when he came inside. I swear Waffles is glaring at me. Jake notices too.

"What's his issue?" he asks.

"I think he's mad at me for taking him away from Iris. She kept an eye on him while Harry and I talked, and I think he has a full-blown crush on her," I answer as I drop my coat over the back of my chair.

"Hm?" Jake says, half paying attention as he flips through a catalogue of flower seeds for the spring.

"Harry Sutton? He owns the law firm near Main Street. Iris is his niece," I explain.

"Oh, yeah," Jake says after a beat, nodding. "I'm with you now. Sorry, Waffles. I'll ask Ace to take you next time they hang out."

I swear Waffles understands because he lays his head down and, with a contented sigh, falls asleep.

I hear you, dude. I like spending time with Iris too.

It's clear Iris is going to be a recurring member of the group, and I don't want things to be weird—not because of me. In spite of what I said to Iris earlier, the sting of her outright rejection is sharp, but friendship is the right option for us. I've known since I met Samantha that we really *should* only be friends, intrigue with her be damned. We're just too different and want different things. I just need to figure out how to convince her this can, and should, work.

I torment myself for a bit longer, determined not to be the source of strife in our group, before I actually focus on my job again.

🐑 🐑 🐑

"How are the Valentine's Day flowers doing?" I ask Jake a bit later as I look over my to-do list.

The second I do, I regret it, because Jake huffs in that dramatic way he does when there's some plant injustice in the world. Valentine's Day is an annual source of agitation for Jake, and it has nothing to do with celebrating the holiday. I think he loves another reason to spoil Alice.

Unsurprisingly, the day hasn't historically been a significant one for me other than the uptick in business.

"They're fine, but whoever decided roses are the flower of Valentine's Day, when Valentine's Day is in *February*, should have their head examined. Roses are not a winter flower."

He's had the same rant every year since we bought the nursery and learned how much work goes into keeping them alive indoors.

"It started with the ancient Greeks and Romans, and Shakespeare reinforced it. They're all dead, so I guess they got what was coming to them," a familiar voice says from the entrance to our office.

Both Jake and I jump, turning to find Grateful Bob leaning against the wall. How he snuck in without either of us noticing, I'll never know. He looks the same as always, long white ponytail hanging down his back and patch-covered denim jacket in its rightful place. Because of the weather, he seems to have added a few more layers under the jacket, but he's otherwise comfortingly unchanged.

"Hey, Grateful Bob," I call over as I stand and approach him.

"Well, it's idiotic," Jake grumbles, still irritated. Grateful Bob and I share a chuckle at his displeasure.

What's family for, anyway? Just like Jake is my brother, Grateful Bob is family to us both. He's a constant in Wilcox Grove and in our lives, a bonus source of advice and friendship.

The old man's grip is strong when he shakes my hand, clapping his other hand on my arm. I doubt I'll ever know how old Grateful Bob is, since he seems to have hit his sixties and simply stopped aging. I'm thankful for that. I need him and his loon obsession to be around forever.

"What can we do for you?" Jake asks, seemingly letting his Valentine's Day irritation go, though the crease between his eyebrows doesn't fully disappear.

"I was headed home and figured I'd stop in to see if you needed me to check on your dog with the weather blowing in tonight," he answers, jerking his head toward Waffles, who is happily snoozing, warming his belly before the space heater. "He seems just fine here."

"Yeah, Eli went to get him earlier so he wouldn't get into any trouble," Jake explains. "I'm going to head back soon since things are getting nasty outside. Why don't you hang around for a bit and come over for dinner?"

"Alright then. Thanks," he agrees.

In spite of Grateful Bob's apparent durability, I know Jake and I both worry about him in his house by himself. It definitely makes *me* feel better knowing he'll be spending his evening with Jake and Alice.

"Eli?" Jake extends the invite.

"Thanks, but I'm going to finish up a couple of things here and then go check on my parents tonight," I explain.

I expect Jake to pack up, but he hesitates. He shuffles some papers on his desk, and I hold off on returning to my own desk.

"Actually, I was hoping to run something by you, an idea I had," Jake finally says, sounding a little unsure of himself.

Grateful Bob must pick up on it too, because he pulls an about-face and suddenly becomes very interested in something at the front of the greenhouse behind him.

"Shoot," I encourage him to continue.

"It's getting crowded in the greenhouse. What do you think about a second one?" Jake asks.

"A wha—?" My brain stumbles to catch up.

"A second greenhouse. I think we could benefit from more indoor space for saplings and potted plants, especially during winter. We have the land for it, and I think we've got the money." Jake stands and unfolds a map of the nursery, pointing to the ample flat space around the office and existing greenhouse. "I ran some numbers on what it might cost to build." He hands me a piece of notebook paper with the figures on it.

I've been encouraging Jake to expand for a while now, but ever since Jake became Scott's guardian over ten years ago, he's been an extremely careful man both in his personal life and with this business. Changes were risks, and stability for Scott was his first and only goal. I couldn't fault the guy for that, so I never pushed *too* hard.

Jake's recent desires to try for more—first by starting a field of Christmas trees fall before last, and now by exploring building a second greenhouse—are huge steps. It's impossible to ignore the positive influence Alice has been on him. Opening himself up to her was a massive risk, but it sure as shit paid off.

I guess things, and people, *can* change.

I know the business's financials inside and out. We're solid and can easily absorb the cost of the greenhouse Jake planned out. The town is loyal, and business is steadily good. Plus, there's Scott's annual reinvestment in the business. Still don't know what the deal is with that.

"I think it's a great idea. If we can get building approvals, I'm all for it," I say, handing him back his price list.

"Ok. So, is that a yes?"

"Yeah, it's a yes," I say, smiling at him. "I'm proud of you," I add. I don't need to say what for. He knows.

When I look over at Grateful Bob, he's carefully examining a very ordinary leaf on a very ordinary plant, but I see a small, proud smile on his face too.

"Shaddup," Jake grumbles, staring very intently at his map as he folds it back up. He clears his throat, now finding the cuff of his sleeve to be fascinating. "I didn't want to raise it with you if it was a non-starter, so I might have already floated it with zoning. We should be able to get the permit quickly. If we could get this up for early spring, it'd be great to start using it for summer tourists."

Jake has always shown his feelings rather than talked about them. I pretend I don't notice his discomfort, so he can pretend he's not uncomfortable. Still, his eyes flash to mine for a second before he shuts down his computer and packs up his things.

"Hey," he says after a few minutes, one hand rubbing against the back of his neck.

"Yeah?"

"Thanks."

I smile and nod. He's just a big softie, after all.

After he, Grateful Bob, and Waffles take off, the wind continues to pick up, and eventually the sleet comes, echoing as it slaps against the roof of the office and greenhouse. When a particularly loud gust of wind shrieks outside, I begin packing up.

My parents aren't frail by any sense of the word, but my dad's back never fully healed after his accident, and it bothers him more on cold and rainy days like today. I like to check in to make sure he isn't overdoing it. I usually pretend I'm coming over just for the free dinner I get out of it, so I don't wound his pride.

I shoot my parents a text to let them know I'm on my way and head out into sideways frozen rain. Having lived all my life, except for college, in Wilcox Grove, I have an SUV that can handle the elements, but I still take it easy, not interested in being surprised by patches of ice.

Mom must have been waiting for me, because the front door to the house opens as I jog up to it with an armful of wood from the shed beside the house. She's bundled up in a thick sweater.

"Eli, what are you doing coming over here in this weather?" she scolds as I set down the wood to remove my jacket and shake out my hair. She takes the jacket and trades me for a towel.

"Oh, you know. Just seeing the sights. Figured I'd look in and check what you're making for dinner." Once I'm dry enough, I pull her in for a hug, and her well-worn smile lines deepen. "Hi, Mom."

As she releases me, the house plunges into darkness. I can barely see light from outside reflecting off her short grey hair.

"Damnit!" I hear my dad's voice from further inside the house.

"Richard!" Mom scolds, shouting right back.

I sigh and take my jacket back from Mom.

"I've got it," I grumble, and head into the storm to hook up the generator and flip the circuit breaker.

Dad is beside Mom when I get back, and I'm now sufficiently soaked to the bone. The appreciative look on their faces makes me not even feel the cold rain. The wood I brought in is gone, and I can hear the faint sounds of a crackling fire from the living room.

"It's good to see you, son," Dad says with a strong grip on my arm. The older I get, the more I see how people say I'm his clone, just twenty-something years younger.

I like seeing with my own two eyes that he's ok. They're both ok.

After I've showered and changed into some spare clothes I keep in my old bedroom, we're seated around the table, enjoying pot roast. My dad is teasing my mom, and she's pretending she doesn't love it.

"You're forbidden from making this roast for anybody other than family. If people find out you can cook like this, they'll steal you away from me, and I'm too old to duel for your hand, Helen," he says sternly.

"Richard," Mom admonishes him again, but her blush gives her away. "You stop it right now."

My parents were high school sweethearts, and even after being married for almost forty years, they still act like giddy teenagers every chance they have. My grandparents on both sides were the same way. I've been surrounded by this kind of green-flag love for my whole life.

After dinner, I help Dad work on the dryer—it's been making a clacka-clacka-clacka sound lately. I ask what else needs fixing around the house, and after some grumbling, he admits the banister for the stairs from the back patio down to the yard isn't in good shape. I promise to come by to help him fix it next weekend.

Mom insists I stay the night, something I'm happy to do. This way I can check for damage outside in the morning. Once they turn in for the night, I quietly unload and reload the dishwasher so it's ready to run once full power is back, tidy the kitchen, and get to work scrubbing the oven.

Then, I settle before the dying fire and flip open the binder from Iris.

CHAPTER 10

Iris

ELI

is this a 3 or an 8

I chuckle at the text and accompanying photograph. I guess I was wrong about Eli not messaging me. Eli has had the binder for a couple of days, and it seems like the biggest hurdle to taxes somehow isn't the IRS. It's Bella's handwriting.

This is the fourth request for help he's sent today. The lack of capitalization and punctuation threw me off at first, but I'm getting used to it now—or at least I tell myself I am. Eli is an unusual man.

He's been surprisingly normal since my mortifying accusation on Monday and unexpectedly funny. His exasperation over penmanship is completely over-the-top but still somehow not obnoxious. I didn't think it was possible, but I think I might *like* being Eli's friend.

ME

It's a 9.

ELI

HOW????

I laugh again when a gif comes through of a cat dramatically sighing.

ELI

im actually getting concerned here. is it possible I learned to read wrong

ME

It's ok. I can bring you some of Sammy's worksheets for writing her letters, and you can learn now.

ELI

your generosity will not be forgotten

After a minute, another text comes through, accompanied by a photograph of several sheets of paper, covered in Bella's scrawl.

ELI

help

I hesitate before answering in case I'm being stupid here but decide to go for it. This is work, and it's my job to help him. Plus, I want to.

ME

This feels inefficient. Are you available around lunch? If we meet up, I can translate them much more quickly.

ELI

youre a godsend. ill be there

are you allergic to anything

ME

Morphine. Why?

ELI

im bringing chinese. any requests

I consider telling him he doesn't need to, but a look at the sad sandwich I'd packed for myself stops me.

ME

Surprise me. And thank you.

After that, the morning flies by.

I usually have a policy not to work while eating—to force myself to take a break—but I don't mind flipping pages with Eli. He's free with expressing his gratitude, and his commentary makes it not feel like work.

I'm drowning a piece of battered chicken in sweet and sour sauce when I catch sight of the perplexed expression on Eli's face as he tilts a piece of paper to the side in an attempt to decipher it.

"Does that say precedent?" he asks, showing me the sheet and pointing to a *p* followed by a squiggle that ends in a wonky *t*.

"You're learning, young padawan," I praise before shoving the bite in my mouth.

"*Yes*," he hisses, pumping his arm in triumph. "This is harder than taking the CPA exam."

I was worried the casual ease of texting would be replaced by awkwardness once we were in person, at *the scene of the crime* so to speak, but he's been just as relaxed since he got here as he was through my phone.

While I'm replaying my idiocy in my head, he seems to have completely let it go. I wonder what it's like to be in his head.

Maybe because I've already mortified myself beyond belief, and it turned out ok, the pressure is off. Maybe my attraction to him has passed.

"How do you like working in law?" Eli asks as he skims

another page of notes, slapping little sticky flags willy-nilly on important lines.

"Honestly, it's been great. I used to dream of being a lawyer, but I'm not sure that'll happen anymore. I still get to help with the cases and interact with clients, so I love it," I dutifully recite what I've told myself countless times. When I finish speaking, I look up and find Eli's paused his page flipping, his focus fully on me like there's no one else he'd rather be listening to. It's *intense*.

My stomach swoops fitfully. *Nope*. The attraction has certainly *not* passed.

"It's great to love what you do, but why do you say law school isn't going to happen anymore?" he asks while picking up a piece of shrimp with his chopsticks.

"I don't think it's in the cards for me. I have Sammy, and she's my priority. Going back to school, especially law school, would be difficult." I try to keep the disappointment out of my voice. I really am content with the life I have now. These are the cards I've been dealt, and while Sammy was a surprise, she's my everything.

"It might be." He shrugs, but I pin him with a look that asks if he's delusional. "Ok, it *would* be. Law school *is* difficult, but I get the feeling that nothing could stop you if you tried. I'd bet you could be a lawyer if it's still your dream."

"You can't possibly know that," I say, even though the compliment makes my chest swell with pride.

"It's just a feeling I've got about you." He shrugs and goes back to fighting to pick up some fried rice.

Sure, I've thought about law school before. A lot. But that ship has sailed. Right?

Eli lets the subject drop. Instead, he asks about Sammy and whether she has any idea about her birthday surprise yet (she doesn't). He asks what I like to do and what I like about Wilcox Grove. When it comes to the tax return, he respects my work and is interested in my thought processes. I think he might even like my meticulous color-coding. He listens and shares and it's easy.

Eli is open without being self-centered. He loves sports and can't wait for spring to come. He doesn't like to cook, but he does love good food. He doesn't know much about plants, but he likes to work with Jake, and he appreciates that the nursery creates life and beauty. He does *not* plan whenever he can avoid it, preferring to take things as they come (I cannot understand this one). He likes working with his hands and is going to do some repairs with his dad on his parents' house this weekend. It's clear he adores them both, so I guess there goes my theory that he doesn't do relationships because he came from a broken home.

It's just really… nice. An hour passes in the blink of an eye, and suddenly Eli is carrying the empty takeout containers to the trash and wiping down the table. He may be disorganized, but he's still clean.

"You have been incredibly helpful, Miss Sutton," he says as he packs up the papers we worked through today. "I'm going to try to make some progress on the smaller returns this weekend, but maybe we can touch base next week?"

"That works for me. Be careful with your dad this weekend, ok?" The second the words leave my mouth, I start overthinking how weird it is for me to say that. He's a grown man, and I'm sure he'll be fine.

Still, I see something flash in his eyes. Something I can't place. It's soft, kind. And it's gone after a second.

"Always am." His hat is a beanie, but he still tips its invisible brim at me. "See you."

Eli

A busy weekend fixing things with my dad turns into a busy week bright and early on Monday morning.

Jake was right about getting permit approvals quickly. After I left my meeting with Iris last Wednesday, I swung by the zoning office with the project plans Jake and I finalized together. Things have been moving nonstop since. By the time I got to the nursery this morning, Jake was already talking to a construction team outside about pouring foundation and expected weather for the rest of the week. By ten, a backhoe's engine was grumbling loudly outside. An excavator joined the party an hour later.

My brain has been rattling in my skull ever since. I think I'm on my way to getting a migraine.

I've been doing as much as I can with the firm's tax return without bothering Iris again, but once I got a list of things to confirm, I switched to some of my other clients. I'm a big personality, and I don't want to take advantage of her help.

It felt like things went well last week. At no point did I find myself reaching for something to talk about. Conversation flowed easily. She's just as nerdy as I am about regulatory stuff, so I didn't feel like I was annoying or boring her while we talked tax. What I do is usually pretty solitary, and it felt good to have a partner to bounce things off of.

I think I just *like* Iris. You know, as a friend.

Today, I'm trying to plow through as much as I can, but my productivity has been at a standstill. I have earplugs in, but the construction outside is shaking my very core—literally. I consider packing up to work from home, but I can't stand the solitude, and I know I'll be distracted by anything that will keep me moving the second I step through my door. Home has my television, video games, snacks, laundry, and dishes that need to be cleaned... endless opportunities for me to avoid working.

I just need to *focus*.

The crash that sounds outside just after I make my vow to buckle down must be a paid actor.

When my phone rattles on the table, I intend to ignore it, but see it's a picture message from Iris, and curiosity gets the best of me. Besides, her initiating contact feels like a good step for our *friendship*.

A laugh bursts from me when I see the image. Two red pandas are on their hind legs facing off. They're the IRS and a CPA. An arrow points to a food bowl the animals are ignoring and reads *Tax issue nobody else can understand.*

IRIS

This made me think of you.

Also, the rest of the account docs are ready.
Could I bring them by the nursery around 4?

I don't dwell on why I like that she was thinking of me. Friendship. With my friend, Iris.

A thundering boom outside makes me jump. Nobody starts screaming, so I assume it's an intentional noise.

Jake comes inside a second later, heads to the fridge, and collects a bunch of water bottles.

"What was that?" I ask after pulling out one of my earplugs.

"We've come across some old roots where we need to pour the foundation and ripping them out is a bit of a process," he explains before taking a long drink from one of the bottles. Despite the cold temperature outside, his face glistens with sweat.

"Is there anything I can do to help?" I feel like a bum sitting in here while everybody is working out there.

"You're helping by making sure this place keeps running and we don't get arrested for not paying our taxes," Jake assures me. It's a conversation we've had before, and I know what I do is important, but it's hard to not feel useless when I'm surrounded by manual labor with visible results.

There's another rumbling crash. This time, the walls shake a little. Without the earplug, the sound bounces around my head.

"Sorry about the noise," Jake says sympathetically when I cringe. "We're trying to get as much done as we can while it's not snowing."

"All good," I assure him, but once he heads back out to deliver the water to the crew, desperation takes over, and I text Iris back, first with a laughing emoji for the meme.

ME

> we have some construction over here and i could use a break. mind if i swing by the firm

Thankfully she sends back a thumbs-up because I'm already packing up my messenger bag with my laptop and the binder. Maybe I'll work at Barefoot Bake or something for a few hours before coming back. Even the bustle of that place has to be better than the explosive noise here right now.

I wave to Tim, who's pruning some succulents at the front counter, when I head out. He seems entirely unbothered by the noise with music blasting through his earbuds. As long as there aren't customers around, music is fine with me and Jake. I let Jake know where I'm headed, and he gives me a quick salute before turning back to his dirt pit.

I drive to Sutton & Associates in silence, relishing the ability to hear my own thoughts and willing the ringing in my ears to stop. Once I'm inside the converted home, the peace continues, so much so that my own footsteps sound noisy in the space.

"Hey," Iris greets me, rising as I turn into the reception space. Her hair is twisted into a long braid over one shoulder, bright gold against the black of her dress.

"Hey. I forgot to say before, the pandas were hilarious." When I speak, I realize I still have one earplug in and remove it.

"It's that bad?" she asks, gesturing to the bit of foam pinched between my fingers.

"You wouldn't believe," I say, shaking my head. I quickly explain the new greenhouse. Then, I gesture to the small stack of files in Iris's hands. "Are those for me?"

"They are." She leads me to the kitchen table we'd shared last week and hands me most of the files once we sit. "Those are all normal. I tried to go through the ones that are Bella's and add notes where I thought things were a little less legible."

"Bless you." I incline my head to her, and she tips her chin down in acknowledgement.

"These are unusual cases, so I wanted to flag them. One person had a name change part way through the year… stuff like that. Maybe take a look at them first, and let me know if they make sense," she says as she hands me the remaining files.

"Thank you," I say.

Iris stands, presumably to return to her desk, and I begin to rise with her. She hesitates, worrying her lip for a moment, so I pause too. Iris seems like the kind of person who likes to be sure in her decision-making, so I wait, giving her a moment to work through whatever she's conflicted over.

"Would you like to stay?" she asks abruptly.

"Huh?" I say dumbly, still halfway out of my chair.

I didn't expect that.

"And work here. If you don't mind using the table, you're welcome to stay. We don't have any other client meetings this afternoon, and it should be fairly quiet. So, stay. Enjoy some peace. If you want to, that is."

My instinct is to politely decline, to avoid putting her out, but when I think of the state of the nursery and the noise of Barefoot Bake, her offer sounds heavenly. Plus, friends hang out.

"Are you sure I won't be in your way?" I ask, giving her a chance to change her mind.

"Positive. Sit," she instructs, and I obediently plop back into my chair. "Coffee?"

"Please," I gratefully accept.

She pours from the already-made pot and sets a mug before me. "We have cream and sugar if you take it. Bathroom's down the hall. I can hook you up to the Wi-Fi if you need it."

"That would be great." I pull out my laptop, and Iris reaches across me to quickly type in the password to connect me. I lean back in the chair, but I can still smell the lavender wafting off of her.

"Thank you for this, really," I say once she straightens up again. Professional. *Friendly*.

"You're very welcome, Eli," she answers. "That's what friends are for, right?"

There's that word again, but I barely notice because I think it's the first time I've heard her say my name.

She returns to her desk and gets to work. I take a sip of my coffee—it's the good stuff—and do the same. For the next few hours, we work in companionable silence except for when Iris makes a few calls, but the sound of her voice is melodic, a complete contradiction to the construction noise at the office. Both Harry and Bella come by to speak with her briefly. They greet me, and we exchange pleasantries, and they don't seem to mind at all that I'm working here. I feel some of the tension release from my shoulders.

I'm able to finish the tax returns for the nursery, the café, and the bookstore.

I don't even realize how much time has passed until Iris starts packing her bag. Once I notice, I begin to wrap up too.

"I need to go get Samantha from after-school daycare, but you should feel free to hang around. Harry and Bella will both be here for a while still," Iris says, but I continue slipping my things into my bag.

"I'll head out with you," I say. "I've gotten *so* much done here. Thank you for letting me stay today."

Considering how different we are, I'm a little surprised by how well this worked all afternoon. I guess at least when it comes to our jobs, we have some common ground.

I follow her out into the hallway where our coats are hanging. Iris again looks like she wants to say something, so I wait for her to be ready.

"I don't know anything about construction or how long it takes to build a greenhouse, but if it's bad again, you're welcome to come back," she says while she tries to juggle her bag and coat. I take the coat and hold it open for her.

"I don't want to be a nuisance," I say as Iris slips her arm into one sleeve, but the idea of working with her is appealing. She's good company.

Jake is my best friend, and I love the nursery, but having somebody else doing similar work makes it feel a little less lonely and daunting.

"Thank you," she says, pulling her braid out of the collar of her coat. "And you're literally the least nuisance person around here. I hardly noticed you were there."

I don't know why that stings, and I force myself to shake it off.

She must still see the hesitation on my face. I *want* to accept the offer, but it feels like an intrusion in spite of her assurances. What if she's just being polite?

"I didn't mean it like that," she backpedals. After a breath, she continues, "I like having you here, and the offer stands. Even if you weren't working on our taxes, I'd offer it, but if you need to use the excuse of working on *our* taxes to convince yourself to come back, please do so."

"Alright," I concede, pulling on my own jacket. "But only if it gets really bad."

Her smile is small, sweet. I hold open the front door and let her walk through first.

It's cold outside, but I feel warm anyway.

She likes having me here.

CHAPTER 12

Eli

I meant what I said to Iris about only turning up on her doorstep when the construction is particularly bad at the nursery. I don't want to be a pain in the ass and make her regret her invitation.

On Tuesday, I split my morning between helping Jake pick up materials for the new greenhouse and walking him through the nursery's return. Then, in the afternoon, I do the same with Leslie, Hannah, and Piper for their returns. After, I continue working late into the evening at home, organizing whatever records I've been given from businesses around town. I'm not entirely focused on work with the distractions I have at home tempting me and the loneliness of solitude, *but* all my laundry is done and the utensil drawer in the kitchen is beautifully organized.

On Wednesday, I'm off from the nursery and head to Barefoot Bake to do some tax work there, but I spend a large portion of the day sampling baked goods, talking to Piper, and helping her move heavy boxes of books instead. It's a good day, sure, but I feel myself falling behind. Again, I'm working well past my bedtime, and I'm a man who likes his sleep.

During my drive into the nursery on Thursday, I tell myself

I'll be able to focus past the construction noises. I have earplugs and over ear headphones. I even pounded an energy drink before I left home to make up for my decreased sleep. This will work.

As I pull into the parking area, I see large piles of pavers being stacked along the side of the office building. Then, somebody unloads a jackhammer for god-knows-what, and I make a u-turn.

Not today, Satan.

Unwilling to show up empty handed—Mom taught me better —I pick up a box of Hannah's pastries—donuts, muffins, and Danishes—before driving over. While I'm waiting for my bakery order, I call the firm. Iris isn't in yet, so Harry answers, and kindly scolds me for checking whether I can come by.

"Eli, you're always welcome here. Don't be ridiculous," he insists.

Grateful Bob pops up out of nowhere again when I'm collecting the large box of pastries.

"Do I need to worry about you and your carb intake?" he teases.

"While I *could* easily and happily eat all of these myself, today I'm sharing," I assure him.

"I'd ask if you were taking them to a lady, but—"

"But you know me," I cut Grateful Bob off and finish his thought for him. "It's all business," I say, but I don't like the taste of that. "And friendship," I add.

Grateful Bob scrutinizes me for a moment, but I guess he doesn't find anything too damning, because he lets me go with a wave.

At the firm, Harry doubles down on the open invitation when I arrive smelling like a confectionary. Iris, who is settling in at her desk gives me an *I told you so* look when I catch her eye before stowing my lunch in the fridge next to hers and Harry's. Harry heads back to his office with a donut in hand, and Iris starts brewing a fresh pot of coffee.

"I don't know if Harry mentioned it, and I should have said something when I invited you to work here, but Samantha comes here after lunch on Tuesdays and Thursdays. She has a playroom upstairs, but she'll likely pop down from time to time in the afternoon. I just wanted to give you a heads up," she says with her back still to me.

"Ok. Sounds good," I say, making sure my laptop connects to the Wi-Fi again.

"That's not a problem for you?" Iris asks, turning now.

I pause. A *problem* for me? She's a kid, not a feral raccoon. And Iris is the one doing *me* an enormous favor by letting me be here.

"No, that's not a problem. The world has kids. I happen to like existing with them. They're usually pretty cool. I'm not here to disrupt yours or Samantha's routines. As long as she doesn't come back from school with a jackhammer, we're cool."

The way Iris softens at my acceptance of her daughter makes me wonder how many people haven't. I think I surprised her with my acceptance. I think about how many times she's had to fight for Samantha to be allowed to take up space. I don't like it.

"You take your coffee black, right?" she smoothly changes the subject. She really does see everything, doesn't she?

"Yes, please." I walk over to accept the steaming mug and then we both get to work.

While I spy on Iris just a little bit while she works, she reminds me of Pepper Potts with how smoothly she runs this office, I still get a lot done, and the morning passes easily.

Lunch is quick and uneventful with Iris and Harry, but I enjoy watching Iris blush when Harry talks her up to me. She's proud of her work, and that's rare.

After we finish, Iris grabs her bag and heads out to pick up

Samantha. Less than half an hour later, I hear their arrival even before the front door is open. Samantha is recounting something for her mother, her little voice raising as she talks faster and faster. Suddenly, I feel nervous. Sure, Samantha and I have met, and it went well, but now I'm in *her* space, and I'm certain this kid has the power to vote me off the island.

"—and then she went *all* the way across the monkey bars! Do you believe that? I want to do the monkey bars. Can you teach me how?" I hear Sam fussing while Iris presumably disentangles her from her winter outerwear.

"Well, it's not exactly monkey bars weather—I don't fully understand why they took you outside today—but when it's warmer, I promise we can practice them. You'll be a pro in no time," Iris reassures her.

"We only went outside for a little bit. Miss Evvie—" Samantha cuts off when she and Iris enter the front room and Samantha spots me.

I wave.

"Why are you here? Do you work with Mama?" Samantha asks bluntly, clutching a stuffed cat.

"Sort of. Where I work is very noisy right now, so your mom is letting me work here," I explain. Then, tentatively, I ask, "Is that ok?"

The girl narrows her eyes at me while she thinks it over, and for a second, I worry she's about to evict me. "I *guess* so."

The implication is clear. I'm on thin ice.

"Do you want a snack before we go to your playroom?" Iris asks, unperturbed by her daughter's intense judgment. "We don't want to disrupt Mr. Eli while he works."

"*Mr.* Eli?" Samantha is offended by the title. "He's *my* friend, and he said his name is just Eli."

Samantha pins me with a stare like she's trying to figure out if I gave her a fake name. I'm not gonna survive this.

"You're right. He did," Iris concedes. "If he's ok with Eli, then you can call him that."

"Eli is fine by me," I say as quickly as I can. To get her focus off me, I gesture to the stuffed cat. "Who's your friend there?"

"Robin," she answers with more authority than I knew a four-year-old could have.

"Robin?" I ask, perplexed. "Isn't that a people name? Aren't cats supposed to have names like Fluffy, Mittens, or Cheese?"

Samantha does *not* like my tone. Her brow furrows, and her lips draw in tight. It's possible I'm about to be beat up by a preschooler.

"Ok, Robin it is." I hold up my hands in surrender. I guess I have no right to argue with anybody about proper naming conventions for a stuffed tabby. I have no clue what to do next to get back on Samantha's good side. "Can I… pet her?"

"No. She doesn't like boys." Samantha tightens her arms around the cat and sharply turns away from me. "Mama, can I have a banana?"

This is going well.

Samantha takes her banana and leaves the room with Iris, who's trying and failing to hide her amusement from Samantha bullying me. Just before Samantha turns the corner into the hallway, she leans back and gives me another scrutinizing look, like she's still deciding if she's ok with me being here.

Once Iris returns, we're back to work as usual until Iris steps out to use the restroom, and Samantha comes slinking back in. She tiptoes over to my table as if she isn't in plain sight in the middle of the open room. I respectfully pretend not to notice her.

"Hey," she says as she climbs onto the seat next to mine. "What are you doing?"

"Right now, I'm working on the law firm's taxes."

"What are taxes?" she asks.

"They're money people and businesses pay to the government

when those people and businesses make money. You also have to fill out a form when you pay the money. I'm helping with those forms." I try to simplify the convoluted system, focusing on income taxes for now. I angle my laptop screen so Samantha can see the spreadsheet I'm working on.

Samantha scrunches up her face. "That's gross. I don't like taxes."

A chuckle huffs out of me. "You're not alone, Samantha."

"Samantha," Iris admonishes as she returns. "Are you bothering Eli?"

"No!" Samantha cries the same time I say she's not.

"It's ok. She's curious about taxes," I say.

"Not *anymore*," Samantha says with a disgusted look on her face as she slides off the chair. "I'm going to play with my Legos."

She pauses when she gets to the door, looking back at me just to announce, "It's my birthday in a week." Then, she's gone.

"Sorry about that," Iris apologizes once Samantha's footsteps have disappeared upstairs.

"Nothing to apologize for. I'm happy to help curate her disdain for bureaucracy from a young age."

Iris seems to be trying to figure out whether I'm being serious or not.

"Ok," she says, retaking her seat.

All in all, it's another really good day at Sutton & Associates.

CHAPTER 13

As an adult it is *hard* to make new friends. So many people have their established groups from college or even childhood, and breaking into them can be incredibly intimidating. I can't point fingers. I have that with Olivia. She's another sister at this point, and I've considered myself lucky to have her. I kind of figured Lemon and Liv were it for me.

But then I get to Wilcox Grove, and suddenly I'm adopted by Piper, and I have Alice and both of their guys. And then… Eli.

Eli's kindness snuck up on me, but he's wormed his way into my life, and I don't want to let go. My prejudice definitely reared its ugly face, telling me that this playboy and I could never have anything in common, but the more time I spend with him, the more I realize he's so much more than a pretty face. And he's no playboy.

His relationships—or lack thereof—might not look like what I've come to expect, but everything about him screams that he respects the hell out of women, especially small ones like Samantha. And it's possible I was being a bit of a judgy-pants just because his life is different from mine.

I get used to having Eli at the law firm. More than that, I look forward to the days when he seeks refuge with me—with us. I always get a heads-up because he insists on checking it's ok each time, in spite of everybody's constant assurances. It's sweet.

I've had a crush on Eli for a while, but spending time with him has taught me that I actually *like* him as a person. He's polite, funny, and has this way of listening to you that makes you feel like there's nothing he'd rather be doing than hearing your thoughts. And in a world that's constantly moving at a mile a minute, it feels good for somebody to choose to slow down for you.

The more I learn about him, the less the no-relationships outlook makes sense. He seems responsible when it comes to work, and he's patient and communicative. He's great with Sam, loves his friends, and is always helping them. Everything about him *screams* boyfriend material. I just can't figure it out.

Everything about him is enjoyable to be around. So, I'm pleased when I get a text on Thursday morning.

ELI

care to take in a stray again? the team is racing against the snow over here

ME

Come on over.

I try not to get my hopes up about the promise of snow. We've had several false alarms already this winter about the white stuff, but it would be pretty special for Samantha to have a white birthday. She'd be *thrilled*.

Not fifteen minutes later, I hear the front door open. When Eli appears in my doorway, he's brushing something from the shoulder of his coat.

"Winter's here," he says gruffly.

I can hardly believe my eyes when I see a distinct sparkle on his hair. I blink to make sure I'm not hallucinating.

Snow.

And it's not the shitty, wet snow we've been getting. Those are full, fluffy flakes.

I gasp at the sight of it, jumping to my feet. I hurry to the front door on stockinged feet, having left my heels that I may or may not have slipped off for comfort under my desk. Shoes are irrelevant when there's snow outside.

"Wha—" Eli starts to say as I slide on the hardwood to pass him, highly resembling a sprinting cat seeking purchase as my feet pitter-patter. I rip open the heavy front door and freeze.

Oh.

"It's really *snowing*," I breathe with awe. Big clumps of snow lazily drift to the ground, where a layer of white is already sticking to the grass.

Eli walks on surprisingly quiet feet for somebody his size, but even though I don't hear him, I *feel* his presence over my shoulder.

"Yeah, it's going to be a mess out there, but it shouldn't be a problem until later this afternoon," Eli says as he leans around me to get a good look at the front yard.

I step onto the patio, feeling a shock of cold through the bottoms of my feet but not caring. I close my eyes and breathe deeply, taking in that unique smell of snow.

The world around me feels quiet and serene.

"Oh…" I sigh out loud this time, smiling blissfully.

Eli doesn't ask what I'm doing standing in my thin dress and shoeless feet on the patio. He just pulls shut the door behind him and stays with me. When a gust of wind shifts the skirt of my dress around my knees, he still doesn't question my sanity. He just slides off his thick Carhartt jacket and drops it over my shoulders. When he retakes his place behind me, we're closer. His chest brushes my shoulder each time he breathes in. Neither of us moves away.

Only when my toes have gone completely numb do I turn away from the scene before me, finding Eli's eyes on me.

"You've got a thing for snow?" Eli asks, with a playful smirk on his face as he holds the door open and steps aside for me to pass.

"You could say that." I smile back before reluctantly heading back inside.

"I don't think I've ever seen an adult who loves snow like you do," he says softly. It almost feels like speaking at full volume would break the spell the snow cast around us.

"It just makes everything feel magical, don't you think?"

"I suppose so," Eli agrees, but I think he just says it to be kind. His expression says he's not so sure about the truth of the statement.

I want to find a way to bundle up and sit on the patio so I can keep watching it, but I know I don't have the right clothes with me here. Begrudgingly, I follow Eli back to my office but am surprised when he walks past his bag, which he had dropped earlier in the doorway, and heads straight to the front window. He quickly pulls back the curtains on both sides, so I have a clear view of the snow from my desk.

Nodding in satisfaction, he retrieves his bag and goes to the kitchen table to begin working. I smile to myself at the small gesture, stealing glances out the window as often as I can.

It's a full hour later when I realize I'm still wrapped in Eli's enormous jacket, surrounded by the smell of earth and leather.

I don't take it off.

I catch myself gazing out the front window for the hundredth time when I get a text from Uncle Harry asking what I'd like on my pizza for lunch.

"You eat everything, right?" I ask Eli.

"I do, indeed," Eli confirms.

"Excellent. Harry is bringing something back for us all."

I answer Harry, letting him know Eli's here too, and force myself to focus until he gets back. Out of the corner of my eye, I can still see the snow swirling around.

Before long, the front door is opening, and a cry of "Mama!" comes down the hallway.

"Happy birthday, lil' one," I say, rising to my feet and scooping up Samantha when she enters the room. Robin is once again wedged in the crook of her elbow.

"Mama, it's *snowing*." She sighs wistfully, suddenly seeming much older than her five years. But then she gently lays her head on my shoulder, and my little girl is back.

"Isn't it *beautiful*?" I ask and feel her head nodding against my neck.

Just like before, I feel Eli's arrival behind me without hearing it.

"Happy birthday, Samantha," he says.

Sam lifts her head, her eyes bright with birthday joy.

"Thank you," Sammy giggles out her reply. "I got snow for my birthday!"

"How special is that?" he asks, a huge smile across his face, and Sam *lights up*.

I catch Eli's eye, and he gives me a little shrug. This is a man who I think *hates* snow, pretending it's the best thing ever just so my kid isn't disappointed. Sometimes, it's the little things that show how much we really care, and Eli is made up of those little moments.

It's a *crime* he insists on flying solo.

"Food has arrived," Harry announces as he joins us in the front room, jolting me out of my thoughts.

He must have collected the troops because Bella and the younger associates, Lynn and Gary, follow the pizza boxes in Harry's hand to the kitchen counter, take a couple of slices each, and retreat to their offices with polite nods, but Harry and Bella stay with us.

I usher Sammy toward the kitchen and reluctantly leave Eli's jacket on the back of my chair. Eli starts to clean off the table, but Bella stops him.

"Don't worry about that. We'll eat on the couches," she says. "It's a special occasion." She winks at Samantha, who, having peeked over her shoulder, beams back at her.

Sam has always looked up to Isabella, and I don't blame her. Bella is the kind of powerful and poised woman I'd like to be. I look up to her too.

As we migrate to the front of the room, I notice Eli takes a spot on the couch with its back to the windows, leaving the seats with the best snow views available for me and Sammy. To my surprise, though, my daughter climbs right up beside Eli and sets Robin on the cushion on her other side, foregoing the most direct view of the snow *and* the chance to bask in Bella's greatness.

"What's your favorite pizza?" she asks Eli, sitting on her knees so she can face him and still see the snow. I'm all but forgotten behind her.

"I'm a simple man. I like pepperoni. What's your favorite?"

"Ham and pineapple," she says, tripping over the word pineapple a little but still getting it out.

Eli flashes an accusatory look toward me, and I gasp dramatically.

"Mr. Chambers, are you a pineapple-on-pizza hater?" I have two slices of ham and pineapple on my own plate. Sam and I share that favorite. I fix him with my best glare, as does Sam from his other side.

After looking between us and then finding no sympathy from either Harry or Bella, he wisely decides to shake his head.

"Absolutely not. I think you two are pizza heathens, but no judgment here," he says, smiling.

"What's a heathen?" Sammy asks without missing a beat.

I look right to Eli. "You said it. You answer her question."

"Uh…" Eli's eyes dart between mine and Sammy's. "I take it back," he stammers out. "Pineapple on pizza is fantastic."

"I know, right?" Sammy is happy enough with his changed opinion to drop her question, and when she takes a bite of her slice, Eli sighs heavily with relief.

"Did you do anything special at school for your birthday?" Harry asks, and Samantha recounts the most exciting snack time, where everybody ate donut holes *and* sang happy birthday to her.

After lunch, when Harry and Bella have returned to their offices, Eli takes our paper plates to the trash for us and returns with a small paper bag stuffed with tissue paper hidden behind his back. I don't even know where he stored it all day.

"For the birthday girl," he announces, presenting the bag to Sam with a little bow. When she pulls out a small stuffed capybara with a ribbon tied around its neck, he continues, "Since you taught me capybaras are friends with everyone, maybe this can be Robin's friend."

I'm stunned. Samantha had only mentioned her birthday once in passing, and Eli hasn't said a word about it. Yeah, little things can mean the world.

Sammy *launches* herself at Eli, flying off the couch and flinging her arms around him. I'm halfway to my feet to catch her, but Eli easily wraps an arm around her and steadies her until she returns to the floor and gets her footing.

"Thank you," she says, squeezing the daylights out of her new toy. "I'm going to call him Eli, and he can be Robin's first boy friend."

The smile on Eli's face tells me he understands how monumental this is for Robin.

"You're welcome. I hope they get along great," Eli says, and I suddenly I think I've got something in my eye.

Once we finish cleaning up, Sammy resists returning to her playroom upstairs, wanting to stay with her new bestie, *human* Eli. I agree to let her sit on the couches and color, but only if she doesn't disturb him while he works.

"I promise," Sammy says, crossing her heart.

To her credit, she *is* quiet as a mouse, entertaining herself and very quietly whispering to Robin and capybara Eli. After a bit, human Eli reveals his true nature as the troublemaker, folding a paper airplane and sending it soaring over my head to Sam, who is pleasantly surprised by its arrival.

"Could you color it for me?" he asks in a whisper voice that's loud enough for Sammy to hear. She dutifully agrees and gets to work.

When I pointedly look at him, I feel like a teacher separating friends in a classroom. He gives me a goofy grin and shrugs. I bet he used the same charm to get out of trouble when he was in school too. I wouldn't blame him. It's very effective.

I remember him calling me *teacher* back at the Corner Post and flush. The teasing dinner feels like ages ago.

For an eternal bachelor, Eli is really good with Samantha, happily calling her over after he notices her shyly lurking. When she presents the brightly colored plane to him, his oohing and aahing at her handiwork is genuine, and she glows. I already know Eli's only "siblings" are the Preston brothers, so I think the kind patience is just part of who he is.

Sam skips back to her couch, and I realize I'm staring at Eli, even after he's gotten back to work, fingers tapping quickly on his laptop keyboard. I pull my eyes away and continue with my case summary.

The light outside has softened when Harry gently interrupts us.

"We might want to all consider packing up. The snow is really coming down out there, and it looks like it's just going to get worse," he says, drawing our attention to the front window, where we can see only white. "Trust me, you don't want your first time driving through snow to be in the worst part of a blizzard."

"It's your first time driving in snow?" Eli asks, surprise written on his face.

I nod. "Other than the slushy snow we've had so far, yeah." When I was in college, I didn't have a car. And when I moved back home, Mom insisted I use a driver any time there was the slightest bit of inclement weather, something I hated and am not inclined to share.

When I stand, I see that while there's significant accumulation on the grass and trees, the snow on the asphalt is still *mostly* melting, but that's quickly changing. Harry is right. It's time to get out of here.

"Let's pack it up, Sammy," I say, and thank Harry for the heads up. I hope the unsteadiness in my voice isn't noticeable to anybody else. I should have left sooner to get Sam home before all this.

"Are you good driving home? I'm happy to give you a ride," Eli offers as he zips his own bag. I guess my nerves didn't go unnoticed by him. "We can pick up your car tomorrow or whenever."

"I think I should be ok," I say, even though I'm feeling anxious. I'll just take it slow. Very slow. "I have to learn sometime, right?"

"I could follow behind you if it would make you feel better," he says, coming behind my desk to retrieve his jacket. He doesn't say anything about me keeping it all afternoon.

"I couldn't ask you to do that," I say even though I want to accept his offer.

"You're not asking. Just let me do this." When I look up at him, his expression is tight, but his eyes are pleading. Is he... worried?

"Ok," I agree. "Thank you."

I'm not used to accepting help from anybody other than family and Olivia, but I like knowing somebody else is looking out for me and Sam. "I'm sorry in advance for how slow I go."

"Go as slow as you need to," he says. "I've got you."

After Gary, Lynn, and Bella leave, with requests to drive safely all around and a special "Happy Birthday, dear" and the delivery of a birthday card undoubtedly filled with cash from Bella to Sam, Harry also asks if I'm comfortable driving home.

"Eli is going to follow behind me as backup, so I'm all set," I assure him.

Harry looks at Eli like he might hug the man, but he just reaches up to clasp his shoulder.

"You both still let me know once you're home safe, ok?" he adds.

We agree once he promises the same and all head out. As warned, I drive annoyingly slow, the unfamiliar sound of tires crunching on snow filling my ears. But the Explorer does well, and having Eli in my rearview mirror every time I check helps loosen the vice grip that seems to have fitted itself around my chest.

After taking at least twice as long as usual, I pull into the driveway behind Olivia's car and take my first full breath since leaving work. Olivia opens our front door before I've even finished unhooking Sammy's car seat and has a cupcake with a lit candle in it on a plate. I scoop Sam up and carry her across the icy walkway. As she blows out her candle, I catch sight of Eli still idling in the driveway.

His window is rolled down, and he's smiling at me. He gives me a nod of approval before waving a quick salute and slowly pulling away.

A bit later I get a text.

His praise makes me feel warm all over. I hug my phone to my chest for a moment before responding.

CHAPTER 14

Eli

Even though I'm an only child, I cannot stand being alone. Growing up in a small town, it was always easy to get a hold of somebody, and they were usually a short walk or bike ride away. Jake and I grew up as brothers, collecting Scott when he was old enough. At college, I lived with roommates, and when I came back home, I settled right back into my old spot.

I live alone, sure, but I spend as little time at my apartment as possible, and when I am there, I play music or put the television on as background noise. I also talk to my pet fish, Phish.

The morning after the snowstorm, most of the town is shut down, including the nursery. Jake and Scott are both taking advantage of the quiet day to spend time with Alice and Piper, respectively. They suggest I enjoy being able to stay home, where it's warm and dry. But I'm crawling out of my skin. Eventually, I can't take it anymore, and I head out, figuring I'll find somewhere to end up.

I head over to my parents' house to shovel their walk and driveway. They live in a neighborhood comprised of primarily older folks, so nobody is out. Leaning against my shovel, I look around, and all I see is white. The sun is thinking about coming out, so there's a soft glow of light reflecting off every surface.

When I'm just about done, I get a text from Iris, and my mood improves at the mere sight of her name.

The message is a picture of Sammy—at least, I think it's Sammy. She's bundled so securely that all I can see of her is the strip of her face around her eyes—beside a snowman as tall as she is. Capybara Eli is balanced on the snowman's head.

> **IRIS**
>
> Sam insisted I send this to you. She says thank you again.

> **ME**
>
> thats a very impressive snowman. please tell her I said so. im glad she's having a good day

As I load my shovel into the back of the Jeep, trying to figure out where to go next, I think about the picture again. Iris's and Olivia's cars both looked pretty snowed in. I should go back home and force myself to work, but maybe they could use a hand.

When I pull up to the curb, Iris, Olivia, and Sam are still in the front yard, and all three look up when I step out of my car. Iris's smile could power a city.

Sam comes bounding over, waddling a bit in her snow gear, with Iris in tow as I head to the back of the Jeep and pull out the shovel.

"Whatcha' doin'?" she asks.

"Thought I might be able to be useful," I answer, gesturing to the shovel. "I noticed your cars were still buried when you sent the picture."

"You don't have to do that," Iris says shyly. She's looking at me like she's trying to read me, and I hope she doesn't find anything bad. "We were going to dig them out eventually."

"Don't be polite, Iris," Olivia calls to us. "Of course you can shovel our driveway!"

Iris's cheeks flush pink. "You're sure we're not keeping you from anything? Don't you have plans?"

"I never have plans. I just kind of do things. I could either do returns or this, and I'd much rather be here," I answer, turning toward the driveway. When I spot the snowman, I add for Sam, "*Sick* snowman, by the way."

She blushes like her mother.

Olivia ends up getting her own shovel so she and Iris can take turns helping me. Eventually, Sam runs inside, returning with her little sand shovel, and begins digging too, flinging tiny scoops of snow over her shoulder. It's fucking adorable.

I won't admit it, but we finish quicker than I'd like. With all the laughter that filled the air while we worked—sometimes throwing snow at each other—it felt like even less time. After I finish salting the driveway and a path to the front door, Iris steps up to my side and places a hand on my arm.

"Thank you for this, and for looking out for us last night." We're all flushed from hard work, but the color deepens on her cheeks again. She looks over at Sam, who's climbing the pile of snow we made. "We're lucky to know you," she adds quietly.

I feel lucky to know them too.

On my drive back home, I think about how Iris said snow makes things magical, and I guess it *is* kinda nice.

Then I get home, step down from the Jeep, slip on a patch of ice hidden under the snow, and land flat on my ass.

I'm still ready for spring...

The following morning, Scott makes sure I remember I agreed to help Piper set up for Samantha's birthday party by calling me before 8:00 a.m., something that should be illegal on a Saturday. I grumble and tell him to fuck off, but I've actually been up for an hour and am already showered.

Now that I know Samantha, helping out isn't an obligation. I'm *happy* to help contribute to that little girl's special day.

A couple hours later, I tie the end of the *Happy Birthday Samantha* banner across the brick archway dividing Barefoot Bake from Literary Lake—as the tallest one here, I got all the high-up jobs—and I think we're done. Sam's fifth birthday party is a rainbow unicorn themed affair. It's loud, colorful, and sparkly.

Everything is where it belongs, I left a card on the gift table, and there's no real reason for me to hang around... except that I see a certain head of blonde hair getting out of an Explorer out front.

I quickly pivot into the café and order a coffee I don't need considering the two cups I've already had today. Even from the café side of the archway, I can clearly hear Samantha's excited squeal when she gets inside.

"A bookstore birthday party?" she yelps before quickly cutting off and following it with a whisper-shouted "Sorry!"

I can't help but laugh and lean back so I can see around the wall toward the ecstatic kid. She's saying it's the best day of her *life*.

"Eli," Hannah calls when my drink is ready, and Iris's head snaps in my direction. So does her daughter's.

"And human Eli *came*?" Samantha's apology for shouting is forgotten as her volume spikes again.

I thank Hannah and collect my coffee before heading toward the birthday girl.

"Happy birthday, Samantha," I say before nodding to Iris with a "Hey."

"But Eli… don't you remember?" Samantha tries to whisper again, but it's still not very quiet. "Today's not my *real* birthday."

"Well, that's ok. You're the birthday girl on your actual birthday *and* at your party. Those are the rules."

Her eyes grow as big as saucers. "They are?"

I nod. "Yup."

Just then, the door opens and a woman with a young girl walks in.

"Can I go say hi to Georgie?" Samantha asks Iris once she spots them, and the other kid starts waving excitedly.

"Go on," Iris urges her.

"Thanks for helping set all this up. It looks great," Iris says to me once Samantha has sprinted off to greet her friend.

I stand and run a hand through my hair. "It was actually pretty fun. Books, birthday parties, rainbow unicorns. Love 'em!"

I've never sounded stupider in my entire life.

"If you're not otherwise engaged, I know Sam would love it if you stayed. We both would," Iris says.

I'm trying to figure out how to act casual with my acceptance when I see Iris's face fall at the sight of something behind me.

"What is it?" I ask, concerned, as I turn and try to identify what she's spotted.

An older couple who looks like they just walked out of a country club is approaching the store. He's tall, with a bald head and a thick neck, and looks like a man who's never said a joke in his life. The woman beside him is short, and everything about her seems… stiff, from her over hair sprayed, blown-out hair to the pointy toes of her heels. They're with who can only be Iris's *actual* twin and some guy whose suit looks like it's too tight.

Who wears a suit to a five-year-old's birthday party, anyway?

"It's my parents, and my sister…" Iris says, though I'm not sure she's talking to me. She's still staring at the group as they reach the door, but her feet are rooted to the floor. "And Samantha's father."

I look back at the furious expression on Iris's face and remember her lack of a wedding ring. The suited man has a smug look on his face that immediately rubs me the wrong way.

Oh, I'm definitely staying now.

CHAPTER 15

Iris

What could have been a nice reunion with my parents and Lemon suddenly has my blood pressure at an alarming level. Just seeing Archer Ringwald's stupid, superior face makes me want to hit him with a two-by-four. Even calling him Sammy's "father" has left a foul taste in my mouth. The better term is "sperm donor" since that man has never fathered anybody a day in his life.

I can only stare in disbelief at the group coming up to the café, since my legs have ceased working. When the door to Barefoot Bake opens, Lemon shoves her way in first, hurrying to me and wrapping me in a bone-crushing hug.

"I'm so sorry," she rushes to whisper in my ear. "We drove separately, and I didn't know he was coming until we parked outside, or I would have warned you. I'm your backup. Whatever you need."

I squeeze her back, grateful to have her on my side here since it's sometimes hard to tell where my parents stand. Right now, they stand physically behind Archer, and the implication of them looking like his bodyguards isn't lost on me.

"What the hell are you doing here," I fume at him the second

Lemon releases me. There's no point in hiding my distaste. When Archer and I last seriously spoke about whether he wanted to be involved in Sam's life five years ago, I made my feelings about his behavior very clear and have repeated that sentiment with my parents every time they pushed me to try to rekindle things with him.

"I'm here for our daughter's birthday, of course," his slimy voice drawls as he lifts a sparkly purple gift bag stuffed with tissue paper.

"Oh, fuck off. That little girl is *my* daughter. She has *never* been your anything. You refused to even sign her birth certificate, and you never came around during the *years* we lived in the same town. You didn't even call her on her real birthday. She's had five of them now, in case you forgot. Do you even know when it is?"

Archer opens his mouth but closes it again.

I always wondered how I'd react if I saw Archer again. I guess now I know. I'm not one to generally fly off the handle, but trying some bullshit with my kid will seemingly tap into a whole new side of me.

"That's what I thought. So, whatever *this* is, I'm uninterested. You need to leave," I snarl.

"Now, Ris, let's not make a scene." My mother's high-pitched voice scratches my brain in the most unpleasant way, almost as badly as the nickname she insists on using. My name is four letters long. Do we really need to shorten it?

Mom's chastising may have been able to keep me in check when I was younger, but I've long since realized her expectations come from a place of catty pride, and they no longer have any power over me. I know who I am with or without her approval, and there are few things she disapproves of more than me having a child out of wedlock.

"A *scene*?" I say, fighting to keep my voice low but feeling outraged she and my father helped this skeevy worm come anywhere near my daughter. "I've got bigger things to worry about than causing a *scene*, like keeping trash away from my kid."

I quickly scan the room and am relieved to see Sammy still chatting away with Georgie on the other side of the store, their backs to us. While there's next to no chance she'd even recognize Archer, I still don't want her to see him. Not today. Not ever.

"Hey now—" Archer starts to protest, but he cuts off.

I feel a warmth at my back before I turn and see Eli has stepped closer to me. I have only a moment to be embarrassed he's witnessed this whole spectacle before he speaks, low and reassuring in my ear.

"Can I help?" His presence grounds me, his palpable anger on my behalf nearly a physical being in the room with us. Every part of him is tense, and I get the distinct feeling he'd physically remove Archer if I so much as hinted that I wanted him to.

"Not if Archer leaves voluntarily," I say, holding my ground. Archer doesn't scare me, but having an enormous man behind me doesn't hurt either. And when Archer takes a step back with his hands up in surrender, I can't help but smile.

"I'm here in peace," Archer lies through his over-bleached teeth. "I never wanted to cause any trouble, so I'll leave this"—he sets the gift bag on the floor—"and go. I was just trying to do the responsible thing. No need to sic your guard dog on me." He smirks, and it's a miracle I don't throw up.

Eli inches forward, and his arm touches the back of my shoulder. I think this guard dog bites.

"Find a short cliff and take a long walk, Archer," I snap. He laughs like it's the funniest joke he's ever heard, wagging a finger at me like we're pals, and I got him good.

"I'll see you around," he says, and it feels like a warning. But then, mercifully, he leaves.

Not that I'm not thankful for his departure, but if he was going to go so easily, why did he even come?

"Iris," my mother snaps. "Was that necessary? He just wants to see his daughter! Isn't that what you've always wanted? And look how well-behaved he was. Especially compared to the feral animal you're acting like."

"I haven't wanted him near Samantha from the moment he made it clear he didn't want her. He doesn't deserve to know her," I say, and I feel a shake in my hands from the adrenaline spike at seeing Archer.

Just as quietly as he arrived, Eli steps away to give me and my family some privacy.

"Well, a girl needs her father." Mom always needs to get the last word in. "Are you going to kick us out now too?"

"Mom, knock it off." Lemon pulls at her forearm, but Mom shakes her off, straightening her sleeve before any wrinkles can set in.

I want to say yes, more than anything else at this moment, especially since she called Archer a "father," but Sammy has finally spotted us. I quickly hook the bag Archer left behind my heel and kick it back.

"Grandma! Grandpa! Lemmy!" her beautiful voice carries across the store. She adores my parents. That's why I invited them to come up here. And she's obsessed with Lemon, obviously, but Lemon's always welcome.

While my family starts to dote on Samantha, happy faces plastered on, I turn to where Eli is leaning against the wall, the opposite of whatever nonchalant is with his arms crossed. Fully chalant?

"You ok?" he asks when I approach him, his voice still hushed.

I press the heels of my hands into my eyes and take a deep breath. I shake out my shoulders as I bring my hands down.

"Yeah. I need to be," I say as I shove the last few minutes to the back of my brain, and steal a quick look at my daughter, but she's fine. "I'm sorry you had to see that."

"Do you need anything right now?" Eli asks, focusing on me and not the fiasco he witnessed.

I look down at the gift Archer left behind, lying on its side by my feet.

"Can you get rid of that?" I ask, nudging the bag with the toe of my shoe. I feel bad asking Eli to basically do a trash run for me, but I can't bring myself to pick it up.

Eli steps around me, snatches the bag up, and tucks it behind his back.

"Consider it done." He leaves to throw it out, and Lemon takes his place at my side, slipping her hand into mine.

She gives me an accusatory look, and I *try* to tell her with my eyes to *drop it* before fixing a pleasant look on my face. She stubbornly nods toward where Eli disappeared, a question apparent there, and I hiss an urgent *later* in her ear.

Once my parents switch into "grandparent mode," I push Archer out of my mind and focus on making sure Sam has the best damn birthday party ever.

Sammy has a blast with her classmates, and I have a good laugh when she introduces her new friend as *human* Eli to each and every one of them. Never once does he explain that the existence of capybara Eli led to him being human Eli. He just easily goes along with his new name.

I've just finished making sure everybody's gotten pizza when Eli finally slides up next to me again, his own slice in hand.

"You've raised an awesome kid," he says, his intense blue eyes boring into mine, like he's willing me to believe him.

"She does that all on her own. I got lucky." I smile at my little girl inhaling pizza like a frat boy.

"Hey, have you eaten?" Olivia comes up on my other side,

holding out a paper plate for me, which I gladly accept. She got here a while ago, a bit late because of work, but, as one might imagine, a kid's birthday party is pretty chaotic, so this is the first we're able to be still together.

"Hey, Eli," Olivia says coolly.

"Yo," he answers automatically. He then asks her something about depreciation elections for the flower shop, and I stop listening.

As I fold my pizza and lift it for a bite, I can't help but watch Eli.

Piper comes over and subtly bumps my shoulder. "Am I interrupting something?" she whispers, looking between Eli, who's happily eating pizza and talking to Olivia about taxes, and me, who she just caught brazenly staring at him.

"No, no. Just having an existential crisis, I think," I murmur.

"Oh, cool. I do that weekly." She nods without batting an eye. Then, she lowers her voice. "I saw a little of what went down earlier, and I just wanted to say I'm very familiar with parental difficulties, so if you ever want to rant or trauma bond or whatever, I'm your girl."

I sigh and heavily flop my head against the side of her arm, but Lemon joins us before I can respond.

Then, Eli looks over at us, smiling when he sees Lemon. With Samantha dragging him around her party all morning, I haven't had a chance to officially introduce them. When Olivia gets pulled away by Samantha, Eli turns back to me.

Lemon immediately holds out her hand to Eli. "I'm Lemon, Iris's sister, in case you didn't put that together already from the face we share."

"I hadn't noticed," Eli says smoothly, taking her hand. "It's nice to meet you. I'm human Eli."

"Oh, I've heard. I don't get it, but I've heard," Lemon answers. "Nice work with dickface, earlier," she adds.

"My pleasure, but I think Iris had it handled pretty well." Eli sidesteps the compliment, raising his plate like he's toasting me.

And when he does, I see the little bits of ham and pineapple on it.

A couple of hours later, with a car loaded full of gifts, I'm strapping a very sleepy Sammy into her car seat. My parents took off earlier to drive to some fancy hotel a couple of towns over, but Lemon will be having a fun little slumby with me, Piper, and Olivia tonight.

"I love you, Mama," Sammy mutters around a yawn just before I close the door to the back seat.

"I love you too, baby," I say, feeling a rush of adoration for this tiny person.

As I circle my car, I spot Eli waving to me from the other side of the Literary Lake front window and return the gesture.

In spite of everything, today turned out alright.

Iris

When we get home, Sammy is hit with a second wind, eager to carefully examine every one of her gifts. Once everything's inside, Olivia, Lemon, and I help her with the kid-proof packaging and let her go to town. Piper will swing by after she's done at the bookstore. Messes are tomorrow's problem. For now, we are all her humble servants, dutifully playing whatever role she assigns.

After an early dinner, Sam crashes hard. She's so wiped from the party that I'm not entirely sure she's fully conscious while we brush her teeth. She's conked out less than a page into our current book.

I sneak out of her room, silently closing the door and tiptoeing downstairs before I fall heavily on the couch beside Lemon before needing to pop right back up to let Piper in.

"You did good today, Mama," my sister says once we're all settled again. "How are you doing with everything that happened before?"

"Waaaaait," Olivia calls, scurrying into the room from the kitchen with three glasses of white wine in her hands and a can of beer wedged between her side and her elbow. She passes the wine to me, Lemon, and Piper, who's draped across the love seat, before sandwiching me in by claiming the cushion on my other side. "I already missed half of the party. Don't make me miss the gossip. What happened *before*?"

"Oh, you didn't hear? Our parents brought Archer, and he was trying to play at being Daddy," Lem says, shoving her finger in her open mouth and fake gagging. Or maybe real gagging. Since she's talking about Archer, it could be either.

Olivia's mouth pops open, and she doesn't even notice the beer she half-opened is hissing in her hand.

"And Archer is…?" Piper prompts, lifting her head to look over at us.

"Shitty baby daddy," Lemon answers, gagging again.

"Got it. Thought so but hoped not. I'm caught up. Please proceed." Piper sits fully up and swings her legs around so she faces us.

"You have got to be fucking joking," Olivia says once she's regained the ability to speak.

"If only." I sigh and drink my wine.

"Why did your parents bring him if he's a piece of crap?" Piper asks.

"They don't think it's proper that an unmarried woman has a child," I say, rolling my eyes so hard I'm likely at risk of them getting stuck in the back of my head. "They have expectations I fail to meet."

The way Piper snorts into her wine glass tells me she wasn't kidding about relating to my situation.

"You know those expectations are *theirs* and theirs alone, right? And all you need to do is keep yourself and your girl happy and safe," she says, a bite in her tone telling me she'd fight my parents on my behalf.

"I do." And I do, but it feels good to hear her remind me anyway.

"So, what happened with Archer?" Olivia leans toward me, eager for details.

"Sis told him to get fucked and then the large man threatened him. It was hot," Lemon summarizes.

"Eli threatened him?" I thought Olivia's eyes couldn't get any wider. I was wrong.

"Eli didn't 'threaten' him. Eli simply existed enormously beside me, and Archer was threatened, so he left," I explain, not wanting to paint Eli as some brute. "But Archer said he'll see me around, so I'm not entirely sure he's done with me."

"Maybe you can get Eli to threaten him more directly next time, so Archer will leave town for good," Piper suggests. "Eli would if you asked him to. He and Jake have very similar moral compasses, and Jake punched Alice's ex in the face for her. I'm told it was hot."

"Ok, one of you has to tell me the deal with this Eli guy. Is something going on between you two?" Lemon directs that last part at me.

"He's my *friend*. We could never be more," I say adamantly, though the mental image of him hitting Archer *is* pretty hot.

"Why never?" she asks at the same time Piper does.

"He's a one-night-stand guy, not a be-with-a-mom guy," I say, pretending it's fine while my body remembers the intensity of Eli's fury when he was standing behind me earlier. I take a drink of wine and accidentally empty the rest of it.

"*I* think you should go for it," Liv pipes up. "A night with Eli would do you good. I would know."

The way she says the last part makes me blush.

"You and Eli?" Piper surmises that Olivia and Eli have a past.

"Only once, and it was ages ago. Obviously just for fun, and no feelings lingered or anything," Liv explains.

"It would be way too weird," I protest.

"Because of our past?" Olivia asks, but I shake my head.

"No. You've made your blessing quite clear. It would just be *weird*. We're too different. Lem, tell them it would be weird."

I look to my sister for support but find hesitation on her face.

"Lemon Sutton, you've got to be kidding me!" I check my volume and lower it so I don't wake Sammy. "There's no way you're on their side."

"I mean…" Lem shrugs. "Not every naked adventure has to be more than that."

"*Thank* you." Olivia is so pleased with the support she's getting. "Get railed, girl."

"Olivia!" I snap, covering my face. "No! There's Sammy to think about."

I may be less uptight than I was when the entire purpose of my existence was to be a perfect student and daughter, but I'm pretty sure I missed out on having my fun fling years when I got pregnant. I need to be looking for a consistent partner who is interested in being a part of my life and Sam's life. Flings are messy and silly, and I can't be making irresponsible choices like that at this stage in my life. That's ok. I accept it.

"Come *on*. I'd gladly watch Sammy for you." Piper waves off my concern. Getting a babysitter was *not* what I meant.

"When was the last time you were taken care of? It might help you relax some," Olivia adds, jumping *right* into the personal stuff.

I part my fingers and peek at each woman, all eagerly awaiting my answer. I don't think it's an answer I'm willing to admit.

It doesn't matter. Olivia takes one look at my expression and knows.

"Oh honey, no," she says softly.

I nod. "Approximately five years and nine months ago."

"Iris!" Even Lemon and Piper are appalled by my lack of a sex life, scolding me in unison.

"Ok, enough," I say, standing and retrieving the wine bottle from the kitchen. "It's not happening, and that's it. Now, are we going to watch a movie, or am I drinking this wine alone in the shower?"

Lemon, Olivia, and Piper share a look but drop it.

"I'll get some popcorn," Olivia says.

Glad that's settled.

CHAPTER 17

When I was growing up, birthdays were formal, impersonal affairs. The *right* people got invited, children were seen and not heard, and the evening inevitably included some amount of business dealings. Mine and Lemon's birthday was always formally celebrated in the fall, since our July 6th actual birth date was extremely inconvenient for our parents' summer travels. These parties weren't exactly about the person whose birthday it was, anyway. It was just how our family operated. It's ok. We'd celebrate quietly with Harry and Kenny, loving the store-bought cake they'd get us.

Now that I make the rules, birthdays are big, spanning multiple days with different events. I don't want there to be any doubt in my kid's mind that her very existence is something deserving of celebration. So, tonight is Sam's birthday dinner with my parents, Harry and Kenny, Olivia, Lemon, and me.

Even from a distance, as our group crosses the parking lot together, I can see the displeasure on my parents' faces.

Sam picked hibachi for tonight, and I know my parents won't consider this a suitable place for a birthday soirée, especially not compared to the white-glove, catered affairs I sat through for the first eighteen years of my life. After the stunt Mom pulled yesterday, my petty side is a little happy that giving my girl what she wants also coincidentally pisses off my mom.

Like most people, I have a complicated relationship with my parents. I was a good little rule follower growing up, but me getting pregnant before I was twenty-one was about as big a diversion from the Sutton plan as I could make. I will forever be grateful for my parents giving me the opportunities I got and for their help when I called my mom sobbing after discovering those two little blue lines, but the way they cling to what is *proper* over what is *right* just doesn't work for me. Not once I had Sam.

I will give credit where it's due, though. Mom and Dad both break into grins the second they notice Samantha approaching and loudly cheer "happy birthday." Once we reach the sidewalk, I release Sam's hand so she can run to my father, who has squatted down to scoop her up. As he stretches to his full height, he easily lobs Sam into the air, just to catch her again.

"Soon you're going to be too big for that," he's saying when Olivia, Lemon, and I walk up. He begins tickling her side, and my mom bends close to kiss Sam's hair. "What are you now, forty? Fifty?"

"I'm *five*, Grandpa!" Sam squeals between giggles. "I told you yesterday."

"That can't be right. Are you sure?" Dad teases.

"Hello dear," Mom greets me with a quick kiss to my cheek. Dad then pulls me in for a stiff, one-armed hug, unwilling to set Samantha down.

"Hi Mom, Dad. Are Harry and Kenny here yet?" I ask, looking around, but Mom shakes her head.

"I imagine they'll be here any minute," she says to me before leaning in close. "Hibachi? Really?"

Either Mom's not as quiet as she intended to be or Sam has the hearing of a bat because she pipes up right away. "You don't like it?"

Mom and I turn to her, and my heart squeezes at the crushed expression on her face.

"Oh, no! I'm just afraid of the fire," Mom recovers. "Will you protect me?"

"Yeah, it'll be ok." Sam nods furiously, reaching for my mom, who happily takes her from Dad, right as Harry and Kenny arrive.

I give Mom a reproachful look from behind Sam's back, but she won't complain about the restaurant again. She won't risk hurting Sam's feelings.

Even though each hub seats ten, and we're only a party of eight, we get a grill to ourselves. The empty chairs let Sam easily seat hop during dinner and spend a little time with everyone. She starts by my dad, but she stays between me and Mom for the whole fire portion of the performance, taking her role as Mom's protector very seriously.

When Dad begrudgingly catches a shrimp flung at him in his mouth, the whole table erupts in cheers, but that's not as loud as the laughter when Olivia completely misses hers, taking it to the cheek instead, nobody chortling as much as Olivia herself.

When Lemon steals Sammy for a bit toward the end of our meal, seating her between herself and Olivia, Mom slides into the vacated seat beside me. I'm immediately on edge.

Danger.

"So, have you reconsidered what we discussed yesterday?" she asks, keeping her voice low and one eye on Sam. There's no way Sam's going to hear anything, though. The restaurant is loud.

I desperately try to think of something Mom brought up that she could be referring to other than Archer. Because I know there's no damn way she's talking about her ridiculous comment about a girl needing her father. Sadly, I come up empty-handed.

"I don't think there's anything we discussed that warranted further thought," I answer, keeping my voice level. There's still a glimmer of hope in me that she's about to bring up some tidbit of a conversation that I forgot.

"It's inappropriate for a young woman to raise a child on her own when the father is alive and well and willing to participate in parenthood. Archer came up here to do the right thing, and you sending him away is an embarrassment. You two need to be married so this whole thing can be put to rest," she hisses, and that hope dies a sad and lonely death.

"Jacki," I snap, knowing she hates when I use her first name, but also knowing it has the effect of telling her I'm not fucking around. "What's inappropriate is that man trying to waltz into my child's life *years* after he made it abundantly and repeatedly clear that he *hates* children and would like nothing more than to ship her off to boarding school as soon and for as long as possible. He's a misogynistic, conceited jackass, and you thinking you get to have an opinion about any of this is a fucking *joke*. So, butt out!"

I don't realize my voice has risen until I finish and find all eyes on me around a silent table. I'm breathing hard and my hands are shaking so badly that my chopsticks are clattering against my plate. I set them down.

My dad's face is red as he glares at me from beside Mom, but Harry looks ready to fight his sister-in-law on my behalf. He's *never* liked Archer.

"Mama?" Sam asks quietly from Olivia's lap.

The fight melts out of me as I take in her little furrowed brow.

"Sorry lil' one. I'm ok. Grandma and I just disagree on something." I don't want her to see things like this. "Ok?"

Sam nods slowly before taking her seat again, but her big eyes look sad. I turn back to Mom.

"I hope you're happy with yourself," she whispers. My father is now on his feet and has placed his hands on her shoulder.

"Not even a little bit, but let me make something very clear. You do not speak to me about Archer again. You do not speak to Archer *about* me or Sam again, and you sure as shit don't bring him anywhere near either of us, or we are done," I whisper back.

"You're being dramatic." She rolls her eyes.

"*Done*, Mother. Do you hear me?"

"I hear you." She huffs. "But I don't need to bring him near you. He's already staying in town."

"Oohs" from around the dining room have me swiveling around toward Sam again. Our server is shielding an elaborate ice cream sundae with five lit candles stuck in it as she approaches our table. I look to Harry, who shrugs while smirking, clearly responsible for the dessert.

All at once, we break into an out-of-tune rendition of "Happy Birthday" while Sam claps and bounces in her seat. She beams when she manages to blow out all five candles with one breath.

"We should get going," my father says the second Sam starts on her dessert, his face stern once again. That's Cornelius Sutton for you, never one to *actually* get involved.

He kisses the top of my head as my mother gets to her feet, and I try not to be disappointed that he didn't stand up for me, again. Mom leans over to hug me like we didn't just have it out in public.

"I just want what's best for you," she says once she pulls back.

"Yup. Have a safe trip home," I manage to say. Even when I'm right, I always feel a massive pit of guilt in my stomach after arguing with my mom. She raised me, and I love her.

But things are more complicated than that.

I watch them dote on Sam and see adoration in her eyes when she looks up at them. With a look back at me, they leave.

"You ok?" Harry asks, now at my side.

I nod. But then I remember what Mom said before the ice cream came out.

Archer is staying in town.

CHAPTER 18

Iris

Monday is a *bad day*. Lem heads back home first thing in the morning, causing Samantha to have a very rare meltdown. It's a struggle for us all to get out of the house, and we barely make it to drop-off on time.

As I'm driving to work, I realize I left my laptop at home and have to go back for it. Then I need to get gas and end up behind my self-imposed schedule.

The reason I can juggle the different pieces of my life is because I stick to a plan. I have lists and schedules and control. Today is out of control from the very beginning, and it makes me feel itchy all over.

If things could stop going wrong, that would be—

Archer is standing on the front patio of the firm when I get out of my car. I stare stupidly at him, praying his figure is a hallucination, but then it speaks.

Fuck. This. Monday.

"Harold dearest wouldn't let me wait inside," Archer says with a lopsided grin like we're on the same side.

"If it were up to me, you wouldn't be let in the state," I mutter. "Get lost."

He steps aside as I walk up, letting me open the door and get inside, but he sticks his leg out and jams the door open when I try to slam it in his face. Without invitation, he slips inside like a noxious gas. Uncle Harry's door is closed, so he's almost certainly on a client call.

"We need to talk," Archer says, his voice sickly sweet.

"We really don't," I say, hanging my coat so forcefully I'm surprised I don't rip the damn hook off the wall. You'd think me storming away *again* would deliver the message that he's not welcome, but no luck.

"Ris, baby. Talk to me," he pleads, and I think I'm going to be sick. That fucking nickname is even *worse* coming from him.

"I have nothing to say to you, and if you call me baby again, I'll cut out your tongue."

"Ok, we'll work back up to pet names. Will you at least listen?"

"I'd rather not," I say, walking behind my desk and unpacking my things for the day.

Archer takes a step toward me, and I realize I've trapped myself between the desk and the wall. I think Archer plans to *force* me to listen to his drivel. I know if I yell for Harry, he'll come running, guns blazing, but the embarrassment of having to do so might end me.

As I look at Archer, I notice he looks just a little bit *off*. His custom suit doesn't fit as perfectly as it should for the price tag I'm sure it had. There's a stain on his collar, his tie is creased, and he's overdue for a haircut. As a vain man, it's very unusual.

Archer moves to take another step toward me, coming around my desk, but he pauses at the sound of the door opening. I feel like cornered prey.

"Heel, boy," a deep but soft voice carries to us, and a wave of relief washes over me.

Eli.

It seems like he's finally gotten over his need to get permission before stopping by, and I couldn't be more thrilled by the development.

As Eli appears in the doorway, I see he's not alone. Waffles is dutifully staying at Eli's side, but both new arrivals spot Archer at the same time. Eli's brows draw together as Waffles's hackles rise, and he emits a low growl.

Good boy.

At the menacing sound, Archer jumps, but tries to cover the reaction by stepping away from me.

"Who's this?" Archer says with false bravado. He squats down like he wants the dog to come to him, but Waffles snaps his jaw, daring Archer to try getting close.

"Waffles! Down boy," Eli's commanding voice sounds, and Waffles's ears pop up from where they were plastered to his head, but he still doesn't take his eyes off Archer.

With the confidence of a man who knows he belongs, Eli walks past Archer and stands beside me, crossing his arms and placing himself directly between me and my ex. It's bold. It's arrogant. It's welcomed.

Waffles comes with Eli but continues right to me and plants himself against my leg.

"Oh, I see," Archer scoffs, facing us with a sneer on his face. "Now you've got *two* guard dogs."

"Maybe I do, but I don't need any help when it comes to you. Get out, Archer. And I don't just mean the building. Get *out* of my town," I say with as much hatred as I can pour into the words.

"I'm here for you, Ris, and I'm not leaving without you."

I see Eli's fist clench under his arm as bile rises in my throat.

"You must have recently experienced a head injury if you think that's anywhere within the realm of possibilities," I say, unable to stop the laugh from escaping me. This whole situation is entirely ludicrous. Archer and I have barely spoken in *years*, and now he shows up just ready to take me back to Newport?

"I've finally come to my senses," Archer carries on, but I don't buy a word of it. "You know we're right for each other. That's why you haven't been with anybody since we broke up. I know. I asked your mother."

I blanch. Of course, he's right that I haven't been with anybody since I found out I was pregnant with Sammy, but it had literally *nothing* to do with him. The disgusting look in his eye tells me he won't believe that, though, no matter what I say.

With Eli standing within arm's reach, a crazy idea pops into my brain. Before I can think better of it, I reach out and slide my hand around Eli's biceps.

"First off, it's gross that you asked my mom. Second off, Mother doesn't know everything," I say, praying Eli won't give me away. His eyes slide down his arm to where my fingers rest, but he doesn't object. Instead, he uncrosses his arms and covers my hand with his.

Archer's eyes travel the same path, and he scoffs again, "Oh, be fucking for real right now, Ris."

Eli smoothly shifts until he's up against my side, so he can wrap his arm around my waist and pull me flush to him.

"*Iris* is so for fucking real right now, Arch," Eli says, his voice laced with menace.

Archer looks like he's going to keep arguing, but Harry reappears in the room and immediately homes in on Archer.

"I told you you're not welcome in my business. You need to get the hell off my property," Harry says, seeming extremely calm, but I can hear the danger in his tone.

"Harry, my man. Ris let me in. We're all good here," Archer starts, turning to my uncle. This man's ego is going to get him killed one of these days, I swear.

"Don't start with me, you cockroach," Harry continues. "I can assure you I know the exact legal limits of how much force I can use to remove you from this building, and I would love nothing more than to exercise those rights. Get. Out."

"This isn't the end of our discussion, Ris," Archer announces, and it sounds like a threat, just like last time.

"I promise it really is," I say, staring him down until he turns and leaves.

CHAPTER 19

Eli

Harry follows Archer out to make sure he really leaves, but neither Iris nor I move. I'm not sure Iris is even breathing.

The front door closes, and Harry reappears in the front room.

"He's gone," he announces. His eyes then catch on my arm around Iris. "Oh! Have you two…?"

Iris seems to remember our predicament and jumps, so I release her and step away. The side of my body that was pressed to hers is tingling. It's happened before when she's touched me, and each time I lie to myself and say it's completely normal.

Waffles gets to keep his spot against Iris's other side, nuzzling his nose into her hand until she bends and begins to absentmindedly stroke his head.

And I am jealous of a *dog*.

"Oh, no, no, no. Eli was just helping me get rid of Archer," she tells her uncle. She sits in her chair and Waffles lays his head in her lap.

Did she have to say *no* so many times?

Harry nods, and his face softens with concern for his niece.

"Are you ok?" he asks.

"Yeah, it's fine. Weird, but fine." She turns to me. "Thank you both."

Harry doesn't look convinced, and I expect my expression matches his. I've spent a grand total of seven minutes with Archer, but I get the feeling he's willing to disrupt whatever he needs to get what he wants.

"Are you sure? I could call Chief Allen," Harry offers, seemingly eager to ruin Archer's day. Or life. He doesn't appear to be picky.

"I'm ok," Iris assures him. "What would we even say Archer did, anyway?"

"Oh, I guarantee I can dig up some crime to get him charged with," Harry says, staring off at nothing and tapping a finger against his lips. I've known Harry for years, but I like him more and more every time we speak. "If you're sure you're ok, wanna get to it, Eli?"

Iris looks quizzically at me, so I explain, "I have a draft of the return to run through with Harry and Bella. Can Waffles stay with you again?"

"Of course," Iris says, and Waffles looks up at her like she's his whole world. Bringing him today was a happy coincidence since I think he might be just what Iris needs right now.

"And for the record, I'm on board with the plan to get that guy arrested," I add.

I follow Harry into his office, and we call Bella, who's working from home, so I can walk them through what I've prepared. We identify a couple of corrections, but it's just about ready to file.

After we wrap up, I head for the front room—Iris's office—but she's on the phone, so I linger in the doorway. She watches me while she speaks into the receiver, and her expression is difficult to read. I overhear her say the ex's name—*Archer Ringwald*.

As always, she's looking at me like she can see every secret I've ever held, but behind that bright inquisitiveness, there's unease.

"Hey," I say softly when she hangs up.

"Hey."

"Waffles," I call him. "Come here. We've gotta get going."

Waffles makes a dramatic groaning sound, but pads around the desk and over to me.

"You're not staying today?" Iris asks, and I think she might sound disappointed. Are we *both* lying to ourselves?

"I think they're finished with most of the tables for the new greenhouse, so the noise should be manageable back at the nursery," I say, also feeling just a bit disappointed. "Plus, I'm about done with the firm's return, so…" I trail off.

"I see," Iris says. Then she takes a breath. "Well, thanks again for going along with my lie before. I'm sorry for pulling you into my issues with Archer. It seemed like the easiest and fastest way to get him to back off since me saying 'no' apparently holds absolutely no weight with him. You were there, and he saw you stand up for me on Saturday, so it seemed like a believable option. I couldn't have him knowing he was right about me being single since him. I'll clear it up—" she rambles until I walk over to her and place my hands on her shoulders.

"Iris," I say quietly but firmly to cut her off. I can tell she's spiraling and likely sharing more than she intends to share with me. "I understood what you were doing, and I don't mind at all. Use me however you need to."

When Iris's pupils dilate and her lips part, I realize what I offered, but I don't take it back. It'd be a bad idea, considering my rules when it comes to relationships and the feelings I may or may not be feeling, but I'd let her anyway.

I clear my throat to break the silence.

"Really, don't worry about it. We're good. It made a tax visit exciting. And that's usually impossible."

Iris gives me a weak smile.

"Thanks, again," she says.

On my way back to the nursery, I pull over to give myself a few minutes to cool down. I didn't want to add to Iris's stress, but Archer talking about her like she's his property makes me want to hit something. I leave the truck running with the heat on for Waffles while I step out, hoping the cold air will help clear my head.

I'm pacing on the sidewalk beside my Jeep when a little Porsche skids to a stop behind it. I immediately know who's driving without even needing to check. I move to my back bumper.

So much for cooling off.

Archer gets out of his car and circles the front of it with his eyes glued to his phone, so he doesn't see me standing in his way and plows into me. He's much smaller than me and stumbles back. I hope it hurt.

"You." He scowls when he looks up and finds me. "Are you following me?"

"Considering the fact that I was here first, I'd be a pretty shit tail if I was," I say, rolling my eyes.

Archer glances over my shoulder to the market.

"Looking for road trip snacks for your drive back home?" I ask, still standing directly in his path.

"Not a chance," he says with more bravery than his expression says he has. "I'm not going anywhere. In fact, I'm going to be in your way every turn you make. Iris is mine and always has been."

Is this guy for real?

Usually, because of my size, I slouch a little, not wanting to feel like the giant at the top of Jack's beanstalk. But right now, I want to look as big as possible, so I straighten up and step even further into Archer's space. When he takes half a step back and stumbles on the curb, I know it has its intended impact.

"Iris is nobody's property, and you're a damn fool if you don't realize that. This *isn't* going to end well for you."

Waffles barks loudly, having moved to the back of the Jeep, and Archer jumps again. He talks a big game, but there's no substance there.

"This is way bigger than you," he says. "I'm staying as long as it takes, and you won't keep me from what's mine. I'm not afraid of you."

I barrel forward to pass between our cars, and he jumps aside, bumping into the hood of his car.

"You should be," I say before I get back in the Jeep and slam the door.

Waffles clambers over the back seat and pokes his head forward.

"Good boy," I say, running a hand down his back, but Waffles doesn't relax until I put the car in drive and pull away from the grocery store.

There's something about the way Archer kept pushing that doesn't sit right with me. There's something more going on here, and I don't like it.

It really wasn't my place to face off with Archer back there, but he didn't know that. He thought I was her boyfriend. And if I was, maybe I could help. I *want* to help.

An alarm bell screams in my head, telling me I'm going down a dangerous path. But for Iris? I'd take that risk.

Iris 

For a while after I had Sam, I had these horrible nightmares that Archer would suddenly show up and somehow take her from me. Eventually, I let myself get comfortable in our lives. I just never thought he'd come back.

Now, I'm teetering between rage and panic. I push myself toward the anger I feel at Archer's audacity because if I panic, I'll be useless, and I can't afford that right now.

Is it healthy? Probably not, but I'll take what I can get right now.

While Eli is meeting with Harry and Bella, I call Samantha's school and confirm her approved pick-up list. The school assures me Archer wouldn't get near her, but that doesn't lessen the intense urge I have to pick Sam up and lock her away at home where I know she's safe.

It's easier to pretend I'm calm, cool, and collected when I'm talking to Eli, but after he leaves, I'm right back in the old folder of notes on my computer where I documented every conversation I had with Archer about Samantha, and his repeated refusals to be in her life.

Thankfully, since Archer never signed Samantha's birth

certificate, he has no rights or proof of paternity. Without my permission, he'd need a court order to establish paternity, and since he's known about Samantha since I first got pregnant, he'd have a tough time getting that. Harry's been having me keep records of *everything* since day one.

When I add notes about Saturday and today, a tiny piece of me cracks. I thought this was behind us.

I take a deep breath and focus. I can do this. I *have* to do this, for Sam.

I quickly look up restraining orders, but unfortunately Archer hasn't done enough for me to get one of those… yet. It would also involve airing all my dirty laundry to the people of Wilcox Grove —and it *would* get out—and I just really don't want to do that. I want this place to remain a safe haven for both me and Sam.

Sadly, I don't think I could get away with just hitting Archer with my car and dumping his body in the lake. That's just a silly fleeting idea anyway, not an actual option.

… right?

Right.

With a groan, I fold forward and let my forehead hit the glossy wooden surface with a soft thump.

After a few minutes, my phone buzzes, distracting me from my murder plots, which keep getting more creative.

ELI

hey. could we meet up and talk later

I check the clock. It's been less than an hour since Eli left the office, so I'm racking my brain trying to figure out what could have possibly occurred in such a short period of time to warrant such an ominous text.

ME

Are you ok?

yeah ive just got a hairbrained idea that i
wanted to run by you

As I pull into the parking lot for Wilcox Nursery just before four that afternoon, I'm buzzing with nervous anticipation. Eli insisted that we talk in person so obviously I've spent the day running through every terrible scenario that could be awaiting me inside.

A gangly teenager looks up from the register as I enter the nursery.

"Hi there. Welcome in," he says with a soft, small smile. I know I've seen him around town before, but I can't remember his name.

"Thanks," I say and take in the space.

Behind the register is a long greenhouse with neat rows of potted plants, small trees, and other leafy thingamabobs. Even in the dead of winter, it smells like earth in here. It's a nice reminder of what's to come in the spring.

Seeing how cramped everything is back there, I understand the desire for an expanded greenhouse. I saw the new structure outside and a team working on finishing it when I pulled up. It looks like it'll connect to this greenhouse behind the building and wrap around the other side.

To my left is an open doorway that seems to lead to the nursery's office space. I can hear someone typing from within but only see an empty desk from where I'm standing.

After watching me look around cluelessly, the young man asks, "Can I help you with something?"

"I'm sorry," I answer, feeling unbelievably awkward. "I was just looking for Eli, if he's around?"

The sound of keys clicking stops.

"He's in there," the worker says, jerking his head toward the office just as Eli appears in the doorway.

"Iris," Eli breathes, grinning when he sees me. I can't help but smile back. Some of the tension I've been carrying releases at the sight of him.

"Thanks, Tim. It's been pretty dead around here, so you're free to take off early if you'd like," Eli says to the boy who checks the clock, nods, hops off his stool, and heads out with a thanks and a wave.

Eli then reaches out his arm toward me, leading me into the office ahead of him with a light touch to my lower back.

Once I've turned the corner, I see a second desk—it must be Eli's—further into the room and across from a small kitchenette. The back wall has two closed doors: the first labeled *Restroom* and the second labeled *Storage*. In spite of the frigid temperatures outside, the room is comfortable. Framed pictures of nature and a large area rug in the center of the space make it cozy too.

Eli directs me to his chair.

"Take my seat," he instructs, before walking to the other desk and stealing that chair for himself. I'm guessing it's Jake's since I know they own the nursery together. I expect Eli to sit across the desk from me, but he pulls up right beside mine. I guess it makes sense. This is *his* desk after all.

"Is it too late for coffee for you?" he asks, and it feels like he's stalling.

Is he nervous?

"Never," I say. It's been an emotionally draining day, and I'm exhausted. Plus, holding the mug will give me something to do with my hands besides fidget.

Eli passes me a steaming mug of black coffee. It's got a grove of apple trees and the Wilcox Nursery logo printed on it. Eli's looking expectantly at me, so I take a sip. I breathe out as the warmth spreads through my chest. Coffee was the right call.

"Ok, Eli, I'm here and coffeed. What's going on?"

"On my way back here earlier, I stopped in town and ran into Archer. That guy's a dick," he starts, and my stomach drops.

"Shit, Eli. I'm sorry. He shouldn't be harassing you. It's because he thinks we're together. I'll talk to him and clear things up." I bring my empty hand up to my temple and press my thumb there, hard. I feel a headache coming on.

"Well, that's actually why I asked to talk to you. What if we didn't?"

I pull my hand back, confused. "Didn't what?"

"Didn't clear things up. About us being together, I mean."

"I mean, if he's going to try to drag me back to Newport, I think he'd figure out I made it up eventually. He's dumb, but not *that* dumb." I'm not following.

"What if there was nothing to figure out? What if we made it so you didn't make it up?"

Now I set the mug on the table, because it sounds a lot like Eli is asking me out, but it was just a couple weeks ago that I was accusing him of that and embarrassing myself beyond belief. I'm not exactly ready to relive the experience. Also, Eli doesn't *date* people, so I must be missing something.

"Eli, I'm going to need you to explain this to me like I'm stupid."

"I have a feeling it wouldn't do you any favors to tell Archer you made up a relationship," Eli tries again.

"You're not wrong," I admit, just imagining that conversation. I expect he'd take it as proof that I'm completely hung up on him.

"So, what if we keep it going until he gets the message and crawls back into whatever hole he crawled out of?"

"He crawled out of a multi-million-dollar mansion in Newport," I point out.

Is Eli suggesting what I think he's suggesting?

"If that piece of shit lives in it, it's still a hole, no matter how nicely it's dressed up," Eli says. "That's not the point though. Iris, what if we let him—let everybody—think we're dating?"

Ho-ly shit. He is.

"You want to date me?" I ask, just to be sure.

"I don't date," he says quickly. Ouch. He must see the hurt on my face. "That's on me, not on you. But if we let people *think* we're dating, I could help you with your Archer situation. I *want* to help you with your Archer situation. There's something about that guy that's got me worried. He sounded like somebody on the edge of losing it, and that's dangerous."

I think back to how Archer looked just a little bit unraveled this morning.

Eli wants to *fake* date me. Considering my very real feelings for him, that feels like a bad idea. But it's also oh so very tempting, and I can't deny having a boyfriend would likely help with the Archer situation.

"You realize how this sounds, right?" I ask, because it sounds insane.

"I do."

"It would ruin your reputation. And you wouldn't be able to be seen with anybody else romantically. I can't have him thinking you're cheating on me. That would be worse than telling him I made up our relationship." I can't believe I'm even considering this.

"It's not like I've got a wife at home who's going to get jealous," he counters.

"I know that, but you love women. You see women. You sleep with women." I mean, he just said a minute ago that he doesn't date.

"From time-to-time, yes. But I have a thousand things going on during tax season. I haven't exactly been hitting the town. I've finished a few of my bigger returns, but I still have a whole list to get through. You're making me sound like a manwhore." He chuckles, but the laugh is tinged with hurt.

"Shit, Eli. I didn't mean that. I just don't want to disrupt your life." I rub at my forehead again. This is a lot.

"You're a damn good reason to disrupt everything," he says without fanfare. "I think you think you need to fight this battle alone. And I want you to know that you don't."

I blink at him, feeling an ache deep in my chest. I've already declined help from Harry. *Do* I think I need to do this alone?

"You barely know me," I whisper, but it feels like a lie as I say it. Our friendship might be new, but it's already important to me.

"I don't think that's true. I'm a trust-my-gut kind of guy. Once I'm in, I'm in. And my gut tells me you and Sam are good people. It also tells me Archer is bad people. I'm not a fan of bullies. Never have been," Eli says, and I imagine him defending smaller kids when he was in school. The picture fits.

I open my mouth to keep protesting but stop when the front door opens. I look up just as Jake comes around the corner and pulls off his beanie.

"Hey." He raises a hand to the two of us but doesn't pry about why we're same-siding Eli's desk or why we're so close together. I'm not even sure he notices. This guy can mind his own business like it's nobody's business.

I look back at Eli to see if he's going to keep going now that Jake's arrived, but I find him waiting on me.

We're so *close together*.

Jake steps toward his desk, and the movement over Eli's shoulder catches my eye. I realize what's about to happen half a second before Jake crashes to the ground, not having realized his chair was missing.

"ELI," his voice bellows from the floor behind the desk.

I jump to my feet, nearly crashing into Eli. I ask if Jake is ok, but the question is completely drowned out by the sound of Eli guffawing. Jake's head appears over the top of the desk as he pulls himself upright. He looks *pissed*.

"We're getting more chairs *tomorrow*," he growls.

As I look back and forth between Jake pulling himself up and Eli running out of air from laughing so hard, I notice the time.

"Hey, Eli," I say, placing my hand on his arm to get his attention. "I have to get going to pick up Sam."

"I'll walk you out," he says, catching his breath.

Eli pulls Jake's chair back to him on our way out, and Jake snatches it from him.

"Sorry, Jake," I mumble, but he shakes his head.

"It's fine. I blame Eli."

Once we're outside, I press the remote to unlock the car, but Eli steps forward and opens the door for me. I don't know what to say about his proposal, and I think he can see that I'm still unsure.

"How 'bout this? Sleep on it and let me know tomorrow," he suggests.

"Ok," I answer lamely. Time sounds good.

He steps back and closes the door.

I briefly look at him through the window, searching his face for any sign of what I should do, but I just find Eli, kind and warm as always.

I think we both know this is a little crazy, but since rationality has apparently left the building, who knows what could happen.

CHAPTER 21

I close Samantha's door after tucking her in for the night, feeling ashamed. I had fully intended to talk to her about Archer today. It would have been the responsible thing to do, so she wouldn't be tricked by him if he tried something, but I just couldn't do it.

Of course Sam's asked about her dad before, but I was able to get away with saying he's not around. How am I going to explain to her that I won't let him know her when he claims he wants us to be a family? How do I make her understand how I know without doubt, in my whole body, that he's up to something? That there's some other reason he's here, and Sam and I are just tools in whatever game he's playing.

How do I break her heart?

When I get downstairs, Olivia is in the kitchen, making two irresponsibly sized bowls of ice cream. I had texted her earlier to tell her Archer had shown up at the firm, but she knew not to ask for the full story until Sam was asleep.

I fall into one of the stools at our counter, and she slides a bowl to me like she's a bartender in an old movie.

"Spill," she demands, and I recount Archer's visit.

"So, that's twice now that Eli has scared Archer off?" she asks when I'm finished and after she's confirmed I'm ok and that she's not allowed to kill Archer.

"And he's offered to do it again," I say. I know the first rule of fake dating is secrecy, but I need advice here. "Eli offered to play the part of my boyfriend while Archer is here."

Olivia chokes on her rocky road.

"You got Eli to *date* you?" she asks, aghast.

"No. I got Eli to offer to *fake* date me," I clarify. "And I haven't said yes yet."

"I mean, shit. That's still more than anybody else has gotten. I thought you've just been doing taxes together. Is that code for something? And what do you mean you haven't said yes yet? Why the hell not?"

"It is *not* code for anything. Eli and I have become friends." I push my ice cream around my bowl. "And I haven't said yes because it feels nuts. It's nuts, right?"

"I mean, maybe not. I know you can take care of yourself, but Eli can help. *We* know Eli is a sweet man, but Archer doesn't. To Archer, Eli is just a guy who looks like he could pop Archer's head like a pimple. There are worse people to have on your side."

"I feel like I'd be taking advantage of him," I say. I'd for sure be getting the better end of the bargain.

"But I doubt Eli would see it that way." Olivia *does* know Eli. "If the goal is to get rid of Archer, I don't know why you wouldn't try to use every tool at your disposal."

She's not wrong. Even though I'll never think of Eli as a tool, I only see how this could help me... as long as it never gets out that it's all a ruse. There really shouldn't be any reason to say no.

When I finally lie down, I run through my day at least a hundred times until I annoy even myself with my waffling. It's not that deep. It probably won't even be that different from how we already interact.

I pick up my phone from my nightstand and open the conversation with Eli.

ME

Yes.

The next morning, I'm in a foul mood because my nightmare about Archer stealing Samantha away came back. When I woke up in the middle of the night, it felt terrifying, and I had to run to Sam's room to see with my own eyes that she's still safe, but in the light of day, I'm back to feeling pissed the fuck off that Archer is getting to me.

When I open the front door to remote start my car, I find a bouquet of cheap flowers lying on the stoop. They're not frozen, so they can't have been there long, but they're not doing great in the cold either. Even before I pluck the card from the bunch, I know who they're from.

For the loves of my life. - Archer

Olivia comes up behind me, bundled up in sweats.

"What's with keeping the door open? It's freezing out there." She looks over my shoulder and spots the flowers and the card in my hand.

"Oh, for fuck's sake," she grumbles.

"At least he knew not to come to you for these," I say as a few petals float to the ground.

I don't care that I'm still in my slippers and I'm not wearing a coat. I scoop up the rogue petals and take the flowers straight to our trash bin. I scan the street and see no sign of Archer, but it doesn't make me feel any better. Because now I know he knows where we live.

I slam the door harder than I mean to when I go back inside.

"You good?" Olivia asks warily.

"I'm just done fucking around." I grab my phone and dial Eli's number.

"What happened?" Eli asks as soon as the line connects. His voice is stern, strong, and I'm thankful it doesn't sound like I woke him up.

"He was at my *house*, Eli. He knows where we live. There were flowers on my doorstep this morning."

"Fuck, are you ok?"

"Yeah. But I cannot have this drag out. I need him to get out, now. Can we get lunch somewhere public today before I have to get Sam from school?"

"Put me in, coach," he answers without hesitation. "Barefoot Bake at noon?"

"Perfect. I'll see you there. And thanks."

"Sammy, five-minute warning!" I call as I head up the stairs once I hang up.

I'm eager to get to work so I can take Harry up on his offer to search for something that can be legally used against Archer. Eli and Olivia were both right. I don't need to fight this battle alone, and it's stupid to let my pride keep me from doing everything I can to get that parasite out of my life. I'm going to assemble a fucking army.

I come back downstairs in a fitted charcoal dress with thick straps and my tallest heels. I'm putting on deep red lipstick when Olivia reappears to have breakfast. I dare Archer to cross me today.

"Oh, you weren't kidding," she says, pride in her voice. "Rip his heart out."

"I plan to."

CHAPTER 22

Eli

I get to Barefoot Bake early so I can claim a table before the entire town descends upon the place. Hannah gives me a perplexed look when I sit down instead of coming straight to the counter like I always do, but I let her know I'm waiting for somebody. That makes the look even worse.

I take a table near the front window so I can keep an eye out for Iris. It also coincidentally makes me extremely visible from the street. If Archer were to wander by on his Sutton-stalking mission and spot me having lunch with Iris, that would just be the funniest little coincidence, wouldn't it?

Fake date or not, with every minute that ticks away, I get more nervous. As each person passing by turns out to *not* be Iris, I find myself needing one of them to finally be her. Even though I have no problem eating out by myself, sitting here waiting for her makes me jittery.

I blame that anticipation for my reaction to seeing her. It's simply relief that causes every thought to leave my brain when I see her coming down the sidewalk. In spite of the perpetual dampness outside, there isn't a single wobble as she strides toward me on stilettos that are at least four inches tall. I know I have about a foot on her height-wise, but those shoes make her legs look miles long, from her ankles to the hem of her dark grey dress.

And I must be short-circuiting because this simple business dress looks anything but on Iris. The way it slides across her hips with each step has me dumbfounded. Her cream-colored coat billows out around her, bright like her hair in the weak sun fighting through blankets of clouds. With her shoulders back, head held high, and those deep red lips tipped slightly up at the corners, she looks ready to kill, and it's a damn good look on her.

I told myself the only reason she took my breath away when I saw her on Alice's birthday was because her outfit was a surprise change from the cozy, clean comfort she usually exudes. But here I am, about to start panting like Waffles.

Get it the fuck together.

I stand as Iris walks into the bakery and turns toward me. When her eyes lock on mine and she smiles, it feels like I've been punched.

Most people in my life believe I find it easy to avoid meaningful relationships with women because I don't let myself have deep feelings for them. It's actually the opposite. Having seen the connection my parents have had my entire life, I seek out that bond all the damn time and then I run like hell from it. Handing yourself over to somebody else so fully is fucking terrifying. But here I am, clearly in trouble with Iris, and I decide to dive in headfirst.

Agreeing to be Iris's fake boyfriend was without a doubt one of the dumbest things I've ever volunteered to do. I fear I'm about to incinerate the decades of protections I've built up for myself.

This is a *bad* idea. And I'm going to do it anyway.

"Hi," Iris says a little breathily as she reaches me.

"Hi," I reply, while I try to think of something better to say.

On autopilot, I move behind Iris and slide her coat off her

arms as she starts to remove it. I fold it over the back of an empty chair at our little table, and we both sit. Iris quickly scans the room before pulling a small notebook out of her bag and putting her game face on, something I recognize from the office. She's focused, determined, and a little intimidating. When she's like this, shit gets done.

"I was talking to Harry about legal avenues we might be able to use to help get rid of unwanted visitors, so let me know if you have any other run-ins, and try to remember as much detail as possible. We never know what will be helpful," she begins, keeping her voice low.

"Of course. If there's anything I should or shouldn't be doing in those situations, just let me know. I—"

She cuts me off, revealing that her nerves are a little frayed. I hate that she's being driven to this.

"I'll check on that, but I assume avoiding unprovoked physical contact is probably a good idea." She makes a quick note on the page before turning it. "I also wanted to go through how you and I should handle our situation around Sam, which is probably something we should have talked about before, so I'm sorry about that. Thoughts?"

"I figured we'd do whatever you'd do if this situation was real." I follow Iris's lead and avoid saying anything explicit.

This makes her pause, though.

"I guess I haven't really thought about what I'd do in that situation because it hasn't happened."

"I'm still your friend, Iris," I say, even though the word feels chalky on my tongue. "So, maybe I just keep acting the way I have been around her. If something comes up where we need to say something more to her, we can address it at the time, and I promise to follow your lead completely."

Iris nods and makes another note. I'm feeling a little like a client at the firm. I don't have much experience, but I expect we look like we're in a business meeting and not on a date.

I take a chance and reach across the table to set my hand on top of hers, covering it completely.

"Iris…" I say softly, and she pulls her gaze away from her notes to look back at me. "I'm down to plan and plot whatever you want, but we should probably look less like we're having a strategy session if we want to sell this."

Iris takes a slow breath in and holds it before letting it back out. I gently take the pen from her hand, wrap my fingers around hers. She watches every movement. I have to remind myself to breathe.

"You're right," she concedes, and when she smiles softly at me, I wonder if it's part of the act.

"Now, whenever I come here, I have the hardest time choosing between the chicken sandwich and the mozzarella pesto panini. What do you say to splitting both?" I slowly rub my thumb across the back of her hand. It really is *so* much smaller than mine.

"Those are my favorites too." Iris moves to stand, but I shake my head.

"Don't even think about it," I warn, giving her hand a quick squeeze before heading to the counter.

Even though there's a line of people before her, Hannah is standing frozen and slack-jawed, staring at me and Iris. When I join the line, she shakes her head and resumes working. When it's my turn, she looks at me with narrowed eyes, like she's trying to figure out if I've been body-snatched.

"Hey, can I please get a chicken sandwich, a pesto panini, and two of whatever the lemonade is today?" I ask, like I don't notice her giving me the most obvious stink eye on the planet.

"It's blackberry," she says, her eyes now darting between Iris at the table and me. "But what is *this*?" she asks, now pointing between the two of us.

"What does it look like?" I ask coyly, glancing back at Iris. As if on cue, she looks over at me and smiles. My insides flip again, and I pretend it isn't concerning.

"It *looks* like a date."

I shrug. "Sounds like you know what this is, then."

I deserve a medal for not laughing at the way Hannah's mouth comically falls fully open, her hands frozen over the tablet screen where she had been entering my order.

"No fucking way," she whispers in awe.

"Yes fucking way," I say back, laughing. The flush I feel spreading up my neck could be a paid actor.

"Damn. Hell must have frozen over. Eli Chambers on a real, live date." Hannah is still in shock for another moment but snaps out of it to glare at me. "I don't know if you know this, but Leslie and I owe a lot to Iris, so don't you dare fuck this up."

"I care about Iris." It's the easy answer because it's true. I pull my credit card out of my wallet. "Is it ok if I get back to her?"

"It is, but I've got my eye on you, mister."

I don't doubt Hannah's threat is real, but she also looks pleased about this. I'm hoping she'll share the big news. She runs the card, and sends me away with the lemonades, promising to bring the sandwiches as soon as they're ready. I feel her eyes boring holes in my back the whole walk to the table.

"What was that all about?" Iris asks, as she takes one of the lemonades from me.

"That was us going Wilcox Grove official," I answer.

Iris's head whips back to Hannah, who quickly spins around and pretends she wasn't still spying on us.

"Oh, so this is *real*?" Iris asks quietly, facing me and taking a sip of her lemonade.

"As real as fake can be," I say and clink my glass against hers.

"How do you like the lemonade? It's blackberry, and the flavored lemonades here are always good, so I went for it. If you're not a fan, I can get you something else."

"No, it's great." Iris gets a thoughtful expression on her face. "If you don't do"—she waves an arm over the table—"*this*, how are you so good at it?"

That one is easy. "I've had a lifetime of watching how my dad treats my mom."

"Huh," Iris says. I'd have figured a line like that—a truth, but a line nonetheless—would have a more emotional impact.

"What is it?"

"Well, it was entirely presumptuous of me, and obviously wrong, but I'd thought maybe you didn't do relationships because your parents had a bad one. Maybe you come from a broken home. It didn't seem likely with how you talked about them, but I still wondered…"

"It's not an unreasonable assumption, but my parents couldn't be further from broken if they tried."

"Was it a bad ex, then? Did a high school girlfriend shatter your heart?" Iris blurts, I think surprising even herself.

"No." I chuckle. "This is my first real date."

I think Iris might ask for an explanation, but Hannah appears with our sandwiches.

"Who's getting which?" she asks.

"Oh, we're going to share both," Iris answers, her eyes lingering on me before she looks at Hannah, like she has to drag her gaze away. It's very convincing.

Hannah nods and sets the plates down, muttering under her breath as she heads back to the counter. "He didn't make it up…"

We quickly swap half a sandwich each, and dive in, but Hannah isn't our last disbelieving visitor.

"Miss, is this man holding you hostage?" a gravelly voice

asks from over my shoulder when we're almost through eating. I recognize the sound of Grateful Bob immediately.

"No, sir." Iris laughs softly. "He's being a perfect gentleman."

"Gentleman? Him? I don't believe it." Grateful Bob claps a hand on my shoulder. "And, please, it's—"

"Grateful Bob. I know. You're kind of famous in this town, you know. Though, I have heard about a dozen different explanations for where you got your nickname." Iris is as charming as ever, and I know Grateful Bob is eating it up.

"Don't believe anything you hear. This town is full of a bunch of storytellers. It's because I'm the Grateful Dead's number one fan." Grateful Bob gives us what I expect is another lie. I doubt anybody knows the real source of the nickname since he's never given the same explanation twice.

"Well, that makes sense," Iris says, and I make a mental note to tell her that Grateful Bob can be the most prolific storyteller in this town. "I'm—"

"Iris Sutton. I'm famous because I know everything about everyone, which is why I can't believe I didn't know a nice young woman like you was spending time with this ragamuffin."

"Geez, Grateful Bob. Give a guy a damn *chance*," I say, rolling my eyes when I look back at him standing over my shoulder.

Grateful Bob keeps an eye on all of us, ready to listen, give advice, or slap us around if we're being morons. I try not to think about which of those most often came my way while I was growing up. He's been a staple in my life, in this town, for as long as most of us can remember. He's also one of my favorite people on this planet.

"I just never thought I'd see the day," Grateful Bob says, and there's pride in his voice. I try not to think about the disappointment that will replace it when Iris and I inevitably break up.

"Have fun you two," he adds before hurrying into the bookstore, his ponytail catching on the patches of his denim jacket as it swishes back and forth.

"Unless you want to be ambushed by Piper right now, we should wrap up and head out," I say once Grateful Bob is out of earshot.

Having him pop up here today was a stroke of luck since he can be one of the biggest gossips in town. He knows where to draw the line, since he's also one of the best secret-keepers we have when he needs to be. Me being on a date? That's the kind of news he won't be able to hold back.

Thankfully, we're good to go, so I drop our dishes and glasses in the bus bin near the trash and make it back to the table in time to help Iris into her coat. As I'm holding the door for her, I see Piper out of the corner of my eye.

"So, do you think that was enough to get the word out?" Iris asks as I place my hand on the small of her back, and we turn toward her car.

I look back at Barefoot Bake and find Hannah and Piper standing side by side on the other side of the front window, Piper's mouth hanging open just like Hannah's had been earlier. Grateful Bob appears on Piper's other side, and it couldn't be easier to read his lips.

I told you so.

As I turn to face forward again, I catch sight of Archer, standing frozen across the street, glaring at us like he's willing me to burst into flames.

"Yeah." I chuckle, nudging Iris and jerking my head toward where Archer stands. "Yeah, I think that was enough."

CHAPTER 23

Eli

I had a date. And it went well. And I *liked* it.

For the first time, I wonder if my fear has been keeping me from something truly great. Iris smiled. She relaxed. She had a good time… at least I think she did. I *hope* she did.

I'm still hoping when I remember this was all a ruse, and it feels like a hot poker in my chest.

I was trying to give Iris a good date, but *she* was just playing a part. Very convincingly, I might add.

I shake my head to dispel those flowery feelings that had been popping up about dating. It felt good because it was played that way.

So, in summary, I like her, but I shouldn't. This is fake. I'm going to get hurt.

I'm fine. This is fine.

Thank goodness.

A little over an hour after I get back to the nursery, Jake comes into the office looking confused.

"What's going on?" he asks.

"Not much in here," I answer with a shrug.

He looks at his phone, his eyebrows furrowing, then back at

me. I think he's going to say something else, but he just sits at his desk.

When it starts getting dark, Marty, one of our other high school employees, pokes her head into the office space to say goodbye before she leaves, but the room otherwise remains in this awkward, silent limbo. I can't explain exactly why it feels weird, but there's an air of suspense. I'm about to finally crack and ask Jake what I'm missing when I hear a car pull into our lot out front, hurried footsteps, and several people talking over one another.

I'm halfway standing, about to check what the commotion is all about when the door bursts open, and Scott hurries in, leading the pack with Alice, Piper, and Waffles right on his heels.

"Eli," he gasps, frantic. "Are you *dying*?"

"Am I—What? No. What?" I look down at myself like I'm suddenly going to see an open wound I casually missed while going about my day.

"Scott, babe, I thought we talked about easing into this and not panicking," Piper says as she comes up to Scott's side. Jake is chortling into the back of his hand.

"Some people seem to be under the impression you're dating Iris, and since that's a little unexpected, we just wanted to come say hey… see what's up," Alice says gently, like this is some kind of intervention, and I catch Waffles's ears perking up at the sound of Iris's name.

I decide to test how believable the date was with the people who know me best and are presumably the most difficult to trick.

"See, the thing is…" I say and look away, feigning sheepishness. "I've been spending a lot of time with her over at Harry's, you know, while I've been working on their return and the construction has been going on here. I… I like her. A lot. She's considerate and funny and so fucking smart. We've been seeing each other for a bit but keeping it discreet. You know how this town can be about stuff like that, and it's new territory for me. We were trying to avoid the added pressure. But with her ex showing up, it felt like it was time to go public."

Starting by talking about the time I've spent with Iris made the lie flow easily because it's born of truth. A *lot* of truth.

The four people before me have very different reactions to my announcement. Piper looks elated, like she's holding herself back from launching at me in excitement. Scott is still looking at me like I've had an emotional break caused by a terminal diagnosis, and Alice is confused. Jake is the only one looking at me with pure skepticism, and he's the first to speak.

"What about your *no relationships* rule? You just threw that out for Iris?" he asks.

"You threw out your rule about not getting close to people for Alice," I counter. And if I were to throw it out… maybe someone like Iris would be worth it.

"I did," he admits. "And it had been a while, but it wasn't that I'd *never* had a relationship before. I was just an asshole."

"Jake…" Alice starts, maybe to contradict his evaluation of himself, but it's pretty spot on for how he was before she broke through that shell. "People can change their minds."

"They can," Jake admits, but I'm not sure he's completely convinced.

"I think it's fantastic that you're a couple. I've seen the potential for the two of you since the first time I saw you together," Piper says, completely buying what I'm selling.

Piper's support, while kind, makes me feel like I've reached my limit on playing into this. I don't know if telling these guys the truth is against the rules of my arrangement with Iris, but I can't lie to them. Plus, I trust them completely. They'll keep our secret.

I know Marty left, and I don't think anybody else has wandered inside, but I get up to check, just in case.

"What are you…?" Jake asks as I flick the front lock on my way back.

"There's more to the story, but it needs to stay among us. *No exceptions*," I say.

"Shit, you *are* dying," Scott says dramatically.

"Scotty, pull it together," Jake grumbles before turning back to me. "What is it?"

"Iris and I weren't exactly on a date today. I mean, we were, but it was planned. Staged. When her ex, Archer Ringwald, showed up at her work, he said the fact that she wasn't with anybody was proof they were destined for each other, or some bullshit. So she told him we were dating," I explain.

"Why you?" Jake asks.

"I was there," I answer before realizing I should be offended. "But why *not* me? I'm great, you know."

"I'm still not getting why you were canoodling at Barefoot Bake today though," Alice adds. "Did you decide to go for it or something?"

"This asshat doesn't take a hint, and he won't leave, like he's going to convince her or something, so I suggested we keep up the ruse until he gets lost." Hearing myself explain this now, I understand why Iris hesitated to say yes. It does sound nuts.

"Are you in a fake dating trope?" Piper asks, looking deflated at learning I wasn't on a real date today.

"A what?" I ask, though based on its name, I can guess what it is.

"You're fake dating Iris," Piper repeats.

"What does that entail, exactly?" Jake asks, looking possibly more skeptical than when he thought I was actually dating Iris.

"We let everybody believe we're dating. We spend time together publicly to help sell the story. We act like a couple," I answer.

"I know you're new to this, but dude, that's just dating." Scott finally participates in a way that isn't just fearing my imminent demise.

"It's different, because she and I know the truth," I argue. I *know* the truth, even if I don't like it.

"It doesn't sound different to me, either." Jake leans back in his chair and crosses his arms.

"We aren't acting on feelings here. We're acting on an agreed-upon plan." It's *different*. Any feelings that exist are irrelevant. We have a goal here, and it's important. It's about her safety and Sam's.

"So, you don't like her?" Piper has that hopeful glint in her eye again, and I feel like I'm being led into a trap.

"I do. As a friend. I'm helping my *friend* who's in a bad situation." I look at each of them like I can will them to understand. Maybe I can will myself to believe that's all it is too. "I'd fake date any of you if you needed me to."

"Suuuure," Piper says, without trying to hide that she thinks I'm full of shit.

"I just think you should be careful," Jake says.

"I've gotten *close* to a lot of women—as close as you can get —and never let myself get caught up in anything serious," I argue. It's the same argument I tell myself.

"Sex isn't the same as intimacy. And intimacy can be a lot more exposing sometimes," Alice offers quietly.

"As much as I agree that people can change their minds, I haven't about relationships. They're not for me, and I'm really doing this to help Iris. Tell me I can count on you all."

"Of course you can," Scott says, and the others echo. "Anything we can do to help with Ringworm."

"Ringwald," Alice corrects him.

"That's what I said," Scott insists.

"I just want to point out that all the romance books with fake dating end with the couple realizing they've got real feelings for each other," Piper says ominously.

"Well, good for them. I'm just helping a friend." I'm adamant. Besides, I've got a lot more experience ignoring my feelings than fictional men do. It's non-negotiable.

Right?

Iris

I don't know if we have Grateful Bob to thank or not, but Eli was right about word of our date getting around quickly. I'm not sure if I'm more impressed or alarmed by the number of people who have brought it up over the past couple of days. While I was able to exist largely under the small-town radar before this week—as a transplant who only periodically visited Wilcox Grove in the past—I'm now tied to Eli, a beloved Wilcox Grove lifer, and this relationship comes with a spotlight.

Thankfully, the town hasn't shunned me. In fact, it's been quite the opposite. People seem thrilled that Eli is finally "settling down" since he's "such a nice man." Apparently, I have quite the catch in him. It's hard not to get swept up in people's interest in our *romance*.

I know this is exactly what I'd hoped would happen, but it does make me feel a little guilty to be deceiving all these kind people who so clearly care about Eli. I already told Uncle Harry the truth about what we're doing, and he looked so disappointed. Like Eli told me he had to tell his friends, I couldn't keep this from Olivia and Uncle H.

As for my family back in Newport, I've taken to dodging

those calls. I've already gotten two from Mom. I don't know if Archer's told her about Eli, but I don't care to find out. It's possible she's calling for a completely different reason, but I've got to focus on battling Archer. I can't be fighting a war on two fronts by going at it with my parents again.

Lemon also tried calling, but I avoided her too, just in case it was about me and Eli. I know Lemon will be on my side always, but I kind of want to keep this here. I won't *lie* to her about it, but I don't want to offer up Eli on a platter either. I texted her, blaming work, and she said she was just checking in, but it's only a matter of time before the rumor makes its way out of town.

As for everybody else… With each new person smiling at me, asking about Eli, or wishing us well, I get more worried about an exit strategy for our situation. However we do it, I refuse to let Eli be the bad guy.

I'm not sure I've ever had somebody step up for me the way he has, so selflessly and without reservation. I can't believe how wrong I was about him just a handful of weeks ago.

Before I need to figure out how to end things, I need to make sure our little plan serves its purpose. And with all the new attention I've been getting, one person has been noticeably silent. This town is not very big, so where the fuck is Archer Ringwald?

I know Eli would have told me if Archer had approached him again, but I'm feeling antsy anyway, like I lost a giant spider in my house and am waiting for it to pop out and terrify me. As I pack up to head home for the day, I give in to my restlessness and text Eli.

ME

You haven't heard from Archer, have you?

ELI

I havent. is something wrong

ME

Just waiting for the rodent to reemerge…

I say my goodbyes and head out to my car as Eli answers.

ELI

be careful what you wish for or hell just pop up.

And when I step off the porch and turn the corner, there's Archer. Leaning against my back bumper. I spot his own car idling in the street. Way to kill the planet, my dude. I fire off a quick reply as I approach my ex.

ME

You don't know how right you are.

"You'd better hope Harry doesn't catch you out here," I say by way of greeting.

"Your uncle needs to chill the fuck out," Archer snaps, the saccharine sweetness he tried last time he was here long gone.

"I'm sure he will when you *get the fuck out*," I answer, crossing my arms. "And get the fuck off my car," I add. My phone, still clutched in my hand, buzzes.

He pushes off it and takes a step forward, but then he just stares at me. I resist the urge to take a step away, not liking him anywhere near me, but I will *not* back down from this scum.

"Well? What do you want?" I have places to go, things to do, a daughter to pick up from school very soon. It wouldn't be hard for him to figure out her school—there's only one preschool in town—but I'm not about to lead him to it.

"I've already told you. I want you. And I want to know why this whole town is suddenly shoving your guard dog in my face. Seems like the new exciting gossip. But that's odd, since you implied the two of you were so solid." There's a healthy dollop of skepticism in his voice.

My stomach plummets, but I do my best not to show any reaction on my face. Even when I'm sure he's about to call me out on my fake relationship.

"I know you saw us the other day. Eli wanted to make sure I was safe, so you made us go public when we didn't want to. Does that make you happy?" I bark, pouring annoyance into every word and hoping he clings to a perceived victory enough that he overlooks the possibility I'm lying.

When his top lip curls, I know it worked. My phone buzzes again.

"Aw, did I cause trouble in paradise?" he gloats, completely glossing over where I called him unsafe.

"Actually, no. Everybody has been so nice and supportive, and now Eli and I don't need to sneak around. I think this might be the best thing you've *ever* done for me."

His face falls at that one, and I tip my chin up.

Point, me.

"I think you have a very short memory. I did a lot of good things for you. You were hardly living before I picked you. And we had a lot of fun together. It's ok, though. I'd forgotten too. I just feel so grateful that I remembered. We can have that again." He's laying it on *thick*, and I'm honestly insulted.

Does he think I'm a fucking idiot? That I'd buy this load of crap and fall into his arms?

He was a college boyfriend, not the love of my life. Yes, I was kind of a homebody before we started seeing each other, but nothing will excuse the way he threw me aside when I told him I was pregnant or change the fact that our relationship was more about superficial appearances to him than actual recognition of me as a person.

"I have a clear memory of everything we were and everything we weren't. That's the problem." I'm getting tired of having the same conversation with this guy. "You need to understand that no means *no*."

"I thought women loved groveling," he plows on.

"What you're doing isn't groveling. And even if it were, there are some things that are unforgivable, and when those things involve abandoning my kid, there's not a shred of hope for you. Cut your losses and go home."

"I just need to try harder. You played hard to get in college too." He shoves his hands in his front pockets and… I think he tries to look cute. It fails.

I glance longingly at my driver's side door and try to figure out if I could get over there, turn on the car, and back over him before he'd have time to run away.

There's a sound from the porch behind me, and Archer's eyes go wide. I think he knows Harry would have him arrested before Archer could *say* the word trespassing. I know the sound is just the branch that likes to scratch on the roof. But Archer doesn't have the same familiarity with this place.

"I'll think of something good. It'll show you that I'm serious about us," Archer says, nodding to himself but also moving with some urgency toward his car.

I realize now that he left it on for a quick getaway. The coward.

"I know just the thing," I say, and he pauses, looking hopeful. "Leave."

"I've always loved your sense of humor," he lies. And for the third time in less than two weeks, I watch Archer walk away.

Once he's out of sight and the sound of his engine has faded into nothing, I get in my car and crank the heat. Without burning hatred to keep me warm, it's *cold* out there. I check my phone screen and see a couple of texts from Eli.

ELI

what do you mean

Iris? are you ok

Crap. I call him.

"Iris?" he asks breathily once the call connects. I wish he were here.

"Hey. I'm sorry. I'm fine. Archer was waiting by my car." I have to speak up because there's some background noise wherever Eli is.

"Hang on," he says, and I wonder if he's going to go somewhere quieter.

But then I hear a vehicle approaching, and Eli's Jeep pulls into the parking lot behind me. He jumps out of his car, leaving it on and his door open as he comes over to mine. At the sight of him, the bridge of my nose stings. I don't know why I feel like I'm about to cry.

"You're ok?" he asks hurriedly, pulling open my door and scanning me from head to toe.

Eli looks... scared. His hair is sticking out on one side like he'd been running his hand through it, and he keeps shifting from foot to foot.

Oh...

"Eli," I say clearly, placing my hand on his arm. "I'm ok."

He takes a long breath in, and it shakes a little on its way back out.

"I'm sorry for overreacting," he says, embarrassed. "I just knew you were with him, and you stopped answering. I shouldn't have come charging over here."

"I'm ok," I repeat softly. "And the charging is ok. If I had needed you, you would have been here."

"Ok." Eli nods. He's still shaken, and his eyes dart around, like he's worried he'll miss something.

I touch the side of his face, and he closes his eyes, taking another slow breath.

"I'm going to get Sam and bring her to Literary Lake to swap a book. Will you meet us there?" I ask. It's selfish, but I don't want him to go yet.

"Yeah," he agrees, looking more like his usual, cool self when he opens his eyes again.

After a long pause that feels heavy with unspoken emotion, Eli heads back to his truck and pulls out of my way, but he waits in the street so I can go first and follows behind me until we get to the bookstore.

As I keep going toward the school, I tell myself it's a good idea for us to be seen all together, especially if Archer is about to double down on his efforts. But I know that's not the only reason I asked him to come with us.

I've never had somebody come to my rescue like that before.

CHAPTER 25

Eli

I stay in my Jeep after I park, watching Iris's taillights until they disappear down the road. I don't realize how tightly I'm gripping the steering wheel until I release it and find every joint stiff and marks from my fingernails pressed into the heels of my palms.

That was close.

If I'm being honest with myself, it wasn't just close. That was a full loss of control.

When Iris stopped answering my texts after basically telling me Archer was there, I didn't think. I left the nursery and was on my way to her before I even realized what I was doing.

Of course I want her to be safe, and I do *not* trust Archer to be a safe guy, but choosing to go check on her is a decision I could have—should have—made rationally and purposefully. It was pure fear that had me speeding across town, and a feeling like that is dangerous.

My mad dash didn't even give the engine time to warm up enough for the heat to work properly, so I can see my breath when I huff it out. The chill is helping to focus me, sharpen things.

Is this what being in a relationship does to a person? Clearly,

I'm doing spectacularly at remembering this is basically a business arrangement.

I turn off the Jeep and head inside the bookstore. Piper clocks me immediately and waves warmly. It might be in my head, but I feel like she's still got that roguish glint in her eye from earlier this week when she told me about her fake dating romance novels.

"What brings you in?" she asks as she approaches me.

"I'm meeting Sam and Iris in a bit." I watch that look intensify as soon as the word "Iris" leaves my mouth and shut it down. "None of that. First, because you're insane, and second, because Sam will be here. And when we're all together, I am just their *friend*."

"Ok," Piper immediately relents, palms raised in surrender. Games aren't fun when they mess with a kid's life.

"Thank you." I spot a bookseller, Mads, not-so-sneakily peeking at me from around a bookcase, clearly looking for some insight into the new gossip. "Can you do me a favor and help me get control of the village people before the girls get here?"

Piper follows my line of sight and shoos Mads back to the register.

"Even the good ones are vultures for info," she says, turning back to me. "I'll make sure nobody says a word about your new *girlfriend* in front of Sam."

I roll my eyes but thank her and head into the café to order hot chocolate.

Girlfriend.

I roll the word around my brain. Like it's a trained response, it still elicits a spike of fear, but when I pair it with the image of Iris's face, that unease feels much less potent.

Leslie is at the register when I get there. She and Hannah used to run the café and bookstore themselves, but Leslie's been able to step back a lot since Piper joined the team. Leslie is a bit of an adrenaline junkie and staying in the stores all day was making her extremely unhappy. Now she works with an outdoor sports group that teaches all kinds of the intense stuff she lives for. She's still ramping up after a bad injury last summer, but she loves it, and as a result, looks much happier when she does help out around here.

"Hey, Eli," she greets when I get to the counter.

"Hey, Leslie. How are the legs?" I ask.

Leslie is a year younger than me and Jake, but we grew up together in this little town.

"They're a little sore with how cold it is, but the doc says everything is doing what it should be, so I'll take it." Leslie pats her thigh.

"Hopefully it warms up here soon. Since that's not today, could I get three hot chocolates?"

It is definitely a hot chocolate kind of day. It's almost March, but there's no sign of winter letting us move on. It's fucking freezing—below freezing, actually.

"Not at all. You have company or should I be worried about your chocolate intake?" Leslie teases as she gets started, reminding me of Grateful Bob's concerns with my pastry order a couple weeks ago.

"I could have six of these no problem, but only one is for me today. The others are for Iris and Sam."

"Oh yeah?" I almost miss the brief pause in Leslie's work. She covers it well, conveying nonchalance. "When Han said something to me about you and Iris, I hardly believed her. But it's a thing? *You're* a thing?"

I chuckle. "We are definitely a *thing*."

Leslie stops stirring the chocolate now, holding one hand up to shade her eyes as she theatrically looks around the café.

"Just checking for flying pigs..." She looks back at me with a smile. "Of course I'm kidding. I think it's a great thing. I never really understood how you weren't a relationship guy. You've always cared so much. I like you having a person. Iris will be good for you."

"Yeah," I say noncommittally. "Iris is a good reason to try something new."

What the fuck am I *doing*.

Leslie smiles, but doesn't respond, nodding her head toward the door instead. I turn and see Iris and Sam walking across the sidewalk.

"Human Eli," Sam greets as she comes through the doorway. "Look." She shifts from side to side so I can see Robin's head sticking out of one coat pocket and capybara Eli's head sticking out of the other. "Now I have both hands for books, but nobody has to stay in the car."

"That's a good strategy, kid," I say with a chuckle, smiling at Iris as she brings up the rear.

"Eli." Leslie gets my attention and sets three paper cups on the counter.

"Would a treat first be ok?" I ask Iris.

"If those are what I think they are, absolutely yes," she answers, breathing deeply. The entire place smells like chocolate.

"That one's not as hot, for Sam," Leslie says, pointing to one of the cups.

"You're the best." I try to give her my card, but she shakes her head.

"On the house. For"—she looks between me and Iris—"good friends."

"Thanks, Les." I balance the cups in one hand and slide my card back into my wallet.

Sam is bouncing on the balls of her feet when I step back up to her.

"Here you go, buddy," I say, bending to hand her the kid-friendly one. I stand and pass a second cup to Iris, but she's staring at the hand that had been holding all three cups. "What is it?"

She blinks and shakes her head.

"Nothing," she says quickly, but there's a blush across her cheeks.

As I take a sip of my cocoa, I see her holding the cup over her own palm, stretching out her fingers, and have to hide my grin.

elping Sam pick out books at Literary Lake this afternoon with Eli was entirely innocent, ordinary, and benign. She's really into stories about space right now, so we collected as many books about planets, stars, astronauts, and adventures in space as we could, including some Ms. Frizzle specials I remember from my own childhood.

We sip hot chocolate, listen to Sam bemoan another classmate bragging about how he can do the monkey bars, and watch Piper continue to terrorize Scott about when he'll be proposing to her. It was a really good way to end the work week.

So, there's no good explanation for why I'm lying in bed, staring at the shadows shifting across my ceiling, and picturing how very small three normal-sized cups looked in one of Eli's enormous hands. Then, I see Eli smiling at Sam, listening to every word she says. *Then*, I see Eli speeding up to the firm because he thought I was alone with Archer.

UGH!

I sit up, smack the shit out of my pillow, and flop back onto it before kicking off my covers. It's the coldest it's been all winter, and I'm on fire. I'm restless and my hormones are confused about what's happening with Eli.

That's *all*.

He's not for us. He's just helping a friend. Don't be weird about it.

Still, on that first "date," once he reminded me to stop treating our little table like a war room, I was feeling a certain kind of way. He was the same ol' Eli, of course, but there was more. I felt seen. Like he's been paying attention to what I do and what I like all this time. I can't understand why this man doesn't date because he seems pretty damn good at it to me.

When I was nineteen, my crush on him was because he was nice to look at. When I saw him in August, I was able to convince myself it was the same. Now I know new parts of him, and I like all of those too.

Because the universe hates me, none of that changes the fact that Eli Chambers isn't the man for me.

Still, maybe Olivia and Lemon were right, and I should live a little. Eli would be safe and good to me. And he's shown he can still maintain a friendship after… Just look at him and Olivia.

I get a pang of guilt at even the thought. I know it's illogical, but I feel like I should devote all of myself to Sam. Having a fuck buddy doesn't really align with that. Maybe I've just moved past the part of my life when I'm allowed to do things like that.

With a huff, I reach off the edge of my bed to retrieve my blankets. I wrap them tight around myself like a hug and tell myself to just keep my eyes closed until I fall asleep.

It's well into the early morning before I drift off.

On Sunday, it starts snowing. It isn't a furious dumping of snow, like last time, but flakes are consistently drifting to the ground around us. With how cold it's been, they stick and collect.

I have a good feeling about this week.

The good feeling disappears when I get a delivery of two dozen long-stem roses at the office part-way through Monday morning. The flowers must have cost a fortune, not just because they're long-stem roses, but because the delivery driver had to come from the next town over. Since I haven't gotten a call from Olivia (or the police station to bail her out), I can only assume Archer somehow got his three functioning brain cells to work together long enough to realize calling her flower shop would be detrimental to his physical wellbeing.

Eli and I already have an afternoon date planned—more hot cocoa and a walk around the park by Barefoot Lake at the end of Main Street to enjoy the still-falling snow—so I take the flowers with me and hand one to each of the first twenty-four people we see as we wander.

I'm hoping it somehow gets back to Archer that I gave away his gift with Eli, but even if it doesn't, I like doling out surprise presents. Everybody is so grateful, and Bets, a kind woman with a thick Southern accent who works at the post office, has tears in her eyes when we hand her our last one. She says it's the first rose she's gotten since her husband passed away a decade ago.

I can feel Eli's eyes on me as we part ways with her.

"What is it?" I ask, looking up at him.

"Leave it to you to bring so much good with a gift like that." When he smiles at me, I make a mental note to call an exterminator for the butterflies in my stomach.

"They were an attempted bribe, not a real gift." I sigh. "The card that came with them said *Something nice for something nice,* and I think I'm supposed to appreciate being called a *thing*. But it's not the flowers' fault, and they were very pretty, so it felt like a nice way to rehome them."

We start heading toward the park that divides Main Street from the lake when I recognize the haughty gait of somebody coming toward us.

"Heads up," I warn Eli. "Incoming."

Eli steps closer to me, but we don't change our trajectory. If Archer is determined to confront us, let him.

"Well, don't you two look cozy," he says once he gets close enough not to shout.

"Yup," I answer, uninterested in encouraging any further contact with this worm.

"I see you made good use of my flowers," Archer continues, looking over my shoulder. I turn and see bright shocks of red where people are holding the roses I handed out.

"What do you want, Archer?" It feels like the eternal question, and it never has a good answer.

"Can't a guy just say hi to an old *lover*?"

The way he says lover makes my skin crawl, like I can feel his clammy hands on my body. He reaches forward like he's going to touch my arm, but I step back, bumping into Eli. I appreciate that he's letting me handle this, but I'm also glad his silent presence is here. Archer's bizarre attempts to get my attention are starting to worry me.

"I'd prefer if you didn't." This is tiring. It's *been* tiring.

"I'll just wait for *this*"—Archer gestures between me and Eli —"to run its course. We both know he doesn't belong, and I just want to make sure you remember *I'm* here, and I'm not going anywhere."

"This is getting a little stalkery, Archer," I say, crossing my arms.

I remind myself that punching him for dismissing Eli so disrespectfully would not be a move in my favor and settle for squeezing my hands into fists instead.

Archer laughs at absolutely nothing and starts walking again.

As he passes by me, he whispers, "I love it when you say my name."

And I resist the urge to trip him. Eli and I turn to watch him until he gets in his car and drives off. Then, Eli's fingers touch my arm, lightly unhooking my arms so he can take my hand and guide me to the path around the lake.

"You can absolutely tell me to fuck off, but I've gotta ask. What did you see in that guy?" Eli doesn't attempt to hide the distaste in his tone.

"I was a very dumb girl," I start.

Eli looks at me skeptically and opens his mouth presumably to protest, but I hold up a hand.

"I know I'm smart now, but that came from learning to be a mom who wasn't a complete failure. I might have been an *intelligent* student back then, but there's no doubt I was dumb as fuck.

"I was such a rule follower that I never questioned anything. I never colored outside the lines. I hardly even lived. I was boring and dull and dumb." I chuckle a little thinking about how much I've grown in less than a decade. "Looking back now, I assume Archer probably thought I was some kind of challenge since I couldn't have been less interested in dating when we met. I'd dated a little at the beginning of college but was underwhelmed and committed to getting into a good law school, so I just studied instead. My college was small, and I developed something of a reputation for being a prude. Archer and I crossed paths a bit into my junior year."

I glance up at Eli to make sure I'm not boring him as we walk, but he looks down at me as soon as I pause.

"I'm still not seeing the appeal, Iris." He chuckles, so I go on.

"Archer was everything I wasn't. He was flashy and outgoing, with a huge group of friends. We had some finance classes together—I thought they'd help me stand out on law school applications since so many lawyers have poli-sci backgrounds—

and he was patient with getting my attention. He focused on class work first, since that was all I cared about. He'd ask to do home-work together or invite me to a study group that I'm pretty sure he put together just to be able to invite me. And it worked. He got me gifts and carried my backpack. He got me to open up and go out sometimes. I was having *fun*, and it was intoxicating.

"My parents loved the idea of Archer. He came from a well-respected family who even had a house near ours in Newport. He was charming and dashing when we went home for school breaks. He was doing all the right things until I told him I was pregnant the summer before our senior year. Then he told me to *get rid of it*. When I decided not to, he somehow came to the conclusion that I must have cheated on him, and he denied any responsibility for the baby. Since he also refused to sign the birth certificate, his lunacy turned out to be the best possible thing for me."

I shudder at the end of my story, thinking of how different things would be right now if he *was* on Sam's birth certificate. Eli notices and pulls me against him, leaving his heavy arm draped over my shoulders. His heat is nice, but his sturdiness feels good for a whole different reason.

I can't help imagining how hot his bare skin would feel under my palm. Would he still shiver if I…

"This guy is a real piece of shit," Eli says simply, and a laugh bursts out of me. I hope it sufficiently hides the path my thoughts were careening down.

"I'm sorry," he continues. "I really couldn't think of anything else to say. I feel like I should make some kind of speech about how incredible you're doing, but I've got nothing but disbelief that he could fuck things up with you so completely. What a bozo."

"I don't need a speech. Calling him a bozo is just fine with me. And speeches would mean talking about him more, some-thing I'm uninterested in doing."

We fall into a comfortable silence as we continue strolling along. Even though we're walking along the sidewalk that traces the bank of this part of the lake, the air is calm and everything is peaceful. With snow falling around us, even the cold doesn't feel so bad… but maybe that's because I'm pressed up against Eli's furnace of a body.

I can't help it. I think again… *what if he wanted to. Just once…*

Would that make me a bad mom? A bad example?

"You're loving this snow, aren't you?" When Eli laughs, I can feel the vibration through my whole body.

Instead of answering, I just burrow deeper into his side, shuffling my feet through the dusting on the sidewalk.

Even though the snow has been falling consistently since yesterday, it's been slow enough that the plows and salt could keep the streets clear while the rest of our little town gets blanketed in white. I look out at the lake and see something small and furry slide across the ice, kicking up a puff of snow, and a thought comes to me.

"Is it safe to skate on the lake?" I ask.

"There might be some questionable parts where it's deeper and the water is more active, but for the most part, yes," Eli answers as we come to stop at the edge of the ice.

"Do you skate?"

"Growing up here, almost everybody has figure skated, played ice hockey, or done both." He catches on to my line of questioning.

When I don't say anything more, he pulls back so he can look down at me.

"Iris, would you like to go ice-skating on the lake?" he asks.

I can't help it, I feel giddy at the thought and at his invitation. It feels like the perfect winter wonderland right now, and I want to be a part of it. I nod excitedly. "I really do."

"Then, it's a date," Eli says with a squeeze around my shoulders.

"Are you sure?" I ask, tipping my head back to look up at him, still grinning. "Even though you hate snow?"

That rumbling laugh shoots through me again. "It's grown on me in the past couple of weeks. I like spring, but I'm not going to do anything that takes that look off your face. So, we'll skate."

"Friday?" I ask. "I can take a half day if you wanna play hooky."

"I think I can swing that. Can you get Sam out of her after-school program too? Does she skate?"

The fact that he so easily includes my daughter sends a different kind of warmth through me.

"Yeah, I think I can swing that," I echo him.

CHAPTER 27

Iris

Unprompted and unwanted gifts from Archer keep showing up, making me more annoyed with each arrival. Archer's strategy continues to perplex me since he hasn't made any more direct attempts to contact me, and his gifts haven't come with any indication that he gives a shit I'm with Eli, even though Eli and I have been seeing a little of each other every day. I'll come by the nursery when there are customers there to see us, or he'll stop by the firm just before we have client meetings scheduled so they can spot him, or we'll just do our grocery shopping at the same time. It's been fun.

When the fourth of Archer's stupid presents arrives at the office on Friday morning—a charm bracelet with charms that have absolutely no discernible meaning to me—I get a flashback to college. Whenever we fought, these baubles would magically appear at my dorm or on my desk in class. What I'd seen then as an apology has only ever been an attempt to distract me with something shiny.

It would appear as though this man has had zero emotional growth.

I drop the bracelet into the bottom drawer of my desk, where it can live with the digital picture frame he sent loaded with images of us from college and the gift card to Papa's he sent a few days ago. Papa's is a delicious Italian restaurant, but when I saw the note—*For dinner with me*—I got the ick and rethought my plan of using the gift card with Eli. Eli and I can go to dinner without any help from Archer, thank you very much.

My phone lights up with another incoming call from my mom, and I handle it the same way I've dealt with the others—adamantly ignoring it. I don't want to talk to her and risk hearing about how she's been helping Archer come up with crappy gifts to assault me with.

When I look outside and see even more snow falling, I worry that Eli and I will need to cancel our ice-skating date. It's been snowing on and off all week, and there must be at least a foot of snow on the lake by now. When I see Eli's name appear on my phone screen, my heart sinks.

"Hey," I answer, knowing I sound morose, but being unable to hide it.

"What's wrong?" Eli asks, concerned. "Is it Archer?"

"No. Nothing like that. I'm ok." I hear him breathe out with relief. "It's ironically the snow. You're calling to cancel, aren't you?"

"Cancel? Not a chance." I can practically hear his smile. "I've got to teach Samantha how to skate."

When I told him earlier this week that she hadn't been yet, he got so excited about showing her. She was equally excited when I told her the plan after school that day. If we can't skate, she'll be crushed.

"But the snow. Isn't it going to be a problem if we can't even see the ice?"

"Don't you worry about that. I'm taking care of it. I was just calling to see if you wanted food before or after."

"What do you mean you're taking care of it?" I feel pretty

sure Eli can't control the weather, but I'm not sure *he* knows that with how confident he sounds.

"I said I've got it covered, so you'll have to trust me," he says, and I really want to. "So, food. Before or after?"

"After," I say.

"And you're trusting me?" he asks playfully.

"I'm trying."

I really, really am.

When I pick up Sam, my plan is to manage her expectations for skating. There's a break in the snow, but I still don't see how this will work with everything that's accumulated. Of course, the second she sees me, she comes flying at me.

"It's time for *ice-skating!*" she cries as she launches into my arms.

Since she's five, that means she basically just plows into me like a wrecking ball. Thankfully, she's not too big for me to absorb the blow.

"Maybe we can just play in the snow at the park," I try, but her little brow furrows.

"No thank you. I want to learn to skate," she says so politely that my heart cracks. "Human Eli is going to teach me."

"Mmhmm," I say and pray that Eli knows what he's doing.

The small lot near the park only has a few cars in it when I get there. Not many people are wandering outside these days, braving the cold and snow.

Sam doesn't seem to feel the bite in the air as she runs ahead of me past the frozen playground. The fact that she doesn't even eye the monkey bars (a continued obsession) is a testament to how excited she is about going skating.

"Mama, what's that?" she asks when a huge cloud of snow appears near the lake's edge seemingly out of nowhere.

"I really don't know, lil' one," I say and adjust our skates draped over my shoulder. Thankfully, my parents had gotten Sam a pair for her birthday.

Sam stays by my side after that just in case we're about to face the abominable snowman. Even from across the field, when I see a figure appear as the snow settles, I know that mountain of a man is Eli. No snow monster here.

A few other people quickly appear around him, and Scott is still shaking snow out of the back of his jacket when we arrive. Jake is manning a snowblower and laughing at what I can only assume was a well-aimed attack on his brother. Eli spots us and makes his way over.

"Hey," he says, taking my hand that isn't holding Sam's, even though the only people here know our secret. And Jake isn't even paying attention. He seems to be headed toward the parking lot.

"Hey," I answer, feeling like a giggly schoolgirl until Sam pulls my hand for my attention.

"Mama, look." She's awestruck, as am I when I follow her pointed finger.

A huge part of the lake has been cleared of snow and is glistening with a shiny, smooth surface. The snowblower suddenly makes sense. Eli must have been out here for ages preparing the ice for us.

"Oh," I breathe.

"I told you I had it handled," Eli says with pride.

"You did *not* have it handled," Scott cuts in, sounding just like a little brother would. "You're lucky I saved your ass."

"You picked up a hose from the nursery. That hardly counts as saving my ass," Eli grumbles, releasing my hand to shove Scott playfully. "Quit stealing my thunder."

"Hey guys!" Alice calls from behind me. I turn and see her walking up, skates in her hand, with Piper beside her.

"The guys *did* help, so we have some party crashers. I'm sorry," Eli says quietly to me.

But I don't mind at all.

"The more the merrier," I say. I even fire off a text to Olivia to see if she can sneak away to join us. The park isn't far from her shop on Main Street, and she and I can swap off using my skates.

"These are for you, little lady," Jake says to Sam as he returns with a stack of five-gallon buckets half as tall as Sam is. He gestures to Scott and Eli. "We all learned to skate by pushing buckets."

Sam looks up at Eli like she wants to be just like him, and when he smiles back down at her, I have to look away before I lose it. Piper stands nearby, adjusting her scarf around her face as the rest of us begin pulling off our shoes.

"You're not coming out?" I ask.

"Oh heck no. I'm enough of a menace on flat ground. Not about to put blades on my feet and step onto ice. I'll leave that to the more coordinated people and stay right here." Piper pointedly looks at Scott who rolls his eyes like this is a battle he's already lost. He also wisely keeps his mouth shut.

When Jake and Eli head onto the ice first to make sure everything is good to go, Scott tells us they've already checked this repeatedly and calls them worrywarts, but when Eli's eyes find Sam as he comes back toward the grass, I understand why he wanted to check just one more time.

Eli had taken the buckets with him, so I help Sam hobble over to the lake on her skates. She looks like a little ice princess in her thick white tights, velvet dress, and white puffy jacket. She seems to be a little less thrilled than before, but her mouth is set in a firm, determined line. Scared or not, she's doing this, and I'm so proud of her.

I take Eli's hand and step onto the ice first, so I can get my bearings. I make a quick circle around Eli and the bucket before turning back to help Sam, but I see her little gloved hands clutching Eli's sleeves as he eases her onto the ice, still supporting her weight when her skates touch the smooth surface.

I pause, watching as he bends down low, steady as a rock, and has her hold one of his hands with both of hers so he can use the other to tap her shoes, her knee, and the side of her hips. She's focusing so hard on him, and he speaks slowly, explaining how to hold her feet and her body, and even warning her that falling is inevitable, but ok.

Sam is looking at Eli like he's teaching her how to fly, and I can only imagine what I look like, especially when Alice comes gliding smoothly up beside me.

"You good, Mama?" she asks, taking my hand.

I don't trust myself to speak, so I just nod sharply. I'm really, really good.

Ice-skating on Barefoot Lake is better than I'd imagined. I'm not sure if Sam actually moves her legs at all, but she loves being pushed around the ice while leaning on the buckets. After a bit, a few people join us on the ice, and Olivia does wander over, picking up Grateful Bob on her way, but they stay by the benches with Piper.

Even with all our layers, it eventually becomes too cold to stay out, though Sam objects to this conclusion vehemently, insisting she can stay on the ice all night long. Grateful Bob stands to free up the bench for those of us who need to take off our skates.

"Thanks, Pop," Sam says out of nowhere and plops down on the bench where he'd been a moment ago.

I blink. As far as I know, she's never met Grateful Bob before. Sure, it's true that kids say the darndest things, and Sam is no exception, but usually it comes from *somewhere*.

"Pop?" Grateful Bob says incredulously. "Does that mean you think I'm old?"

Sam looks from Grateful Bob's snow boots up to his face before answering.

"Yes," she says without further explanation, and begins pulling at the laces on her skates, likely making the knots worse.

I hear a snort of laughter from beside me, and spin around to find Eli trying his hardest to hold it together.

"Samantha!" I admonish, but Grateful Bob is laughing too.

"You've got me there, kid. I am old. My name is Grateful Bob," he says.

"Why?" Sam pauses her lace pulling, and Piper swoops in to help before I have the chance.

"Well, Bob is short for Robert, and I added Grateful because I thought it sounded more lyrical. I've always wanted a song to be written about me," he fabricates.

Sam looks at me, not at all buying what Grateful Bob is saying, but I give her a stern look, intending to remind her to be polite, especially after calling the man old.

"Oh," is all she can find to say.

Once Sam is back in her boots, I take her seat, and Eli drops to his knee to begin untying my skates. As I look down at him, the image of him glancing up at me sears into my brain.

"Was it everything you'd hoped it would be?" he asks as his fingers make quick work of my laces.

I'm worried my feet will be gross and warm, but Eli doesn't hesitate to wrap both of his strong hands around my socked feet, one at a time, gently squeezing them, a heavenly feeling cutting through the soreness that sends goosebumps up my legs, multiple layers of clothing be damned.

"It was more," I answer while he pulls my boots on for me. I could easily do this myself, and I feel a bit self-conscious as a grown woman getting help with her shoes, but it's so sweet that I decide I don't give a crap about being embarrassed.

"What do you say to Papa's for dinner?" he asks, and my laugh cracks through the peaceful park at the irony of his choice. He gives me a questioning look, not knowing about the gift card in my desk, but I shake my head.

"Papa's sounds just perfect."

"It's Friday," Sam says quietly from her place beside Eli. "Can we look at books first?"

I catch Eli's eye, and he gives a subtle nod, brow furrowed like he's saying *of course*. After all, swapping books at the library on Fridays is tradition, and Sam's books from last week are in the car.

"Sure, lil' one," I say as Eli taps the side of my boot, signaling I'm all set.

After quick goodbyes, the three of us head to pick up Sam's books from the car before walking to Literary Lake. Sam is excitedly recounting her first time ice-skating to Eli like he wasn't beside her the whole time. Patient man that he is, he listens like she's telling him groundbreaking news.

The two are so focused on each other they don't see Archer lingering back by the park. I shudder, wondering how long he's been there. Was he watching us? If he was, how did I not notice him? How did *none* of us notice him?

I see his shoulders shake with laughter. When he raises his hand in a little wave, it feels like he's saying *I see you.*

CHAPTER 28

Eli

Papa's has always been a favorite of mine, but sharing dinner with Iris and Sam changes the experience completely. Sam is so excited to be in a "fancy" restaurant and keeps fidgeting on the half-moon booth seat to make sure she's sitting up as straight as possible, smoothing her skirt every few minutes.

The restaurant is all deep, rich colors, and soft, crushed velvet. Lights are turned low, and tea candles flicker on each table. Crisp white tablecloths are spots of brightness in the cozy and welcoming space, and the whole place smells like garlic and oregano.

We eat slowly, tired from skating and in no rush to leave. Part way through our meal, I realize how *easy* it is to spend almost my whole day with these two people. Conversation isn't forced, and nobody seems to be counting down the minutes until we part ways. We're able to just be.

Being here reminds me of dinner out with my parents when I was a boy, something saved for special occasions since it wasn't an expense we could regularly afford. Mom would have all of us dress up, and Dad and I would each take one of her arms, escorting her like we were rolling up to a damn gala. Those nights were far from extravagant, but I never knew that. I felt like the luckiest kid alive every time.

I snap out of my reminiscing and look over at Iris when I realize I've been quiet for too long. She doesn't seem to have noticed and is watching Sam dozing against her arm, the candle on the table casting soft light against Sam's wind-burned cheeks. I slip out of the booth to find our server and pay.

Iris is trying to wake Sam when I return, but I shake my head, bending to scoop the sleeping girl up instead.

"I've got her," I whisper as Sam's arms automatically loop around my neck, and her head flops against my shoulder.

When Iris stands, I offer my other arm to her, and she loops her hand through it, hugging my bicep just like Mom hugged Dad's.

A longing ache runs through me, a strange emotion that feels a lot like "this could be nice."

I remind myself this is temporary, *and* that that's a good thing, as we head out to the parking lot. Snow is coming down a bit heavier, but it's still not unmanageable. It's supposed to get worse as the evening progresses, but it looks nice now.

I release Iris so she can open the door by Sam's car seat. The poor kid doesn't even stir as I transfer her into it. I prop her head up with Robin, who had been waiting in the car, but step back so Iris can properly strap Sam in.

Iris leans across the driver's seat to start her Explorer and flick on the heat before turning back to me.

"Thank you for today. It really was perfect."

When she looks up at me, I can see snowflakes clinging to her eyelashes. As they fall around her, I completely buy into her belief that snow is magical. And she seems to shine with it.

I might be imagining it, but I think she leans toward me. She shifts and her hair slips from behind her ear. I *don't* imagine the soft sigh she makes when I brush it back off her shoulder. I keep my hand against her neck and touch my thumb to the corner of her jaw. I might be playing with fire, but I want to kiss her.

"You deserve perfection," I say, and I step back because I know I can't give her what she needs.

She smiles without it touching her eyes and gets in her car. I close the door after her and head to the Jeep.

Once inside, I drop my head against the steering wheel, wishing I could be wired differently. Behind my eyelids, where it's safe, I envision another life for myself, one beside somebody like Iris, raising a great kid like Sam. Going to their games and recitals. Watching them graduate and having a partner by my side through it all. I imagine loudly celebrating wins and enjoying each other's company in those precious, quiet moments.

But then I hear the slow beep from a heart monitor and the smell of antiseptic fills my nose, and I know I can't handle the danger that comes with that life. Liking Iris more with each passing day doesn't change any facts of reality. And the reality of our situation is that I'm no good for her.

A sharp tapping on my window has me jolting upright, embarrassed at being caught daydreaming of a life I can't have, until I see Iris's worried face on the other side of the glass, her car idling behind mine.

I lower the window as quickly as it'll go.

"What happened?" I ask.

"What do you know about heaters? Olivia just called, and I guess ours died."

CHAPTER 29

As Eli follows me back to the house, I try to think of contingency plans for the night if we can't get the heater going again. With enough blankets, we might be ok to stay in the house, but if we get snowed in and stuck there tomorrow, it could get pretty bad. Harry and Kenny would probably take us in, but they have a small house perfect for two and maybe one guest. My eyes flash to the rearview mirror, where I see Sam still sleeping peacefully.

Even though Eli pulls into our driveway behind me, he's out of his car and at my door before I've collected myself. One hand holds a heavy-looking toolbox. How on earth…?

"I keep it in my car, so I have it when I go see my parents," Eli explains after seeing my confusion. "Pretty happy about that right now."

Since he's carrying that, which likely weighs more than Sam, I bring her inside and set her on the couch under a thick blanket. I don't know how long the heat has been down, but it's already cold inside. *Shit.*

"Hey," Olivia greets us quietly, looking relieved when she sees Eli and his tools. "You brought backup."

"I can't promise I can fix it, but I'll do my best," Eli says as Olivia leads him to the thermostat in the downstairs hall.

"Both this one and the one upstairs are blank. I checked the circuit breaker, and it's not that, but that's all I've got," she explains.

"And the furnace?" he asks.

"In the garage."

Eli sets down his tools and follows Olivia to our disaster of a garage. We use it as more of a storage area than a car home, with boxes of decorations, Sam's baby things—I wouldn't leave them at my parents' place—leftover boxes from her parents, and who knows what else piled in there.

I hang back as Eli starts disassembling things without hesitation, checking this and that. I have no clue what he's doing, but I really hope he does because this feels like it could be dangerous. He moves with confidence, pulling off his jacket and sweater after a bit, shoving the sleeves of his shirt up to his elbows.

Olivia catches me blatantly ogling once he does and flashes me a teasing look. I mouth for her to *knock it off!*

When she turns back around, though, I look some more, and it's a good view. I try to be more discrete watching his strong back muscles moving under the thin fabric stretched across his shoulders, I flash back to our almost moment in the Papa's parking lot.

I wanted him to kiss me, and for a second, I thought he might.

Eli cleans off our mesh filter and replaces it before reassembling the furnace and heading back to the thermostat. Olivia flips the circuit breaker to cut power to the hallway while he works, but I'm still nervous he's about to electrocute himself as he fiddles with wires under the faceplate.

Olivia and I have been watching silently, so we don't distract him, but half an hour in, I can tell she's as anxious for an update as I am. I'm about to ask if it's a lost cause when I see Eli's lips tip up in a cocky smirk.

"Ok, turn the power back on," he instructs, and I hurry to flip the switch.

When I return, he's clipping the faceplate back on the wall. He presses and holds two buttons at once, and numbers appear on the screen. Fifty-nine degrees. He presses the button for heat, and I think we all hold our breath until a low rumble sounds from the garage, and warm air blasts from the vent overhead.

Olivia runs up the stairs to check that it's also working up there while I fling my arms around Eli's neck. His arms band around my back.

"You saved us from freezing to death," I say and plant a kiss on his cheek before realizing what I'm doing. I spring away from him a moment later, and his hand remains outstretched toward me, hovering mid-air.

"Sorry," I mutter, embarrassed.

"Nothing to be sorry about, and I wouldn't have let you freeze. If I couldn't get it going, you'd all have stayed with me." He says it like it's the most obvious thing in the world.

"Mama?" Sam's sleepy voice calls from the living room as Olivia comes back downstairs. Eli follows her back up to reset the upstairs thermostat screen while I collect Sam to put her to bed.

"Good night human Eli," she mumbles as we pass him and Olivia on the way to Sam's room.

When I make my way back downstairs, Olivia and Eli are arguing near the front door.

"Don't be stupid. You have to. It's dangerous," Olivia says in an urgent whisper.

"I'll be fine. I don't want to overstay," Eli says back.

"What's going on?" I interject before I'm caught eavesdropping.

"Eli is trying to leave during a white out." Olivia huffs,

flinging open our front door for effect. Sure enough, all I see is white.

"It's not that bad. I've driven in storms before," Eli says, but his argument is severely undermined by the angry gust of wind that blows directly inside. Olivia shuts the door quickly.

"Eli, don't be stubborn," I say, immediately siding with Olivia. It's *nasty* out there. "Our couch is big enough even for you, and it's very comfortable. At least stay until it's light out. Please?"

Eli looks between us, and Olivia crosses her arms. I match her stance.

"Ok. I'll stay until morning."

"You gave us heat. You're good to stay, Eli," I say, padding over to him. "Come back inside. We'll put on a movie, and nobody will die in a ditch on the side of the road."

"I'm going to shower and crash. I was up early this morning, and I'm beat," Olivia says, yawning to punctuate her point. "Thanks for saving us, Eli, and good night."

Eli ventures out to his car to swap his toolbox for a gym bag that he says has been untouched in the back of his Jeep for longer than he cares to admit.

After only a couple of minutes outside, he comes back completely covered in snow.

"Ok, you two might have been right about how bad it is out there," he admits as he brushes it off and removes his coat and boots.

"Told you so," I tease. We head to the couch, and I hand him the remote, but he holds it back out to me.

"You can pick," he says.

"I don't even know what's good. I feel like I only watch kids' movies these days." I smile as I say it, but it's the truth. "I'm just a mom."

"I don't think there's anything *just* about it. You are so much more, Iris." Eli has gotten serious.

I'm ok with being a mom. I'm *happy* being a mom.

"Everything I do is for her," I say proudly.

"You have every right to do what you want to do for *you* sometimes. You can be a good mom *and* be good to yourself at the same time," he says, and I can feel his eyes boring into the side of my head.

"You sound like Olivia and my sister." I chuckle to break the tension that feels thick around us.

"You should listen to us all," he says and finally looks back to the television.

I pick a horror movie. I've always loved them, but haven't put one on since having Sam, worried she'd walk in and get traumatized for life. Out of the corner of my eye, I can see Eli smile at my selection.

Even with tense music and jump scares that have my adrenal gland working on overdrive, it's impossible to ignore Eli's refrigerator-sized body beside me. He still radiates heat, but in the most pleasant way, especially as the house slowly warms back up.

The couch shifts every time he startles, and I feel attuned to his every movement. I swear we sat down with some distance between us, but somehow, we've ended up right next to one another, and every time any part of me touches any part of him, it feels electric.

Yet again, I find myself thinking back to our almost moment earlier today. The more I fixate on it, the more I convince myself I'm blowing it out of proportion.

But when my hand lands on Eli's thigh after a particularly sudden scare, he covers it with his own, and we stay that way for the rest of the movie. If the brief touches were electric, this feels like a frayed wire resting on a damp street, live and dangerous.

I fake a yawn as the credits roll, even though it's not particularly late, and I'm anything but tired. We had a busy and active day, and I guess it wouldn't be too unbelievable if I went to bed. I reluctantly peel my hand from beneath Eli's and go upstairs to get spare blankets and pillows. When I return, he's changed into basketball shorts and nothing else.

I've never seen this much of Eli before, and I can tell he's built his body from years of working with his hands. Maybe at the nursery or from helping his parents with their house. He's made up of broad planes, and there's a jagged scar on his ribs that I want to know more about. His muscles aren't cut with sharp lines, but he's firm and so very *big*.

My mouth goes dry, and I resist the urge to press my thighs together, though the muscles in my abdomen clench anyway.

I do my best not to stare while we make his bed for the night, but it's impossible not to keep glancing at the faint line of blond hair on his lower stomach leading to—

"Thanks for this," Eli says, snapping me back to reality.

"You're very welcome," I say awkwardly as he sits on the couch once we finish. "Good night, then." I head for the stairs with my head full of *what ifs*.

"Hey, Eli?" I turn back before I lose my nerve. I *have* to know.

"Yeah?"

"Were you going to kiss me before? Outside of Papa's?"

"I was certainly thinking about it. I'm sorry." He looks down. "I got caught up in the day and the snow."

I think about how it would have felt if he went through with it, and I just *know* it would have been good. I remember what Eli said about doing what I want to, and I feel brazen.

"Eli?" I say again, to get him to look up at me as I walk back to the couch. Dutifully, he does. "I want to do something for me."

I slip my hand around the back of his neck and thread my fingers in the hair I wanted to touch seven and a half years ago.

Eli's lips part in surprise a second before I press mine to them. He's as warm and pliant and perfect as I'd imagined. His hand falls to my hip, and he lightly squeezes my soft skin there, pulling an unexpected sound from me. His tongue slides into my mouth like he wants to devour that noise.

Ever so slightly, he tugs me toward him, and *damn* do I want to crawl over him, but I've already crossed a line between us tonight. I don't want to take too much, so I clench my hand in his hair for just a moment before releasing it and stepping back.

"Good night, Eli," I say, breathy and dazed. And then I scurry up to my room like a coward.

CHAPTER 30

Eli

I stare at the base of the staircase where Iris disappeared until my eyes lose focus. I think my brain may have liquified. Dumbstruck, I look down at my hand where it fell to my leg when Iris fled, closing my fingers around air and feeling the ghost of her under my touch.

Remembering my brain needs oxygen, I take a deep breath, but it doesn't help. It might make things worse because all I can smell is the lavender that seems to follow Iris everywhere. I roll my lips together, and I feel soft skin and demanding pressure.

What just happened.

I know what just happened. Iris kissed me. It was unexpected, sure, but more importantly, it was incredible. It took everything in me not to pull her down, lay her on this couch, and press her body into it. I drag both of my hands through my hair.

I've been telling myself for weeks that anything physical with Iris was off the table, but it's feeling very *on* the table right now. Then, I'm picturing Iris lying back on a table and—

And now I'm painfully hard on her couch.

Great.

I adjust my shorts and lie back, pulling the blanket over me, even though I feel like I'm on fire. I stare blankly at the ceiling and try to think of *anything* but the sound Iris made into my mouth.

How the fuck am I supposed to fall asleep now?

Somehow, I do manage to drift off, but I dream only of Iris and wake up the next morning no less frustrated than the night before. Based on the soft light coming in the windows, I can tell it's still early. The house is quiet.

Should I go before anybody wakes up? Does Iris want me to go? Are we going to talk about last night? Is she going to pretend it didn't happen?

I drag myself off the couch, pull on yesterday's undershirt, and pad to the downstairs bathroom to splash cold water on my face and brush my teeth. The little reset does help, but when I open the bathroom door, I find myself confronted by a very stern-looking Sam.

"Morning, Sam," I say, but she makes no move to step aside and let me pass.

"You're a boy in the house," she observes. "We don't have boys in the house."

Based on what Iris had said about being *only* a mom and not having been with somebody since Archer, I shouldn't be surprised she hasn't brought men around here. I guess Olivia doesn't either.

"I am a boy in the house. The snow made driving dangerous last night, so Olivia and your mom invited me to stay. Is that ok?" I really don't know what I'm going to do if she says no.

"Can you make pancakes?" she asks, narrowing her eyes and tilting her head.

"I can." It's possible I've never been more grateful for my parents teaching me how to cook the basics.

"Ok." Sam turns and walks away without an explanation.

Unsure of what to do, I follow her into the kitchen, where she's already taking milk out of the fridge. When the carton of eggs teeters in her hands, I reach over her head and take them from her.

"Are we making pancakes?" I ask.

"Duh," she answers. And that's how I end up making breakfast in my fake girlfriend's house.

I expect Sam doesn't know how to make pancakes, but she scrutinizes me so intently as I work that I can't be sure. I'm just hoping she's not about to get me in trouble for invading the kitchen like this. I get the feeling she'd throw me right under the bus.

"Hey." Iris's soft voice from behind me makes both me and Sam jump and spin toward her.

"Human Eli wanted breakfast," Sam says quickly.

I *knew* it. The traitor.

"I'm sorry. I can replace everything." I sound like a kid caught with his hand in the cookie jar.

"It's ok." Iris laughs, though she still won't make eye contact with me. "I know Sam conned you into it. Girl *loves* her pancakes."

Sam doesn't even try to object, sliding off the stool she'd been occupying and running to the living room to turn on Saturday morning cartoons.

"And what about you? Do you like pancakes?" I sound like an idiot, clearly grasping at anything to talk about.

I don't know what to say, what to do. I've never had a morning after like this. When I'm with a woman, expectations are always clearly communicated before anything. Here, though, I'm flying blind.

What did that kiss mean? Did that kiss mean anything? Was it just for fun? For curiosity?

"Where do you think she gets it from?" Iris says, her eyes flashing toward me for just a second.

When she looks down, I can see a flush spreading quickly across her perfect skin and down her neck to the triangle right above her chest peeking out of her silk button-up pajama top. The matching oversized pants cover her feet, and with a messy bun of hair on top of her head, I'm not sure she's ever looked more adorable.

I flip my current batch of pancakes onto the plate I've made a mountain on and turn off the stove. I walk up to Iris and touch a knuckle under her chin to lift her face until she's looking at me.

"We're ok, Iris," I say. Communication is always a key element when I'm with a woman, and I see no reason to change that part of things. "We don't need to be weird around each other. We can talk about things or not talk about things. Whatever you want to do. I'm still with you for this Archer situation either way, so don't worry about that."

"I—" Iris starts, but she's cut off.

"Morning!" Olivia says loudly as she comes around the corner, and Iris teleports across the kitchen before I can blink. "Do I smell pancakes?"

"You do, indeed. Sam insisted, and I'm here to serve," I say, trying to subtly catch Iris's eye, but she's back to staring at anything *but* me.

"Good man." Olivia claps before diving into the fridge for butter, syrup, and juice. "You two have fun last night?"

"What?" Iris squeaks a little too animatedly to be natural.

Olivia's head appears around the fridge door again.

"The movie?" she clarifies, setting everything on the kitchen island.

"Oh. It was good," Iris says, and I pretend not to notice Olivia giving her roommate a suspicious look.

"Oh, honey, I think you got burned when you were skating

yesterday," Olivia says, leaning forward to examine Iris's pink cheeks. "You're very red."

Olivia's smirk tells me she knows damn well Iris's color isn't from the sun.

Women are *diabolical*.

CHAPTER 31

Iris

After breakfast, Eli helps us dig out the driveway again—ok, Eli digs out the driveway *for* us. I don't know how so much snow could have fallen in just one night, but fresh powder comes up high enough to cover the Explorer's tires, with much more piling up on the lawn from throughout the week. Everything is bright and glistening as far as I can see.

I've finally been given my snow globe.

I stay outside with Eli while he works even though he won't let me help, but I can't think of what to say. It doesn't seem like he's upset about the kiss, and that's good, but what now?

Did he like it? Does he want to do it again? Do I?

I *definitely* do.

A nagging feeling lingers deep in my mind. It tells me I shouldn't be fooling around. That it's irresponsible when I have a kid because it could introduce instability for her and could mess things up with a great man who has been good to both me and Sam.

But, maybe for the first time, Olivia, Lemon, Harry, Kenny, and even Eli's reminders that I'm allowed to want something for myself too, talk over that feeling.

Am I allowed to want *this*?

Eli steals glances at me when he thinks I won't notice, but he doesn't pressure me to get talking. It's like he knows I need to find my words. I can only hope that my internal dialogue isn't written all over my face. I expect I'm not so lucky.

After he finishes flinging the last clump of snow to the side, Eli walks up to me and leans on the shovel handle. He's standing so close again, and after shoveling my whole driveway, that uniquely Eli smell is everywhere, and it's intoxicating. I think it's addling my brain like a drug.

"You doing ok?" he asks, and I think he really wants to know.

"Yeah," I say, and decide to go with honesty. "I'm trying something new for myself, I think. Seeing if the world ends if I do some things I want to do just because I want to do them. That's why I kissed you. And I don't regret doing it. As long as you don't. We don't have to *not* talk about it."

"No, Iris. I don't regret you kissing me." The way he looks at me makes me feel warm even in the middle of my snow-filled yard. "I'd actually very much like to do that again."

No, I don't think he regrets it at all.

As I take him in, all I feel is that want, want, want. And not just physically, even though my own horniness right now is embarrassing me.

He makes me want to do more for me.

"In the spirit of your new take on life, I'd like to do something for you today," Eli says, and I'm suddenly horrified that I said my thoughts out loud. "Do you think somebody could watch Sam this evening? I'd like to take just you somewhere."

I'm intrigued. My instinct is to ask for details, but I resist it. Maybe it's ok if my new take on life includes surprises that I don't have complete control over.

"I'd like to go," I say, and the way Eli grins at me makes my head swim. "Let me see if Olivia has plans."

"Yo," Olivia calls from the front door, still in her pajamas and cradling a mug of coffee in her hands. "I've got a kid in here that is about to rip through the walls to get into the snow. Are you two done with whatever moment you're having out here?"

She has the subtlety of a tap-dancing bull.

Eli's smile widens and a dimple appears on the right side of his face. He leans the shovel against the side of his Jeep and bends to scoop up a handful of snow.

"Send her out," he hollers back.

Olivia steps aside, and we can hear Sam's squealing war cry before she comes barreling out of the house, which Olivia retreats back into. Sam's barely reached the lawn when *smack!*

Eli's pelted her square in the chest with his snowball. Sam grinds to a halt and stares down at her torso like she's just been shot. When she looks at Eli, her mouth is still hanging open. Eli just raises his eyebrows at her in a challenge.

"Mama's on my team!" Sam yells as she launches herself sideways into the pillowy cloud of snow, safely flopping into the mound and quickly making small, lumpy snowballs to lob back at Eli.

Eli pretends he's trying to sneak up on her so he can be close enough for her projectiles to have a chance of hitting him, and he somehow makes the way he launches into their paths look like accidents.

I come in as Sam's backup, holding nothing back as I attack the man with snow. While he only throws snowballs *near* Sam, he has no qualms about hitting me with them directly. Even teaming up against him, and him dramatically taking fire from Sam, he could bury us if he wanted to. But Eli seems as unwilling to end the game as Sam does, just enjoying the fun of rolling around in the snow.

When Eli finally flops onto his back, feigning defeat, Sam charges forward and launches herself on him. I wince at the huff of air she pushes out of Eli when she lands with her knee on his stomach, but he doesn't give any indication that he's bothered.

"Hurry Mama! Get him!" Sam calls for me.

"Yeah, Mama," Eli practically growls. "Hold me down."

And I think I perish on the spot.

I *don't* end up holding Eli down, but he does surrender gracefully to Sam nonetheless. We stay outside a while longer, until Sam is shivering, and her lips look a little blue, even though she continues to insist she's "f-f-*fine*."

We head in, and Eli says it's getting to the point in the day where no grown man can respectably exist without a shower, still wearing yesterday's clothes. Once Olivia confirms she's happy to hang with Sam tonight, Eli confirms the heater is still working and says he'll be back to get me at 8:30.

When I walk him to the front door, he pauses and looks down at me, and I think he's going to kiss me goodbye, but he seems to catch himself and gently kisses my cheek instead.

Now it's less than an hour until Eli will be back here, I have nothing to wear, and I've realized I'm not even a human. I'm a grimy bridge troll masquerading as a person, and Eli is going to realize I'm gross and not want to spend any more time with me.

Ok, what's really happening is that Olivia keeps trying to dress me, and I keep resisting her suggestions. Eli hasn't told me where we're going tonight, but he has told Olivia, and I just can't believe that whatever it is calls for the tiny-beaded bodice and skirt she keeps trying to get me to put on. Why does she even own that?

Olivia gets more exasperated each time I try to pull a chunky sweater over my head, insisting wherever we're going will be warm, even though it's freezing outside. As I keep ignoring her, she finally snaps and full-on tackles me to yank the offending yarn from my grip. We land on my bed but bounce right off, thudding to the floor in a mess of limbs. I kick out and my shin connects hard with the dresser. I yelp out a sound that's shockingly similar to those goat screaming videos that were insanely popular when we were in high school.

Then Olivia and I are laughing, and when we spot Sam standing in her pajamas in my bedroom doorway, looking at us like we're completely off our rockers, we fall further into our pit of madness. When we eventually pull ourselves together, I tuck Sam into bed while Olivia takes another tour through both of our closets. As I reenter my room, I hear her gasp.

"This is the one," Olivia says, holding the hanger up.

It's a short black dress hanging from two straps so thin that I worry an aggressive sneeze would make something snap. I remember trying on this dress ages ago. It's fitted from the sweetheart neckline through my torso until it flares just above my hips into a skirt that's made for twirling. Of course, with that skirt ending above the middle of my thighs, I'm not sure twirling would be wise. The material is soft and smooth and there are thin strings to tie into a dainty bow between my breasts. It could honestly double as modest lingerie.

This is one of my B.S. dresses—before Sam. I bought it just before finding out I was pregnant, so the tags still hang from the back, taunting me. The longer I look at it, the less sure I am. I *love* this dress. That's why I never got rid of it. But…

"Are you sure, Olivia? Isn't it—"

She doesn't let me finish. "I'm positive. And since it's already 8:15 and you still have to do your makeup, you don't have the time to fight with me. Put it on now, or I'll tackle you again, and Eli will find us fighting on the floor like feral beasts."

A quick glance at the clock tells me that Olivia wasn't exaggerating, and I'm seriously out of time. I snatch the dress from her and pull it on. I try to contort myself to pull up the zipper, but Olivia swats away my hands and does it for me. When I turn toward her after, her whole face lights up.

"Yup. That's the one," she says, smiling brightly at me.

I close my closet door and stand in front of the mirror hanging on the back of it. The dress is even better than I imagined. My body has changed since the last time I put it on, but the curves I've developed are no more or less beautiful than my former shape.

When I shift, I spot Sam's reflection, her little face peering around my doorway again, having crawled out of bed with curiosity, and I smile. This body has done incredible things.

"Hi Mama," she whispers.

I feel like a woman, and I feel beautiful.

"Hi baby girl," I say back. "Promise me you'll go back to bed for Liv once I go."

Sam nods energetically. "Promise."

Olivia, the only one still focused on getting me ready, scurries to the bathroom only to return a moment later with mascara, my signature red lipstick, and her favorite teardrop pearl earrings.

"Just these. Trust me. You don't need anything else."

I take her advice, put them on, and am finger-combing my hair when I hear a knock.

Olivia, Sam, and I head downstairs, but Olivia lightly catches Sam's shoulder, holding her back when we get to the bottom of the stairs so I can approach the front door alone. I see Eli's Jeep through the window, so I pull open the door.

Eli is leaning an arm against the door frame, looking casual and perfect in dark jeans, a button-up, and a black wool coat, but he straightens up when his eyes fall on me. His gaze licks over every inch of me as it travels down my body and he breathes out a soft "Oh."

I feel simultaneously embarrassed and empowered, so I try to cling to the strength.

"Hi," I say quietly.

"Hi," Eli says back. "You look incredible."

"You can thank Olivia for that," I deflect.

"No," he objects. "I think I'll thank you."

He reaches for one of my hands and raises it to his lips, pressing a soft kiss there. I feel a tingle all the way to my toes.

"Ready?" he asks, and I can only nod in response.

I hurry back inside to grab shoes and say goodnight to Sam when Olivia pulls open-toe black heels out of nowhere. She buckles one around my ankle while I get the other, and when she hugs me, she whispers "Get it, girl" in my ear.

When I get back to the door, Eli is holding my peacoat out for me.

"This one, right?" he checks, and I slide into it.

Eli offers his arm to me as we walk to the car, and I'm eternally grateful he cleared the walkway this morning. He opens my door, helps me into the Jeep where he kept the heat on full blast, and closes me in.

I'm so thoroughly enjoying how this feels like a date from a rom-com that it takes me a minute to notice we've left Wilcox Grove and are on the highway.

"Where are we going? I'm not sure Archer will hear about our date if we go out of town," I say as snow-laden trees rush by.

"This night isn't for Archer. This night is for you."

CHAPTER 32

Iris

We don't drive for long before Eli pulls into the parking lot of a nondescript brown building with an LED sign out front that reads only *Restaurant and Bar* with the *and* part flickering. Even from the back of the lot with our windows rolled up, I can hear the rhythmic thump of a prominent bass. When Eli cuts the engine, I check the clock, and it's barely 9:00, but this place is already in full swing.

"Eli, where are we?" I ask once he circles the car and opens my door.

"This"—Eli sweeps out an arm toward the structure like he's presenting a piece of priceless art—"is a dive bar. It has the most incredible fried food, cheap drinks, and an enormous dance floor."

The grin on his face has me excited even if I'm a bit skeptical of our destination. Eli must see the uncertainty I'm trying to hide, though.

"How old were you when you found out you were pregnant with Sam?" he asks.

"Twenty," I say. I was about a month along when I figured it out, and that was around two months before my twenty-first birthday.

"And did your rule-following ass have a fake?"

"God no," I scoff at the prospect. Even once I started spending time with Archer, I still refused his pleas to get a fake ID. Drinking with friends was one thing, but I was *not* going to bars and risking getting caught.

"That's what I figured. You deserve to experience something like this." Eli's excited, and it's a little infectious. "I could tell you weren't the most thrilled to go out for Alice's birthday, but I think you ended up having at least a little fun."

He pauses, and I tilt my head side to side in reluctant admission.

"Try this with me," he continues. "Try to get out of your head for a little bit. If you hate it, we leave."

"Are you sure I'm dressed right for a place like this?" I ask, eyeing the worn wood exterior.

"You're dressed perfectly," he promises.

A pair of girls spill out of the front doors, bringing a burst of music with them. Sure enough, they're wearing dresses not too different from mine. They're a tangle of limbs, giggling and hunched together. One presses the other against the side of a car and kisses her passionately. They're young, and happy, and I want it.

I'm young. I'm happy. I can have it.

"Let's go," I say, taking Eli's offered hand and hopping down, landing steadily on my heels.

"You won't want this," he says, removing my coat even though there are piles of snow all around the parking lot. He folds it with his own and lays them on the passenger seat of the Jeep.

Goosebumps erupt on every inch of my skin, and even under the dim light of the lot, I expect from the way Eli's eyes linger just a second too long when he looks down that he can see my nipples pressing against my dress.

I remind myself I'm just a twenty-six-year-old woman on a date tonight—fake or not—and let him look.

While the short walk across the parking lot, even giving the two women a wide berth for privacy, is exceedingly cold, the second we step inside, I understand why we left our coats behind. The building is packed with warm bodies—at the bar or dancing with sweat-slicked hair stuck to their skin, while even more fill high-top tables that are crammed into every available space. String lights crisscross messily across the ceiling, lighting the place in soft, inconsistent blotches of light.

Televisions above the bar show college basketball games and highlights, bright in the dimly lit room with cheers and heckling adding to the volume in here.

Winter or not, air conditioning is blowing in a desperate attempt to keep the temperature down, but it's still hot and a little humid.

Eli's eyes sweep the room, and I briefly wonder what it looks like from so high up, but then I'm just grateful for his vantage point as he takes my hand and leads me to a table the second it's vacated. It seems like laws of the jungle rule in here, and having one of the biggest creatures on my side has its perks.

He somehow catches a server's eye and bends low as the man works his way over to us.

"Anything you *don't* want?" he asks, picking up the little tent from the center of our table and showing it to me.

I skim it as quickly as I can and shake my head. I'm hungry, and everything looks delicious. I do pick out a fun-sounding cocktail and point to it. I can't hear what Eli orders, but the server nods his head and disappears back into the throng of people with Eli's card secured between two fingers.

As we wait, I can't help but bob to the music. I can feel it thrumming in my pulse. Yes, it's loud, and the table is a little sticky, and the air smells like stale beer and sweat, but every face I see is smiling. Drinks come quickly, and I beam when I find my blended something-or-other has a cherry and a little umbrella in it.

This feels like a rite of passage I'd drifted on past when my life took a nontraditional turn. Not drinking this cheap liquor that I'll regret in the morning. Being messy and free and probably a little stupid.

Something about tonight is different than the few times I've gone out since becoming a mom. It's even different than dancing on Alice's birthday. I'm not worried about fitting in or making sure everybody is happy. I'm not watching my friends' drinks or being the water police. I feel safe.

Tonight, I lean into release. I can be a responsible adult again tomorrow.

Because of how busy it is, people keep bumping into me as they dance or even just try to walk past, but Eli's eyes narrow when I jolt forward for what must be the fifteenth time and some of my drink sloshes over the rim of my impractical glass, adding to whatever's coating our table. He shifts toward me until he's behind me, my own human shield.

He leans the heel of his hand against the table on one side of me and holds his beer bottle next to my glass on my other side, effectively caging me in. I'm sure he must be getting jostled as much as I had been, but he doesn't shift an inch, and I remain untouched.

Archer first said it as a criticism, but maybe Eli *is* my guard dog. And maybe I like it.

Even once our mozzarella sticks arrive, Eli stays wrapped around me. At some point, a new drink appears before me with a water for Eli and some sliders, and he closes our tab. He leans forward each time he goes for a bite of food, and his chest brushes against my back. My heels eat a bit into the height difference between us, but he's still just so *big*.

After we finish eating, we're still touching. He doesn't step away, and neither do I.

When I tip my head back to drain my glass, I let it rest on Eli's chest. He looks down at me, his eyes dark. When I look back down, the hand he had leaning against the edge of the table is now gripping it hard.

"Dance with me," I demand.

Though I'm sure he can't hear me over the music, Eli nods and takes my empty glass from me. Setting it beside his on the table, he laces his fingers with mine and lets me lead him into the throng of people that's only grown since we arrived.

Eli bumps against me when I stop, surrounded by people. I pull our still linked hands across my body until his fingers graze the material covering my opposite hip. And then we move together. I feel alive, my skirt brushing against my legs until I become so damp it sticks to me. My cheeks ache from laughing at nothing.

All I do is feel. Feel the music, feel the energy from the people around me, feel the strength of Eli at my back.

I release Eli's hand to reach up for his neck behind me and find his skin as slick as mine. His hand remains banded across me, and his fingertips press against my soft belly. I have a flash of his hand on my hip when I kissed him last night, and I wonder if he's thinking of that moment too.

Boldly, I press into him and feel his hardness against my back. I should pull away, but I don't.

I like knowing I did this to him. I like him knowing I know.

I force myself not to think about how I'm a grown woman grinding on this man behind me like a college student and instead lose myself in how good I feel in his arms.

His other hand comes around me, trailing down my skin from

my shoulder until he can grasp my hand. He lifts it above my head and turns me. His enormous hands find my full hips, and it feels like puzzle pieces snapping together.

He's bent over me, and he's *so* close I can feel his breath against my face, and I can tell when it hitches. He tears his eyes away from mine and looks up at the ceiling. If I didn't know better, I'd think he's struggling with this as much as I am.

"Eli?" I ask, but he can't hear me. I reach up and touch his face.

Hesitantly, he looks down at me, torment in his eyes, a brewing storm he's keeping at bay. I smile, trying to reassure him this is ok. But I want to talk to him. I want to know…

He jerks his head toward the front door, and I nod. Even though we're not drunk, we stumble our way out, like walking normally after being in that mass of bodies is jarring. When we tumble out the door, I remember those two women from before.

The rush of cold air is heavenly on my skin.

"You ok?" Eli asks, a little louder than is necessary. I think his ears are ringing like mine.

"Are we still just friends?" I blurt without warning or preamble.

Eli's eyes soften as he looks at me, and I feel a rush of fear that he'll reject me, in spite of what I felt inside.

"We have to be. I can't give you what you deserve." His voice is deeper than I've ever heard it, and heat pools low in my belly at the sound.

"What if I've changed what I want?" My voice is small, but I'm not unsure. "What if I want you? Would you want me too?"

"*Fuck*, Iris," he says, putting his hands on his hips and looking up at the stars. I can hear him breathing purposefully slowly, like he's trying to stay in control.

"Would you?" My heart is thumping so hard in my chest, I'm

sure he can hear it. I'm sure the whole *bar* can hear it, even over the music from inside.

He moves quickly now, turning and bending his enormous frame over me again, his hand landing on my lower back and pulling me toward him.

"More than you know," he breathes.

I tip my chin up, and he presses his lips hard against mine, swallowing my gasp. When my fingertips connect with his abs, I feel the muscles tighten, and I press my hand against them.

He pulls back abruptly.

"I need you to be sure, Iris. I didn't bring you here to pressure you into this. I need you to know that."

"I know that. I want this. I want you."

I want to keep feeling *more*.

Eli

I try not to dwell on the laws I break driving back to Wilcox Grove. The roads are deserted, and Iris pulled my hand onto her bare thigh as soon as we got into the Jeep, so I really don't think anybody would fault me for going a few—or many—miles an hour over the speed limit.

Iris's legs are pressed together, but the tips of my fingers are firmly held between those perfect thighs, and it takes everything I've got to keep from sliding my hand up. I can't help tightening my grip on her leg, though, especially when she gasps at the pressure.

She's always so tightly wound, and I want to unravel her completely.

I feel like I should say something, but I can't find any words. Each time I look over at Iris, she's completely relaxed, smiling at my hand on her leg. When she begins tracing the outline of my fingers with one of her nails, I feel myself harden and press down harder on the accelerator.

When I finally park outside of my condo, I realize I need to say *something*. That's how I make sure nobody gets hurt. It feels different with Iris. Not that I've never gotten here with somebody who was a friend first (or a friend after), but this is just *different*.

"I haven't changed my mind," Iris says, possibly misinterpreting the look on my face. "Take me inside, Eli."

Upstairs. We'll talk upstairs.

"Then, let's go," I say, getting out of the Jeep and circling the hood to meet her on the passenger side.

She's already out of the car when I get to her, leaning back in to get her coat, and showing me an extra inch of skin as her skirt shifts up with the movement. After a quick glance, I force myself to look *anywhere* else. The smirk on her lips when she turns to me tells me she knows exactly what she was doing. I don't try to deny what I did.

I looked, and I liked it.

We head upstairs, and I hold open my front door to let Iris in. The one-bedroom condo has always been good to me, but when I look around now, I can only wonder what it looks like through Iris's eyes. I take our coats and drop them over the back of the couch.

The living room and kitchen are divided by a half-wall counter. Stools on the living room side eliminate the need for a dining room table, though I do have a desk with a hutch against one wall. My television in its entertainment center takes up the wall that divides the living room and my bedroom. The shelves are filled with books, pictures, and Phish's sizable aquarium. A small hallway leads to a laundry room at the end, with my bedroom and bathroom doors facing one another just before it.

Thankfully, I've never been a particularly messy person. It's a lived-in space, but it's clean.

"That's Phish," I introduce when I see Iris's gaze pause on the tank. When she looks at me, skeptical, I realize Phish is being shy, and remaining completely out of sight. "I swear there's a fish in there... named Phish with a ph."

"You sure you don't just have an empty tank of water?" she asks, looking at me like she could have just walked into the home of a serial killer.

"No, I swear—he's—"

She smiles, and I realize she's teasing me.

"You are a mean woman," I say, coming to stand before her, moving closer than is appropriate and forcing her to tip her chin up to maintain eye contact.

"Nothing changes between us," I say. "We're going to have fun, and if anything isn't fun, we say so, and that's that. This is safe. *You* are safe."

"This is safe," she echoes back to me as I trace her jawline with my fingertips. "Nothing changes."

She turns her head into my palm and plants a featherlight kiss there before looking back at me. She reaches between us, and her nails drag along my stomach as she hooks her fingers behind my belt and pulls me toward her.

Like the tether in me has snapped, I tip her head further back and crash my lips to hers, needing, pulling, demanding more from her. She doesn't hesitate to give it to me, opening her mouth and sweeping her tongue against mine. I groan, wanting to drink her in, wanting to make her scream.

I release her face to cup her full ass with both my palms, lifting her until I feel her legs clamp around my waist like a vice, her arms band around my neck, her thin heel digs into my back. The sting of pain shoots through me, and I feel myself throb in my pants.

Reluctantly, I break our kiss just so I don't crash into anything, but Iris isn't satisfied. She pulls the collar of my shirt aside and licks from the juncture of my neck and shoulder to under my ear, where she leaves a sharp bite at the same time she rolls her hips against me.

We are *not* being gentle tonight.

How I manage to walk to my bedroom without blacking out from this woman wrapped around my body is beyond me, but I somehow do. When I'm standing at the base of my bed, I release one hand to reach around me and unhook her ankles. Before she can fight it, I toss her from me, right into the middle of the mattress, where she bounces once, her hands propping her up and her legs landing parted.

I see a shadow of dark fabric between her thighs, and I'm hypnotized.

"I think," I start, pausing to lick my lips. "I think you're used to being in control. Tonight, I want you to not have to think. Let me take care of you. *Trust me* to take care of you."

Iris's eyes darken at my offer.

"I do," she says simply and nods. "What do you want me to do?"

"Touch yourself," I instruct, my eyes falling back between her legs.

I think I stop breathing completely when Iris's hand slides over that fabric, and her knees fall even further apart, forcing her skirt to hitch up. She drags two fingers over her center deliberately, and I would happily waste away watching her like this.

"Do you want to touch me, Eli?" Iris asks, but it sounds like she's under water with the blood rushing in my ears.

"I want *you* to touch yourself first," I somehow rasp out. "Show me what you like."

Iris's beautiful giggle bounces around the room.

"Do you like how I look?" she asks.

"I adore how you look, Iris," I say truthfully. "Now put your fingers in your perfect cunt," I demand, stepping forward until my knees hit the bottom of the bed.

"Ok," she breathes, her fingers pressing against herself through her underwear, drawing slow circles. "But can I see you?"

I look up at her face and see her cheeks stained a vibrant pink, determination in her eyes. I know it's been a while for her, and I'm thrilled by her eagerness.

When my hands find the top button on my shirt, she pulls her plump bottom lip between her teeth. I notice her lipstick, which made it through dinner and drinks, is smudged from my own mouth, and I consider just ripping the damn buttons off. Fighting the urge to rush, I pull the hem of my shirt out of my pants and push it off my shoulders.

Iris scoots up my bed until her back is propped against my headboard. I keep my eyes on her as I continue, tossing my undershirt to the floor with my button up and unhooking my belt.

As I push my pants to the ground and step out of them, kicking off my shoes in the process, Iris lifts her hips and bunches her dress at her waist. Midnight blue panties are all that are in my way now.

Just as my eyes devour Iris's core, hers work down my body, and when they get to my waist, I push down my boxer briefs and take off my socks. When I stand, completely naked and with my erection bobbing before me, Iris's lips pop open, and her hand slides over her perfect thigh and over the center of her underwear again. I resist the aching desire to grip myself, afraid I'll come just from the touch. I retrieve a small box from beneath my bed and drop a strip of condoms from it on the bed for later.

"My shoes," Iris says suddenly, like she's just noticed they're still on.

"Leave them," I growl, my gruff voice stopping her hand that was reaching for one of the buckles. "And touch yourself."

Obediently, Iris moves her hands up and down over the dark fabric again. Her other hand bunches in the waistband of her underwear and pulls sharply up until the fabric stretches taught, slipping between her folds and giving me my first glimpse of her wet pussy. The soft moan she makes as she rolls her hips against the taught material nearly breaks me.

"*Fuck*, Iris," I groan, my hand flying to the base of my cock and squeezing hard. "Do you know how amazing you look doing that?"

She's absolutely glowing at what she's doing to me, and she tentatively rolls her hips up again, pressing her clit into the rough fabric once, twice, three times, humming in appreciation at the friction. I stroke myself hard, just one time, desperate to relieve some of the tension spreading through me.

Iris hooks a finger under the fabric barely covering her now and pulls it aside as she releases her other hand and slides her two middle fingers completely into her mouth. When she makes eye contact with me, I nod, encouraging her to keep going. I imagine I'm pushing myself between those red lips instead, and I release myself, just before I tip over that edge.

Iris pulls her fingers out of her mouth with a *pop* and buries them deep into her cunt in one smooth motion. She throws her head back, hitting it against my headboard with a thud that she doesn't seem to feel. She rolls her thumb over her clit as her fingers pump into her over and over again. The sound of her wetness has me clenching my jaw so hard I'm surprised I don't hear something crack.

"You are so fucking perfect," I say.

I need to be closer to her. I kneel on the bed and crawl toward her. She separates her legs even farther, making room for me to fit between them. I place a hand on the inside of one of her thighs, pressing the outside of her knee into the mattress. The hand that was holding her panties flies to my wrist, gripping so hard I can feel her nails digging into my skin.

Iris's whole spine is bowed off the bed, every muscle clenching tight. She's still pressing her head into my headboard, but she's looking down at me, her mouth open as she pants gasping breaths. She looks like a perfect mess, her hair caught behind her head, and the tiny straps of her dress hanging limply off her shoulders.

Her hand speeds up. I can't stand it. I need to touch her. I suck the pad of my thumb into my mouth, thoroughly wetting it with my tongue before I bring it to her clit and replace her own. While she frantically drives her fingers into herself, I roll firm circles over her.

Her hips buck off the bed, jerking against my thumb and pulling her fingers deeper inside her. I grind harder into her, and her gasps become whimpers, and it sounds like she's trying to hold them in.

"I want you to come, Iris. Can you do that for me?" I ask, and she nods frantically, eager to please.

"I want you inside me, Eli," she pants.

"Soon," I promise.

I lean close to her pussy and spit on it, watching it drip from my thumb down to her opening. All at once, Iris's hand clenches hard around my wrist before letting go to grab the pillow beside her head, and her thigh muscle spasms beneath my palm as she comes undone before my eyes.

She cries out in spite of her attempts to keep quiet, her eyes squeezed shut, and her hips rutting against our hands.

With my thumb still working her clit, I use my other hand to snatch one of the condoms, tearing it off the strip and ripping it open with my teeth. I roll it on myself and move over Iris, gripping the headboard for stability with one hand and pulling her hand out of her with the other so I can replace it with my cock, slamming halfway into her in one push.

Iris moans again, a broken, needy sound, but I claim her lips again and palm her ass when she drives her hips up to take more of me. One of her hands grips my shoulder, where her nails scratch against my skin, and I can feel her wetness paint me there.

"You're going to take more," I tell her as I release her lips, keeping our sweat-slicked foreheads pressed together. "I know you can."

I know my size. She's tight from her orgasm, but I can feel her stretching for me, and it feels *so fucking good.*

"I can," she says, lifting her hips again while I use every ounce of control to remain still.

When she lowers them to the bed again, I sink down with her, sliding another inch into her. Her leg hooks around me, and that sharp heel bites into my back when she pulls me down and lifts her hips once more. Again, I chase her into the mattress until my hips are flush against hers.

"Look at you," I say, eyes on the place where we press together. "You were made for me."

I rock my hips forward, and we groan in satisfaction together.

"Yes," Iris hisses, shifting so she can kiss my jaw, just under my chin.

Ever so slowly, I pull out until just my head is still inside and inch back into her. When Iris arches her back, I move my hand up to the neckline of her dress and yank it down along with her bra until her gorgeous breasts are trussed up above the fabric, tight nipples begging to be touched. I keep moving slowly, ignoring Iris circling her hips in an attempt to get me to speed up, and lower my lips to one of those perfect dusty pink nipples, drawing it into my mouth and biting to earn myself a yelp. Iris's hand shifts into my hair, where she tangles her fingers and squeezes, pressing me closer to her chest.

I alternate licking, biting, sucking. One breast and then the other, gradually picking up my pace as Iris's breathing devolves into little pants once more. When I'm fully driving into her, Iris tugs on my hair to pull my lips back to hers, dragging her teeth across my bottom lip.

When she tightens her muscles around me, it's my turn to yell out. I can feel Iris's satisfied smile spread against my lips as she repeats the movement.

"You're a *wicked* woman," I chastise. I turn my head just enough to wet my fingers again, lifting up so I can reach between us to play with her clit. The next time she clenches around me, it's sharp and quick, and I can tell she's close again.

Thank *god*, because I can't hold on.

"You can let go," I breathe. "I've got you."

Iris's eyes are closed, and we're sharing the same air as I spill into the condom, continuing to piston into her until I feel her walls fluttering around me. I keep moving, riding our orgasms out for as long as I can before stilling and falling to my back beside Iris, the sides of our arms pressed together, and all of our tight muscles releasing.

For at least a full minute, the only sound in the room is our ragged breathing.

"Wow." She sighs, her chest heaving.

I rotate my wrist between us until I find her hand to hold.

"Yeah," I agree. *Yeah.*

CHAPTER 34

Iris

T'm still trying to sort out up from down when Eli grunts and stands up, dropping the condom in his bathroom trash and washing his hands before continuing to his kitchen.

That was an out-of-body experience. When I agreed to trust Eli, I thought it would be difficult to let go, but in his hands, I was able to let my mind go quiet for the first time in a *long* time. With him, I could just feel, and his constant reassurances made sure I never had to question whether what I was doing was alright. This was an excellent decision.

When I hear Eli rummaging around in the fridge, I swing my legs over the side of the bed and test my weight on them. They feel a little wobbly, but they hold me up without collapsing, so I'll take it. I'm righting my dress when Eli returns.

"Where do you think you're going?" he asks as he hands me a sports drink.

Cute.

Still, I open it and take a long gulp.

"I just need a minute to use your bathroom and get my things," I say, shifting my underwear back into place. Unfortunately, there's no graceful way to do that, and I remind myself not to be embarrassed after what we just did.

"No, no. I don't think so," Eli says, and his deep chuckle has goosebumps erupting down my arms and legs. He chases them with a gentle touch of his knuckles running from my shoulder to my wrist. He raises his own bottle of electrolytes to me.

"Just let me finish this and give me half an hour. I'm hoping we're not done here, but if you'd like to rest, I'd still never kick you out. I want to take care of you." He pauses, concern touching the edges of his expression. "Unless you *want* to go?"

Oh.

"I don't. I just figured…" I trail off, not wanting to insult Eli by saying what I figured.

"That we'd fuck, and I wouldn't even let you stay the night?" Eli guesses anyway. "C'mon, Iris. I'd never. Especially not with you. I want you to stay with me."

I try to not let that *especially not with you* burrow too deeply into my mind.

"Ok," I say dumbly, happily.

"So, you'll stay?" Eli says, invading my space again.

"I'll stay," I agree.

"Good." Eli takes my drink and sets it with his bottle on the nightstand before reaching around me to pull the zipper of my dress down.

I let my arms fall, and Eli drops to his knees to tug the material over the flare of my full hips. A second later, he's removed my bra too. When he looks up at me, his eyes are dark pools that make me press my legs together.

"You are stunning, Iris Sutton," he says without exception or qualification for my soft stomach, many stretch marks, or any other flaw I see on myself.

With him kneeling before me, it feels like a prayer.

He urges me to sit on the edge of his bed and pulls my underwear down my legs. He taps my ankle until I spread my legs, running his fingers over the strap from one of my heels, still secured around my ankle.

"I don't need to wait half an hour for this," he says.

Then he devours me like I'm fucking dessert.

The next morning, I wake early, sore, and sweaty. Even though he's completely uncovered and we aren't touching, Eli is somehow even hotter when he sleeps, and he seems to turn the whole bed into a giant heating pad. I look around for something to put on and settle on Eli's undershirt since there's no way I'm about to put my dress back on.

After a quick stop in the bathroom, I venture into the living room to say good morning to Phish, who has finally come out to say hello, and into the kitchen to find something to eat. After a late and active night, I'm *starving*.

I consider making pancakes for Eli like he did when he woke up first at my house, but I simply cannot wait that long. Toast will have to do. I'm eating a slice with peanut butter on it when Eli emerges from his bedroom. He did *not* feel the need to dress and comes into the kitchen in all his naked glory.

And it is *glorious*.

"Morning." Eli's voice is all rough gravel before he presses his lips to mine, not a drop of embarrassment over morning breath or my peanut butter-covered lips.

"Mmm," he hums. His eyes are half-lidded, and the sound is deep. He licks his lips after we separate, and I don't think it was peanuts that caused that response.

"I like this on you," he says, looking at my torso in his shirt with blatant approval. He holds some of the fabric at my shoulder, rubbing it with his thumb in a way that has me thinking of that thumb elsewhere.

I'm glad he's happy to carry this little conversation one-sided, because I'm loving just watching him take me in this morning. I feel sexy, and it feels *good*.

I shift on my feet and suddenly Eli's brow furrows, and displeasure crosses his face. He points down to my shin.

"Did I do that? Did I hurt you?" he asks.

I glance down and find a purplish splotch toward the inside of my lower leg. Even now, I still feel delightfully silly at the memory. I shake my head.

"No, that one is care of Olivia tackling me off my bed yesterday," I say, but I like his protectiveness, his caring.

"Well, I'm glad you went home with me instead of her," he jokes.

I hold up my second slice of toast to him.

"You hungry?" I ask and have only a second to brace after seeing the mischievous glint in his eye.

Next thing I know, I'm scooped right into the air, bear-hugged by this bear-sized man.

I'm short, but not a small woman. Eli moves me with ease and over the past twelve hours, I've learned he appreciates every curve, ridge, and dip on my body. It makes me not mind at all that he's hiked the shirt up my back. It makes me *want* to be on display for him.

"Eli!" I squeal as he begins carrying me back to the bedroom. "Hang on! Let me at least put down the toast before I get peanut butter in your hair."

"Bring it with you," he growls. "You'll need your strength."

An hour later, I'm showered and leaning up against Eli's headboard, eating that piece of toast while Eli's head rests against my stomach.

"You are one hell of a woman." He sighs with contentment.

"I try," I say with a laugh, running my free hand through his hair. He's practically purring.

Still completely content with his own nudity, Eli is sprawled on top of the covers with an arm lazily laid across my hips. I take this quiet moment to get my fill of him, though I'm not sure I'd ever get tired of looking at him like this. When he shifts his arm, I spot that scar on his ribs again.

I reach down as far as I can and tap the side of his torso near the raised ridge.

"What happened here?" I ask.

Eli peels open an eye and twists until he can see the mark before flopping back on me, pushing the breath out of me in a whoosh. He chuckles, and it's like I've got a motorboat attached to my side.

"That was care of Jake being a moron when we were younger, and me following right along with him," Eli reminisces. "Jake is almost four months older than I am, and when you're kids, age basically determines seniority, especially when he was ten—a *double digit*—and I was still only nine. It was summer vacation, when we were at our worst, and that year, Scott was almost two, loud and needy, as babies can be.

"So, Jake was all about anything that took him out of his house. It had absolutely *poured*, and the entire town had become a mud pit. Jake thought it would be cool to go biking in the mud in the woods, and I saw no issue with that. We were sliding everywhere. All fun and games until he crashed into a tree, and I crashed into him, nearly impaling myself on his kickstand. If you look very closely, you can still see the edge of the scar at his hairline on his forehead. He needed like seven staples. Our moms yelling at us was twice as scary as the crash."

I like watching him tell the story. He's animated and happy, looking dreamily at nothing like he can see his childhood in his mind. It also makes me think of the dumb things Lemon and I would get up to. Of course, as the *older* twin, they were mostly my doing.

This moment feels remarkably coupley, and I have to remind myself that it isn't. We have a deal, and forgetting that is a mistake. Pain waiting to happen. I tell my heart to simmer down and try to just enjoy the moment. I'm not even sure it'll happen again.

When Eli sighs again, I expect our time is up.

"Time to go?" I ask.

"You're more than welcome to stay if you'd like, but I need to get some tax stuff done. Filing deadlines are looming, and I'm kind of behind," Eli says, unable to hold eye contact, like he's embarrassed by the admission.

I still, thinking about the last couple of weeks and realizing how much time Eli has given to me and our arrangement. He had said this was usually an extremely busy time for him, and I feel guilty for not realizing I've been keeping him from his responsibilities.

"Hey, Iris." Eli pulls me out of my thoughts. "None of that. I'm a big boy, and I can manage my own time. Everything will get done. I just need to buckle down."

"Ok," I say, taking him at his word. Also, it takes a lot for me not to agree with his assessment of himself as a "big boy," but I manage to keep my yap shut. I should get a point for that. "I should probably still get home, for Sam. I can find a ride."

"I'm driving you home." It's not a question.

"Ok," I say again and drag myself out of bed.

I'm looking at my dress with displeasure—it's really not a Sunday mid-morning fit—when Eli chucks sweatpants at me. They're almost as long as my whole body, and I cannot wait to leap into them. He also wordlessly brings me a clean t-shirt and a sweatshirt, both equally enormous. I'm about to be the coziest I've ever been in my whole life.

I start climbing into everything, and extra material is bunched everywhere. When I turn to Eli, I find him standing in his boxers, staring at me.

"What?" I ask, waving my arm and the sleeve that hangs several inches past my fingertips at him. "Don't I look good?"

"You always look good," Eli says, coming over to help me cuff my sleeves. "I'm just trying to stop myself from getting hard knowing you're in my clothes without anything underneath them."

I like how blunt he is. It leaves no room for doubting myself or questioning how he feels about my body. That kind of assurance is incredibly freeing.

"I'll just have to reserve this mental image for next time," he says.

So, I guess there will be a next time.

Eli pauses, rolling up my second sleeve. "There could be if you want there to be. *I* want there to be," he says, making me realize I blabbed my thoughts.

I take a page out of Eli's book of honesty. "I'd like that very much."

CHAPTER 35

Eli

When I drop Iris off at her house, handing her off to Olivia—who's wearing an expression that says she's about to grill Iris for every detail the second I pull away—I fully intend to go straight home and start working on taxes. I just need to focus… on taxes.

I wasn't lying about having a long list of things to get through before the partnership filing deadline in a week, but mostly I needed to give myself a little breathing room.

I had a great time last night… and this morning. The sex was amazing. Of course the sex was amazing. Iris is amazing. But spending time with my friend was also really, *really* fun. I think of how both Jake and Scott talk about their partners as their best friends, and I know I'm wading into dangerous territory.

Everywhere I look, I see her. On my bed. In my shower. Against my kitchen counter in just my shirt. I can still smell her on my skin. Feel her hands in my hair.

A little bit of distance will help me clear my head, remember my rules, and keep everything safe for myself. It was incredible sex, and incredible sex is bound to muss things up in my brain.

That's all that's happening here. That's why it's convincing me to get attached to Iris and never let her go.

If I want to keep my sanity, this will have to stop once Archer is gone. Then maybe I'll take a trip until I can get my head back on straight. I'm sure I can convince Jake and Scott to spend time in the woods. We can get a cabin or something. It doesn't really matter where. Scott's been yapping about some town in Massachusetts called Merrymount that's apparently got a lake or river or something and warmer weather than Wilcox Grove. Maybe we go there.

And when I get back, Iris and I can go back to being friends.

This is fine. We'll be fine. I'll be fine.

With a solid plan that will absolutely work—if I say it enough times, maybe it'll be true—I sit at the desk in my living room and get to work.

Sheer stubbornness keeps me going until it starts to get dark out and my body demands food.

Wandering into the kitchen, I catch sight of my bread and peanut butter, but shove it aside, doing my damnedest not to think about this morning *again*, and pull one of those pre-made meals you can get delivered out of my fridge. Curry it is. I inhale my food and get right back to work. It's well past midnight when I finally fall into my bed and pass out.

I've never been one to have vivid storytelling dreams. I always only get bits and pieces of scenes or memories, but what sticks with me when I wake up is the feeling the dream gave me. An arched back. The smell of lavender. Fingers in my hair.

With the state I wake up in, I know *exactly* what I was dreaming about. *Who* I was dreaming about.

Fuck.

Knowing I'm going to see Iris for coffee at Barefoot Bake before work doesn't help my situation at all. My morning shower is *very* cold.

As I walk across the sidewalk from my car to the café, I try to picture as much of that video they showed us in driver's ed in high school to scare us into being good drivers—anything to keep my mind away from the image of my hands on her hips.

No.

I open the door to Barefoot Bake, pulling a blast of warm air from inside. Like she's as drawn to me as I am to her, Iris's head whips around, her blonde hair sliding over her shoulders, as her mismatched eyes find me. Her deep red lips part before smiling, and when the door closes behind me, I swear the café becomes a vacuum.

After all, that's the only logical explanation for why I feel so lightheaded all the sudden.

It's just the incredible sex.

My legs move me to Iris on autopilot.

"I already ordered your coffee, but did you want anything to eat?" she says once I get to her.

I look at the case of pastries, even though I've been here more times than I can count. For some reason, it seems like making a decision is outside my capabilities today.

What the fuck is wrong *with me?*

"Uh…" I say without a thought in my head.

"You're getting a breakfast sandwich. Clearly you need fuel." Leslie saves me. Apparently, my idiocy is obvious.

"Sounds great. Thanks." I try to hand Leslie my card, but Iris hip-checks me.

Because of our size difference, it isn't an effective move, but she shoves my hand aside anyway, passing Leslie her debit card instead.

When she finishes paying, we move down the bar to wait for our order, standing near the wall to be out of the way. Barefoot Bake is *the* place for this town's caffeine supply in the morning, so the café just gets busier by the minute, and Iris and I drift closer together.

When the back of Iris's hand brushes against mine, she pulls it back like she was burned.

"Oh, sorry," she mutters, the prettiest pink color spreading across her cheeks as she looks down and tries to shuffle to make space.

I can't take it. I'm about to crawl out of my skin standing this close to her, not touching her, thinking only of her skin, her sounds, her smell, her *taste*. Her. Her. Her.

Maybe just a bit more of her will take the edge off.

Suddenly, I couldn't care less that most of Wilcox Grove is in this room. I turn toward Iris, wrapping my arm around her back and pulling her off balance against me. She looks up at me in surprise, and I give in, bending to kiss her, needy and hard, because I think I might die if I don't.

When Iris's hands slide up my chest and grip the edges of my jacket, I pull her tighter against me, like I can pull her right into me.

"Iris and Eli!" one of the baristas calls from behind me, ready with our order.

Just as abruptly as I kissed her, I pull back, keeping my arm around her as she stumbles from the sudden movement. Her eyes are bright, and her lipstick is smudged. I hope it's stained on my mouth.

When I look up, the people closest to us turn away and pick up conversations that had been cut off moments earlier.

"Sorry," I say, breathless. "I—" I don't have an excuse.

"No." Iris shakes her head, smiling. "Me too."

She purposefully leans forward, pressing her hip into my growing erection.

In the fucking café? What am I, a teenager?

Thankfully, my jeans are thick and my jacket hangs a little long.

"Iris and Eli?" the barista calls again, and I can feel his eyes on the back of my head. It's hard to hide when you're as tall as I am.

"Yeah," I say gruffly as I turn and take the cups and bag of food. "Thanks."

Iris stays close behind me as the crowd parts to give me a path to the door. She shifts around to hold the door for me and then walks beside me to her car, parked on a quiet side street. I set one of the cups on the roof of her car so I can open the driver's door for her. She ducks under my arm and hops into the seat.

I reach across her to set her coffee in the cupholder in the center console, and my eyes catch on the hem of her grey knit skirt, stretching across her thighs. Obviously still out of my mind, I put my hand on her leg and slide it up, my fingers getting caught when she shifts her thighs together.

When I turn my head, I find her pupils so wide that her eyes look nearly black, even the hazel one.

"If I touched you right now, how wet would I find you?" I ask quietly.

My body and the door are blocking her entirely from view, and the street is deserted, but there's no denying this is a brazen move. If anybody were to look closely enough at her windshield to see past the glare bouncing off it, it would be obvious what is happening.

When Iris hesitates, I think I pushed too far, but there's the tiniest smirk on her lips telling me I haven't.

"Tell me, Iris," I instruct.

"Soaked," she whispers, holding my eye contact.

"Let go," I beg, lightly massaging her inner thigh with my fingers. "Let me touch you."

With a sigh, she releases her muscles and tips her knees apart, letting her head fall against the headrest as her whole body relaxes. I push my hand under that skirt, letting it bunch around my wrist until I find her just as she promised, completely drenched. I hook my fingers in the scrap of material, and when Iris lifts her hips up, I yank her underwear down her legs.

When I straighten again, Iris has spread her knees even further. I hold my two middle fingers before her lips.

"Suck," I instruct, and she eagerly obeys, sliding her tongue over my fingers as she pulls them deep into her mouth. When she sucks hard, I pull them back out with a soft *pop*. "We don't have time," I chastise.

When I put my hand back under her skirt and find her clit, Iris's entire body jerks. I've barely touched her, and she's already close. The mewling sound she makes when I stroke the bundle of nerves nearly brings me to my knees.

Without warning, I move my fingers down and drive them into her, curling against her front wall while my thumb reconnects with her swollen clit.

I lean my other forearm against the door frame, so it'll look like we're just having a private conversation to anybody who might wander down here, and Iris presses her forehead against my shoulder, her breaths coming out in little pants.

I know it won't take long to get her there, now familiar with the way her eyes close and her breathing changes just before she comes. I keep working her, chasing those soft sounds she makes. She was made for this, made for *me*.

"Eli," she pants, her walls squeezing my fingers. "I want you."

"I know," I answer. "But we can't right now, so give this to me. I want to feel you come on my hand."

Iris's hands fly to my forearm, squeezing and adjusting me to right where she wants. When I feel her start coming around me, I bend over her, pouring my need into our kiss, devouring her as she rides my fingers. I stay inside her even after she stills and releases my arms. I can feel her pulsing around me and commit the feeling to memory.

Slowly, I pull my fingers out of Iris, reverently stroking her as I do. A full-body shiver is my reward.

"You did so good," I praise, pressing a kiss to her hair before I bend to retrieve her thong. It's grey like her skirt. Instead of putting it back on her, I clean my fingers on the material before balling it and shoving it in the front pocket of my pants.

"I'm keeping these," I say, and Iris looks at me like she's wondering where I got the audacity.

CHAPTER 36

Iris

Ho-*ly shit.*

When I wake up the next morning before my alarm, I still can't believe I spent all day yesterday going commando. All because Eli *stole* my underwear!

I'm hot and frustrated, but when I slip my own hand into my sleep shorts, it feels like a sad replacement for what I really want. I know I could still get myself there, and it would feel nice and maybe even give me some relief, but I want the anticipation of not knowing what Eli will do next, the weight of his body, the warmth of his touch, the comfort of his instructions.

I can't sleep. I can't even relax. My mind just keeps showing me the look of desire in Eli's eyes when he watched me come. I've never felt more wanted. When I couldn't stop hearing the sound of Eli's groans on Sunday, I started to think I'd lost my mind.

But if Eli's feeling this too…

The morning absolutely crawls by. I know checking the clock every seventeen seconds doesn't help, but I can't seem to stop. I try to focus on work, but I'm all over the place. I still do good work—I care too much about this job not to—but I'm not nearly as productive as I can be.

As soon as it hits a reasonable time to take lunch, I let Harry know I'm heading out and basically sprint to my car. I just need to drive around a little and clear my head.

Unsurprising to probably anybody but me, I pull into the parking lot for Wilcox Nursery. It's quiet when I walk inside, with nobody behind the register.

"Hello?" I call out.

"Iris?" Eli's voice answers from deeper in the greenhouse a moment before his head appears over some small potted trees.

"Hey." I wave and begin making my way toward him. "What are you up to?"

"What should have been done weeks ago." Eli huffs, a terra-cotta pot held in each of his strong hands. I pick up a third and follow behind him as he explains, "There were all these little things that needed to be finished in the new greenhouse, and we kept getting distracted by other projects, then Jake couldn't decide on a table layout, so we never got around to moving the plants into the new space. I was going crazy staring at my computer and made this my break."

We turn the corner at the back of the structure, and I get my first real look at the new greenhouse. It almost triples the space they used to have, wrapping around the back and other side of the office space like a U. Even with most of the new tables only sparsely covered with plants, the space is warm and damp, causing the glass to fog until it's nearly opaque against the cold outside.

Eli sets his plants down before relieving me of mine. He finally turns to fully look at me.

"Hi," he says with a coy smile that lazily spreads across his lips. "And thank you. But I expect you didn't come here to move ferns. Is everything ok?"

I really don't have a reason for coming other than wanting to see Eli… or touch him… or lick him. But that feels inappropriate to say, and I don't think it's within our agreement.

"Oh, uh. I just wanted to… see you," I admit sheepishly. "Is that ok?"

He smiles in a way that makes this all feel real. "It's more than ok."

"I can't stop thinking about yesterday," I say. "You know, in my car?"

Eli leans back against the long plywood table. He rubs his thumb against his fingertips between us like he's remembering the feeling of my wetness there.

"Trust me, I remember." His line of sight seems to get unfocused, as I expect he replays the memory.

"It was unexpected… and exciting." I nod. "I just—"

I don't know what to say that won't ruin this, but I can't keep existing like this, wondering what's real and what's part of our act because it all feels pretty fucking real.

I huff out a breath in frustration before I just go for it.

"Is this more? With us. Is it… something? Am I crazy?"

Eli's expression tightens, and I immediately regret my question. I should have just kept my mouth shut. We were clear with expectations up front.

He looks skyward, taking a minute to collect himself. At least I can take comfort in the fact that it's seemingly not easy for him to let me down. That's something, right? He looks back at me, his eyes full of emotion.

"It's more," he says, and I swear the world stutters around me. *It's more.*

"And I don't know what to do with that. I don't do more. I don't think I *can* do more, but we're here, and you're not crazy. It's more," he continues.

"What does that mean?" I ask, trying to stay grounded and not skip off into la-la dream land on him admitting he feels something too.

He roughly drags his hand over the lower half of his face.

"I don't know. I don't exactly plan things in my life," he admits, looking helpless. "But I don't want to stop, and I know that's not fair to you but—"

"I don't want to stop either," I interrupt. I don't want to know what comes after that *but*. I'm being selfish, clinging to what's good now—I know that. But I want to be a little selfish right now. "I like this too. I don't want to drag you into something you don't want, though."

"Iris, you could do whatever the fuck you want to me right now, and I'd let you," Eli rasps. "I don't stop thinking about you. Ever."

Oh. This is *more*.

My instincts kick into high gear, and a thousand questions flood my brain. Is he trying? Will he stick around after Archer leaves? Does he want to?

But there's panic in Eli's eyes, so I don't ask any of them. I swallow down what I want to know—some of which I deserve to know—and touch his arm. He tracks my every movement with such intensity that I might as well be laid bare before him.

"So, we continue," I suggest.

"We continue," he parrots.

I want to say more, but we hear the front door open at the same time.

"Eli? Whose car is out front?" Jake calls back to us.

Neither of us responds, but I nod at Eli, trying to tell him this is ok.

"Oh, hi Iris," Jake says as he comes around the corner.

"Hi Jake," I answer, unnecessarily shifting my bag further up my shoulder. I feel fidgety. My phone buzzes, and I ignore a call from Lemon. I've been squirrelly with her for a couple of weeks, and I think she's getting suspicious. "I should actually get going."

Jake's eyes narrow as he takes us both in, especially when Eli doesn't look away from me.

I squeeze Eli's arm before I step back, turning and hurrying past Jake to the front of the nursery.

"What was that?" Jake asks quietly.

When I look back over my shoulder, Eli is still watching me, but he makes the smallest, almost imperceptible nod.

This is going to be ok.

CHAPTER 37

Eli

I blew Jake off yesterday when he tried to continue questioning me about Iris's visit. I admitted to her that I felt more, but I'm not ready to tell anybody else, not even Jake. It already feels too real in a way that terrifies and thrills me at the same time.

Maybe I can do this. With Iris… maybe I can do this. But I want to find out for myself without the pressure of anybody else's expectations.

I plan on hurrying past his desk before he can think about re-raising his line of questioning from yesterday, but the expression on his face stops me in my tracks.

"What is it?" I ask without greeting.

"There's a letter for you from the CPA board," he says from his seat behind his desk, holding out the envelope for me.

I'm not up for renewal, so a weight drops into my stomach, and it grows when I see the word *ethics* in the return address. I rip into the envelope and unfold the pages inside so urgently I almost tear them. My eyes fly over the sheets before I read the top page again more slowly.

This can't be happening.

Somebody's filed a complaint against me for a potential ethics violation. Words like *integrity* and *conflict of interest* and *objectivity* stand out like they're screaming at me.

Even before I flip to the page with the complainant's contact information, I know in my soul who filed it.

"Eli," Jake starts cautiously as he gets to his feet. "What is it?"

"Iris's ex is coming for my license," I summarize. "He's claiming I created a conflict of interest by becoming personally involved with an employee of a business I provide tax services to, and that there's a further conflict because Iris is Harry's niece, and Harry is my client."

"Dumb it down for me. What does that mean practically?" Jake circles his desk and takes the letter from me, eyes darting down each page like mine did.

"*Practically* it means I have to do bullshit paperwork." I drag a hand down my face. This guy is a real piece of work.

Mentally, I start cycling through everything I know about the ethics rules. I know I did everything above board. Disclosure of the relationship, quality of the work, consistency in fee for the return… I don't fuck with those rules.

"He's got nothing?" Jake surmises.

"He's got nothing. But I still need to answer the complaint and provide evidence that I didn't do anything I shouldn't have. And I doubt it looks good to have an ethics complaint against me, even a completely frivolous one." I put my hands on my hips and look up at the ceiling, breathing slowly in through my nose and out through my mouth so I don't give into the urge to find Archer's stupid little sports car and slash all four tires.

He's coming after my *livelihood*. I can't lose this license.

Jake's strong hand grips my shoulder and helps ground me.

"I'm sorry, Eli," he says, ever the calm and rational one. "If you need anything—character witness statement, whatever—I've got you. This whole town has got you."

"I know." It doesn't mean I don't want to drive into the woods and yell as loud as I can.

After a lot of internal debate, I decide not to tell Iris about the letter over the phone—it doesn't feel right. I consider not telling her at all since I don't want to add to her stress, but I don't want Archer to have anything he can try to surprise her with, to throw her off balance.

Plus, I'm new to it, but I'm pretty sure *more* means I shouldn't keep this a secret from her.

On Thursday morning, after only a few hours of sleep, I get up and out of my house early. I need to see Iris.

Since I don't have a lot of time—I still have a ton of work to do, *and* I need to compile my response to the complaint—I decide to intercept her between school drop-off and work. First, I swing by Barefoot Bake for a bag of pastries and enough espresso to fill a large to-go cup. I park near the cluster of schools on Main Street and lean against my hood to wait.

I watch Iris's Explorer join the kindergarten drop-off line and raise my hand when she spots me. I ignore the feeling in my torso when she smiles through her window and will my heart rate to slow the fuck down when she parks behind the Jeep after leaving Sam at school.

"Hi," is all Iris has a chance to get out when she walks up to me before I wrap an arm around her waist and squeeze her to me, eliciting a small *"oomph"* from her when she falls against my chest.

I tell myself I don't know why I did that. I came to talk, but first, I just needed to feel her, to hold her, to breathe her in. When she slips her arms around my middle, all the tension I've been holding releases, and something calm spreads in my chest.

"I've missed you," Iris murmurs so quietly I wonder if she meant to say it.

"Me too." I *know* I mean it. "I have to buckle down again today, so I wanted to at least bring you breakfast," I say, lifting the paper bag off the hood of my car and handing it to her. "And, I have to tell you something."

"Ok…" Iris says, dragging out the word before her brow furrows a beat later, and she guesses where I'm going. "What did he do?"

I decide to take the direct approach, like ripping off a Band-Aid. "He filed a complaint with the CPA licensing board claiming I've violated my duty to act with integrity."

"He *what?* What does that mean for you? What's going to happen?" Her fingers begin working the paper of the pastry bag, folding and unfolding the top flap. I place one of my hands over hers to still the movement.

"Nothing. Nothing is going to happen. I have to answer the complaint, but since I didn't do what he's claiming, it will get dismissed." I spent yesterday going back through every line of the code of conduct, so I'm confident I'll be ok.

"It's still an ethics complaint against you. I assume that's not good." When she looks up at me, the expression in her eyes is a battle of anger and sorrow.

"It's baseless, and I can show that. I just wanted you to know in case he tried to use it to prove I'm a bad guy or something."

Iris scoffs. "I know the type of man you are, Eli."

Her shoulders slump like she's been hit with a wave of exhaustion, and I wrap an arm around her again, urging her forward until she can lean against me. I wish I could carry this weight for her.

"I'm sorry. He's doing this because of me, and I'm so sorry."

She presses her face into my jacket, like if she tries hard enough, she can hide from this whole mess. After being so strong for so many weeks of this, I don't blame her.

"No. He's doing this because he's a shit human being. This is not your fault." I smooth my hand over the back of her head. "This is a desperate attempt by a pathetic man."

"I'm a little scared, Eli," she confesses.

"I know. We'll get through this." And when I say it, the word *we* doesn't scare me like it usually does.

I want to stand with her like this all day, but we both need to get to work, and she steps back after another minute.

"Are things still very busy?" she asks.

"I'll be able to finish in time." I evade her question. I *will* manage.

"Should I be worrying about you and how much you're working?" Iris asks, touching her fingertips to my jaw.

With her touching me, I can't find it in myself to be bothered by a single thing.

"Nah." I shake my head. "I'll be alright. This is temporary. But what about you? We talked about my Archer update, but has he bothered you anymore?"

"He sent more flowers to the office on Tuesday, so I think he's officially cycled through all his 'romantic' ideas. Uncle Harry threw them out before I even got in." She shakes her head in frustration. "I really thought he'd give up by now, but going after you is unbelievable. I'm going to talk to Harry more about our legal options. Considering how long this has gone on, we might have something now, and I don't want Archer escalating further or showing up during Sam's school break next week."

"If you decide to confront him, just promise me you won't go alone. I know you can handle yourself, but I don't want you taking any risks. That means not doing anything about this CPA complaint either. I've got that covered."

"I promise," Iris says before leaning up on her toes to reach for a kiss. I want to melt into her. "You should go, though. Finish up so I can see you again."

If that's not motivation, I don't know what is.

After Iris pulls away, I get into my car and back to work.

CHAPTER 38

Iris

I think of Eli for my whole drive to the office. I worry, not for the first time, that I'm taking advantage of him. This business with his license makes it feel, now more than ever, that his life is being wrecked, and for what? For me?

For… more?

When I walk into the firm, I hear Harry in my office.

"Hello? Is anybody there?" he asks, but it doesn't sound like he's talking to me.

When I poke my head around the corner, I see him setting the phone back on the receiver.

"Iris," Harry greets when he spots me. "Your phone's been ringing off the hook for the last five minutes, but it's a blocked number, and there's never anybody on the line. I don't know if it's a problem with the phone or somebody who has taken up prank calling."

"That's not good," I say, getting a bad feeling. "If it keeps happening, I'll call the phone company."

The phone starts ringing again, and Harry groans in frustration.

"I've got it," I say with a sympathetic smile. I see *Unknown* flash on the caller ID, and I know in my gut it's not a problem with the line.

"Sutton and Associates," I answer, my skin prickling with anticipation.

"Iris?" Archer's unmistakable voice answers.

I *knew* it.

"What the hell game are you playing?" I ask, a bite already in my tone. My eyes flash to Harry, who quickly figures out who I'm talking to from the way I answer.

"I've been waiting for you to get in. Your uncle kept answering," he says, like it excuses his behavior. "I tried your cell, but it wouldn't go through. Did you change your number?"

"I blocked you. Take a hint."

Harry holds a finger to his lips before he points to the speaker button on the phone stand. I nod, pressing the button and setting down the receiver so Harry can hear everything Archer says too.

"We need to talk," he says, irritation clear in his voice. "I'm *trying* to show I'm responsible, and you're making it really fucking hard."

"I cannot be any clearer. You and I will never happen." It feels like I'm talking to a brick wall.

"You don't understand what I'm dealing with. That isn't an option. Is this about your townie boyfriend?" Archer's voice gets sinister when he brings up Eli.

"You don't want to go there," I warn. I keep my voice calm even though I feel anything but. It's only a desire to avoid making things worse for Eli that keeps me from tearing into Archer about the ethics complaint. That, and I promised I wouldn't. "My relationship with Eli is none of your business. *Nothing* about Eli is any of your business."

"It is when you're making out with him outside of Samantha's school. It's an embarrassment for the both of us. This quarter life crisis with him needs to end," he seethes.

My head starts to swim as Archer's voice rises. How *dare* he comment on who I spend my time with or what I do with them? I'm a grown-ass woman and—

I feel a prickling sensation on my cheeks as all the blood drains from my face and realization dawns on me.

"How do you know Eli and I kissed this morning?" I ask, but I know the answer.

"I—" Archer cuts off, apparently realizing his mistake.

Harry realizes it too.

"What were you doing outside of Samantha's school, Archer? Are you following Iris?" he cuts in.

"Harry, this has nothing to do with you. I'm being *responsible*. Just because Iris is resisting this, it doesn't mean Sam wouldn't want her father. I have every right to see my daughter, to try to bring my family home," Archer snaps.

"Actually, you don't." Harry's tone is curt, furious.

"What, but some guy who has no kid in that school can linger across the street like a fucking creep?" Archer's volume keeps going up.

"Eli has more ties to *my* daughter than you ever will." I find my voice again.

I can't believe he got that close to Samantha. How often has he done that? Has he seen her? Has he spoken to her?

"You don't understand what I have at risk here," Archer yells again, unraveling. "I—"

"No. You *nothing*. I'm done playing whatever stupid game you think is going on here. Get it through your thick skull. You and I are *finished*. Stay the hell away from me and my kid. It's harassment, Archer, stalking. And I'm done fucking around." I lift the phone and slam it back down to end the call.

I look back up at Harry. "Anything we've got a chance of getting to stick, I want to throw it at him," I say. I want him gone. "I don't know if he's following me or trying to get contact with

Sam, but I've had more than enough. Also, he filed a bullshit ethics complaint against Eli with the CPA licensing board. This has to stop."

"He did what?" Harry starts, but I hold up a hand. I can't get into it right now. Harry nods, understanding. "Isabella and I will handle it personally," he says with a squeeze of my hand before he heads straight to her office.

I call Samantha's school and must sound like a lunatic when I demand the receptionist check with her teacher and the drop-off and pick-up attendants for this week and last week to make sure nobody has tried to get to Samantha. I probably seem unhinged when I refuse to get off the line until she asks them all.

"Miss Sutton, I've personally checked with everybody. Nobody has gotten anywhere near Samantha. Nobody has come in asking about her."

It doesn't make me feel better. I describe Archer's car. If he was there and nobody saw, that might be worse.

Her voice is muffled as she likely sets the phone down to ask about the car.

"We have noticed the car before, but it's never been in school limits. Is something happening? Do you need to come get Samantha?" the woman asks in a small voice. I think I've frightened her.

"No," I answer, even though I want to say yes. I don't want to scare Sam. I'm terrified enough for the both of us.

I'm probably rude when I hang up, and I'm sure I'll feel guilty about it later. But not now.

I want to call Eli and tell him what happened, but he's already prioritized me and this Archer situation over himself far too much. He looked so tired this morning, and I feel awful about it.

I take a few deep breaths to focus and pull up my old research on restraining orders. I just wish I knew what to do next. I want to be trained, prepared. I need to do more.

After work, Uncle Harry follows behind me to Sam's school. I feel like I'm going to give myself whiplash with how much I look around. Thankfully, neither Harry nor I see any sign of Archer or his car. Under the premise of joining us for dinner—which he does do—Harry also follows us home.

Long discussions and a lot of thinking today led me to finally decide to pursue a civil restraining order against Archer. I will not risk Sam's safety, and knowing Archer was outside her school… no. No more.

I think I'm going to be on edge until we get the court order, and I appreciate that Harry saves my pride and protects peace in our home, insisting he's hanging around just because he misses Sam and not because anything's wrong.

Still, I need her to be safe, so during dinner, Harry and I try to naturally ask if she's made any new friends or met any new grown-ups. She says she hasn't and miraculously doesn't notice our unusual line of questioning. We remind her of the rules about not talking to strangers and about never going anywhere with anybody, even if they claim to know her or tell her Mama or somebody else said it's ok.

"Mama, I know that." She rolls her eyes, but I ask her to repeat the rules back to me anyway. Maybe she *can* tell something's up because she does so without objection.

It's a good thing I barely touched my food because having to go over this with her makes my stomach roll.

After Sam's gone to bed, Harry heads home. He hung around until Olivia got here and insisted I stay on the phone with him in the morning from the moment I leave my house until I get to work. As soon as Olivia's gotten in the shower, I finally text Eli.

ME

Hey. You have a minute?

I watch the dots indicating he's typing bounce at the bottom of my screen, but they disappear after a moment. Bounce… gone. Apparently, Eli gives up on trying to write something, because my phone buzzes with his call.

"Hey. You didn't need to call. I don't want to disrupt your flow," I say.

"Breaks are good for me, and I like hearing from you. What's up?"

"I decided to move forward with filing for a civil restraining order against Archer," I say.

Silence fills the line in the wake of my announcement.

"Iris, is this because of the complaint? I don't want you feeling like you have to do things you don't want to because of me." Eli sounds more serious than I've ever heard him.

"There's more. He flipped out because he saw us kiss outside Sam's school. He's been hanging around outside Sam's *school*." My voice breaks on the last word, and I cough to try to hide it. Nothing happened, and it makes me feel weak to react so strongly to what is essentially still nothing.

"Fuck," Eli bites out. "Is Sam ok? Are you ok?"

"We're both ok. As far as I can tell, he hasn't approached her, but something about his tone today felt off. He kept saying I didn't understand what's at risk—and I don't—but I'm not about to wait around and see what he's willing to do."

"I don't want to say something that will make me sound like an asshole or make things worse, but even if you get the order, what's stopping him from doing something drastic anyway?"

It's a fair question. Will a piece of paper stop him from taking Sam? Is that what he plans to do?

"It'd be the threat of ruining his life. His dad is a very proud man with a pristine reputation. And he's somebody who would react out of spite. I wouldn't be surprised if he'd write Archer out of his will if Archer embarrassed him," I explain.

"If that's the case, have you considered calling him to tell him what Archer is doing now?" Eli suggests.

"I have," I admit. "But Mr. Ringwald is not a kind man and never took my side with Archer. It would very likely backfire. He's also never sought any rights with Sam, and I like having him completely out of my life. He's much smarter than Archer, and with his money and influence…"

Olivia trips upstairs and I gasp. She closes her bedroom door, and the house is silent once again.

"What? What's wrong?" Eli asks, concern lacing his voice.

"Nothing, I'm sorry. It was just Olivia upstairs. I'm a bit jumpy."

I rub my fist into my chest over my heart, annoyed by how it's thumping so hard. There's another pause on the line while I do.

"If I came over right now, would you kick me out?" Eli asks.

"Eli, I know you're still working. Sam and I are safe here with Olivia."

"Would you kick me out?" he repeats, ignoring my protest.

I know he won't come without permission. It's selfish and dumb and way beyond the scope of what he signed up for, but I want him here.

"No," I say in a small voice.

"I'm on my way."

I expect Eli to hang up, but there are a few moments of rustling before I hear Eli's keys, his front door open and close, footsteps on stairs, and him getting in the Jeep.

We don't speak on the drive, but the soft sound of his rhythmic breathing is comforting. I jump to my feet when I hear his car outside, but Eli still doesn't hang up until I open my front door, and he sees me with his own eyes.

When I step aside to let him in, I see he has a small overnight bag as well as his laptop bag, and I worry again about taking him from work.

"I can work just as easily on your couch as at my place, so stop feeling guilty," Eli says with a half-smile like he's reading my mind. "It'll make me feel better to be here. Just in case. Ok?"

I nod, but something cracks in me. I feel a rush of emotion and that telltale tightness in my chest, so I step toward him and wrap my arms around his waist, pressing my face against him so he won't see me start to cry. The quake in my shoulders is a dead giveaway anyway.

Eli's hand comes to my hair, smoothing it back over and over, while the beat of his heart against my ear is the drum I use to center myself again.

"Do you think you could work in my room instead?" I ask quietly when I finally think my voice won't sound wet and pathetic.

"I'll be wherever you want me to be," Eli whispers back.

I hastily wipe a hand across both of my cheeks before leading Eli upstairs to my bedroom.

"Pick whichever side you want," I say. "I'm just going to let Olivia know you're here in case she didn't hear you come in."

I knock and crack Olivia's door. She starts to get up when she sees what I expect is my very splotchy face peeking in.

"It's ok," I say to stop her. "Eli came over, and I had a moment. He's going to stay tonight if that's ok."

Olivia continues crossing the room to me anyway.

"Of course it is. I want you to feel safe," she says, wrapping her arms around me.

After basking in her strength for a moment, I head back to my room to find Eli changed into pajama pants and propped against my headboard with his laptop open. Only the small lamp beside him is still on, and shadows stretch across his broad torso.

He looks up, and I stop. He's wearing black-framed glasses that I've never seen on him before, and in spite of the emotional roller coaster I've been on today, I can appreciate how they look on him.

"What?" he asks, and I wonder how stupid my expression became when they saw his slutty little glasses.

"I like your glasses," I say as I continue to the bed and climb in on the other side.

He chuckles, enjoying the reaction.

"Blue light glasses for the longer days," he explains.

I feel his eyes on me while I set my morning alarm. When I'm finished, he lifts the arm between us, and I slide over until I'm tucked against his side. His wraps himself around me, and it feels like nothing can touch me here.

"Don't you need that arm?" I ask.

"No. It's where it needs to be," he says.

I didn't expect to be able to sleep tonight after everything that's happened, but I suddenly feel exhausted.

"Goodnight Eli," I murmur, and I'm asleep before I can hear his answer.

CHAPTER 39

Eli

I work late into the night, but with Iris's warm breath brushing against my side every few seconds, it isn't so bad at all. Eventually, I close my laptop, set it aside, turn off the light, and slide down in bed, careful not to wake Iris. I remember the time of her first alarm and set my own for fifteen minutes prior. Then, I fall into the deepest and most restful sleep I've had in a while.

When I'm pulled back awake by my phone buzzing on the nightstand, I feel content, and I see the hazy memory of Iris and Sam smiling together on the frozen lake.

Reluctantly, I drag my eyes open and reach for my phone to silence it before it disturbs Iris. She's already shifting against me, though, so I know I wasn't quick enough.

"What time is it?" she murmurs softly, her hand tightening around my biceps.

"It's early. I'm going to slip out before Sam wakes up."

Iris doesn't object, but the pout on her face tells me she's unhappy about it anyway. When I rub my hand up and down her arm, her sleepy expression softens. It tugs at something deep within me, and I very badly want to stay here with her.

"Don't worry," I assure her. "I plan on taking her to school with you and then driving you to work, so I'll be knocking on your door in just a few minutes. I'm going to be sticking to you when you're alone, if that's alright, at *least* until you file that restraining order. I'd apologize for being overbearing, but I'm not sorry."

To my surprise, she doesn't fight me. In fact, she melts a little further into me.

"It's alright with me. I feel better having you as Sam's bodyguard." She pauses. "Mine too."

I curl over her and kiss her hair before extracting myself from her bed and dressing as quickly and quietly as I can. When I look over my shoulder at her, I find her blatantly watching me. I give her a reproachful look, but she just shrugs like *what do you expect?*

Even though I can still hear Sam's even breathing through her cracked door, I tiptoe through the house and don't put on my shoes until I'm by the door. As I'm tying them, I spot Iris's keys on a small table and quickly push the button to unlock her Explorer.

The sun is up, but the light is soft, and the world is still waking up around me while the house behind me comes to life. Even though it's just over a week until the first day of spring, it's still bitterly cold, the crystallized snow shows no sign of melting, and only a few birds have migrated back, so things are still and quiet.

I want to give Iris a few minutes to get Sam up and going before I make my "arrival," so I pass the time by moving Sam's car seat into the Jeep.

My whole life, I've considered myself a relatively intelligent man with decent handyman skills, but after an indeterminate amount of time doing a full-out battle with this car seat, I feel incompetent. No matter what I do, it doesn't feel tight, and I'm certain it isn't supposed to lean to the left like that. When I jiggle it to check for stability, it flops forward against the back of the passenger seat.

Frustrated and getting nowhere, I take the L and make a mental note to ask Iris to show me the secret before Sam gets in the damn thing.

As I turn back toward the house, I see Iris innocently holding back the curtain at the front window, looking radiant as ever. She's gotten dressed in a white flowy top with a bow tied at the top of her sternum, and I have the indisputable urge to unwrap her.

She jerks her head, telling me to come back inside, and who am I to disobey?

I head to the front door and knock for showmanship. Even though I know she's standing right on the other side of the door, Iris waits a few minutes before opening the door, like she wasn't expecting me.

"Good morning," she says, with a knowing glint in her eye.

As a smile threatens to break out on my lips, I do my best not to think about how nice it was to wake up beside her. My eyes flit down, and there's that bow, tempting me.

That's *much* worse.

"Eli's here," Iris calls to the other occupants of the house.

Olivia comes downstairs first, waving and not at all letting on that she knows I was here all night. Perfect.

"I'm glad you're here, Eli," she says.

"Do me a favor and be careful too, ok?" I don't want to be irrational about my concern, but I don't know Archer well enough to know what he is or isn't capable of.

Olivia pulls a pair of pruning shears out of the pocket of her fluffy pink robe without hesitation.

"I dare him to try me," she says, flicking off the locking mechanism lightning quick and brandishing them with a menacing grin that has me both comforted about her safety and a little afraid of her.

I don't have to guess what she'd be cutting off if Archer came for her.

"Do you have those on you all the time?" I ask.

She's still in pajamas and fuzzy socks, but she's packing those?

"Yeah, why?" she responds, looking honestly puzzled by the question.

Sam's clopping steps sounding on the stairs save me from having to get into a discussion about standard robe pocket contents with Liv.

"Hi human Eli," Samantha greets me with a gigantic yawn on her way to the kitchen island, where she crawls her way up onto a chair. "Why did you leave and come back?"

She plops Robin on the counter and starts pouring cereal into a bowl, spilling a not insignificant amount of it on the counter in the process.

Iris, Olivia, and I all exchange alarmed looks. *Busted.*

"What?" Iris asks her daughter.

"Eli was here, and then he left, and then he came back," Sam says slowly, like she doesn't understand why we're all dumb.

I never heard her wake up. I didn't leave anything out. I can't figure out how she knows, but she knows.

"Oh," Iris continues tentatively. "Is that… ok? That he was here?"

"Do you want breakfast?" Sam asks, twisting in her chair to look at me and ignoring her mother's question entirely.

"Sure," I say with a shrug, walking up to stand at the counter beside Sam as Iris slides a bowl to me with a shrug of her own.

I think we're just going to go with it. But Olivia needs to put her eyes back in her skull before her expression invites more questions from the most observant kid on the planet.

Sam happily fills my bowl before I top both of us off with milk. Any concern I had about this being awkward now that she caught me in her house dissipates. She's acting like this is the most normal thing on the planet.

And maybe it is.

Once we're ready to head out, I sheepishly admit to Iris that her car seat got the best of me. Of course she reaches in and locks it into place with one forceful movement. Easy-peasy.

"It's all in the wrist," she teases, tapping the center of my chest with the back of her hand after checking Sam's harness.

I roll my eyes as I yank open the passenger door for her.

"Get in the car, Iris."

She obeys, chuckling with satisfaction as she goes.

The car is quiet on the drive over to Sam's school, and I know Iris's eyes are cycling from one mirror to the next just like mine are. I don't know if it's because she can feel the tension in the car, but Sam stays silent too.

Iris hops out of the Jeep when it's our turn in the drop-off line, helping Sam down, taking her hand, and walking her right into the school. Looking at the cars in front of and behind me, I can tell that's not always standard procedure, but we're not taking chances here.

The haunted look on Iris's face as she gets back into the car will stay with me for a while. She breathes a heavy sigh as she clicks her seatbelt in, and I wish I knew what to say to make this better. The ugly truth is that words can't help here. She's scared for her kid, and I expect there's nothing comparable to that feeling.

I can't...

So, I reach across the console and hold her hand, silently telling her I'm with her. I will help her keep Sam safe. And my mind runs wild trying to come up with ways for me to do more.

Once I get to the firm, I pull as close as I can to the porch and wave when Harry opens the front door, ready to collect Iris like a relay racer. I hate that we have to do this, but I appreciate that she's got people looking out for her.

"I'll be here by four to pick you up," I promise.

"Thank you," Iris says, giving my hand a squeeze before she lets go. "And I'm sorry for disrupting your life. I could ask Harry for a ride or—"

"Let me help you," I say, willing her to agree.

"Ok," she accepts. "I'll see you at four."

I stay until she's inside and the door is closed. Is it overkill? Maybe, but I'm not willing to take the risk.

CHAPTER 40

Iris

When 4:00 comes around, I'm finally feeling the first breath of relief I've had since Archer came to Wilcox Grove almost a month ago, and it's a stark contrast to how I've felt for the last day and a half.

Harry and Isabella worked their asses off so Harry could file the restraining order today. Harry even called Allen, our police chief and one of the most discreet people Wilcox Grove has to offer, and got him to agree to serve Archer first thing Monday.

This is far from over, but it finally feels like I'm a step ahead, acting on offense instead of constantly defending. And it feels good.

Archer hasn't called all day. He hasn't shown up. It wouldn't be in his interest to do so either, and assuming he understood my threat yesterday as truthful, he knows that. I'm cautiously optimistic he finally understands his situation with respect to me and Sam.

Isabella waits with me by the front door until Eli's Jeep pulls into our lot and swings around to pick me up. She gives me a quick hug for strength before I bound toward the car, ready to tell Eli the good news.

"Something good happen?" Eli reads my excitement as I buckle myself in.

"We filed the restraining order. Archer is getting served on Monday." I'm practically bouncing in my seat.

I'm *extremely* grateful we haven't started driving yet when Eli's hands find my face and guides me toward him. I don't even have time to breathe in before his lips are on mine, hungry and smiling. Then, we're laughing into each other's mouths, and he's pressing his forehead to mine, and I can feel his eyelashes against my cheekbones.

"Congratulations, Iris," he whispers, his lips still against my skin. "I wish it didn't come to this, but today is a very good day."

I nod as much as I can, my face still cradled in Eli's capable hands.

"Let's go get Sam," Eli says, and he's making all of this sound so much like a "we" that it hurts.

Sammy is always happy when I collect her on Fridays—it's new book day—but with this one being right before her March break, she's particularly excited.

"Hi human Eli!" Sam exclaims when I open the back seat door for her.

Eli braces a hand on the passenger seat headrest to help him pivot in his seat toward Samantha.

"Hey, kiddo," he says back. "How was school?"

As Sam answers him, my eyes fall on Eli's hand. Everything with Archer had me twisted up in knots last night, but seeing him in this moment, giving my kid his undivided attention, being protective and supportive of us both…

He dropped everything to just be by my side last night, this morning, now, in spite of his own shit going on.

I swallow hard, knowing I'm in deep trouble with this man and his *very* nice hands.

Him spending the drive to Literary Lake animatedly talking to

Sam about her day doesn't help my situation in the slightest. I'm a package deal, and he has never even blinked about the fact that Sam is here too.

As soon as we head over to the bookstore, Piper waves at us from the desk.

"Head on upstairs. I'll get our cocoa and come meet you in a minute," he says to me before handing Robin off to Sam. Eli had been dutifully carrying the cat at Sam's request.

"Put her in your pocket so you don't lose her," he instructs.

The lending section of the store is peacefully quiet. Mads is shelving a few rows over, but the upstairs area is otherwise deserted.

Once she sets her old books on the bottom shelf of the return cart, Sam makes a beeline for the kid's section, starting with picture books like she always does. She'll move on to chapter books after and pick some things for me to read to her.

While she falls into her routine, I sink to the floor on the opposite side of the aisle, leaning back against the shelves and breathing in the perfect smell of books.

It's been a while since my thoughts have been quiet, and the relief from today hits me hard, making my limbs feel heavy, and my head feel light, like I could just float away. I look over at Sam, sitting on the floor with her legs stuck straight out, flipping pages on books she can't read yet, and I know I'd walk through fire for her.

When I hear footsteps coming closer, I don't need to turn and look. I know by now what Eli sounds like, quiet and gentle. He folds himself nimbly, dropping to the floor beside me, and that smell of wind and earth and leather wraps around me with a bonus of chocolate this time.

I take my cup from him, enjoying the warmth through the paper. Without a word, I let my head fall against his shoulder, and after a few moments, our breathing aligns, and we watch Sam thriving without a care in the world.

Eli is what I've always wanted in a partner. I've tried not to let myself want it, but I do hope he stays after things are done with Archer. He's a part of us now, but if more is too much…

The thought creates a lingering ache that won't quite let go. These last few weeks have taught me I'm far from alone in this life, and the years before have taught me I can handle more than I expect, but I don't want to have to handle him leaving our lives.

As Sam puts her choices in a neat pile, I lift my head off Eli.

"Are you sad, Mama?" Sam asks as she comes up to me, her little head tilted to the side.

"No, baby girl. You make me very happy." I squeeze her against me before taking Eli's hand and letting him pull me up.

Sam leads the way back to the stairs while Eli and I follow behind her.

As I walk beside Eli, I'm struck with how little time we may have left as a couple. With Archer getting served on Monday, we're going to have to talk about this. Maybe I am sad after all.

Of course, Eli notices. While Sam takes her books to Piper like a big girl, he leans close to me.

"You ok?" he asks.

I nod. A lie.

"I'm exhausted," I say. Not a lie. "I think I want to stay in with Olivia and Sam tonight."

I feel a pang of guilt at my passive-aggressiveness, but I think I need a beat alone.

Eli presses his lips to the top of my hair.

"Whatever you need," he murmurs softly. "Let me take you two home."

After an extra-long reading session, Sam finally falls asleep. I head to my bedroom and quietly close the door. Sitting in the middle of my bed, I make a call I should have made weeks ago.

"Hey Lemon," I say when my sister picks up. "I've got some things to tell you."

Lemon isn't one of those "I'll stay quiet until you finish" kinds of people, so the story of me and Eli takes a while to tell. Then, she scolds me for a not insignificant amount of time for not telling her sooner about Archer sticking around and all the juicy details of what it's been like to be with Eli—though I still decline to tell her a lot of that, much to her dismay.

"I just hope this gets Archer to give up." I sigh. "Even *his* pride can't matter that much, right?"

"Tsk, tsk, tsk," Lemon clicks her tongue loudly, reminding me of our childhood arguments. "This is why you shouldn't dodge my calls, Sis. Because I think I might know something about your situation."

While Lemon moved out of our parents' house during college and hasn't moved back, she does still live in Newport and often gets insight into things that don't reach me up here. I wait for her to tell me whatever it is she thinks she's got figured out, but in typical sister fashion, she lets the suspense grow.

"Any day now, Lem," I grumble.

"The biddies around here love to gossip, and word is Earl Ringwald might be working to kick young Archer out of the family business. *Apparently*, he's sick of Archer continuing to act like a child, and unless he shows some real stability, he's out." Lemon lets her bombshell land.

It's always been assumed that Archer would follow in his father's footsteps at the hedge fund, inheriting more money than anybody needs. At least in Archer's mind, it was a foregone conclusion, no matter what happened.

"But wait," I say, realizing a flaw in this news. "If he needs to show his dad he's stable, what the hell is he doing gallivanting around Wilcox Grove? Shouldn't this be more reason for him to get back there and get to work?"

"Iris, you don't get it. I think you and Sam *are* the stability. No matter how much he denied it, everybody knows he abandoned you and a child. I think he thinks if he came home with a wife and kid in tow, he could show Daddy he's an upstanding family man and get back in without actually having to do any work."

That's insane. It's absolutely insane. But Archer is sounding a little insane these days…

Oh my god.

I think of Archer's outbursts, what he has to *lose*. Knowing what I do about Archer, it's not so insane that this would all be about his money. I sure as shit knew it wasn't about me and Sam.

That son of a bitch.

CHAPTER 41

Eli

Since Iris and Sam are safe at home with Olivia, and Alice and Piper kicked their guys out so they can do some craft for Alice's wedding, my brothers and I head to my parents' house for dinner. Jake is bringing Scott and Waffles. I'm bringing a pie from Barefoot Bake. Scott is bringing… vibes, I guess.

My parents adore him, and he's the youngest. It's fine.

It's been a while since I've visited home with everything going on—construction at the nursery, taxes, helping Iris—and Jake, Scott, and I haven't all been back together since Christmas, so it's long overdue. I love spending time with my family, even if I've been dodging my parents since Iris and I went public because I'm chickenshit.

I end up behind Jake's pickup a few minutes from my childhood home. Since he drove Scott, we all walk up to the house together. As if waiting for our arrival, like always, Mom opens the door before we can knock.

"My perfect boys." She beams, pulling us all into a hug at once, while Waffles dances around our feet, always a bundle of chaotic, happy energy.

Mom's been this way since we were kids. And their parents, June and Daniel, were the same. We were all their boys. Of course, the group hug is a bit tougher to accomplish with us guys being so big now, but we'd all die before we said anything to deny Mom.

"I was hoping next time you came home, you'd bring your new friend," Mom says quietly to me, taking my hand as we step inside. Jake, Scott, and Waffles follow behind.

That didn't take long.

Like most moms, she's been waiting for the day that I settle down with my own family. She's never pressured me to give her grandbabies, but I think she's afraid of me ending up alone. I try to explain to her that I can't be alone in this town, but moms will always worry about their kids.

"Mom…" I warn. "Iris is my *friend.*"

It's not that I don't want Iris and Mom to meet. I think they'd get along great. It's just that I'm still trying to figure out how this is going to go, and meeting the parents feels… big. These days, everything feels big. I've tried my hardest not to think about what comes next since Iris and I talked about more, but that doesn't mean it hasn't lingered… loomed… terrorized.

"I never said I was talking about Iris. You jumped there all on your own. For all you know, I meant that boy from the nursery." Mom purses her lips, and I feel like a kid again.

"Tim? Tim's been working for us for over two years, so he's hardly a *new friend*. We both know who you were talking about, Mom."

Mom huffs in a way that reminds me of a mother hen ruffling her feathers, indignant but bearing it.

As we turn the corner into the main part of the house—a large, open room that serves as a living room toward the front of the house and a dining room and kitchen splitting the space toward the back of the house—my dad raises his hands in cheer for our arrival, the electric knife in his right hand, sending bits of roast beef flying when he fails to release the trigger.

"Richard!" Mom scolds, ducking behind me to avoid the food projectile.

"Don't worry. We got this," Scott says, releasing Waffles's collar.

The pup finds every piece of roast in record time before planting himself right at Dad's side, hoping the man will drop more. Scott follows behind the dog, wiping up the slobber spots with a paper towel.

"You've always been our sweetest boy," Mom says, patting Scott on the cheek before heading to the fridge. And she's right. Scott is the nicest of us all, always has been.

"Aww, our sweet, sensitive Scott," Jake says, coming up behind him, starting with a tender pat on the shoulder before grabbing Scott around the back of his neck and violently ruffling his hair.

When Scott lived in New York, he'd kept his hair buzzed short, but he's let it grow out on top and in the back since he came home, and his curls are on full display. A sharp pang goes through my chest when I remember his mom, the source of those ringlets. I wonder if Jake thinks of their mom when he sees Scott too.

"You leave him alone," Dad scolds, brandishing his electric knife again. Waffles starts drooling on Dad's socked foot.

"But he's my *brother*," Jake whines, becoming as close to youthful as you'll ever see him when he's at the Chambers' house.

The bravado is all for show. There's nobody on this planet more protective of Scott's bleeding heart than Jake. Jake can poke fun, but if anybody else does? It ain't pretty.

Mom emerges from the fridge with three tall glasses of apple juice and passes them to me, Jake, and Scott, just like when we were little. There are even bendy straws in the glasses. Mom doesn't baby us—she treats us like grown men and expects us to know how to act like them—but these little hints of days long gone are always going to be special.

"What can we help with," I ask, but Mom waves us all off.

"Nothing," she says, gesturing to the table across from the island that Dad's cutting at. "Sit. Tell us what's been going on. How are Alice and Piper?"

Ignoring her request for us to sit and get served, we start setting the table, but we do abide her request for updates.

Jake goes first, talking about the changes at the nursery, wedding planning, Alice's classes at the college, Waffles's puppyhood. Then Scott takes his turn. He and Piper have been making major updates to their house—which used to be Alice's mom's when she was living in Wilcox Grove—so they no longer have to count how many lights are on to avoid blowing a fuse, and so the water actually comes out hot from the shower without having to wait ten minutes.

When it comes to me, I realize I don't know what to say. Somewhere along the way, Jake and Scott got these full, domestic lives that seem to make them both the happiest I've ever seen, and I've got… taxes? I don't want to worry Mom and Dad by talking about my ethics complaint, and I don't want to offer up any of Iris and Sam's story without them here. So, silence stretches, and all eyes fall on me.

"Same old," I awkwardly say when I realize nobody else is going to say anything until I do. "You know how tax season is. Debits, credits, deductions… Good stuff."

"Oh, come on," Scott scoffs. "You've had a lot more going on than just that."

I shoot him a sharp look, which he sees and blatantly ignores.

"Did you know that just last week, Eli cleared a huge part of the lake in town so he could teach Iris's daughter how to skate?" he announces, looking pleased with himself in a way that only a younger brother could.

"It wasn't just for that. We saw Archer earlier, and Iris asked if—" I try to explain, but Scott plows on, hearts forming in Mom's eyes.

"He took Iris *and* Sam, that's her daughter, to Papa's after. And they're always visiting each other at work," Scott continues, happily spilling everything he knows.

I don't even know how he found out about the work visits. I glare at Jake, since he's got to be the source of that gossip.

"That's nothing," I try to interject again. "We have to be seen—"

Again, it's like I'm not even there.

"*And* he's started driving them around—"

"Scott!" I finally shout to shut him up. "Enough."

"Eli!" The chorus of my name being shouted by Mom, Dad, and Jake slams back into me. When Waffles dips his head and makes a shamed whimper at the noise, all the fight flies out of me.

"Sorry, Scott," I immediately mutter. "It's just… You don't understand. Iris is in a dangerous situation, and I'm just trying to help her and Sam stay safe. Making it into some romantic joke isn't funny."

Scott looks just as deflated as Waffles does. Jake looks pissed, but he isn't about to get between us. Sometimes, brothers just need to work shit out. He knows that.

"I don't think it's a joke," he says back, sounding like his spirit's been broken. "I think what you and Iris have is really great, and it honestly makes me happy to see you opening up with her."

I haven't been hiding things well at all, it would seem. With everybody's eyes on me, I also feel their expectations for me and Iris, and it's suffocating. What if something happens? What if I mess up? What if…

There's just so much that can go *wrong*.

I never should have admitted there was more. I should have kept my distance. I—

"Eli, help me get firewood," my dad announces, handing the platter of beef to Mom.

When he turns, he winces, his hand going to his lower back. It still twinges when he moves wrong, even now. I'm at his side in an instant, but he swats at the arm I was going to support him with.

"Be right back," I mumble vaguely, turning back to the room and catching sight of the sizable stack of chopped firewood beside the wood-burning stove.

Dad doesn't say anything as I follow him out to the shed. Once we're in front of it, he gestures for me to open the sliding door for him. It's rusty and often gets caught. I wonder if his back is hurting more than he's letting on.

"You ok, son?" he asks as I reach inside and begin collecting wood, placing a few pieces into his waiting arms.

"I'm good," I say and sigh.

Dad pins me with a look saying we're standing out in the cold until I fess up, so I continue.

"I don't know what I'm doing," I admit.

"Son, none of us do. We just keep going anyway. I understand wanting to help however you can, even in the face of that uncertainty," he answers.

Of course he does. My dad is one of the most selfless people I've ever met. Everything he's done has been for me and Mom, or Jake and Scott, or… anybody but himself.

"I do care about her," I admit.

"As a friend?" Dad asks.

"A really good friend," I say. The words feel like chalk on my tongue.

"And that's what you want?"

I've never talked to my dad about my relationship status. My mom will ask regularly without shame, but Dad's always let me be. It's been better that way because it's always felt like he's had the ability to read my mind, and this isn't something I want him to see into. I can't have him blaming himself.

"I don't know what I want," I say, yanking the shed door closed.

"I think you do." Dad nods once, and that's that.

CHAPTER 42

On Saturday, I wake up feeling restless and decide to do all the domestic things I've been neglecting. When I finish all my laundry, vacuuming the entire house top to bottom, and cleaning all the windows, I start on more obscure, but no less important—or so I tell myself—tasks.

Obviously, it's essential I empty all the cabinets in the kitchen and deep clean them immediately.

Keeping busy helps me resist the urge to text Eli. After all he's done for me, I don't want to commandeer more of his time. I don't want to be annoying. I don't want to push him.

It'll be ok.

I'm in the middle of telling myself that everything is so normal, fine, great when there's a knock on the door. I jump, smacking my head on the top of the cabinet I've half crawled into. Fear shoots through me for just a second before I hear Eli's voice on the other side of the front door.

"Iris? Olivia? It's me." His deep timbre settles somewhere warm in my chest.

I look over at Liv, who's been following me from task to task, eyeing me warily for several hours, but she just shrugs.

"I texted him for you. You've been a fucking menace all day. If you want to see him, just see him," she says before giving me a knowing look and heading upstairs to make herself scarce.

I want to act incredulous, but of course she's right. I do want to see him.

That's the problem with friends who know you maybe *too* well. They're happy to call you on your shit.

And just like that, when I open the door, I feel like I can breathe fully again.

"Olivia told me to come by, but if you don't want me here, I'll go," Eli offers, but I step back.

"Get inside, Eli."

"And I didn't even have to bribe you with food." His lopsided smile leaves me winded. "My parents don't believe in portion control, so Jake, Scott, and I all got enough leftovers last night for several days. I thought I'd share."

I take the bag from him and begin unpacking the Tupperware.

"It'll have a good home here," I say with a smile before taking a deep breath to call Sam down. A gentle hand lands on my arm.

"I can go get her," Eli offers, and my heart stutters. I nod.

Quietly, Eli heads upstairs.

"Human Eli!" Sam's excited squeal reaches downstairs. From the soft thump I hear after, I just know she's tackled him.

… And shit.

I think when I wasn't looking, I fell in love with Eli.

Olivia also joins us for dinner and sits with us for the first part of a movie but offers to put Sam to bed when the kiddo starts yawning. A bit later, we hear Olivia close Sam's door and go to her own bedroom.

"Do you want me to go?" Eli asks once we're alone.

I scoot along the couch until I'm pressed into his side. Almost as if it's instinct, Eli's arm lifts and wraps around me. I shake my head. I want to know what's going to happen after Archer is served Monday, but I also want this night with him, so I keep my mouth shut.

Eli squeezes me against him, like he wants to be closer too. I turn, leaning away and look up at him in the soft, blue glow from the television. I try to read his expression, but I can't untangle the turmoil in his eyes.

The house is dark and quiet, and it feels like a place where secrets are safe.

"Iris…?" Eli questions, shifting like he might get up.

I shake my head, planting my free hand on the center of his chest and pressing him back into the cushions before I climb over him, spreading my knees far to fit around his thick thighs. I release his hand so I can slip my fingers into his hair, and his hands find the backs of my thighs. With his head tilted back against the couch, he looks up at me almost reverently.

"Iris." My name again falls from his lips like the ghost of a word.

"Shhhh," I breathe before lowering my lips to his.

The second we touch, I feel each of his fingertips pressing into my skin, like a jolt of electricity went through him and back into me, and I need more. I sink down until my body is flush against Eli's.

I hear a needy groan in my ears, but don't realize it's mine until Eli responds, raising his hips to meet the heat between my legs.

"Ah," I gasp, and Eli greedily takes the invitation, sliding his tongue into my mouth, pulling my very soul out of me.

"Upstairs," I plea against Eli's mouth.

Not needing to be told twice, he stands, taking me with him. I squeeze him between my thighs, but it's really not necessary. He has me.

I scrape my nails down the sides of his neck and over his shoulders before my lips find those red marks, kissing, licking, biting beneath his ear. Eli hisses quietly in response and slides one hand up my thigh until his fingers press against my core through my leggings. I know he can feel how wet I am for him, how badly I need him right now.

He doesn't bother to turn on the lights when we get to my room, so once the door snicks shut, we find our way entirely by touch. Eli keeps me astride him when he sits on my bed, releasing my legs so he can yank my shirt over my head. Finding my breasts unbound, he descends on them, pulling my nipple sharply between his teeth while his hand kneads my other breast, pulling a muffled cry from my lips.

Eli's other hand flies to my mouth, abruptly cutting off the sound without even the slightest hiccup in his attention on my chest. I begin clawing at his shirt, needing to feel more of him. With a frustrated groan, Eli releases me and pulls off his shirt, flipping us so I'm on my back and he can take off his pants.

No matter how many times I see him, I'll never get my fill of him—powerful, strong, and mine.

I lift my hips and try to peel off my leggings, but they're tight and my entire body is hot, and they stick to me like a second skin. Eli sees my struggle and reaches for the front, right along a well-worn seam. The echo of material tearing bounces around the room, and I can only stare in shock as he pulls the fabric from my body. I didn't think people actually did that in real life.

A moment later, that and every other thought flies out of my mind when Eli's tongue drags up my opening, and I have to cover my *own* mouth to keep from waking the house.

"I can't stop thinking of this, of you on my tongue." Eli sounds strained, and I realize how undone I've made him.

He drives two fingers into me, stretching me, working me like I'm his plaything. His tongue is a beast, spearing into me with his fingers and then dragging over my clit in just the right way.

"Eli, please," I beg.

Please what? I don't know.

"I need you to be good for me and keep quiet, so we don't wake your whole house." His voice rumbles low in his chest and fills every inch of me.

After a stinging bite to my inner thigh, Eli stands, pulls a condom from god knows where, rolls it on, and prowls over me. When he kisses me, I can taste myself on his tongue.

I expect him to fuck me hard, urgent like the rest of this night has been, but he slows, trailing his fingertips down my sternum. He follows the path with unhurried kisses, before his lips find the pounding thud of my heart, placing a lingering kiss above the spot as he slowly enters me.

Full. I am so fucking full as he bottoms out inside of me, rolling his hips against mine, like he's searching for a way to be just a little bit closer. The pressure on my clit has me mumbling curse words and dragging my nails down his back. I want to come so fucking badly.

Eli slowly pulls out and rolls back into me, shifting so his lips are by my ear.

"You are everything, Iris," he breathes, but my fractured brain can't form a response. With Eli, I don't need to. I don't have to think or worry or put on a show. I can just feel. I can just *be.*

Instead, I lift my hips on his next thrust and hook my heel around his back so I can pull him into me.

A sound builds deep within Eli before he begins speeding up, and I take all of him. I feel him tensing, but when I turn my head toward his, I don't find his eyes squeezed shut. He's watching me, like he doesn't want to miss a thing.

I squeeze my muscles around him, and he releases his breath all at once.

"*Fuck.*"

I can feel him pulsing inside of me as he comes, though he doesn't slow.

He wants to take me with him.

He shifts onto one elbow and moves a hand between us, spreading my wetness over my clit while he continues to pound into *me*.

"Come, Iris," Eli says, and it's like his demand pulls a trigger, setting me off.

My back arches off the bed, a tightly strung bow, and I clamp around him inside me, pulsing and pulling him deeper. I think I stop breathing entirely.

I gasp for air when Eli pulls out of me, my chest rising and falling as rapidly as Eli's.

"Perfect," Eli whispers as he kisses my temple.

"Perfect," he repeats, kissing over my closed eyelids.

"Perfect," once more when he kisses my lips.

Eli removes the condom, balling it in a tissue from my nightstand, and though I don't want to, I drag myself out of bed and throw on my robe so I can hurry to the bathroom, hoping Eli won't have fallen asleep before I return. But the second I come back, he's lifting the covers for me. I drop my robe on the floor and crawl in, nuzzling against his warm skin. He wraps me up and buries his face in my hair.

Though we don't speak, I know we both lie there awake for a while.

Tonight felt different. It felt like more.

But maybe tonight is just goodbye.

Far too early the next morning, Olivia is knocking on my bedroom door. The sound is urgent, and I immediately leap out of bed, dragging the blanket with me.

Has Archer done something? Is he here?

"Iris?" Eli's sleepy voice carries to me as I fly to the door, opening it just enough to see Olivia.

"I'm sorry. I told her to wait downstairs, but…" Olivia steps aside, retreating to her own room, to reveal the last person I expected to see today.

"Mom?"

CHAPTER 43

Eli

*S*orry... *Mom?*

As in, Iris's mom?

"Ris, I am trying to surprise you for Sam's school break. The least you could do is have some clothes on to greet me."

I immediately recognize the snippy tone even though I can't see its source. Iris's mouth pops open just before she slams the bedroom door shut in her mother's face. Quickly, she flips the lock on the handle—a good move since the knob begins rattling a moment later.

"Iris. Iris Sutton!"

Iris covers her face with her hands, inadvertently letting the blanket that was wrapped around her fall to the floor.

It's really *not* the time, but I look. She's so fucking beautiful it would be wrong not to.

I untangle the sheet from my legs and pad across the room to fold Iris in my arms.

"I'm happy to stay locked in here until she leaves," I whisper once her head is tucked under my chin.

Iris wraps her arms around me and nuzzles her face into my chest. I think she might be considering it.

"Grandma?" Sam's sleepy voice carries from the hallway, and Iris groans. So much for building a bunker in here.

"My girl!" Iris's mother squeaks. "At least *someone* is happy to see me. Iris, I will be feeding your child downstairs. I hope you'll grace us with your presence after you're finished throwing this tantrum."

Once the sound of them heading downstairs fades away, Iris pulls her head off my chest.

"I need pants. I gotta rescue my kid," she groans. "What the fuck is my *mother* doing here?"

"What does she know about what's been happening here?" I ask while I search for my discarded clothing. I brought a change of clothes, but the bag is still sitting in my Jeep out front.

My wrinkled, second-day clothes don't exactly give the best impression, and I could also really use a shower, but I already feel like I don't much care if Mrs. Sutton likes me. As it stands, I'm not too fond of her myself.

"I don't know. I've kind of ignored her calls over the past few weeks," Iris says, also sorting through the discarded fabric around her room. After a second, she chuckles.

When I turn to her, I find her holding her destroyed yoga pants from last night, nearly torn in two.

"Sorry," I say, but I'm grinning because I'm not sorry. I'll buy her new ones.

Iris shakes her head before balling up the fabric and dropping it into her little trashcan, pulling a different pair of leggings out of a drawer. When she pulls an oversized sweatshirt over her head, with nothing underneath it but those leggings, I have to remind myself again that her mother is right downstairs, and this is *not* the time.

Being with Iris has given me time to learn her body in a way I haven't learned others, and I've decided it's my favorite. I know where to touch to pull sounds from her, when to speed up or slow down, and I find myself wanting to know every inch of her. I want to know everything.

It makes me want her all the damn time. I'm completely consumed by her.

Like a bucket of cold water is being dumped over my head, I'm reminded that's why I've resisted getting close to someone like this.

I look away from Iris to find a mirror and attempt to fix my hair.

"Ready?" Iris asks.

"As I'll ever be," I answer, trying to sound normal.

Mrs. Sutton *must* hear us come downstairs, but unlike Sam, she doesn't turn to greet us, and stays standing at the kitchen sink, washing our dishes from dinner last night.

"You shouldn't let dishes sit overnight," she scolds, still with her back to us. "You know—"

She finally turns, spots me, and cuts off abruptly.

"Oh." She turns to Sam. "Why don't you go find something on TV?"

Sam looks among all the grown-ups but does as she's told.

"Mom, you remember Eli from Sam's birthday party. Eli, this is my mother, Jacki," Iris says, looking a little smug at her mother's apparent displeasure at my presence.

You'd think Iris's state of undress would have tipped mother dearest off to the possibility that her daughter wasn't alone. I expect it's a dose of active ignorance.

"'Lo," I say with a half-hearted salute. Confirmed. I'm entirely uninterested in impressing this woman.

"Yes, I remember." It seems to pain Jacki to admit it. "That explains the green monstrosity outside and some of the rumors I've heard."

The Jeep is hardly a *monstrosity*, but just to tick her off, I happily say, "Yup!"

"Hm!" Jacki tuts at me.

"Mom, what are you doing here?" Iris asks but doesn't take her mom's bait about "rumors."

"I came to spend time with Samantha during her school break," she repeats.

"And you didn't think to *call* first?" Iris snaps.

"I didn't think I needed to call before coming to visit my daughter and only grandchild. I also didn't think you'd answer," Jacki snaps right back. But then she takes a breath, visibly forcing herself to calm down. "I didn't come here to fight. And I'm not here for anything having to do with what we... discussed in February. I haven't been speaking with *that person*. I just thought you'd be working and maybe I could watch Sam for you and visit with you. I got a room at the inn and rented a car."

She shifts uneasily on her feet before adding, "I miss you and Sam." She looks thoroughly annoyed about having to admit she actually experienced a feeling.

Iris looks back at me, her eyes pleading with me to tell her what to do, but I can't. I reach out and take her hand, squeezing it.

I've got your back.

Iris takes her own deep breath, looking shockingly like her mother in that moment.

"Trial basis," she says, turning back to Jacki. "And we do *everything* my way. You need to understand how serious this is." She lowers her voice and steps closer to her mother. "Archer has been following us and hanging around outside Sam's school. I got a restraining order against him on Friday, and he's going to be served tomorrow."

"A restraining order?" she says, dumbfounded, her eyebrows high with surprise. Maybe she was telling the truth about not having spoken to him. "This seems so unlike him."

"Not really. If you had listened to me at any point in the last five years, this wouldn't be that much of a surprise. We've got a lot to talk about." Iris rubs her forehead.

"Do you want me to stay?" I ask. It feels like Iris and her mother might need some time to themselves.

Iris shakes her head. "Can I call you later?"

"You'd better," I say, eyeing Jacki.

I want to believe Iris's mother has had a come-to-Jesus moment since her last visit, but even if she has, I still don't like her. She brought Archer here, and I'm not sure I can forgive that, even if Iris does.

But Jacki isn't *my* mom, so I can keep on hating her.

"I'll head out with you," Olivia says, finally coming downstairs. "But call me or Eli or Harry if you're going out, ok?" She directs that request to Iris.

Iris agrees, and before I realize what I'm doing, I've bent and quickly kissed her. She looks a little dazed, cheeks pink when I straighten back up. I like it.

Before I change my mind and decide to stay, I collect my coat and open the front door to let Olivia ahead of me.

Out of nowhere, the sun is blazing down on us, and it's got to be close to fifty degrees. That might not seem warm, but after weeks in the twenties, it's basically a pool day.

"Huh," Olivia says, when we stand on the porch, shading her eyes with her hand. "I guess spring is finally here."

CHAPTER 44

I smile at Eli's text before snapping a selfie and sending it back.

That pulls a full laugh from me, drawing the attention of my mom and Sam from their place on the couches near the window. We're four days into spring break, and Mom has honestly been… great?

Even though Archer has gone ghost protocol since Allen served him, I haven't felt comfortable letting Sam go too far, but Mom's been fine with coming to the office with me and playing with Sam down here, in the playroom, or in the small yard while I work. Since I told her how Archer has been behaving, she's been looking out for him like a damn hawk, and she even apologized for helping him come up here in the first place. She's sworn she hasn't taken his calls since she got back home.

Harry was just as apprehensive as I was when I told him Mom was here, but she's making an effort to get on his good side too. She volunteers to pick up lunch and makes more coffee when the pot is empty. For somebody who doesn't typically lift a finger, it's kind of monumental.

On Tuesday, Eli came by for dinner, to celebrate filing the last of the business returns he had to do, and Mom was almost pleasant to him. She was still stiff and asked awkward, personal questions about weird stuff like income prospects, but that's just her on a good day. She's still a stuck-up, rich woman.

I think she's *trying*.

That's more than I've gotten from her in a while.

I look over at her and Sam as they build a castle with magnetic blocks on the coffee table up front and can't help but feel all warm and fuzzy. Sam is *thrilled* to have Grandma in town.

"Hey, master builders," I call over to them as I hold up my phone to take a photo. "Smile."

They both completely cheese out. It's sweet.

I fire off the picture to Eli, promising that things are going well, and I'm not sending it under duress. When I look up, I find Sam peeking over the edge of my desk at me expectantly.

"Yes, my love?" I ask.

I can tell she is going to ask for something, so I glance at Mom for a hint, but she's focused on fitting the blocks back into their little carrying case.

"Can we try the monkey bars?" Sam asks in the littlest voice.

It's been getting warmer each day this week, so Sam's been begging to finally go to the park. It's still chilly out, but spring has sprung seemingly all at once.

We tried on Monday, but there was still so much filthy snow, and everything was so wet from what had melted that the entire park was basically a mud pit. Then, it rained Tuesday, clearing almost all the snow, but making the mud worse.

Yesterday and today, though, have brought nothing but dry sunshine. That, coupled with my kid's enormous, mismatched eyes staring at me full of hope, is enough to warrant another try.

"We can go look, but if the park is still in bad shape, we'll have to go back when it's dry. Deal?" I offer.

"Deal!" Sam's face splits into the biggest grin. "Now?"

Oh, this kid.

I check the clock, but Harry surprises me from the doorway.

"Go," he says. I'm not sure how long he's been standing there, but it was apparently long enough to understand what's being asked of me. "And take tomorrow off. Enjoy Sam's last day of break away from here. You work too hard."

"Uncle Harry…" I start, but he won't hear it, turning and heading back to his office with a wave over his shoulder.

"Ok, lil' one. Put your toys away and get your shoes," I say, surrendering and shutting down my computer. "I hope you're ready for the park, Mom."

As much as Sam loves snow, it's hard to believe she's not a spring kid with every peal of laughter out of her today, even when she repeatedly falls from the monkey bars. As she lands once more on her feet before stumbling to her hands and knees, I'm grateful the ground is still a little soft.

"I did three that time, Mama! Did you see?" This little powerhouse isn't the slightest bit discouraged by falling. Her little hand goes to a lump in her pants pocket that I have a sneaking suspicion is Robin the cat, who was *supposed* to stay in the car.

Maybe she's just a happy girl in any season.

Sam brushes off her knees and runs up to me.

"Can I have a snack?" she asks.

When I check my watch, I'm surprised to discover how long we've been out here.

"It's probably time to head back and have dinner instead," I deliver what's considered devastating news for a five-year-old.

"Noooo," Sam whines. "I'm doing so good! Can we stay?" She points to one of the picnic tables around the park as my mom comes over to us.

It's a beautiful day, and it won't get dark for at least another hour. Maybe sandwiches from the grocery store are a good idea.

"Alright, how about you pack up so we can get sandwiches now, then we can come back and stay until it gets dark?" I offer.

"That will take *forever*," Sam says, looking toward Main Street. The store must seem like it's miles away to somebody her size.

Mom turns toward me and speaks quietly enough that Sam won't hear.

"I can stay here. It won't be long, but then we don't have to pack up. I'll watch her. I promise," she offers.

I eye her warily. I don't like the idea of separating from Sam, but this week has gone well. Mom's been so attentive and helpful and has changed her tune about Archer. If I hurry, I can probably be back in fifteen minutes, and it'd take a lot longer if all of us went…

"Ok, but don't you take your eyes off her for a second. Do you understand?" I say to Mom as Sam starts cheering.

"We'll be fine," she swears.

I kiss Sam's head before she goes back to the monkey bars with my mom right behind her. I take off at a jog toward the store.

Just fifteen minutes.

The small grocery store isn't busy, and I quickly grab stuff from the deli. As I'm paying, I see the sky showing beautiful streaks of gold and pink around the fluffiest clouds. This picnic might just be the perfect way to end today.

As I reach the end of Main Street and cross back toward the park, I see Mom standing with somebody. It looks like they're arguing. I'm squinting to figure out who, when Mom shrieks—not out of anger or excitement. It's one of those sounds of pure horror that burrows deep into your bones and haunts your nightmares.

The bag of sandwiches is already falling from my hand when Mom screams Sam's name and takes off at a sprint toward the lake. I look toward where she's headed and force my legs forward, even though it feels like I'm wading through molasses.

The second the lake comes into view, I expect to feel some level of relief. Anything has to be better than not knowing. But then I watch somebody drop through the melting ice and vanish.

"Eli, I'm at the hospital. There's been an accident. I need you." I barely get the words out before it feels like my very soul cracks in half.

CHAPTER 45

Eli

I'm just pulling into a spot outside my condo when I see Iris's name on my phone screen. Immediately, a smile spreads across my face. I want to see her all the time, talk to her, simply be *near* her. It's intoxicating and overwhelming and terrifying, but for now, it's my truth.

"Hey." I answer the call and hear a sniffle on the other end of the line.

It feels like the very blood in my veins freezes, starting from the top of my head and working its way down my body inch by inch. I hear a mechanical announcement in the background, an eerily familiar bustle and beeping of machines.

Before she speaks, I know where Iris is, and I'm reversing my car out of my spot at an alarming speed.

"Eli, I'm at the hospital. There's been an accident. I need you." Her voice is broken, and I've never felt a fear like this before.

"What happened? Are you ok?" I drag in a ragged breath before I can continue. "Is Sam?" I croak out.

"I'm ok," Iris says, gasping for air. I can only catch some of her words. "Sam… I think she's… But Grateful Bob… I don't know. Can you get here? Are you coming?"

Grateful Bob?

I slam on the accelerator, flying through a red light.

"I'm coming, baby," I whisper before Iris's sobs are all I can hear.

I pull up to the curb at the hospital and barely throw the Jeep in park before I yank the keys from the ignition and practically fall out of the vehicle.

I must look like a madman approaching the receptionist desk because the woman seated there rears back as I approach her.

"I'm sorry," I breathe out. "The Sutton room, please. Samantha or Iris Sutton."

The woman turns toward her computer, tapping furiously. "I'm sorry. There's no room assigned to a Sutton. Nor are they in the ER or any of our other units."

That doesn't make any sense. I check the shiny letters on the wall. I'm at the right place.

Wait. She said Grateful Bob. Even when I was a kid, I never called him anything other than Grateful Bob. He wouldn't hear of it. What the *fuck* is his last name?

Like it's being pulled from fog, the name hits me.

"What about Mason? Robert Mason?" The name sounds foreign on my lips. He's *always* Grateful Bob. And he doesn't belong in a *hospital*.

The woman goes back to her computer and nods. She's barely finished telling me the room number before I'm thanking her and taking off down the hallway.

My head is swimming so much that I can barely see the numbers on the doors as I pass. I know I can't show up behaving like this. That's not what Iris needs. I skid to a stop and brace my hand against the wall, forcing myself to take a few deep breaths.

As I'm staring at the white, linoleum floor, the sharp,

distinctly *hospital* smell consumes me. I feel a wave of nausea slam into me as I'm thrown back into the last time I was here. It's been almost two decades, but I'd really hoped, perhaps stupidly, to never have to come back.

I squeeze my eyes closed and switch to breathing only through my mouth.

It's ok. Breathe. You can't fall apart.

"Mom! I don't want to hear it!" I suddenly hear Iris's angry voice from around the corner, and pull myself together, headed toward her.

"You don't understand. I wasn't helping him. I told him to stay away. I was trying to protect her." When I catch sight of them, Jacki is gesticulating wildly.

"I don't *care*. You brought him here. You were distracted and my *kid* fell in a *frozen lake*. I just need you to go. I will call you when I'm ready." Iris has become steely in her resolve, but her words ring in my ears, and I feel gutted.

Sam fell in the lake?

Jacki hurries past me, her bowed head not doing much to hide her defiant expression.

"Iris," I call out, breaking into a jog until I have her in my arms. "What happened?"

While she was angry moments ago, Iris's shoulders shake once I'm folded around her. Over her head, I can see through a small window into a patient room. Grateful Bob's room.

Somebody's lying in the bed, covered with the pale blue hospital blankets. It must be Grateful Bob because the person fills too much space for Sam's little body. I have a sudden flash of my father lying in one of these beds.

I rub my hand on Iris's back, and when we pivot, I see Sam sitting in a chair beside the bed. She's awake, alert.

She's ok.

I fight the very real urge to crumple to the floor, my legs only holding me up because I know Iris needs me.

"Sam…" I start. I don't know what to say. Nothing makes sense. "You said she fell through the ice? She's—"

I'm looking at her. And I'm like ninety percent sure she's not a ghost. And what happened to Grateful Bob?

Iris pulls away from me to open the hospital room door, pulling me inside by my hand with a quiet "c'mon."

"Hey lil' one," she says weakly, and Sam looks over at us.

"Hi Mama. Hi human Eli," she says with a happy wave.

Everything seems normal, except she's in a pair of those hospital socks with the grippy bottoms, and they're so big on her they go up to her knees.

My eyes dart to the bed, where, sure enough, Grateful Bob is sitting, wrapped in thick, lumpy blankets, though he's been relegated to a full hospital gown and looks mighty displeased about it.

I give him a questioning look, but he just presses his lips together and gives a sharp nod. He's telling me he's ok.

But he doesn't look ok.

"He saved her life," Iris says, looking at Grateful Bob while her eyes well with tears again.

Grateful Bob's scowl melts away.

"Hey now. No crying, little lady," he says softly.

"Are you warm enough? Do you need anything?" Iris asks.

"I'm fine. I just need to get out of here and back to my own home," he grumbles.

"I'll ask," Iris says, but it sounds like she already knows the answer to that inquiry.

I follow her back into the hallway, desperate for an explanation.

"I wanted you to see them," she explains. "My head is all over the place. I'm sorry."

"It's ok," I say, rubbing her upper arms. "Can you tell me *what happened*?"

"Sam wanted to learn how to do the monkey bars. She's been obsessed for weeks. There was some kid at school—it doesn't matter. It was nice today, so Mom and I took her. I went to get some sandwiches, and when I got back—" Iris cuts off again. Her eyes keep flying back to the door we just came through. I know she wants to get back in there.

"While I was at the store, I guess Archer came up to Mom, yelling about the restraining order. I think he thought she'd help since she brought him to the birthday party? I don't know. I don't care. But Mom took her eyes off Sam to talk or fight or whatever with Archer, and I guess Sam saw the part of the lake we had skated on, and didn't realize how much had melted, so she stepped on it and—" Iris's voice cuts off in a choked sob. I reach forward, but she shakes her head, like she needs to get the story out now.

"Grateful Bob saw her out there and tried to get her. When he stepped out to grab her, the ice broke, and he went in, and he cut his leg *really* badly. Sam slipped, but he got her. Eli, she could have *died* if he wasn't there. I can't keep doing this with Archer. I just *can't*. Looking over my shoulder for him is going to kill me."

I don't know what to say. She's right. Today could have very easily gone extremely different. I want to reassure Iris, but I have no words. I'm relieved. I'm angry at Jacki. And I'm so fucking *grateful* for Grateful Bob—jesus christ, I don't know what I'd have done if he wasn't there.

It feels like there's an entire fucking war going on in my head and in my chest. And I feel goddamn *useless*.

"Are you here for Mr. Mason?" a nurse asks.

Before I can say yes, Iris is furiously nodding.

"He said he wants to go home," she relays.

"I'm just here to check on his pain levels. At his age, he's very lucky things weren't worse. The water is still extremely cold, and we need to monitor that leg. The doctor wants to keep him overnight," the nurse says. "Why don't you come in with me."

They go back in, and I mutely follow behind. I need to *do* something.

Iris goes to Sam and stands in front of her daughter while the nurse talks to Grateful Bob. Iris turns toward Sam and holds her face against her torso, with a hand over Sam's eyes so she can't see when the nurse uncovers his leg.

A thick layer of gauze covers him from knee to ankle, but dark red has already begun to seep through. The nurse gingerly peels back the tape to get a better look, and Grateful Bob hisses sharply. My eyes bounce from his leg to his pained expression, to Iris's eyes squeezed shut, to Sam hugging her mom around her middle.

Suddenly, the battle within me breaks, and one emotion silences all the rest.

"Iris, I need to do something," I say suddenly.

Grateful Bob furrows his brow when he catches my eye. Ever so slightly, he shakes his head. I think he knows what I'm thinking. I turn and leave anyway.

I'm sorry.

Suddenly, I remember the paperwork Iris showed me over the weekend. The court documents granting her restraining order, listing details for a hearing, and the information about the person being served. His name… and his address.

Archer Ringwald has caused *enough* damage to my town and the people I care about.

Next thing I know, I'm tearing out of there and back to my car, somehow neither towed nor ticketed in its very illegal spot by the hospital door. I don't remember the drive across town, parking, or walking up to the door.

I *do* remember pounding on it, and the sharp pain on my hand from punching Archer's stupid fucking face with all the force I could muster.

He lurches backward, his hand being ripped off the doorknob he was still holding as he tumbles to the floor. He looks small and frail crumpled in a heap, but I can't summon even a drop of sympathy for this toxic waste of space.

"Hey, asshole," I say, calling his attention to me.

His eyes swim for a second but they seem to focus. I crouch down before him and balance my forearms on my knees.

"I need you to pay attention. Look at my face right now and know that I mean this with my whole fucking soul. If you go anywhere *near* either Iris or Sam ever again, I will fucking *kill* you," I snarl, and he just blinks back at me.

"Do you understand me?" I ask and wait for him to nod. "This isn't a threat. It's a promise. I will *kill* you."

CHAPTER 46

A thin sliver of light stretches across Samantha's room as her door opens and Eli creeps inside. He catches my eye for a moment when I look up at him from my place on the floor leaning against her closet door, but he silently moves across the room to Sam's bedside. When he gets to her, he ever so gently brushes her hair back from her cheek. Even in the darkness of the room, I can see his shoulders shudder. I look away to give them a moment.

A silent minute stretches into two before Eli turns back to me and falls heavily beside me.

"What are you doing in here?" he asks barely above a whisper. "Is she ok?"

I nod. "She's perfect. I made the doctors check twice. But I can't bring myself to let her out of my sight." My voice is as unsteady as I feel. "When I think of what *could* have happened today…" I trail off, unable to say the haunting thought out loud.

Eli wraps his arm around me, and I fall against his warm chest. I press my ear to his shirt, the sound of his heart a steady drum.

"Where did you go before?" I ask.

"I'm sorry," he whispers. "I went to see Archer. I don't think he'll bother you again. I know it's your business to handle, but I was just so *sick* of him hurting—"

I cut him off by pulling his face down to me and kissing him fiercely.

"Thank you," I say against his lips.

I do like to handle things myself, but I don't mind Eli taking things into his own hands this time. I've said my peace over and over, but Archer was never going to hear me. I'm learning I'm not an island. I don't want to be. I wrap myself back around Eli.

"Is he why you came here? Did he do something else?" I ask, but Eli shakes his head.

"I just wanted to see her again with my own eyes," he says. "Make sure she's alright, you know?"

"I know. I will owe Grateful Bob for the rest of my life," I murmur against him.

"He won't think of it that way for a second," Eli assures me, and I can hear the deep sound come from him.

"How did you get in here?" I ask, suddenly realizing how late it is.

"Olivia let me in. She's not sleeping either. Your little girl has a lot of people who care about her."

My heart squeezes at his words. I know she does.

We fall into silence, and I find myself counting Eli's breaths. They're slow, steady, strong.

In... two... three. Out... two... three.

"Months ago, you asked me why I didn't do the relationship thing, and I completely blew you off," Eli says just when I think he may have fallen asleep.

One hundred and eighteen breaths.

"It was something really personal to ask. I'm sorry," I reply, but he shakes his head again.

"It wasn't that. I was embarrassed by the reason, so I didn't want to tell you. I wanted you to think I was Mr. Cool Guy." His laugh comes out as a silent huff.

"Well, you should have told me, then. I've never thought you were cool," I tease.

"Ouch," he breathes, but when I tip my head back to look at him, he's smiling. As I watch him, the smile slips.

Eli nods toward Sam's bed. "This is why I don't do relationships," he says.

"You don't want kids?" I ask, confused.

"It's not that." Eli shakes his head. "I love kids, and the fact that I'd probably never have any as a result of avoiding relationships was the biggest downside to the plan, actually."

"Then what do you mean?" I press.

"Like I told you before, my parents are madly in love with each other. They have been my whole life. They argue like normal couples do, sure, but they're solid. My grandparents on both sides were the same way. I grew up surrounded by the lifelong kind of love you usually only get to see in movies," Eli starts. He takes a deep breath before continuing.

"When I was thirteen, I got pulled out of class and called to the principal's office. I remember being terrified, because I too was a real rule follower. I couldn't imagine what I'd done wrong, especially nothing bad enough to get called to the *principal's office*. When I got there, my mom was standing in the hallway, and she was crying.

"I've never seen anything like that before. She was wholly shattered, and when she looked at me, I didn't even recognize her. She couldn't speak, so the principal told me there had been an accident at my dad's job. He worked at a lumber yard, and one of the machines had broken. He was hurt… badly."

Eli leans his head back against the closet door and closes his eyes. I reach across my torso and thread my fingers into the hand that's wrapped around me. When I give a gentle squeeze, he begins speaking again.

"Somebody must have taken us to the hospital since Mom was in no state to drive. I honestly don't remember, but the image of my father in that bed and the sound of the slow beeps coming from the machines around him will stay with me forever. Almost every inch of him was wrapped up.

"He had been crushed, and he was in that bed, unconscious, for weeks. I swear everybody was just waiting for him to die. It felt like nobody had any hope, even though the nurses kept encouraging us to keep our spirits up. It—it got bad.

"I just remember thinking *You can't die, Dad.* And it wasn't even for myself. He had to live because if he died, I knew Mom would die too. During those weeks, I watched her become a husk of herself, even though she did her best to hide it from me.

"That kind of love is something fierce and strong. But the pain of losing somebody you feel that much for is also the scariest thing I could ever imagine. When Dad finally woke up and the doctors said it looked like he'd pull through, my mom crumbled. I'll never forget the sound she made. I vowed on that day I wouldn't let anybody close enough to have that level of control over me. More importantly, I couldn't handle the pressure of having somebody else's happiness tied to *me* like that. What if I made a mistake and destroyed them?"

Silence falls over the room again. Eli's arm tightens around me, and I burrow deeper into him.

"I understand that. It *is* the single scariest thing to live tied completely to another person," I finally say, my eyes falling on Sammy's rising and falling chest. "My entire heart lives outside of my body, and it's fucking terrifying."

"How do you do it?" His voice is barely above a whisper. "Every single day. How do you know what to do?"

I could make something up about instinct and learning from past mistakes, but I choose to give him the truth instead.

"Guess and pray."

"I don't know if I can do it," Eli whispers so softly I could have imagined it.

We stay sitting there so long that I fall asleep right on the floor, propped against that closet door. I wake up when the first rays of sunshine force their way past Sam's blinds and land on my face.

I'm exhausted, stiff, and alone.

Eli's gone.

CHAPTER 47

Eli

It's been three days since the accident at the lake.

I haven't slept, but I don't feel tired. Actually, I don't feel much of anything. After the stress of the hospital, this is strange, jarring. As I pace back and forth across the floor, my condo feels too small for the first time since I bought it. I don't know how I was so careless to let this happen.

My phone buzzes on my desk with a call from Iris, but like the others, I let it ring out. A few texts from her over the last few days also sit unread and unanswered.

IRIS

Eli, where are you?

Are you ok?

Piper told me you're alive at least. What's going on?

Please don't do this.

There are even more messages from my brothers, expressing a range of worry, anger, and frustration. I don't blame them. I'm acting like a real piece of shit right now. Even I'm pretty pissed with me.

All I want to do is go to her. The second I left her house, it felt like a mistake. But I know it'll be worse the longer I let this go on.

I should have known better. I *did* know better. This thing with Iris has always been too fucking dangerous.

My phone buzzes again, but it's not Iris.

Grateful Bob.

I launch toward my desk and answer.

"Are you ok?" I ask, frantic.

"I'm *fine*, my boy. You need to answer your damn phone. They're letting me out of this place, but they won't release me unless somebody comes to get me."

"I'll be right there," I say.

"Bring me some pants, would you?"

Pants in hand, I head back down the stark white hospital hallways, my shoes squeaking every few steps and angry, fluorescent lights beating down on me from overhead. I really hate these godforsaken hallways.

I knock when I get to Grateful Bob's door, and he calls me in. He's already sitting in the chair beside his bed, looking as menacing as somebody *can* look in a blue hospital gown. His lower leg is still wrapped, but just in a thin bandage rather than the thick, bloody wrap from the other day.

"'Bout time," he grumbles, reaching for the bag of clothes I brought him.

I help him to the attached bathroom, but he just shuts the door in my face when I ask if he can change alone. He emerges a moment later, my massive clothes barely fitting the thin man only a little better than they fit Iris.

Iris.

My traitor of a brain supplies me with the image of her in my sweats, the sleeves rolled up half a dozen times each, her hair a mess from my hands, and a goofy smile on her face.

I clear my throat, like removing a tickle that doesn't exist from my throat will make this hurt less.

Grateful Bob is observing me with his eyebrows raised. Sometimes I *hate* how he seems to notice everything.

"I want a cheeseburger," he says out of nowhere as he transfers the contents of his pants pockets into the pockets of the sweats I gave him.

It looks like the doctors had cut the black jeans off him. He balls up the mangled fabric and drops it in the trash can by the bed.

I was *sure* he was going to say something I don't want to hear about my feelings, or some great truth he knows that I should have realized. He has a habit of doing that.

"A cheeseburger?" I question. "Are you sure that's a good idea right after getting out of the hospital? Don't you want to go home and rest, or at least get your own clothes?"

"Just because I'm an old man who was in a hospital, it doesn't mean there's something wrong with what I'm eating. In case you forgot, I'm here because I fell in a frozen lake, not because I had a heart attack." Grateful Bob marches toward the door. "You can order takeout. I want a cheeseburger."

Because being an adult in charge of my own free will does not extend to contradicting Grateful Bob, in no time at all, I'm carrying a bag of food from the Corner Post to my Jeep. We drive in silence back to his house, where I help him to his couch and prop his leg on a loon print pillow.

"Sit," he instructs when I try to take the burger he insisted I order for myself and leave.

I sit.

"What the hell are you doing?" he asks, more anger on his face than I've ever seen.

I look back at him, ashamed. Even before he explains, I know he knows what I've done.

"Iris and Sam visited me this morning. I didn't realize you were such a coward," he says. I wish he'd have stabbed me instead.

I can't find words, and I'm not sure I'd trust myself to speak if I did.

"Eli, I've known you your whole life, and you have one of the biggest hearts I've ever seen. I need you to explain to me why you're running from this because I don't understand, and I don't think either of you deserve it." Grateful Bob leans forward.

"I didn't think I could do it," I choke out. "When Iris called me and asked me to meet her at the hospital, it felt like the world stopped. What if it hadn't turned out ok? What if one of you had died? I left, and now I don't know what to do."

"Why?" Grateful Bob asks without beating around the bush.

I meant it when I said I love Grateful Bob, but I don't get how he's not getting this.

"I didn't think I could take the risk of putting my heart in their hands, so I ran. Iris and Sam are *everything*, and I panicked. I don't think I can do this." I feel my voice rising and take a breath. It's not his fault. It's mine.

"Boy, I think you've already been doing it. And you've been doing it for other people your whole life. You love Jake and Scott and your parents and, damnit, even me. Don't you understand that kind of love is just as important? Don't you understand you're already taking risks in letting them in and letting them love you back? And you've been surviving. Why have you singled out just one type of love as the dangerous one? All love is risky, but I think it's worth taking that chance."

All at once, I feel like a fool. Of course I love them all. I'd do *anything* for them.

"So, do you love Iris and Sam?" he asks when I don't speak.

I don't need to think about my response. "I do."

"So, you keep going."

"And what if she doesn't forgive me for leaving?" I ask. I've made a real mess here.

"What are you *willing* to do?" he asks.

"Anything," I answer immediately.

"Then, you try. And you keep trying."

"Doesn't that make me no better than Archer?" I argue. He didn't know how to take no for an answer.

"Well, don't stalk and harass her. Jesus christ. I didn't think I had to tell you that."

I try.

CHAPTER 48

Iris

Like I've been doing for days, I just stare at Sam while she watches television. I'm dreading the idea of sending her back to school tomorrow, but I already kept her home for her first day back.

I'm just not sure I'll ever be able to breathe normally again. That moment when I'd thought she was the one who dropped into the lake? I expect that feeling will wake me up in the middle of the night for a long time.

It's been a rough weekend.

When Sam woke up Friday morning, she realized Robin was missing. I remembered the lump in Sam's too-small pants pockets when she was on the monkey bars, so I had little hope, but we tore apart the house and checked at the hospital and the park anyway. There was no sign of her.

Sam's been clinging to capybara Eli, but she's devastated about Robin. She's had that cat since she was born.

I also haven't heard from Eli since he left. I tried texting and calling, but it became too pathetic to keep reaching out when it was clear he wasn't reaching back.

My fear for Sam has helped dull the pain of my disappointment in Eli, but it's still there. I wanted him to be better. I *thought* he was better. If he was going to walk away, I didn't think he'd do it like this.

Turns out, I'm just naïve.

"Come on, baby girl. It's time for bed," I say, clicking off the television.

"Maybe Robin will come home tomorrow," she says as she stands from the couch, and my heart breaks. "Maybe she's with Eli."

What am I going to do?

When I come back downstairs instead of isolating myself, I consider it a win. I really wanted to crawl right into bed.

"Iris," Olivia says to get my attention.

I look at her, but she nods to something outside the front window. The sun is setting, casting a golden glow over everything, and I can clearly see a dark green Jeep parked in the street, a hulking figure leaning against the side of it.

I'm ashamed when my heart squeezes with relief. I think I hate him right now, but I also fucking *missed* him.

"I can tell him to leave. Just say the word," Liv offers.

I shake my head. "I'll go."

With sweats and slippers as my armor, I walk down my driveway toward Eli.

"Did you know I basically had a fight with my sister, keeping her from rushing up here to be with me after everything that happened? She just wanted to be near us, here for us if we needed anything, or if we didn't," I say once I'm near him. The sun is behind him, leaving him in shadow, but I can tell he's slumped against his car. "So *you've* got a lot of nerve showing up here after dropping off the face of the fucking earth after all that."

"I know. It's not enough, but I'm *sorry*." He sounds gutted.

Good. I hope he's fucking miserable

He pushes himself off the Jeep, and there's a weird squelchy sound. I shade my eyes to see him better and find him looking lumpier than normal. He's sopping wet.

"Eli, what the hell?" I automatically step toward him, concerned, before I stop myself.

"I, uh—" He doesn't finish the thought, instead raising his arm. Sitting small, soaked, and a bit smelly in his large hand is tiny little Robin.

"Oh my god," I gasp, snatching the cat from him to make sure it's really her. "How did you…"

"Piper told me, after yelling at me for a while," he says. "Since Sam and that cat are inseparable, I went on a hunch and stayed until I found her. Robin is her best friend. I had to try."

"You went in the lake?"

He nods.

"Fully clothed?"

"I haven't exactly been thinking straight." There's no laughter in his tone. He sounds like a broken man.

My eyes snap back to his. "Yeah, well you deserved Piper yelling at you. And more."

"I know. She told me I was a fucking moron for messing things up with the best woman I've had in my life. I also had Grateful Bob telling me I was a damn fool, if that helps." There's no fight in him, but that *does* help. I bet Grateful Bob can guilt trip like the best of them.

"Iris, I got scared of how badly this could hurt if something happened to one of you or if something went wrong. I ran because I thought it'd be better—for you, for me, I don't know and then I knew I had to do something to make up for it. I'm *so* sorry. I made a mistake," he continues.

My eyes sting, and I'm mad at myself for crying. I wish I wanted to tell him he lost his chance. I'd be in my rights to do so. But I don't. Because he hasn't. There's been a lot of good that he's shown before this, and it's not nothing.

"I deserve better," I say, a tear falling down my cheek.

"You do."

"You can't just fucking leave like that. What the hell was I supposed to tell Sam? And what about me? Do you know how that *felt*?" I can't help it. I step forward and push him against his shoulders.

"I know. I have no excuse. I fucked up." He looks down at my palms still pressed against him, Robin squished under one. He wraps his cold fingers around my hands.

"I'm not asking for your forgiveness because I don't think I've earned it. We started this whole thing together because we *had* to. I'm asking for a chance to try and show you that I want to. I want you. I want Sam. I want the good days and the bad days and the terrifying days. I want it all. And I want to prove to you that I'm worthy of you."

I feel my resolve cracking, and I worry I'm a bad example for Sam. If a man came to her like this, I'd probably tell her he blew his chance. But my heart is screaming for me to give him one more. My head falls forward.

"I'm still fucking furious with you."

"Valid."

"And if you take off again, I'll fucking murder you."

"There are many who would handle that for you."

"I'm not inviting you in."

"Ok."

I pause, looking into his blue eyes for any hint that this is the huge mistake I know it could be.

"Come back tomorrow?" I ask.

"Ok."

And I know he will.

Eli

After work, once I know Iris and Sam will be home from school, I head back to Iris's house. Olivia mutters that she's got her eye on me when she opens the front door, but she does let me inside.

Sam is sitting at the counter, bent over a worksheet with a freshly-laundered Robin and capybara Eli dutifully watching over her. Iris is at the stove, stirring something in a large pot. She looks over her shoulder at me while I'm taking off my shoes.

"Eli, can you help Sam with her numbers?" Iris asks, and Sam spins around at the sound of my name.

"Human Eli!" she cries, nearly falling out of her chair to wrap her arms around my middle when I get to her. "Mama told me you were looking for Robin for me, but I missed you."

My eyes jump back to Iris, who's giving me a knowing look. She covered for me with Sam, and it's a kindness she didn't have to offer.

"I missed you too, kiddo. I'm glad Robin is back home with you," I say, talking around the fresh stab wound in my chest. I'm lucky to be back here, and I'm not about to take advantage of that. "What are you working on?"

As Sam explains they're learning adding and take-aways, I mouth *thank you* to her mom. Iris nods, and I think there might be a small smile on her lips when she turns back to the stove.

APRIL

Thankfully, Archer finally got the hell out of town after I punched him in the face. I guess after he fled back home to Newport, his life fell apart, something that Iris and I take guiltless pleasure in.

To try to make up for what happened at the lake, Jacki called Archer's father and made sure he was well aware of the fool Archer had been acting and the restraining order. It was announced the following week that Archer was no longer affiliated with the family's hedge fund. Iris and Jacki are still working on mending their relationship, but I think Jacki's loyalty to Iris is solidified now. At least, it had better be.

So, this becomes our routine. Some days I come over to the house. Others, the girls come by the nursery or even over to my condo. We don't talk about my few dark days again, and I keep showing up for them—something I'll do as long as they'll let me.

Sam thinks it's so cool that my house is on top of somebody else's. Her mind was blown when I explained how college dorms work, but Iris looked a little pale at the prospect of college not being *so* many years away.

That gets me thinking though…

"Can you pass me the butter?" I ask Iris. It's another ordinarily perfect day, and I'm making grilled cheeses for me, Iris, and Sam.

"Mmhmm," Iris agrees, but she freezes when she opens the fridge. I hear her unstick the Post-it from the inside of the fridge door. "What's in June?" she asks, after reading the date I'd written down.

I didn't need any more butter.

"Hm?" I feign ignorance, but she knows I'm faking it right away.

After just a couple seconds of thinking, I can see Iris figure it out.

"Eli… what did you do?"

I slide our sandwiches onto a plate and turn off the stove, unable to keep the smile off my face.

"You've always wanted to, so why not give it a go?" I ask, pulling an LSAT test prep book out of my bag along with a book of prior exams.

"I couldn't," Iris starts, but there's no bite to her words. I hope she's realizing she *could*.

"Things feel like they're settling here. I've got a good handle on Sam's schedule, and I'm happy to help with her when you'd have classes. I know I wouldn't be the only person to offer to help. Harry would *love* for you to take over his firm someday, so you know he'd support this. I think you can, and you should." When I pass Iris the books, the look of longing on her face is unmistakable.

"I'd never be ready for the June exam. It's like two months away." But Iris is already opening the prep book, flipping through the first few pages.

"I think you could. You can always take a practice test and see where you're at. If you need more time, there are other testing dates. Next objection?"

"I—" Iris doesn't have anything else to say.

She starts studying that afternoon.

JUNE

"You have your bag?" I ask for the third time today as I pull up to the college that Alice works at. It's serving as an LSAT testing location today.

"Yup." Iris holds up her gallon zip-top bag.

I still think it's ridiculous that something as professional as a law school entrance exam has a Ziplock bag requirement, but Iris checked over those rules diligently to make sure everything she's got is above board.

"Extra pencils, eraser, ID, a granola bar," I list off, with Iris confirming each item.

"I think I'm ready," she says, psyching herself up.

"I know you are," I say. I lean across the front seat of the Jeep and kiss her hard. "I'll be out here when you're done."

With a nervous look, Iris hops from the car. She's only a couple of feet away when I jump out too.

"Iris!" I call.

She stops and pivots back to me as I jog up to her.

"One more thing," I say, my heart suddenly hammering in my chest as I look into her beautiful eyes.

"I love you," I say.

Iris's mouth pops open.

"Eli," she starts. "I can't believe you said that right before I'm about to take the LSATs! I'm already nervous!" She playfully smacks my chest, but she's absolutely beaming.

"Well, don't let it distract you, because I'll only keep loving you if you get a good score," I tease back at her.

"Eli!" she shouts now, but I bend and wrap an arm around her waist, lifting her to her toes and pulling her against me.

"You know I don't mean it," I say when my lips are a breath away from hers. "I'd love you even if you were dumb as rocks."

She's laughing when I kiss her.

"Go get 'em," I say, turning her back toward the college and swatting her ass to send her on her way.

When she's nearly at the door, she spins back to me.

"I love you too!"

CHAPTER 50

Iris

"Where are we going?" Sam asks from the back seat, and Eli looks over at me with his eyes narrowed.

"Did you put her up to this?" he asks.

"I didn't!" I lie.

He's refused to answer me the half a dozen times I asked him about our plans for the evening, and I thought Sam might have more luck.

While I've calmed down a lot since meeting Eli, I'm still a control freak, and it's driving me nuts that Eli won't tell me where he's taking me tonight. When I saw he had a bottle of wine, I thought we might be going over to Jake's or Scott's for dinner, but we're driving in the wrong direction.

"It's a surprise," Eli answers Sam. "Trust me, you'll like it."

"Okie!" Sam says, clearly *not* as anxious as her Mama. Good for her, but bad for my curiosity.

Eli turns up the music before placing his hand on my knee. The way he squeezes it silently promises me it'll all be fine.

The rest of our drive is quick, and we pull into the driveway of a house on a quiet street. I recognize Alice's CRV and Scott's Range Rover parked nearby.

Before we're out of the car, a short woman in her fifties or sixties with straight, shoulder-length grey hair emerges from the house. She's wearing an apron over her dress and a bright smile on her face.

"Eli, where are we?" I ask just one more time. But the question proves needless when an aged-up version of Eli comes to stand beside the woman a moment later. There's no question in my mind that this man is Eli's father and the woman beside him must be Eli's mother.

Eli opens my door, already having gotten Sam while I was creepily staring at his parents.

"Come on, Mama," he says, offering his free hand to me. His other is holding Sam's hand.

I grab the wine bottle and clamber out of the Jeep.

He brought me home to meet his parents... and I think his mom is crying.

Eli's mom quickly wipes at her face before we reach her.

"Mom, Dad, this is Iris and Sam," Eli introduces us.

Sam is half hiding behind his leg, like she used to do with me when we'd meet new people, and Eli's hand is protectively resting against the back of her head.

"Mr. and Mrs. Chambers, it's a pleasure to meet you," I say, offering the wine to Eli's mom.

"Please, dear, I'm Helen, and this is Richard," she introduces. Richard plucks the wine bottle from my hands a second before Helen folds me into a warm hug. "And we couldn't be happier to have you and your little girl here today."

"Waffles, stay!" Jake's voice carries from inside a second before Waffles comes barreling down the front hallway, sliding on the smooth flooring. He crashes into the screen door behind Helen and Richard but doesn't seem to notice. Sam certainly does, though.

"Puppy!" she squeals, even though she could basically ride that "puppy" like a horse into battle. He's gotten so big.

Helen releases me with a laugh. "Would you like to go inside, dear?" she asks Sam, who nods eagerly.

"Yes, please," she answers. I reach around Eli's back and tap her shoulder to remind her of her manners.

"Oh! And hello," Sam adds, waving to both Helen and Richard.

Eli reclaims my hand as we follow them inside, and I know this meeting is just as important for him as it is for me and his parents.

Once we turn the corner, I find the great room filled with my friends and a dozen balloons. A large cake sits on the counter, *Happy Birthday* written across the top in careful script. My mouth falls open as my eyes jump from face to face. Jake, Alice, Scott, Piper, Leslie, Hannah, Harry, Kenny, and even *Lemon* surround me.

"I hope you like chocolate cake. Your sister picked so we could surprise you," Helen says from my side, and I realize she made us our very first homemade birthday cake.

"Everything is perfect," I say, feeling emotional myself, now. I turn to Eli.

"How did you know?" We haven't discussed birthdays.

Eli looks pointedly at Sam, who's wrestling with Waffles, but when she catches us looking at her, she looks anywhere *but* back at us.

Lemon makes her way over and wraps her arms around me.

"Happy Birthday, Sis," she says.

"You too, little Sis," I joke.

The guys have started helping Helen and Richard prep food, opening the back door to the patio where Richard will be manning a grill, and Alice has started opening wine bottles. Lemon keeps her arm around my back as we watch everybody happily moving around each other.

This is my family.

EPOLOGUE

AUGUST

"Mama, let's goooooooo," Sam's voice carries up the stairs to me. "You can't be late for the first day of school!"

My little girl is still the anxious academic, but she's not talking about *her* first day of school. She's talking about mine.

It's orientation, actually.

For law school.

I'm going to law school. Today.

Ever since Eli pulled an LSAT book out of his bag in my kitchen, it's been a whirlwind of moving pieces. I was late to register for the test, late to start studying, late for most school applications… but somehow here I am. I got in to a school I can commute to from Wilcox Grove, and I'm going to be a lawyer—after three years of classes and, you know, the bar exam.

"One minute!" I call back, and I can hear her huff all the way from my room.

I check my outfit in the mirror for the fiftieth time. It's a favorite of mine—my pencil skirt and my flowy white button up with the tied bow at the top. I won't need to dress up for classes, but I want to make a good first impression and have a good ID picture. Plus, I feel good in this.

I feel strong.

When I get to the bottom of the stairs, I see Sam standing beside Olivia—Olivia with her phone out, taking pictures, Sam with both arms wrapped around Robin.

"Look at our student, all ready for school!" Olivia squeals.

She instructs Sam to stand with me for another few photos, then we take selfies all together before Sam's patience runs out, and she demands I leave immediately.

"Ok, ok! I'm going. I'll see you this afternoon," I say, slipping on some black heels and pulling open the front door.

Standing on my porch as he has so many times before is Eli, his arms full of a gorgeous bouquet of sunflowers.

"Eli," I breathe, taking the flowers from him, but immediately being relieved of them as Olivia scoops them out of my arms and takes them inside.

"Your chariot awaits, esquire," he says, leaning forward to quickly kiss me.

"You can't call me that yet," I protest. "I'm not getting in trouble for representing I'm a lawyer when I'm not before I even start law school."

"Aw, come on. We can have matching ethics complaints." Eli beams at me.

"Shut up," I say, but it's with a smile as he bends to catch me behind my knees and sweeps me into his arms, carrying me to his Jeep. Laughing, I wave over his shoulder to Olivia and Sam standing in the doorway.

Eli gently kisses me after depositing me in his passenger seat.

"I am so fucking proud of you," he says. "I love you."

"I love you too."

Eli

BONUS EPILOGUE

OCTOBER

"**A**re you *sure* you left it in your desk?" Iris asks me for the third time as she dumps out the contents of the bottom drawer on the floor.

"I'm pretty sure?" I answer, making the mistake of glancing at her and pausing my search through my work bag.

Iris's organization skills have yet to rub off on me, and it might become a real problem today if we can't find Jake and Alice's marriage license I was supposed to be holding onto.

Iris's hair is braided and twisted, swept back from her beautiful face and pinned up. She shifts her sheer wrap up over her shoulder, but it slips right back down as she rummages through the pile of folders slowly spreading across the carpet.

"I found it!" she exclaims, hopping to her feet, not a single wobble in spite of the tall, pinpoint heels she's balancing on.

Fuck she's sexy.

As she straightens up, the silky fabric of her long, sage green dress tumbles around her ankles, pulling over her ample curves, and short-circuiting my brain.

"Eli?" she says, looking up from the folder in her hands to me when I continue to stare silently.

"Sorry," I mumble, shaking my head and going to her, confirming the marriage license, my notes, and my officiant registration paperwork is all in the folder.

Once I have, I set it on my desk, and sweep Iris into my arms, bending her in a low dip as I kiss her.

"What would I do without you?" I ask, still bent over her.

"Crash and burn," Iris answers, her eyes shining as she smiles up at me.

Her hand slips inside my suit jacket and grips the material of my dress shirt at my side. When her eyes drop to my lips, I quickly check the clock. There really isn't time, but...

I straighten up and quickly lift Iris, sitting her on the desk beside the folder. I bend to kiss the exposed skin on the side of her neck.

"Eli." She giggles. "We can't. Somebody could walk in."

I groan against her but get an idea.

"Ok," I say slyly. "Come on, then."

I take her hand and pull her behind me through the office, nursery store, old greenhouse, and deep into the new greenhouse. Plants of all sizes tower around us, and a thick layer of fog covers every pane of glass.

We weave between the tables until I find the empty space I'd been looking for. Jake and I have been building new tables to best use the space, and there's a brand new one just waiting for us. It's a bit low for me, but approximately the perfect waist-high level for a five-foot-five spitfire.

I spin toward Iris, wrapping my palm around the back of her neck, careful not to disturb any of the many pins in her hair and tipping her head back so I can claim her lips again. She moans and arches her back, molding against me.

"We can't. There's no time," she hisses against my mouth, but her hands have once again found my shirt, and they're pulling me flush against her.

"Please, Iris," I beg, kissing along her jawline again.

One of her hands slides down to the front of my slacks, finding me hard and ready for her already.

"Ok, yes..." she moans again, quickly looking around to find us completely secluded. "But we have to hurry."

I release her and flip her around, guiding her to the empty table and slowly pressing one hand between her shoulder blades until she bends over it. Her hands are flat on the surface beside her face, one cheek resting on the wood and those perfect lips parted.

Dropping to my knees behind her, I carefully collect the fabric of her dress and draw it up her legs and tuck it under her until it's gathered at her waist and her smooth ass is on display.

We won't have to worry about being quick. I could come just from looking at her like this.

I pull off her thong and let it slide down her legs until it's stretched between her parted knees. I waste no time unbuckling my belt, opening my pants and sliding on a condom. I run two fingers over her opening and find her just as ready as I am.

"Hold on, Iris," I instruct as I line myself up behind her.

Once we're both looking generally respectable again, we hurry back into the office where I chuck my handkerchief, wash my hands, and grab the folder from my desk.

Then, we're running across the fields, where a panicked wedding planner starts berating me for being late before basically pushing me down the aisle. Iris slips around the outside of the rows of chairs, staying crouched as she sneakily takes her seat.

I take my place in front of a carefully constructed wooden archway, draped in vibrant red, orange, yellow, and gold fabrics. As a very fitting ode to Alice and Jake's first season together, we're in the middle of the pumpkin patch, grown carefully this year to leave a space in the center for the ceremony to take place. All around us are twisting vines and pumpkins of all sizes, and far behind me is our largest apple orchard.

An enormous tent awaits us in one of the empty flower fields, twinkle lights strung every which way for when it gets dark later, because Alice has vowed that the dance floor will remain packed all night long. When the wind shifts, I can smell cinnamon and maple from the delicious dinner awaiting us.

The air is crisp, but the sun is shining, and somewhere, somebody is burning wood in their fireplace. The day could not be more perfect.

Jake eyes me suspiciously as he walks down the aisle a few seconds later with Scott. Once he's situated to my right, he leans in close.

"Where's your handkerchief?" he asks, looking me up and down.

"Oh," I say, trying to sound casual. "I must have forgotten it. I'm sorry."

Jake's eyes narrow, and he breathes in deeply.

"You smell like sawdust," he says.

"Oh, do I?" I quickly straighten my lapels as realization dawns on his face.

"Dude, in my new greenhouse and on my *wedding day*?" he asks, incredulously.

I can't help but chuckle, my eyes finding Iris in the first row, Sam seated between her and Grateful Bob.

"Sorry, man," I apologize, but I don't mean it.

"No, you're not." At least Jake knows.

"I'm really not."

"Will you two shut *up*?" Piper scolds us as she takes her place a few steps back on my other side, looking radiant in a burnt orange gown.

I remember I have a job to do, and motion for everybody to

stand as the string quartet starts playing an acoustic version of "A Thousand Years."

Alice appears from wherever the planner had her tucked away, and I hear Jake suck in a breath. She looks beautiful. The gown is soft and sheer, the layers moving like water around her. Intricate lace that looks like plants winds around her torso and over her shoulders. The most beautiful part of her, though, is the glowing smile on her face when her eyes find my brother's.

My eyes sting, and I wish I'd grabbed a new handkerchief. I seek out Iris again, finding her with a tissue already balled in her hand.

As Alice gets toward the end of the aisle, Grateful Bob steps forward and hugs her before taking one of Jake's hands and placing Alice's in it.

The music fades and everybody sits back down.

"Hi," Alice whispers to Jake, who I can see visibly shaking.

"Hi," he says back, his voice thick with emotion.

They both look to me and nod.

"Hey there, everyone," I start. "I'd do introductions, but we all know one another here. That's one of the special things about Wilcox Grove, I think. It makes families where there might not have been ones before. And today, I gain my first sister.

"I could not be more honored to get to stand up here among the most important people in my life while Alice and Jake pledge their love to each other forever.

"Those of you who know Jake might be a little surprised to find that we made it here. As you know, he can be a little bit... grumpy. But that didn't scare Alice. In fact, I'm not sure anything does. She is one of the bravest, strongest, kindest people I've ever met.

"And these are all important traits when dealing with Jake, who can be growly, stubborn, and sometimes rude. But he is also the most loyal, dependable, and one of the best men on this planet, and I don't know what I did to get to call him brother.

"Alice and Jake finding one another was nothing short of fate, so that's enough of me talking. How about we get these two married?"

Hours later, I'm holding Iris in my arms as we sway on the nearly full dance floor—Alice was right. Sam is nearby, giggling as Grateful Bob balances her patent leather shoes on top of his toes.

Over Iris's head, I catch sight of Piper and Scott at the dessert table again, his hand wrapped around her waist. She laughs brightly at something he says, and he kisses just under her chin.

We slowly rotate around, tinkling notes whispering with the rustle of the leaves. I see Mom and Dad, Leslie and Hannah, Ila and her husband, Marty and Tim. There's Mads with one of the new booksellers. Olivia smiling dazed at a woman from the catering company.

Then there's Alice and Jake, looking the happiest I've ever seen them, staring into each other's eyes as they dance on their wedding day.

And I don't think my heart has ever felt so full or so safe.

Acknowledgments

My first thank you has to be to you, reader. When I was a little girl, I had the crazy idea that I'd be an author someday, and it never would have become a reality without you. These characters, this place, these stories—they're all here because of you. Thank you for giving them a home.

To my partner in life, Ben, thank you for doing all you do so I can do this. Thank you for listening to my rambling half-ideas, for living in an apartment that had an end table made of boxes of my books, and for supporting me on every step of this journey.

To my best friend, partner in crime, sister author, Ila, thank you for sharing this crazy thing called life with me. I don't want to think about where I'd be without you, so yer stuck with me forever. You have made me a better person.

To Mads, Jessi, and Marissa, for being my ride-or-die crew, and for never judging when I crash out in the group chat.

To my parents, for always believing in me and for telling anyone who will listen that you've got an author for a kid.

To my sister, Georgianna, for always being my cheerleader, even when you're bullying me for early book secrets.

To Robin, Emily, and Mel for being brave enough to dive into the unedited first draft of this book, and for taking such amazing care of Iris and Eli with me.

A HUGE thank you to another absolutely incredible group of women who helped bring this book, Iris, and Eli to life: Annie, Hannah, Sam, Nicole, Kenzie, and Fozi. Annie and Hannah—you both know this book was *tough* for me and having you both as friends in addition to editors is a priceless gift I'll never take for granted.

Lastly, a special thank you to whoever made the meme of the red panda that I have Iris send to Eli. The original had "tax lawyer" instead of "CPA," and that meme helped me explain my job as a tax lawyer to many people, including my parents. It's beautiful, hilarious, and accurate. I am so grateful for your creativity.

Somehow, I feel like I've known Wilcox Grove my entire life, and that we *just* started this journey a moment ago. Even back when I was tapping out the first words Barefoot Lake, I knew I wanted to write three stories, for the three brothers: Jake, Scott, and Eli. Now that I've done that, I can't say goodbye, so know this is just *so long* to this motley crew for now.

We'll be back someday.

*Content Warnings
and Spice Guide*

Guess and Pray includes references to the following topics:

Abandonment of a child
Parental disapproval
Parental pressures
Off-page parent death (one from cancer and others from an accident)
Serious injury of a parent/parental figure, hospitalization
Anxiety

Explicit sexual scenes can be found in the following chapters:

Chapter 33
Chapter 34
Chapter 35
Chapter 42
Second Epilogue

After nearly half a decade of practicing law, Kim Swizz is now a recovering attorney, living her best life writing small-town romance. Kim has always had a passion for creative writing and has come a long way from the book she wrote and had bound in first grade, a titillating story entitled "The Cat is Eating."

A forever Jersey girl turned former Arizona resident, Kim now calls Boston home with her husband, though they love to travel together.

When she is not writing spicy scenes or making her readers cry, you can find her crocheting tiny things, knitting, embroidering, cross-stitching, bullet journaling—you get the point.

Kim is never without her emotional support Kindle and is an

avid F1 fan, keeping up with news on all the drivers, but mostly Carlos Sainz.

Kim is an unapologetic Disney adult who loves the smell of fall, small animals, and dancing her heart out (and Carlos Sainz).

Website: kimswizz.com
Facebook: Kim Swizz
Facebook Reader's Group: Kim's Swizzles
Socials: @authorkimswizz